Total Human Extinction is hours away...

Desperation began to drain the life from his face as he listened to the horrific news being played all over the world. He stared with disbelief as the global news broadcasts poured in.

"Over 100,000 dead in the city of Beijing. Riots have begun in the streets. Shops robbed, public buildings destroyed. A frenzied crowd armed with knives, broken bats and firearms is attacking anyone who tries to stop them from fleeing the city filled with sickness," a newscaster announced. "Tiananmen Square is littered with dead. No one has been spared. Women, elderly and children lie among them."

NINE DAYS TO EXTINCTION

J.B. SUMMERS

WWW.JBSUMMERS.COM

First edition, March 2010
NINE DAYS TO EXTINCTION
ISBN 978-0-615-34729-5
ISBN 0-615-34729-0
Copyright © 2010 by J.B. Summers
www.JBSUMMERS.COM.

STONE
LIGHT
PRESS

All characters in this book have no existence outside the imagination of the author and have no relation whatsoever to anyone bearing the same name or names. Any resemblance to actual events, locals, organizations or persons, living or dead, is entirely coincidental.

Cover design by Clay Gootgeld

Printed in the U.S.A.

In loving memory of
Mary Fitzingo-Mastasova, Joseph Fitzingo Sr.
and Joseph Fitzingo Jr.

ACKNOWLEDGEMENTS

I would like to thank my husband Jerry and my daughters Jamie and Jennifer who believed in my work more than me at times. Thanks also to Mark, my son-in-law, who graciously updated me on "Kindle news."

Citing acknowledgements of those individual who have help my dream come true over the last ten years has been one of greatest feelings of accomplishment I could have as novelist. I have worked with three great people who have supported my novel, *Nine Days to Extinction*, and stood by my side in the darkest of hours. Without them I might not be the author I am today. They are talented, skilled professionals who I could not have completed the novel without. Their knowledge, editorial observations and literary skills have enriched this novel and added color to this tapestry of words.

My thanks to my private editor, Paul D. McCarthy, an editor and New York Times best-selling author with 38 years of combined experience in book publishing as an acquiring senior editor, a creative editor, a consultant, a literary agent, a publisher and a book critic. He has worked with nine #1 *New York Times* and international best-selling authors. His comments have always helped to clarify and deepen the content of my novel. He truly took my novel to a higher level.

I thank the man without whom my career change from academic to author might not have been possible, top writing instructor Tom Bird. He has shared his gift of writing and his method with me and kept me on track. Without his constant encouragement and belief in my writing this novel may never have come about. After many, many rejections, he always kept his cool and said, "Don't worry, it's gonna happen." And yes, it has.

A warm thank you to Jenna Porter, my copyeditor, who has a gift for vision and grammar. I am honored to know her. She has been a true blue friend and polished professional with a heart.

I would also like to thank the following academics and medical professionals who were so gracious in donating their time and creative energy. Their knowledge, observations and stimulating conversations helped enrich and sharpen the contents of this novel:

John Amspaugh, MD
Douglas C. Broadfield, PhD, Biological Anthropologist, Florida Atlantic University.
Dr. Stacy S. Conrad, Premier Sports Chiropractic
Marcus A. McCray, DC, ATC, CCEP, Carmel, Indiana
Andrew S. Holzman, Family Tree Counseling Associates, Carmel, Indiana
Michael Harris, PhD, Cultural Anthropologist, Florida Atlantic University

My thanks and appreciation to:

Jen Babicz: Make-up designer and photographer.
Clayton Gootgeld, web designer, cover designer, book trailer (www.clayg.com)
Cliff Ehrhart, original drafts of the logo and creative suggestions
Cameran Gilliam, junior proofreader.

A final thank you to all my friends and family who supported me with many acts of kindness and made me laugh when I needed to: Don Fontana, Anna Babicz, Lavern Detloff, Sherry Roberts, Louise Sauvageau, Pierre Girard, Christopher Schranz, Bob and Jan, Sue, Tom, Stacy, **Abuelo's**, Carmel, Indiana (special thanks to Lori and staff), **Carrabba's Italian Grill**, Carmel, Indiana (special thanks to Todd Melton, Steve Briggs, Sarah, Chuck, Mike), **Mitchell's Fish Market**, Carmel, Indiana (Bob, managers, staff and chef; special thanks to Grace and Keith Parish, Jamal), **La Peep's,** Carmel, Indiana (manager, staff and chefs). Never forget to thank the source of all great successes, small and large. Love.

NINE DAYS TO EXTINCTION
By J. B. Summers

CHAPTER ONE

Day One. 12:01 a.m. Moscow Time (MSK). The Fennoscandia Formations. Lake Ladoga.

The faded green and chukker-brown Ka-25 Anti-Submarine helicopter lowered and hovered at his command. The air was crisp, clean. It was a perfect day for his meeting. The whirling wind from the propeller blades blew his sandy brown hair away from his handsome face. His icy gray eyes stared upon the chilly waters of Lake Ladoga. Russia's White Nights had lit it up as if it were a sheet of shiny glass. His body was a perfect icon of a man, god-like. Russian Federal Security Service officer Yuri Nevsky inhaled one last time from his unfiltered cigarette, flicking it out the open bay door.

Death came easy for him. He was familiar with death. He liked death so much that he would frequently walk among the dead that lay rotting in the overfilled makeshift morgues of Russia's poor camps near Tula. It was a forsaken place few cared about. He had lived with death at Tula for three years, breathing in the stench of rotting corpses as if it were as fragrant as the dried, withered rose he kept in a jar on his kitchen shelf. It had belonged to his mother. It was the only pleasant memory he had of her: Her death.

FSB Lt. Commander Nevsky turned his solid six-foot frame to his guests and transformed his evil grin. He smiled charmingly at the pair, one a Russian who demanded his attention and the other a composed, thin Syrian who wore a swastika tattooed in his nations colors hidden just above his heart. Raising his hand, Yuri brushed his wind-tossed hair into place. He had prepared for this moment over the last four years. It was finally here. Vengeance.

The old ex-Soviet general restlessly stirred his compact body in the seat. He was a burly man who showed little sign of having once been a high-ranking USSR military man. His skin was weathered from years of service to a failed political system. He had given everything he had to that way of life. He could not let go of the past. He felt at odds wearing his Russian Federation uniform, though it, too, he thought, was one he would soon retire to the shelf of dusty relics he owned. The old man reached for a case he kept covered by his trench coat.

Yuri spit at his feet but remained attentive, listening to General Pachen's complaints until the general finally pressed him for assurances.

"Yuri, I need an answer from you. We provided you with enough money to blow up half of Europe. A small fortune, I might say. Without my connections to your father, you wouldn't be riding with us in your latest request for air transportation." The general waved his calloused hand along the floor of the fully armed helicopter. "And now this little deadly item." He clicked open the metal clips on a weathered black briefcase. Turning it to reveal its contents, he pushed two metal tubes toward Yuri, one with a red warning seal, the other simply marked in blue. Four Russian-coded Cold War-era medical vials were secured in each tube.

Pulling the case closer, Yuri snatched up the silver tubes, securing them in a streamlined biomedical case lined with specialized thermal foam. The side was marked with bold red letters reading *Dispose of Properly* under a metallic green biohazard symbol. No one except Pachen seemed to take notice of the unspoken warning.

"It's a bad move, Lt. Commander. With one drop, the world will change forever. Possibly cause the extinction of all life, if not controlled. You *do* know that, don't you? I was there when that deadly bug was created. Does your father even know what you're planning to do with these? This isn't right." Pachen, bitterly disappointed, criticized, "We are unhappy with your progress in overthrowing the present government. In return for our support, we have received nothing but empty promises. We warned you. This trip had better be worth our money or your very powerful brother will find out your dirty little secrets. Now is the time to restore Lenin's dream, to restore communism to its glory days."

A devilish grin froze on Yuri's face. He snapped the case shut. The time had come to unleash his plan on the civilized world, one that would satisfy his thirst for power and erase his past. Yuri glanced at the Syrian adjusting his *taqiyah*. He slid the bio-case under the chopper seat and flatly said, "Communism was nothing more than a scab on Mother Russia's ass." He stood to face his guests. "Where Lenin failed, I will succeed. As we speak, your comrades are all sharing the same fate as you, my old friend."

A straightedge razor dropped from Yuri's sleeve into his hand. With one yank, he jerked the old general up from his seat. The old man blinked as he felt the cold metal edge of the razor slit his throat. Fresh blood sprayed Yuri's newly laundered shirt still scented with starch.

Pachen gasped for air. Yuri seized his Federation uniform's collar and dragged his paralyzed body to the open cargo door. Disbelief left Pachen numb. The horror-struck general gave a last look into his assassin's cruel eyes and caught a glimpse of an unearthly evil within them he had not seen before. Yuri's hands pressed against Pachen's bloodstained chest. It was the last thing he felt as Yuri pushed his body out the helicopter's door. His eyes shut as the blackness of death overtook him. His lifeless body plunged into the icy waters that shimmered under the Russian White Night.

The Syrian smiled, revealing several crooked gold crowns as he opened a case on his lap neatly packed with crisp U.S. hundred dollar bills. "Payments will continue as our cause meets with continuing success," he cautioned.

Yuri gave a cold, calculated look as he slammed the case shut. He sat down, shoving it next to him. "Prince Adar, your cause will be successful as long as your payments continue. Make sure your half-brother Mus'ad understands that before we meet today." Yuri wiped the bloodstained razor clean on the Syrian's shirt, tapping the edge on the patch of fabric that hid the swastika. The Syrian held his breath in unspoken comprehension. The helicopter banked hard left to return to St. Petersburg. The men sat in silence as they returned to Russia's mainland.

"Two-ten a.m. Moscow Time. St. Petersburg. On schedule," the pilot radioed Yuri.

Yuri clapped his hands together in approval, rubbing them. His hands dropped to his side searching for the biomedical case. He felt the chopper set down hard on the black asphalt at St. Petersburg's Pulkovo Airport. The sudden landing shifted Yuri and Adar to one side. Recovering the cases, Yuri pushed the open bay door wider. The two stepped off the chopper. The smell of jet fuel filled their noses, wafting over from the leaking engine of a newly renovated Pulkovo Airlines plane alongside them.

Yuri frowned. "Piece of junk." The jet fuel fumes burned his lungs. Yuri dragged his handkerchief from his back pocket and placed it over his nose. Adar hastily wrapped the tails of his headdress around his face to stop from choking. Yuri passed one case to his armed bodyguard who was pointing the way. They hurried toward two Volgas sitting at the baggage loading strip, waiting for their arrival. Yuri hopped into the back seat of one of the gunmetal Volgas as the bodyguard climbed in the other side.

The Chechen driver started the engine. He tapped his finger on the wheel, keeping perfect rhythm with the Russian rock song blaring over the radio. He awaited his next orders.

Yuri unfolded the new white shirt waiting for him on the back seat. Swiftly, he unbuttoned, removed his bloodstained shirt and slipped on the clean shirt. Stuffing the shirt and wrappings in a paper bag, he handed it to the mafia bodyguard sitting next to him. "You know what to do. Burn this. And take care of the spoiled Syrian 'prince'. He is our new friend. Give him whatever he wants. I have a small errand to run before I meet up with him at Nevsky Prospekt."

The taller, nimble bodyguard nodded and stepped out of the front seat, slamming the door. He headed toward Adar and the two mafia security men at their post. "This way, Prince Adar. Your brother has already arrived." Adar was escorted to the black Volga.

The Chechen pulled away along the old airport's pitted back road and headed toward St Petersburg. "Drive faster," Yuri ordered. "We have to have enough time to make the switch." Frustration filled Yuri. The drive was taking too long. Yuri's temper flared as the car's speed dropped. "Why are you slowing down? You are becoming useless to me." Yuri fingered his gun.

Nervously, the Chechen pointed at the military police staked out at the mafia henchmen's old lair.

Yuri cursed, then ordered, "Detour to the other side of the Neva River, opposite the Smolny Cathedral. That should save us half an hour." His trigger finger left his gun and his hand rested protectively again on the biomedical case.

They drove past buildings that showed their Soviet heritage despite recent renovations. This was not the St. Petersburg of the days of the Lenin. This was the new Russia and it was growing. He gritted his teeth. A fresh Russia under the influence of his step-brother, the forward-thinking President Stepanov.

Yuri, growing impatient at his driver, bellowed, "Now what is the problem?"

"Damn!" The car slammed to a halt. The Chechen driver hit the palm of his hand on the radio face. The rock music stopped.

"Why are we stopped?" Yuri demanded. "This case has to get to my man within the hour. We have to finish the testing tonight, before the oil tankers leave dock. I never trusted Pachen. I will not miss this opportunity to carry out my plan because of a lousy driver."

"The bridge, boss." The shaky driver twisted, placing his arm over the seat. "We can't cross. It's after two a.m. The bridges are raised for merchant ships until five a.m. We are stuck until then."

Yuri looked at the dirty river. Leaning over the seat, he placed the tip of his gun between his driver's eyes. "Well, there are no ships now. Get the bridge down."

"How? What if there is nobody at the controls? Not every bridge has an operator posted this time." The driver quivered.

"Stop your bitching. I want the bridge lowered. Pay off the watchman."

"Wait. I'll do it," the bodyguard broke in. "We need him to drive. And I don't want him pissing in his pants again, boss." The hefty man left the back seat and silently shut the door.

A minute later the bodyguard reappeared and waved them forward. Yuri reluctantly put his gun away. "Hurry!" he commanded.

The driver nervously obeyed. He stopped briefly to pick up the bodyguard who was stuffing a few rubles in his pocket. The henchman tossed an empty wallet into the river as they pulled up. "Get in," Yuri said harshly. He took his seat beside his boss. Yuri noticed the strangled bridge operator still seated at the controls. He glanced to his bodyguard for an answer.

"It was cheaper to kill him." The bodyguard straightened his suit and leaned back.

"You and your fuckin' money. Well, it saved time." They passed the bridge unnoticed.

The Chechen let his guard down. Turning the radio on, he mused at the successful assassination of General Pachen. "I can't believe you pulled this off. With Syria's underground leader in town, you are now the most powerful Russian mafia boss ever. And the beauty is that your brother doesn't even know."

"Shut up. You talk too much. What my brother does or doesn't know is none of your business. You are paid to drive." Yuri mumbled to himself, disgruntled, feeling the sting of his role in life. "I should have had his mother's blood." He always felt he failed at the expectations of being a bastard son to a Stepanov.

Yuri hit speed dial on his satellite phone. "Professor Mikovich," he began. "My men are on their way. Get busy on the test site. I have personally cleared all the arrangements. The countdown starts tonight." Patting the biomedical case, he said, "I have the vials. Yes, they are still intact after all these years. I will need three more test subjects. Pick them from among new recruits." He hung up.

They made their way around the backside of town. They passed the square and drove to a rundown area named Nevsky Prospekt. It was where the red light district conducted its business in the open. Stale perfume hung in the air. Yuri liked sharing a name with Saint Nevsky. His twisted mind imagined himself to be like a saint. He waited for his best man, Misha, to arrive.

"Right on time!" Yuri relaxed, hearing the familiar un-rhythmic banging of a tailpipe against the pavement. A half-broken-down cab appeared. Misha slipped out of the driver side. He casually walked up to the open window. "Hi, boss. You look good. I see you got the shirt I sent ahead." Misha knew his boss's quirks. He made it his business to know.

Yuri ignored his comments and handed him two cases, one the thermo case, the other Adar's cash installment. "I sent a few men ahead of you in case you needed back up. Take care of this tonight. I want all the Swiss bank accounts under this name." Yuri handed him a note. Misha nodded as he took the cases and note. "Get Pachen's name off of them. When are you going to stop driving that piece of shit?" He pointed to the rusty cab.

"Never." He glanced at the old cab. "Best way to pick up information on the streets." He padded the Volga's car door and added, "I'm on my way."

"Good. Don't disappoint me," Yuri callously said. Misha walked back to his cab and shut the tinted door. With one last look at his rearview mirror, he maneuvered around the Volga and sped off.

"We're not far from my place." Checking his watch, Yuri said, "Adar should be there by now. Take the short cut."

The Chechen driver pulled up to a rustic restaurant. Yuri's bodyguard scanned the area as he stepped from the car. "It's OK, boss."

Yuri strode into the restaurant and greeted the assembled guests. There was an aura of rudeness in the air. He walked past several of customers eating and watched them silently glare at him as Adar was escorted past Yuri. "You're late," he complained to Adar. "I'll meet you downstairs in a minute."

The bartender tossed Yuri an unopened bottle of vodka. Yuri grabbed a clean shot glass off the bar top and turned to his bodyguard. "Tonight we find out if Pachen and Mikovich were lying." He said to his bodyguard, "Keep me posted." The guard nodded.

Yuri motioned several of his men waiting in the wings to join him. He strolled past a small storage room to a deadbolted door that led to a cellar. Music filled the stairway from below as the unlocked door swung open. Yuri's men followed him down to the underground room.

A gypsy girl sang "Paranya" in a velvety voice. Yuri watched Adar as he stepped off the last step. Adar was more impressed by her half-clad body than her song. He pushed the two whores off his lap and approached her. Mus'ad sat in silent disgust of his brother's disrespect for tradition.

"Nyet!" Yuri yelled. "Maria belongs to me. Any other one, you can have. No one touches her." Yuri came fully into the room filled with the stench of liquor and smoke.

"I see, Adar, you've made yourself at home rather quickly?"

"Never turn a gift away as a diplomat, father said," Adar replied with a laugh.

"Shut up," Mus'ad spat back. "Father is a weak Syrian living the fat life with the Saudis who bargain with the West. Take that headdress off. You are a Syrian. Act like one."

Yuri quickly noticed the brothers were like night and day. Mus'ad adhered to his Muslim traditions with an evil twist; his brother, hiding his terrorist activities behind a veil of diplomacy for a country that was not his, had grown to like the pleasures offered to him during his days representing Saudi Arabia on behalf of his father at the United Nations.

Adar sat back down. He pulled the two whores back to him. Yuri took a seat next to him. He kept his eyes on Mus'ad, gauging if he would be a problem in the future. He tapped a cigarette out of his pack. He struck a match and lit it. He inhaled deeply. Smoke poured out of his mouth. "I have one last test to do. Misha is handling that for me tonight," Yuri said.

"When can we take control of the satellites?" Mus'ad asked impatiently.

"Soon. Not all of my men are in place. I'll give you the word when. I will need Syria and Iran both out of our way before the next step takes place. That is your and Adar's job. I have to take care of a little problem in the States. New York needs to be taught a lesson. They have not been agreeable with my terms." Yuri exhaled with a ring of smoke. "After that, the vial goes to the highest bidder."

"And then you keep your contract with us," Mus'ad reminded him. "Syria receives the vial regardless of who the highest bidder is. After the fool makes payment, of course. You get your Russia as it was under the Soviet Union, China and the Americas. We get the rest." Mus'ad motioned to his bodyguards to step back as Mus'ad stepped closer.

"Sure, Mus'ad. Sure." Yuri's voice temporarily reassured him. "But first we'll see if all the test vaccines and vials are good. I had Pachen inject three men with the virus and vaccine the day he stole the canisters. Two of my men, unfortunately, will not have the correct vaccine injection. We'll know soon enough if Pachen was lying to me about the virus's potency and the vaccine's value. We must also wait on this morning's final test result on my family's private land. We must make sure all the vials are effective."

"Yes, or else it's all worthless," Adar agreed, leaning forward to snort a line of cocaine as the whore beside him lined up another on the table. "And if all goes well," Adar slapped the young woman's backside, "one drop of that liquid will bring -"

Yuri finished Adar's sentence. "Me an extreme amount of wealth and power."

Mus'ad snapped, "You mean *us*, Yuri. It is *us* who will own the world. Three way split."

Yuri gave a devilish smile. "Of course." He pushed a bag of cocaine closer to Adar, whose eyes glazed over as he inhaled another line.

Appalled at his brother's careless attitude, Mus'ad snapped callously, "When do you see Nikolai?"

"Tomorrow. I fly to Moscow." Yuri cracked open the premium vodka.

"Why not today?" Mus'ad asked abrasively.

Yuri poured himself a drink. "With the vials safe in our hands, we have time. We move when the tests results are in."

"But are the vials safe?" Mus'ad coldly dictated, "Before I kill a third of my countrymen off for this plan of yours, I demand to see the test outcome first."

Yuri shot down the glass of liquid fire at hearing the arrogant demand. His teeth clenched, he calmly suggested, "Relax, my friend. Enjoy the music." He lifted his empty glass to the young woman to play a new tune. "It is not a good idea to throw threats at me." His eyes narrowed at the Syrian. Yuri's voice hardened. "If I were you, I'd pray to that God of yours that the tests succeed." Yuri placed the glass on the table. He wiped his lips and warned, "Should the tests fail, neither you nor your brother will leave this place alive."

Mus'ad was rendered speechless. Music filled the air once more.

CHAPTER TWO

Day One. 6:12 a.m. MSK. Pechora, Russia.

"Eleven bodies have been found. One gravesite." The head medical inspector adjusted his biohazard suit as he began the briefing. "We are treating it as a biohazard scene. No evidence of who committed this mass murder or why." A ripple of discontent rolled over him. "Local residents directed members of our team to the site. The victims were all employed by Stepanov Oil Company and most live in the town south of the oil fields. This one will be hard to cover up for the President." Damp mud clung to the cuffs of the short, heavy man's pants as he trampled the moist earth. The tall, elegant man beside him listened intently. "This light mist is not helping our investigation," the inspector complained.

"What is the level of decomposition?" Dr. Petro Glazkov, Professor of Forensic Medicine and Criminology at St. Petersburg State University, questioned.

"Several different levels of decomposition were noted among the corpses." The inspector pulled out a burgundy cap and placed it over his gray hair, giving it a small tug. His upper lip was wet from the mist. He stooped down to scoop up a handful of dirt, sifting through it with his latex-covered fingers. "The spilled oil doesn't help. Worse than the mist. It's all over everything. It is slowing us down and has contaminated most of our samples. See?" He let the last clumps of dirt fall to the ground. "The level of decomposition depended on where in the grave the body was taken from." He stood and unconsciously wiped the dampness from his lip. "The bodies found on top and along the sides of the shallow grave were decomposed into a mass of liquefied flesh. We will be able to separate the skeletons, the bones, but are uncertain as to the reason for their rapid decomposition." The inspector continued, "The bodies taken from the middle of the grave had no soil contamination, were moist, covered with lesions, but easily identified as male or female. None of the bodies showed any signs of insects or remains of insects that could date the time of the burial." His lips curled. "It's a fresh grave. We've concluded that the burials took place within the last 12 to 24 hours."

Glazkov frowned. "So basically the bug larvae haven't gotten to them yet." He tugged at his face mask. "We know natural ground bacteria can cause rapid decomposition where the bodies had direct contact with the soil, but nothing like you're describing, not in that time frame." Glazkov was dissatisfied. He needed more answers. "What turned up in microbiological sampling?"

Grabbing his medical note pad, he touched the blue screen and entered Case #SSO498, Stepanov oil gravesite. He had been called only hours ago to investigate the discovery of the bodies on the President's family owned oil lands. Glazkov added the briefing's information to his file. He left his medical bag in the black sedan bearing the coroners' license plates. He'd thought he wouldn't need it. This was understood to be a routine check of a homicide gravesite. But it was fast turning into a medical mystery. He had a bad hunch he would need that bag after all. Glazkov rechecked the facts. None of the dead had decomposed at a normal rate. No blunt trauma, puncture external wounds. No traces of struggle. Just open sores. They had just died.

He looked up from the screen and faced the medical inspector squarely, eyes tense and serious. "Well, what do you think you have?"

"We don't know." The medical inspector awkwardly continued, "All our tests are coming up with negative pathogen matches. We're treating the site as infectious until we know what they died from. We targeted deadly microorganisms that even included Ebola, Marburg and Lassa fever viruses. My guess is it's some kind of biological pathos related to the genus orthopox virus. Possibly vaccinia."

Glazkov shook his head. "No, inspector, it's something else. More than a pox. The graves are too fresh for the 10 - 12 days incubation period for pox. You said these victims were working a few days ago. This is worse." Glazkov's voice grew quieter. "Let's take a closer look." Glazkov motioned toward a mound of wet oily muck.

The two men arrived at the partially exhumed site. Glazkov stooped to examine footprints in the oil-discolored soil. "More than one suspect. Looks like three. You missed these, inspector." He motioned to the forensic photographer. "Take some shots." Glazkov stood. "We need some pictures of what they used to bury them, too." Glazkov turned and pointed to a roped-off tractor. "They used the backhoe loader over there to dump them. I want a complete set of photographs."

Glazkov was not a happy man as he walked over to the far side of the shallow grave with the medical inspector. He was repulsed by the smell and sight of the grave. "The few bodies were scattered on top of each other," the inspector explained. "We have not exhumed all the corpses. There may be more. It was fortunate we even found them. Whoever buried them here was sloppy. They had no idea a drill site was moved to this location hours before we suspect the murders occurred. Otherwise, it would have taken months to find. It had to be someone who knew the Stepanov oil land and knew where to dig. The company authorities tried to help, so the site has been tampered with." The medical inspector pointed west, near a stack of unused oil pipes. "There is another site over there."

They walked toward the exhumed corpses. "Mostly adult males ranging in age from 18 to 50 and three adult females." The inspector hung his head, rubbing his neck. "Among them, one child, one dog," he explained.

"Have you notified the President with the new information?" Glazkov asked.

"No," the inspector replied. "After we finalize the report today he'll be informed through traditional contacts that it appears to be some kind of mass murder for political statement. It's on his land..."

Glazkov was not as sure. "Everything is not always what it appears to be. We can't snap to judgments until the evidence is examined. Something is terribly wrong here. We will tell him after I have your full report and we're sure of what to tell him."

"Here, come quickly!" A young man's voice rang over the open field, his footsteps sounding on the disturbed soil. He stumbled and fell to the oily muck, the blanket-wrapped bundle in his arms falling from his bloody hands. Glazkov and the medical inspector hurried to approach him and found him frozen, staring at what the fallen blankets had revealed.

"Get an immediate biohazard wash down for this man!" Glazkov ordered. Both men suppressed a gag at the twitching bodies of young woman and her child. They were fighting for their last breaths. Blood and bile colored foam poured from the child's mouth. Then nothing.

The man wept at the death of his family, his hands and face covered with his own blood from newly burst lesions.

Glazkov was shaken as he felt a sense of familiarity wash over him as he viewed the man's disfigured skin. He had seen these symptoms before. "Damn! It can't be. Not after all this years. It's has to be tied into the old Siberian site," Glazkov mumbled to himself.

Glazkov abruptly turned to the troubled inspector. "Check with whoever has records for our 1940-1960 bioweapons storage sites. Find out if any pathogens are missing. Check the shutdown Western Siberian germ warfare labs." He felt a knot in the pit of his stomach as the inspector snatched up his phone. He looked at the twitching young man in front of him. He would be dead in seconds; there was nothing any doctor could do for him. Glazkov could only watch as the young man's life left him. "Ice them," Glazkov ordered one of the forensic assistants as he made his way back to the black sedan, the medical inspector trailing close behind him, his phone pressed to his ear.

"Da. How many missing?" The inspector's face went white. "Glazkov," he said, slamming his phone off. "Your hunch was right. The Siberian lab was breached three days ago. Several canisters of a special pox strain were taken."

"Check the old DNA samples against the one found here immediately. How soon can we have the results?"

"In a few minutes. I am linking into the cyber lab now." The inspector paced around the site. His phone droned.

Glazkov waited impatiently. He did not have to wait long. The inspector handed him his phone. Glazkov's eyes fixed on the tiny screen. "This is bad. It's not a match, but it's close, too close not to be related in some way." He unclipped his own phone from his belt, anxiously punching the buttons. He listened eagerly for a voice on the other end.

"Dobroye utro," a female voice answered. "Good morning, how may I direct your call?"

"Get me President Stepanov," he demanded. "This is Dr. Glazkov of St. Petersburg State University. We have a biohazard emergency."

"Dr. Glazkov, a moment please. I'll transfer you to President Stepanov's office immediately."

Glazkov silently kicked the back tire of the coroner's sedan, listening to the clicks, clacks and hum of the call being transferred.

"Dr. Glazkov. President Stepanov here. What did you find out?" a solid male voice asked.

Glazkov gripped the phone tight. His speech was cold and frank. "Mr. President," he began. "The mass grave appears to be a test site for one of our Cold War pathogens." Glazkov paused. He felt a sickness overcome him as he spoke his next words. Beads of sweat formed on his brow. "What we have, Mr. President, is the start of a pandemic if we can't contain it here."

"A pandemic! It 'appears to be'? Are you sure? What did the tests conclude?"

"There is no exact match. It is similar to one I worked on years ago, but, I can't be sure. It may have mutated over the years. This new virus taken from the grave site is not in our databanks."

President Nikolai Stepanov listened hard. A man of great power, a former FSB officer himself, he was stunned. He was a man in charge of himself and had the respect of his friends and enemies alike. But this was an enemy he had no experience dealing with. "Tell me more, Dr. Glazkov," Nikolai demanded.

Glazkov's body temperature suddenly rose as sweat poured down from his brow, mixing with the mist and oil-tainted air. "At this moment, until we know exactly what pathogen we are dealing with, your land has become a Petri dish for this virus. We will need international help. A virus like this could be outside of Russia within the week. If that happens..." He paused. "We will not be able to contain it."

Nikolai's adrenaline streamed through his veins. He stood in his Moscow office troubled. He waved to his aide to get his right hand man, General Serebrinsky, in his office immediately. Nikolai clutched the phone firm with the news. "Keep working on it. Update General Serebrinsky with any new findings," he directed Glazkov. "I will put in a call for the help you asked for. We will see who will extend themselves under these conditions."

Glazkov listened grimly to the President's words. "Yes, Mr. President." He swallowed, ending the call. Glazkov was not sure if his team would come up with anything new in the next few hours, but he was certain if they did not, everyone in the contained area will be dead in the next few days. Including him.

Alarm bells overtook Nikolai. The professor's concern was well-founded. He glanced at his watch. 7:00 a.m.

General Sergei Serebrinsky, walked in tense and pessimistic. "I've heard. The canisters were stolen three days ago. The military was handling the investigation through the usual *slow* channels. If our forensic scientists cannot identify the pathogen, what do you intend to do Mr. President?" Sergei sat in a chair across from his President, leaning back in it. He tossed a file on Nikolai's desk. The man much older than his President fixed his eyes on Nikolai. This was the one man Nikolai trusted beyond his special operations team. A war hero, a friend of his father and of himself. Any one of those titles allowed Sergei the right, Nikolai felt, for his informalities when dealing with his office.

Nikolai pushed the intercom button. "Get U.S. President Brice on a secure line," he ordered his aide.

"Maybe you should wait a day?" Sergei suggested.

"No. A breach at an old Soviet lab three days ago now tied into my oil land can't wait. Glazkov said it could spread quickly. We have to know what we're up against. People have died under my watch."

The room fell silent as the implications of the events weighed on them. Nikolai opened Sergei's file and began to glance over its contents. "Mr. President, President Brice is on the line," his aide announced a few moments later.

"President Brice," Nikolai began.

"President Stepanov. What kind of problem do we have?" President Brice questioned. He was not a man to be taken lightly. His 10-year service as a leader with the Navy Seals and two terms as Vice President gave him an edge. Brice was no fool and Nikolai knew that.

"Brice, I always liked the way you never minced your words," Nikolai replied. "So, I'll get to the point. Three days ago a pox strain from the Cold War turned up missing. We put our best undercover agents on the weapons' black market to see if the canisters would turn up, but we had no luck. This morning a mass gravesite was discovered in an oil field. My scientists can't identify the pathogen involved in the deaths. The stolen canisters and the grave sites may be linked." Nikolai felt a distant ripple of unrest run through his body as he spoke his next words. "My government is requesting that your government send your top pathologist, virologist and epidemiologist to find out what killed the victims. We need to find the match and the virus is not in our data banks. It could be in yours. Brice, we don't have time to waste. Whatever this virus is, my team at the site informed me it is fast and deadly."

Brice was clearly agitated. "President Stepanov, are you telling me a biological weapon was released on civilian land? Stolen from under your nose?"

Nikolai felt the sting of Brice's words. He gritted his teeth and put his pride aside. He had no choice. "Look, Brice. We need your help to stop the virus here in Russia. There is a high possibility it could spread out of my oil fields and beyond the Russian borders within days."

Brice narrowed his eyes. "Your oil fields?"

Nikolai pursed his lips. His stomach tightened. "Yes. The gravesite is on Stepanov family oil land." He snapped back, "The location has nothing to do with the urgency of the matter. We can't get enough facts, which is why we need your help. Who can you send?"

"That would be Dr. Blake."

"Elizabeth Blake, William Blake's niece? You only offer one medical expert! Are you sure her medical qualifications are adequate for this operation? Can she be sufficiently removed from your administration to give an impartial report, knowing her family connection to that office?" The niece of the U.S. Secretary of State was not a stranger to him. She was, however, the last name he thought he would hear from Brice.

Brice hid a slow burning anger as he spoke in her defense. "Dr. Blake *is* the head of our Centers for Disease Control and Prevention. That alone would make her more than just another pathologist for your needs." Brice took a breath to calm down. He coolly continued, "I'll make a call to Secretary Blake. We do not want to wait on this. I'll put Dr. Blake on a jet immediately heading to Moscow. But if what you are saying is true, that this virus is only an old small pox strain, we should have a quick match and getting the antiserum out of storage would provide the solution for both of us. We'll need access to your old data."

"Of course," Nikolai said. "We'll send our records, but we'll need yours as well. And you should know this: My scientists claim it may not be the old pox virus. This virus is something new."

"Something new? Not the old germ warfare strain? I hope to God it's not, for both our countries' sakes. That would be a political nightmare. Keep me posted." Brice hung up without a goodbye.

Nikolai looked at Sergei. "A political nightmare would be the best that could happen."

CHAPTER THREE

Day One. 5:45 p.m. EST. The Pentagon. Arlington, Virginia.

Warning sirens blared in the hallway of the Pentagon. Hustling through the corridor, Dr. Elizabeth Blake, America's leading pathologist in bio-warfare and current Director of the Centers for Disease Control and Prevention, pushed her newly-trained biohazard first responders. "Hurry, soldiers! You have less than five minutes to seal off this area before you and everyone in it is exposed to the latest Machupo virus."

Three Marines lowered the three-inch thick airtight Plexiglas barrier. One Marine stood out, rash but effective, as he compromised himself to seal the barrier. Emergency oxygen poured into the newly-sealed area from specially designed reserve ducts.

"Reckless! But effective..." Elizabeth glanced down at the unit leader's name tag. "Special Operations Officer Benjamin P. Harrison. You even have a minute to spare."

"It's Big Benny," Harrison shot a cocky half-smile at her approval. A handsome man, he was one of the rare breed of soldiers who felt they had something to prove. He glanced beyond Elizabeth. Admiral David Kullens was rapidly approaching. His smile faded. Harrison slipped off his hi-tech bio-gear helmet and stood at attention. His unit quickly followed his lead.

Kullens gave his Marines a hard look as he stopped and stood next Elizabeth. They saluted. He returned the salute and sharply ordered, "Harrison, new orders. I need you out of that gear immediately. You have been reassigned as Dr. Blake's escort. You have five minutes." Kullens shot a sharp glance of admiration at the remaining Marines for a job well done. "Men dismissed."

Harrison pulled open the snaps on his biohazard suit. He never glanced back at his men as he started for the dressing room.

Elizabeth studied the robotic Kullens. She thought it was out of her scope of duties when he personally requested her help to create a specially-trained team of officers for the protection of the Pentagon. He would take no chances with the current threat that some home grow terrorists might breach its walls again.

"Dr. Blake, you will have to terminate your tests for now. File your report with my office later. The Secretary of State has requested to see you immediately. A military escort is waiting."

Cocking her head, Elizabeth glanced at the floor where her medical bag sat and wondered what her uncle might want from her that could not wait until tonight. He knew she would be attending the family event later that evening. William Blake was not one to order a military escort for a social call. Stuffing her note pad into her medical bag, she frowned. "What's going on, Admiral Kullen?"

"Harrison will escort you to your uncle's estate. That's all I am allowed to tell you," Kullens said. "If you will follow me, Harrison will meet us outside." Kullens turned, leaving Elizabeth to follow in his wake. She took one glance at the remaining soldiers who could only speculate what was on her uncle's mind. She followed Kullens in silence. He squinted as they step outside into the sunshine. There was Harrison, waiting in full military dress beside a State Department limousine. Elizabeth grew concerned as she climbed into the back seat. She watched Kullens pass Harrison sealed orders. With a quick salute, they were on their way.

The drive was smooth, the weather beautiful. Lush green trees lined the road outside the city limits. The summer clouds whisked by. Leaning back, Elizabeth glanced over the front seat. Harrison was in a hurry, breaking the speed limits. So much in a hurry, that she found herself standing alone inside her uncle's office within 30 minutes of their departure.

Elizabeth rubbed one slender finger against the cherry wood post that held the Blake family crest, a symbol of the present-day political powerhouse. It had been a long time since she had lived in that house. She took in the familiar smell of fine leather and moss wood that filled the air, acutely aware that this was more than an ordinary man's office.

Glancing toward the sound of solid rapping on the door frame, Elizabeth glimpsed her uncle reaching for her face. He swept a small lock of her silky hair back in place behind her ear. Elizabeth smiled gently at him. It had been some time since they had seen each other. Both of their jobs kept them busy. She thought it had been too long, noticing the streaks of silver-gray feathering his hair. His eyes were the same. Elizabeth looked into his steely eyes, knowing that as difficult as any one man could be, he was also one of the most understanding and compassionate men she knew, except when it came to politics and polices. Elizabeth grew serious. She looked at her watch.

"It's the Russians again?" Elizabeth asked her uncle, breaking through her own thoughts.

"Yes." William paused. "A mass grave site was found on President Stepanov's family oil land. Men, women, children. All dead."

"Another old Soviet kill site unearthed?" Elizabeth grumbled. "Why are you telling me this?"

"With the recent global security issues, our countries agreed to quietly help each other." William turned toward his desk. "The Russians suspect a stolen cold war biological weapon may have been used on the victims. And you know very well that if it has anything to do with biohazard materials, my dear, it means you. You are the best we have to offer. Their top scientists have only concluded that it's an unknown pathogen. See for yourself." William handed her several photographs of the victims.

Her face hardened as she studied the photos. "What else?"

"They want to keep it hushed until we all know what it is. President Brice has considered that the fact that it could be one of our old formulas, sold on the black market." He handed her a notepad. "Here take this. It's my personal notes from my conversation with Brice on the subject. I'd just hung up with the White House when I asked Kullens to send you to my office. Study them."

Elizabeth coolly reached for it. She scanned it. Her head shot up. "This is not good. I can see why they would like to keep it hushed. It looks like a pox virus. Can't be sure until I do the tests myself." She placed the notepad in her medical bag. Shaking her head, she locked on to her uncle's troubled eyes. "It looks like what we all feared has finally happened with that Cold War garbage the world's been storing in old bunkers," Elizabeth added. Her sapphire eyes held a challenge.

William tightened his lips around his empty Ashton pipe. There was a small tone of rebuke in his voice. "I am afraid you're right. I know how you feel about 'war waste'. But leave the politics to us."

"Do you think President Stepanov will have any issues with me being a woman?" Over the years Nikolai had seemed to hold female Russians in a certain dim light. She bit her lip slightly as she abruptly recalled the single glance of intense admiration that had passed between them during that first encounter fourteen years ago and seemed to linger the few times their paths had crossed since then. His intelligence coupled with his willingness to put his pride aside for his country had always impressed her. He was an honorable man, much like her uncle. But, he was Russian. One she would have to be careful of.

Brushing the feeling off, staring at William, she asserted, "And when are you going to throw out that pipe? You gave up smoking years ago. Besides, you know it's not good for you." She scolded him, walking toward his desk. She fumbled inside the medical bag she had casually placed on top of a stack of official papers.

"After all these years, I doubt he'll have a problem." William grimaced. "And I don't have to inhale the damn pipe to obtain enjoyment from a habit I once took pleasure in. That is, before you became a doctor." William removed the pipe and cradled it in his hand. "Don't try to change the subject. Elizabeth," he advised her. "As head of the CDC you have a job to do. They made a good choice putting you in that position. If my memory serves me well, you two got along during my stint as an ambassador to Russia. Besides, times have changed and I'm sure he's grown with them." William tapped his pipe in his other hand before slipping it into his pocket. He sat in his overstuffed leather chair and wondered, not for the first time, if Nikolai Stepanov knew what he was doing.

Elizabeth eyed him intensely, then swiveled her head back to her medical bag. Pausing, staring at the contents of her bag, she asked, "How much cooperation will I get from the Russians?" She frowned at the thought. Elizabeth tugged on her Armani suit and glanced back at her uncle. "Well?"

"You will have to deal with that when you arrive. Brice made it clear to Nikolai that they need to be open with our country."

The Russians open? Absurd, she silently declared. Pulling out her sleek Droid phone, she closed her medical bag. "Fine," she conceded. With a touch of her finger, the phone's virtual files system pulled up her calendar. "How soon do I leave? Tomorrow?"

"You leave immediately. Officer Harrison will escort you to Moscow. President Brice has given you the use of a new prototype medical plane. Everything you need will be on that jet. See if you can pick up some international information from this old report." William had over a classified military file. "Start checking databases. Brice wants you to see if anything similar has happened elsewhere." He paused. "Liz, are you sure you are okay with this?"

She hit the sleep button on her phone and put it away. "I see. This is serious." Taking the file, Elizabeth slipped them into her bag. "Not to worry. I'm ready." Elizabeth gave a reassuring wink and a thumbs up to her uncle. She grabbed her medical bag and walked briskly back out into the fresh June air. Harrison opened the State Department limo's back door. Elizabeth slipped into the back seat once more. Shutting it behind her, he swiftly took his place behind the driver's wheel. Harrison glanced in the rearview mirror. Adjusting it, they sped off for Bolling Air Force Base.

The sun reflected off the sleek black hood as the limo pulled onto the runway. The air conditioner's hushed whir was the only sound within the Lincoln. Elizabeth stared out the tinted glass windows, viewing the experimental Stealth One Jet Lab waiting for her. It was an atypical stealth, single wing, Payne's gray in color. She wondered when the government had begun such a clearly expensive project and how it would even fly.

Peering in the rearview mirror, Harrison caught her disbelief. "Her name is Eclipse," he offered. "One of a kind and one hell of a jet. Only six pilots trained to fly this baby. I was the first of those elite six to take her out on her classified fledgling flight and I'll be your pilot for this mission, Dr. Blake."

Elizabeth said, "I can see why they have put a lot of faith in you after observing your," she paused, "less than conventional methods of getting a job done."

Harrison cocked a half-smile and continued. "She hits speeds upwards of Mach 10. She's silent on radar and more. Like an eclipse she disappears into total blackness. Her skin's a beauty, the next generation of metamaterials. The mesh is made of nanofibers less than a thousandth of a millimeter. They bend visible light waves to the point that it defies the laws of physics. Basically, she can cloak herself in war time and not be traced. This is the President's hospital in the sky. A full medical lab with increased payload capacity. She even has a morgue." Harrison took a deep breath and exhaled. "Damn, she can even fly herself home with a press of a button."

The limousine pulled to a stop. Harrison jumped out of the driver seat. In perfect valet form he opened the door, offering a hand to Elizabeth as she stepped out. Elizabeth clutched her medical bag. It was the one item that took on the form of an extra appendage for her. The black leather bag never was out of sight or reach. Elizabeth followed Harrison up the open ramp and entered the Eclipse.

Elizabeth's eyes widened as she took in the interior of the futuristic jet. It seemed to come from a sci-fi movie than reality. Glancing around, she noticed it was outfitted with nanotechnology within as well as without. Her brow rose with anticipation at recognizing the next generation of medical robotics, synthetic biology devices she never thought she would see in her days as a doctor. Elizabeth sat at the main console, listening to her escort continue to ramble on about the marvels of the Eclipse. It was even fitted for emergency surgery with a sterile operating room. Gazing out the open ramp door, she observed the loading of laser guided bombs. She realized this was an aircraft that could save life as well as cause death.

Harrison caught the look of surprise on her face. "We are going to Russia. Regardless whether we are on peaceful terms at the moment—"

Elizabeth shot a hard look at him. "I take it I have no say in the matter."

"Correct." Harrison explained, "I do not expect we'll use them on this mission. They're just a precaution. Don't worry, Dr. Blake. Besides, this sleek baby has longer mission range, more nimble maneuverability, but her key element is vertical life and jet capabilities. A masterpiece of aeronautical design. She's also the first of her kind using cold fusion nuclear power in a jet. Experimental, yes. Hydrogen back-up gives her an unlimited range within the Earth's atmosphere. She's an ozone skimmer."

Elizabeth smiled, watching Harrison run his hand over the console of the prototype jet as if it were a long lost lover.

"The need to stop and refuel is now nonexistent." Harrison sat next to her. He unlocked a Plexiglas case and pointed. "If there is one thing to remember from this briefing, Dr. Blake, it's this: This one-control button. Press it once and the Eclipse goes on emergency autopilot. She'll take you back to the Area 52 base where she was born. After you hit the button the only way to stop her on her course is to blow her up." He moved toward a row of lockers. "The G-suits are stored here. They double as biohazard suits. I'd like to meet the genius who married the two suits."

Elizabeth smiled. "You just did." She'd never realized when she developed the suits that this was where they would end up. "Where is the lab equipment stored?"

He reached for what appeared to be an ordinary head set. Handing it to her, Harrison warned, "Keep in mind, Dr. Blake, this equipment is not like any you've used before. No key pads, no outdated monitors. You'll control everything through this head set." He pointed to one corner. "In case of a shut down, the back-up unit is stored in there." She glanced at the wall hutch.

Elizabeth slipped on the metallic gray headset. Visions danced before her eyes, equipment sliding out of hidden cabinets, then back in. "What the heck?" She ripped the head set off. The holographic images ceased.

"You'll get the hang of it," Harrison encouraged. "Everything is remote-controlled using your own brain waves. The headset taps into your brain's Transcranial Magnetic Stimulation. The TMS energy output telekinetically controls the equipment. If you prefer, you'll have hands-on capabilities. There are three master computers onboard to take over if the plane loses its pilots. We only need a single nano chip to fly her. The rest is for all the medical components." Harrison's eyes fell on the long-legged doctor. Time was getting tight. "The briefing is over." Harrison threw her a flight suit. "Put this on." He took the pilot seat.

Shaking her head, Elizabeth watched the payload doors close. Within minutes she was out of U.S. airspace, over international waters and in contact with the Russian forensics team.

CHAPTER FOUR

Day Two. 4:22 a.m. MSK. Zhukovsky Airport, Russia.

Elizabeth sucked in her breath, feeling her stomach flip at the sudden drop of air speed. The uncommonly bright Russian white nights warmed her skin as the light filtered through the four optical windows of the Eclipse. "When do we land in Moscow?"

"In ten minutes." He smiled and added, "Sorry about putting the brakes on fast." Harrison's voice held a tone of humor.

"I bet you are," Elizabeth fired back. She was not the type of women who would take flashy displays from a man for the sake of stroking his ego. "I'd appreciate it, cowboy, if you'd keep your recklessness under control while we are acting under the President's orders," she huffed.

Harrison frowned. She was right. He should have known his flying exploits would not impress her. The long-legged doctor was out of his league anyway. Harrison shook Dr. Blake out of his head. He reminded himself of flight class 101. The primary objective for this mission, or any flight, was to get from point A to point B and complete the assigned mission with the least amount of trouble. He had put her in jeopardy with that fly boy stunt. Pissed at himself, he switched communications channels. His brawny Montanan voice called out over the small transmitter fixed against his ear. "Flight U.S. Eclipse A101 requesting permission to land."

"Granted," the U.S. Ramstein Air Base flight tower radioed back. Harrison turned off stealth mode. "We'll track your landing. Moscow's base is an uncontrolled aerodrome. No flight towers. You will have to land without voice commands."

"Not a problem. I've landed on dead lake beds with dust cutting my visuals to zero. No towers? Easy."

"Okay, Harrison. Put that big head of yours on check. Your Russian contacts are already on the ground as of 0400 hours local time. Moscow will provide flight information for the investigation site once you arrive." The U.S. controller was to the point. "One more thing, Harrison. You have been reassigned back to the States. Deliver Dr. Blake and then hand over the Eclipse's controls. Two pilots have been assigned to take over the mission."

What is this about, Harrison silently questioned. The whole damn Air Force knows I don't like anyone else flying the Eclipse, but especially on her first big mission. Not her or any of my planes for that damn matter. The air was dead quiet as Harrison entered the landing coordinates.

"Hey, Harrison! I know what you're thinking." The controller broke the silence. "It's an order from the White House and you don't own that jet. Geez, you're the one guy in the military who thinks he *is* the military."

Shit, Harrison silently lipped. "Must be big or suicidal. Orders received." Harrison raised one brow as his mind turned to Moscow's hidden air base. "No towers," he mumbled to himself. He adjusted his headset to speak to Elizabeth. "Close up shop. We'll be on the ground in five minutes."

Elizabeth reached for the computer keyboard as it slipped out of sight under the thin mirrored screen. She turned sharply right to see the dual-optic microscope retreat along with all other open equipment. She lunged to catch it but jumped back as silver metallic doors slammed and secured themselves all at once. In less than 15 seconds all the equipment was securely stored. "I'll never get used to this telekinetic technology," she sighed.

Harrison glanced at his flight controls. The wind speed was off. He was dropping too fast. He pulled up her wings for a vertical landing and fired off all vertical propulsion cylinders. Harrison's hand passed over the holographic control panel for wind speed correction. It was enough of an adjustment for him to relax. The otherworld-looking jet touched down smoothly.

Elizabeth's attention focused on the sophisticated computer while waiting for Harrison to unlock the hatch doors. She took pride knowing she had personally overseen the development of the unique interactive medical storage program during her days working with the Pentagon, but held a slight bitterness that they had apparently added auxiliary support to her design without her. The Pentagon could have at least told her what she and her team were working on for two years of her life before the CDC came along.

"Dr. Blake," a female computer-generated voice called. "New information is requesting upload access."

Elizabeth, still not quite familiar with Eclipse's voice recognition system, uncomfortably ordered, "Upload date on screen." She shook her head, forgetting her headset was still on as her mind rambled. "They could have given it a name."

The computer responded, "MARY. My name is M.A.R.Y., Dr. Blake. Military Advanced Research and Yellow-alert response program. And yes, Officer Harrison is quite a pilot."

Elizabeth whipped off her headset. "If I wanted to let a computer know what I was generally thinking, I would have manual entered it. This is way too personal," she complained, staring at the headset. This was something she would have to work at. Putting the headset back on, she took a breath in. Exhaling, she focused on the incoming information. Blinking typescript, photographs and cryptic medical jargon whizzed by as an atypical computation of intercontinental data appeared on the holographic monitors. One screen caught Elizabeth's attention. It was the Head of Pathology at the University of Peking. MARY's multicolored screens danced with imagery from the database around her.

"Dr. Blake, we have new information that may be useful to the Russian team." The auto-translator kicked in and then abruptly cut off the Beijing report.

"MARY, reconnect," Elizabeth requested.

"Cannot comply, Dr. Blake. Programmed to override incoming date for all vital international news announcements." Elizabeth listened as Radio News from BBC World filled the room. She grew unease at the image on the floating screens. The news boomed, "It is surfacing that the Russians have restarted testing of biological weapons. The world must know why and, more importantly, if we can trust President Stepanov based on these new reports."

Elizabeth slammed her hand on the counter. "Who leaked the information? And what do they know about the grave sites?"

MARY interjected, "I am not programmed to find that data. Please restate request."

Elizabeth fumed. "I wasn't talking to you."

"I detect some hostility. I have been programmed to block any threat to the assigned mission. Are you angry with me, Dr. Blake?"

"Hostility!" Elizabeth calmed her tone. "MARY. I think I will have to look over your master boards. It will be just between us girls." A little makeover to reprogram her attitude was needed. Elizabeth tossed her headset on the tabletop.

MARY did not reply. She silently cut off the BBC feed and turned on the exit lights.

"We'll continue this later," Elizabeth told MARY. She watched as the images faded. Rising from her seat, Elizabeth headed off to meet her contacts.

The moist summer air left droplets of dew on her flight suit as she stepped off the Eclipse. Squinting, she saw three FSB commanders exiting their black Mercedes and approaching her as if they had a claim to her. One officer stayed back as he opened the trunk of the car bearing Russia's Presidential flags. All three were large, intimidating men. Two of the men she was familiar with: Ivan and Dmitry Stepanov. She had met them years ago at a government-sponsored dinner between her uncle and the then Russian president, the same night she first met Nikolai. She frowned. "I had forgotten how the Russian special service teams were iron-like."

Elizabeth noticed the one odd FSB officer blatantly staring at her. No doubt measuring her character, she thought. She nodded, acknowledging his presence. Her eyes held a slight contempt. There was iniquitousness in his eyes. Rolling her lips together, she proceeded with her assignment while Harrison waited on the Eclipse. Elizabeth unclipped the phone. The latest virtual communication technology made her whirlwind life a breeze as she pulled up her Russian contact's name. She mumbled a voice command under her breath as a photo popped up, a perfect match to the unpleasant FSB officer. "Lt. Commander Yuri Nevsky."

"Dr. Blake," Ivan greeted her. "Commander Ivan Stepanov. Please to meet you again. I am sorry this meeting could not be as pleasant at the last."

"Commander Dmitry Stepanov. I, too, wish it was different occasion."

"I wasn't expecting either of you," Elizabeth said. "How long has it been? Fourteen, fifteen years since I've seen you?" They nodded. Elizabeth glanced past Nikolai's brothers, her eyes falling back to the third officer. "I assume that is Lt. Commander Nevsky?" She flashed Yuri's photo as it appeared on her phone.

"Yes," Ivan confirmed.

Elizabeth watched him. His body was stiff, rigid; his face was etched with arrogance as he spoke into his phone. She noticed he was a handsome man, not unlike the other two.

Yuri held his temper in check as he listened to his panicked head scientist, a professor of genetic biochemical engineering, Stefan Mikovich. He was intent on Mikovich's conversation, but not so single-minded as his cold eyes swept over Elizabeth, accessing her capabilities, first as an American, then as a female scientist. Tightening his lips, his face turned to stone as he listened to the rambling on the other end of the phone. He turned away from the scrutiny of her glance. Elizabeth noticed his attempt to hide his displeasure as his hand tightened around the phone.

"We have a problem with the test subjects injected with the virus." The professor hid his anxiety.

"I do not have all day to listen to you whine. What is the problem?" Yuri wiped a small sweat bead from his neck.

"The virus is unstable. I can't be certain you can control the rate of contamination. It's inconsistent. I am requesting to be pulled off the project."

"*Nyet!*" Yuri angrily denied him. "You are not going anywhere, professor. This is good news. Yes, good news. The faster the virus works, the faster I get to sell the vaccination on the black market and have the world at my feet. Good, good."

Professor Mikovich's voice cracked. "Yuri, as your friend, I have to tell you that you do not understand! Even the mice with the vaccination are dying. Slower than the unvaccinated mice, yes, but most are dead already and the rest will be in hours. Nothing we've tried can save them."

Yuri paused. He smiled and asked, "Are my vaccinated men dead? Do they have the pox marks?"

Mikovich swallowed hard. "No. Your men seem fine, but the med techs are not. Humans and mice do not always produce the same results upon exposure. I'm not sure what the actual cause of these deaths is, or why the human assistants are sick when they were wearing biohazard clothing. Yuri, something is very wrong!"

"What do you think is wrong, Mikovich?" Yuri glanced back at Elizabeth. The call was taking too long. He had to deliver her to the grave site immediately or his plan would be compromised. If his men were not so careless, she would not be here, he considered.

Mikovich paused before answering. "Either this pox virus is new or the vaccine isn't working." Mikovich hid his doubts that it was a new virus. Yuri would kill him for sure. It would be a painful death, one he had to escape from. Yuri was unadulterated evil to those who knew him. In truth, Yuri owned him, and Mikovich knew that. He had already made plans to leave when the testing was completed and as far as he was concerned the tests were completed to Yuri's demands. Mikovich had hoped his call would somehow stop Yuri, but it had only given him a reason to plan his disappearance sooner. They had been working together for a long time. Mikovich now knew it was a mistake to trust they were friends all those years.

Yuri repeated icily, "Are my men dying from it?"

"No, but—"

"Then I see no problem with the vaccine's effectiveness. *My* tests have succeeded. It's for men, not mice or your lazy inept assistants. We're going with the original plan. After I am done escorting the American pathologist to Shapkino, I will be flying out to meet you at the lab." Yuri abruptly hung up without another word. His attention switched on how to use this news to gain control of the few remaining splintered Russian mafia gangs not under his control already.

Yuri hurried toward Elizabeth. He was late. Angry Mikovich had delayed him, his temper etched lines on his face as he forced a diplomatic smile. It disappeared as quickly as it appeared.

Elizabeth offered her hand as he approached her. "Lt. Commander Yuri Nevsky. Dr. Elizabeth Blake with the United States CDC. I was told Moscow's newly established health organization will be meeting me and providing updated data."

"We will meet their representatives at the grave site." Yuri's sweaty palm took her hand. Pulling her hand back, she stuck her hand in the pocket where she kept a dry wipe sanitary cloth and wiped the sticky dampness from her palm. "The three of us will be escorting you there and we are behind schedule," Yuri continued. "I suggest we get on that fancy plane you arrived in and try to make up some lost time."

"Before I can let you on, I need to see your security clearance. And the medical research files, please. The material you sent my staff is not current. It's only a location report. You do have your forensic team's latest reports, don't you?"

Damning her silently, he opened his brief case, snapped up the cyber files and silently handed them to her. He had planned to dispose of those files.

Glancing at the two brothers, she said, "Commander Dmitry Stepanov, Commander Ivan Stepanov, I need your clearances as well."

Ivan and Dmitry smirked as they reached for their security tags.

Yuri's cold eyes washed over her face and rebuked her. "Remember, Dr. Blake, that if it weren't for President Stepanov and us, you would not be standing on any Russian military base. Without the clearance provided by us, you and everyone else on board your fancy American plane would be dead." Yuri disliked her boldness and wondered if she was a threat. Looking at her womanly frame, he pushed the thought aside. *She is just a woman.* He had disposed of many during his life. She would be no different if she became a problem. Everyone was disposable.

Yuri flashed his security IDs for her to see. Swiftly, he placed them back in his shirt pocket. Yuri reassured himself as he mentally worked out the timing for his next move. He would turn the investigation at the mass grave site over to Ivan and leave as soon as they arrived. They could handle babysitting her. He had more important matters to attend to. Yuri nodded toward Dmitry and Ivan.

"Lt. Commander Nevsky." Elizabeth, irritated by his rudeness said, "I find your diplomatic protocol irregular. But, in the interest of time," she momentary looked at Ivan, who she trusted, "let's proceed."

The four entered the Eclipse. Twenty minutes later the team was over the Shapkino oil field.

CHAPTER FIVE

Day Two. 5:35 a.m. MSK. South Shapkino Oil Field, Pechora.

"The Stepanov oil land is far larger than I had imagined." Elizabeth viewed several hundred drill towers dotting the stripped Russian landscape. "So this explains how President Nikolai Stepanov could afford to beat his predecessor," Elizabeth commented. "He's a rich man."

"That is he is," Harrison agreed, the cockpit doors slid shut behind him. A whiff of her jasmine perfume filled his nostrils. The scent caught him off guard. His attention was divided. He had to think. *Lock the cockpit. Get the gear.* He pushed through the scented air, reaching into the overhead bin. He tossed his belongings into his standard-issue khaki duffle bag and zipped it up. He shouldered his gun and ordered, "MARY, secure the cockpit." A soft click was heard.

Elizabeth raised a brow. "Going somewhere, Harrison?" She slipped into her cyber-biohazard suit, checking the digital armbands.

"Back to the States." He stared at the form fitted bio-suit. "You have two new pilots. They are escorting the Russian medical inspector on board as we speak."

"Why?"

"I don't get to say no to orders, doc. You, on the other hand, do not have to go when called. The Eclipse delivered you to Stepanov's oil field and it will remain with you to ensure you have its testing facilities available. God, I'll miss this baby." Harrison gave the Eclipse's side control panel a sorrowful glance as he grabbed his duffle bag and swung it onto his shoulder.

Elizabeth half-mocked, half-joked, "Are you sure you can leave your love?" Her eyes swept around the interior of the Eclipse. Reaching past him, they bumped. Her smile faded. Elizabeth disregarded the flash of chemistry between them. She pulled several evidence bags from a small bin next to him.

Harrison replied in what was becoming a familiar drawl, "Oh, I'm not worried. We were meant to be together." He paused. His eyes fell hard on Elizabeth. "And we will be." He changed the subject. "By the way, those three pitbull FSB officers who are waiting for you will need new clearances if they fly with you again. They only had a one way ticket with me to get you here." He looked up at a silver panel. "MARY, no one is, other than Dr. Blake and my authorized pilots will have access to this area or any area of my plane. Eclipse's lab is off limits, too." He stared at Yuri through the hatch, sizing him up.

Elizabeth questioned, "*Your* plane?"

Harrison ignored her. He pointed to Yuri on the other side of the hatch door. "I don't like that one. What's his name? Nevsky? Dr. Blake, I'd watch myself around him. I can't put my finger on it, but he's bad."

It was Harrison's gut reaction, kneeing him in the pit of his stomach. It was never wrong. Well, it had been once. He hung his head in disgrace, struggling to shut out the pain he would carry for the rest of his life. An entrenched memory. Sucking in a breath, he pushed the painful old images aside. Harrison's head shot up. He strolled forward, adjusting his backpack one more time.

Elizabeth tilted her head, questioning his sudden quietness. Harrison said nothing. She would not understand. It was his burden. He kept moving.

"I think Yuri is benign," Elizabeth replied. To put him at ease, she said, "He is my Russian contact and was cleared by both Presidential offices. He seemed to be interested in only himself and that travel chess game I noticed him playing with during the flight. Not a word on what he knew about the mass grave site when I questioned him. Just moving white pawn to black knight. Russians and their chess! But, I will keep in mind what you said Harrison."

Elizabeth followed Harrison to the exit lab hatch. He passed his hand over a small iridescent glass plate.

The security doors slid open to a posh interior, a fine leather couch at one side. Deep first class flight chairs lined the other wall. Yuri sat alongside the single armed Marine escort.

"Come, time to go. Tell me you were not sleeping on the job." Harrison grabbed the Marine's arm. He pulled him up from the leather seat. "No time to waste." The Marine snapped up his pack, feeling Harrison's grip drop. "I'll finish securing the Eclipse and meet you outside. Stand guard."

The Marine walked down the flight stairs taking up his position at the foot of the flight stairs.

Harrison turned and smelled smoke. His jaw line tightened as his eyes followed several smoke rings up to the ceiling of the Eclipse. Harrison stared at its source. The men locked eyes.

His face etched with arrogance, Yuri snuffed his cigarette out on the fine leather armchair, leaving a small black hole in the seat meant for a president, an American president. A dare. Anger filled Harrison as he placed one hand on his semiautomatic sidearm and patted it twice, breathing in the odor of scorched leather. Yuri's lips pressed together maliciously, his gaze cold. He was a man with no soul.

Their wordless exchange of threats and counter threats passed between them within seconds. Finally, Harrison slammed the air sanitizing unit's control panel, the dare answered. The smoky carcinogenic haze was sucked away. Clean recycled air replaced the polluted air in seconds.

Yuri tapped out a fresh cigarette, leaning deep into the leather chair, and put it to his lips. He patted his shirt pocket, looking for his lighter. He flinched in surprise when Harrison snatched the dangling cigarette out of his lips and broke it in two. Harrison placed the fragmented tobacco halves in Yuri's shirt pocket. "This is a no smoking area."

Yuri's face turned antagonistic. His hand sought out his blade. "Shit," he cursed under his breath. His favorite razor was not in place. Of course, he remembered. The American's security systems were too advanced. The scanner would have detected it, even his latest Hawk blade. He let his hand relax. "Maybe so. But Russia is not." Yuri's words held a harsh tone.

"As long as you're on the Eclipse, you are in America." Harrison made it a point to deepen his cowboy accent.

Yuri's eyes held contempt. His voice was threatening. "I guess we'll have to share a smoke together, fly boy, on another day." Yuri silently marked him for dead and added, "I will see you again, my new American friend."

Harrison knew what he meant. He gave a brazen half-smile and withdrew, stepping backwards, keeping his eyes on the Russian FSB officer, mentally recording Yuri's face and mannerisms. He made sure he knew who his enemies were and Yuri had just been added to his list. "I'll remember never to show him my back," he said under his breath. Reaching the exit, Harrison quickly turned and walked down and down the Eclipse's stairs, passing three of Russia's most significant men boarding the Eclipse without a greeting: Ivan, Dmitry and the newly-arrived youngest Stepanov brother, Anton.

"Well, well, all of President Stepanov's brothers, all top government security officials. Only in Russia. What I can't figure out is Yuri. Where does he fit into this team?" Harrison muttered as he nodded to them. The brothers returned the nod of acknowledgement. Harrison's reputation did not go unnoticed in top circles overseas. The medical inspector followed closely behind the commanders.

Yuri stood. "Commander." He acknowledged Ivan.

Elizabeth offered the four men a seat. "Men, let's get busy. I will need all your current forensic reports, samples, and all completed data."

"And who are you?" questioned the inspector. "And the American pathologist? Where is he?"

"He? I guess you were not aware I was a woman." She managed a smile. "I'm Dr. Elizabeth Blake, Head of the CDC."

Yuri tugged on his suit jacket. Glancing at Elizabeth, he callously introduced her. "Dr. Blake is at your service, inspector."

Elizabeth pointedly corrected Yuri. "I am not at your service, inspector. I was requested to head this investigation by President Brice and President Stepanov. I can't believe you were not properly informed."

"Paperwork must have been delayed," Yuri said, enjoying the moment of discomfort between the inspector and Elizabeth.

The medical inspector grumbled, disappointed by the fact that help from the West had come in the form of a woman. He rolled his eyes at Yuri. "Why her?" he grumbled in Russian.

The air grew somber. Elizabeth pressed forward. "Inspector, let's get started. I understand you have orders from President Stepanov to cooperate with me?"

The inspector hesitated. "I don't think so. This information is too critical to our country."

"Inspector, President Stepanov personally requested her specifically because of her expertise with bio-warfare agents," Ivan informed him. Let me remind you of who really is in charge here. You are dispensable. Dr. Blake is not." His hands slipped into his trouser pocket, exposing his security badge. That was the reality of this meeting. The inspector understood. He took a seat.

Ivan quickly summed up the introductions, fearing delays. "This is one of our top medical inspectors." Ivan threw a hard glance at Elizabeth, withdrawing his hands from is pocket.

The inspector took out a handkerchief and wiped his sweat-covered brow. "Too hot for me today." He tucked it away. His skin paled. "OK, OK. Nice spy plane you Americans have. We have one too, but it's in a safe house now."

Elizabeth doubted there was actually a Russian version of the Eclipse. "She is a medical sky lab," was her only correction.

"What's this?" The medical inspector rudely pointed to a glass case marked "emergency only" that held several odd handheld medical devices, one a defibrillator. "Looks like something from one of your space movies." He mocked. "Too fancy to work, *nyet?*"

"Can we move on to the Russian team's forensic report? Let's not waste time, inspector." Elizabeth exhaled deeply. Her temper in check, she said, "You haven't give us much to go on to figure out what killed your people. Do you have anything else?"

The inspector handed her several photographs. He feebly pointed out, "One looks tortured. The female was stripped naked. We should have all the forensic conclusions and the completed examinations in a few days. We expect-"

Elizabeth, exasperated, shot in, "The cause of death of the exhumed corpse was clearly a deadly fast spreading pathogen. Let's not waste time. And those reports will be ready by the time I leave this site. I am sure your president would agree." Elizabeth snapped, "I need to see the victim's bodies. I find it hard to believe that all of your scientists are having trouble identifying a variation of this pathogen. Let me make this clear. I am not here to determine who murdered who in your country but to find the cause. I have been in contact with my staff at the CDC and several other key international scientists to gain access to their data banks. I have approval to form a five panel international team to help discover the cause. Inspector, this can't be covered up. Have you not heard the news that was leaked?"

The inspector's eyes darted at Elizabeth. "There has been a leak? I see." Sensing he would only look more incompetent providing her his files, he added, "I appreciate all of this." He glanced drearily at the interior of the Eclipse. "However, the challenges of the cyber forensics investigation before you are new. Our established methods are enough." He clenched his papers tighter.

"Even though your report is incomplete, it contains critical first responder insights. Let me reiterate that several international scientists have been asked to forward their data banks. They are in the process of being linked up to the Eclipse's communication systems." Elizabeth sighed. "Send them what you have. The rest of the specialized team will be on system network within the hour. The team will be headed by me per both our president's orders. I can't believe you haven't taken this pathogen seriously," she scolded. Snatching medical gear off a nearby shelf, she said, "Put these on. Standard safety procedures." Elizabeth handed out several cyber biohazard suits. "MARY, secure all areas except the presidential exit."

"Secured, Dr. Blake."

Dmitry seized Elizabeth's shoulder, "Stop. Who is this Mary? We were informed only that you, Dr. Blake, would be arriving, and only you have clearance."

"MARY is not human. M.A.R.Y. is the master communications system on board." Elizabeth gently put her hand on Dmitry's and slid it off her shoulder, picking up her forensic case. She headed for the exit

"Inspector," Ivan said glancing at his watch. "Time to go."

The inspector was exasperated. Looking for any way to delay Elizabeth, he jostled his files, spilling them across the floor of the Eclipse.

"Clumsy!" Ivan ridiculed. Yuri smiled.

Elizabeth glanced back and grimaced at the Eclipse's floor covered now with his report. She sighed. "MARY, provide the inspector with a tech pad." She shot the inspector a hard look. "I hope you know how to use one." She abruptly turned to the Marine on guard. "Stay with the inspector. He's not allowed in the restricted areas. Escort him off the Eclipse after he is finished cleaning up."

Elizabeth's attention focused on the team of forensic scientists before her as she stepped off of Eclipse. Leaving the inspector to juggle through his probably useless papers, she adjusted her cyber biohazard gear. She focused on a small glowing holographic screen, she checked her vital signs. Scanning the rest of her group, she confirmed that all the medical scanners were linked directly to MARY. She glanced back at the Eclipse and saw Harrison jump into one of two F 35C lightening jet fighters nearby.

He turned the jet to face her. Confident he would see her again, he lowered the hood. Grasping the fighter jet's controls, Harrison gave them a familiar squeeze and fired up the engines. In typical Harrison cowboy style, he was airborne within seconds.

Elizabeth hid her feelings of unease. There was something about Harrison's risky boldness that was comforting on this mission. Elizabeth hated to acknowledge that he had more... more of just what she could not put her finger on. She pushed Harrison out of her mind.

Elizabeth hiked toward the yellow barrier tape that held back a growing mixture of journalists, photographers and locals who came out to get a look at the dead. "I'm with the CDC. I am here to meet with Dr. Glazkov." She handed her tag to the Russian officer directing the uninvited guests to stay behind the tape. Elizabeth, feeling agitated by the loss of time, pressed him. "Dr. Glazkov, please," she repeated in perfect Russian. She adjusted her face protector.

"There he is. The tall man." The officer pointed.

Elizabeth stepped under the barrier tape to stand before Glazkov. "*Dobroye utro*," she addressed the doctor. "*Menya zavut* Dr. Elizabeth Blake."

Glazkov nodded in approval of her Russian. "Good morning. This will make my job much easier, Dr. Blake, my English is limited." He waved off his interpreter. Looking over her shoulder he saw the top FSB Stepanov commanders behind her. "I have to admit, I was getting impatient waiting for your arrival. I've heard good things about you, doctor. I see the president *has* taken this seriously if he sent those three."

Elizabeth felt relieved that she would no longer be dealing with the inspector. Glazkov, if nothing else, was generally concerned.

Glazkov pointed to a small group of men excavating a site. "We will start there." They walked toward the restrained forensic team. A quiet buzzing sound filled the quiet air. Elizabeth glanced toward Yuri as he snatched his phone. He glanced at the screen.

"Crap," he said under his breath before deleting the text message. Yuri shoved passed Elizabeth, slipping his phone back into his pocket.

"An 'excuse me' would have been nice," she admonished, regaining her balance.

He chose not hear the good doctor's comment. He was mad. Dangerously mad. Mikovich had disappeared. *How could he slip out that easily? He has to still be in Russia.* He texted Misha back. *Hunt him down. Stop him before he leaves Russia.*

"Ivan." Yuri pressed Ivan forward. "We have to talk. Now."

"What the hell is so important you're interfering with a Presidential order? Again!" Ivan asked, irked.

"I have just received new orders," Yuri lied.

"What orders? From whom?" Ivan questioned. He never trusted Yuri.

Yuri paced a few more feet away and motioned for Ivan to join him. "From General Serebrinsky. He knows I have a snitch in the Russian mafia, and my inside guy has a lead on who may have stolen the canisters and why they used them at this site." Yuri's boldfaced lies were getting him deeper that he wanted to be. Getting Ivan to believe him could prove difficult.

Ivan hesitated, and then called Serebrinksy. A minute he snapped off his com link and he said, "What's with General Serebrinsky covering your ass? Go, but report to me as soon as you get the information. It better be good. I plan to follow up with the general."

The confrontation stirred up Yuri's hatred for his half-brothers, but his ploy bought him time to find Mikovich. He would deal with them later. The two men walked back to Elizabeth and Glazkov, who were approaching a newly uncovered grave.

"Dr. Blake, I leave you in the capable hands of my Commander, Ivan Stepanov." Yuri left her without another word. Stalking away from the scene, he pulled his phone out. He sent a final text to Misha before leaving the site. *Put out the order: Find Mikovich alive tonight. I will personally see to his punishment for this betrayal.* Scrambling into a black sedan, Yuri headed for the airport.

Arriving at the disturbed grave mound, Elizabeth found Glazkov's forensic team hard at work.

"Gentlemen, take a break." The Russian flowed from her tongue. Several Russian forensic specialists took a look at Elizabeth. Questions filled their eyes. She was definitely not Russian.

"Who sent you?" one questioned. He refused to move.

"I have orders from President Stepanov." She glanced backward toward the Stepanov commanders. She turned back to the team of scientists hovering over their specimens. The three Stepanovs stood in stiff contrast to Elizabeth's elegance.

"OK, we'll go." One team member stood and brushed the dirt from his gloved hands before heading into a canvas tent. The rest followed suit.

Elizabeth hiked up to the canvas-covered dirt mound. She sorted through their specimens. The sound of a helicopter flying overhead drew her attention. "Now what?" Looking back to the mess before her, she tugged on each gloved finger, making sure the glove was a snug fit. She put her forensic case down on a canvas next to the others that were left behind.

She began to slowly sift away the dirt. "What do we have here?" she asked herself as she bagged a four-inch long dirt covered specimen. Elizabeth held up a plastic bag with partially decomposed human skin. She quickly put it back. "Useless." She looked around and found nothing in the collected specimens that could give a clue about the pathogen.

Glazkov agreed. "It's useless."

"I have to start over. I'll take these onto the Eclipse for analysis. With your permission, of course, Dr. Glazkov."

"Yes, anything," he agreed. "I see why President Stepanov agreed to have you come. You have the right combination of scientific skills and trained intuition that promises to work well for us. I wish you could have come sooner. Damn. I do not know what is with the inspector and his obstructive behavior."

Elizabeth endlessly repeated each step of her investigation, collecting fresh forensic material to be added to the data collected by the Russian team. Glazkov observed her skill and detail; he was determined he would not interfere with her investigation. Elizabeth abruptly stood and walked around the grave. Something caught her eye. She stopped to look at one particular exhumed corpse lying on the side. She was startled. She saw this corpse as the first of many to come, looking across the rotting human carcass to Glazkov.

"Dr. Glazkov, this one has small pox-like lesions, but the incubation period and the time of death do not agree."

"I know," Glazkov replied. "It's what led me to suspect the old biological warfare operations site at the western Siberian site. Years ago, as a young scientist, I worked on a virus that had similar symptoms. But I can't be sure. The DNA doesn't match the virus we're dealing with on site."

"Why wasn't this mentioned to me before I arrived?" She didn't wait for an answer. "I will need this male and that young female for immediate autopsies onboard the Eclipse. Can Moscow Central Clinical Hospital's morgue contain the virus if we transport the bodies to them for autopsy?" He nodded. "We must keep the others secure and on ice here. Order refrigerator trucks if you have to. It can offer the sterile environment needed to contain the virus."

Elizabeth saw a peculiar carefully wrapped body bag tagged for storage. "Who is in there?"

Glazkov shrugged his shoulders. "The inspector tagged this one."

Walking over, she read the tag. Turning to Glazkov, out of curiosity, she asked, "Did you know?" Glazkov's brows lowered and he shook his head. Stooping down, Elizabeth inspected the unlisted victim. "Why is this man wearing a military security uniform on company land? And he has no signs of small pox. See? The body is well-preserved."

She no longer maintained any illusion that his would be a one-day investigation. Someone had something to hide, someone high up in the political Russian hierarchy. She called out, "Ivan, come take a look. I think that we have a mystery man here. Looks like one of your men." She stood next to Glazkov. "That soldier is here for a reason. He may give us a clue to the canisters." She looked at Ivan. "We need to know who and where he was in service."

Ivan was concerned. He recognized the uniform. He was pissed the inspector did not inform him or anyone on his FSB team. He would have a talk with him before he left the site. And it would not be a pleasant one. Ivan hustled away, pulling out his phone. He hit one key on his com link to reach General Serebrinsky. "It seems someone got very sloppy. General, Dr. Blake has uncovered new information to pass on to President Stepanov. We have a dead guard from the Cold War storage site. I recognized the uniform. I haven't confirmed it with Dr. Blake. What are your orders?"

"Keep it to yourself. Do nothing. Watch Dr. Blake and see if more clues come up. Let her do her job. Keep me posted. I will inform the President."

"Yes, general." Ivan broke off the conversation quickly. He hurried back to Elizabeth's side.

"I'll start with the interviews of the employees. Anton, please ask the employees to meet under the canvas tent." She turned to Ivan, "Call me as soon someone finds out where this guard was stationed." Ivan nodded.

Elizabeth found herself holding her breath. Walking by the exhumed sites, she realized that this was nothing like what she had expected. Every corpse she had seen had blood-stained noses and mouths and pox marks. All had vomited blood. She had thought just this one time it would be simple. Just pull up some data banks, match the DNA and, viola! The Russians would have their pathogen mystery solved. But something different, something new, had killed these people.

Her worst fears overcame her as she approached the tent where Anton had gathered the oil workers. Elizabeth froze in her tracks. She noticed pox marks on the employees' faces. It was spreading quickly.

"Stop. Stop!" she called to Anton. She ran back to Dr. Glazkov. "Who on your team has been vaccinated for small pox?" she demanded.

"I have been. As for the rest, I can find out." He unclipped his cell phone.

"Everyone on this site is infected except for those of us who arrived suited up. This bio-suit is impermeable to 100% of pathogens. How on earth did you miss this and why was nothing done to quarantine these people? And your medical inspector is on the Eclipse. He has to be quarantined here. The plane has to go through automatic sanitization before anyone gets back on board again."

Elizabeth radioed her pilots. "Initiate total sterilization. Scrub down all the passengers aboard, military and non-military. MARY, prepare a small pox vaccine and with this pathogen unknown, provide everything else available, for such plague-infection known in our records to cover our bases. Start with the inspector and all on the site. Generate recommendations to the CDC and Moscow, Office of the President. Use the bifurcated needles from my medical station desk. Leave the vaccines at medical station 1A."

"Yes, Dr. Blake," MARY responded.

"Added order: Escort the inspector to meet Glazkov after the biohazard procedures have been implemented."

"The inspector has been vaccinated, as has my team," Glazkov said, replacing his phone.

Elizabeth shook her head. "This could turn into a real plague. A pandemic."

Glazkov paced back and forth a few steps. "What do you want to do?"

"I need you to order mass vaccinations and medical supplies issued immediately. What is the quarantine area?" Elizabeth's blood raced through out her limbs. She was alarmed that the virus was spreading faster that originally confirmed by the Russian team, that it was already too late to contain it at the site. Small pox lesions would normally show up days later, not mere hours after infection. Either the people had had small pox for days or this virus was running amok. At this rate, it could spread across all of Russia in just days. It had to be stopped here.

A Russian team member placed a hand on her. He showed her a clipboard that held a map of the quarantined towns.

"No! This should have been tripled in size. You knew you had a pox virus to deal with. Get the quarantine for a wider area approve immediately!" She slapped the clipboard back into his hands, walking toward the Eclipse. "Let's get moving. Now!" Security followed behind, carrying the bodies for autopsies on stretchers. A team member and Glazkov followed with the others.

"Dr. Blake, President Stepanov." Ivan waved her over with a phone in one hand.

She reached for his phone. "President Stepanov. Dr. Blake. I have to have your Russian investigation team take me to visit the nearby towns. They may have signs of a pathogen mimicking small pox."

"Small pox!" Nikolai's voice was harsh.

"Mr. President –"

"What the hell is going on?"

"The unidentified virus is spreading rapidly, Mr. President. The Russian Ministry of Health needs to be called in. I have requested the quarantine be broadened. However, you're the one who will have to implement some military enforcement to contain it to this area. Have you been vaccinated for small pox?"

"Yes."

"And your men?"

"Yes. Of course!"

"I suggest all personnel and healthcare workers who have not been get vaccinated within the next two hours, if you can."

"I see." Nikolai hit his fist on the polished desk top. "What do you need from our government?"

"To start with, the Ministry of Health must update the Russian people with the new information. I will place calls for more international assistance. I already have access to global medical databanks." Thank God for the Eclipse, she thought to herself. She would need all of its technology.

"How?" Nikolai demanded.

"President Brice assigned the U.S.'s newest technological jet lab to this mission. It will serve as our mobile base," she explained quickly, getting back to the point. "My concern is keeping the virus contained in this area until we know what kind of pox it is. This must be seen as an international threat."

"We do not go public with this new information. My government wants to keep it out of the international press for a bit longer," Nikolai remarked.

"You mean you want to keep it undercover. Just like all those years ago? Well, Mr. President, that is your prerogative. Mine is to stop this from spreading. Goodbye, Mr. President."

Elizabeth paused before passing the phone back to Ivan. Her personal history with Nikolai might be an issue after all. She couldn't just hang up. Elizabeth had heard the worry in his last statement. She waved off Ivan and placed the com link back to her ear. She calmly said, "Nikolai - President Stepanov - I am sorry for my personal outburst. We'll find out what it is. I'll be in Moscow today with my report. I am shutting down my on-site investigation as we speak."

Nikolai ran his hand through his black hair and pushed his half-filled glass of coffee cup aside. He asked, "How soon?"

"I hope to have something for you within five hours."

"I'll see you in Moscow. Goodbye."

Elizabeth passed the com link to Ivan. He checked the line, then slipped his phone in the case clipped to his belt. "Dr. Blake, we have five hours to be back in Moscow. Do you think you can complete your report?"

"The initial one, yes, but we have to move quickly. Have your team placed all of the collected specimens on board the Eclipse."

Ivan turned to Dmitry. "Anton, get on it. Find out what you can, and then get back to Moscow when you finish. Keep us updated." Ivan turned to the others. "We need to board the Eclipse immediately."

Ten minutes into flight, Elizabeth made the Y-cut on her first cadaver.

CHAPTER SIX

Day One. 9:40 p.m. EST. Atlantic Ocean.

The *Dostoyny*'s stern fell hard into the wild waves. The oil tanker struck with such violence that the crew was tossed about as the ship hit the deep, swelling waters. It was as if it had hit solid stone rather than fluid sea. The ocean's torrential waves rushed with great force up onto the deck and receded back into the ocean as the waves claimed anything that was not fastened down securely. The winds increased the size and force of the waves with each pass. The 108,000-ton petroleum tanker rolled and pitched in rhythm to the sea.

"The sea rolled high today," Captain Mokotoff commented. He took in a deep breath of the salt-dampened air in the dimly lit cabin. He casually spoke to his chief mate who looked up from the bridge's master control panel with red, tired eyes.

The chief mate nodded. "Yes, sir. The weather is not cooperating with us." A steady rain fell against the window panes of the *Dostoyny*.

"What is our ETA for pulling into Port Everglades?" Mokotoff asked as he turned his head to the chief mate.

"Four hours, sir."

The dirt and the smell of the oil on the ship were things that Mokotoff had to get used to. Mokotoff, having spent nearly half his life in the pristine Russian Navy fleet, was already used to dealing with the rough seas spilling over the bow. "Would not have found a speck of dirt about my ship then," he thought aloud. He owed his life to Nikolai Stepanov for providing him the opportunity to captain his oil fleet after the fall of the USSR.

Beneath his strong veneer of man, the conflict between his loyalty to Nikolai and his distrust of Yuri Nevsky weighed heavily on Mokotoff. He hated the fact that Yuri had special oversight privileges. He had a knot in the pit of his stomach with each voyage of the oil tanker. He had a nagging feeling about his cargo, 100,000 tons of oil. The weather wasn't good. The delay in departure was unusual and to not go through a final inspection seemed out of place. Still, the weather aside, it had been an uneventful trip and he was nearing his port of call. He walked about his small bridge and poured himself a hot cup of black coffee. He unwrapped the dark rye bread sandwich his wife had made him before he left port.

"Captain, we have a problem."

Mokotoff swallowed a bit of his sandwich. "Well, what is it? Something small, I hope."

His neckline prickled with an unnatural tingle as he heard his chief mate say, "We have a breach in the double hull. A small puncture-like hole in the inner lining. We can patch it."

"A puncture? How much oil are we losing?"

"It looks like a small explosion unit might have done it," a crew man said. "It's a slow leak sir."

"Fix it!" he exclaimed. His hunches were validated as he heard his crew radio about the problem in the hull. He felt confident that the oil leaking into the outer shell would not pose a threat of an ocean spill. Taking another bite of his sandwich he quickly washed it down with a gulp of coffee. He finished the sandwich. With one sweep of his calloused hand, he cleared away the trash, making room for the ships' logs.

"There is a call for you, sir. It's from Dmitry Stepanov."

"Dmitry? Not good. If he took over the command center..." Mokotoff let his words hang in midair as he took the radio transmitter and held it up to his bearded face. "Captain Mokotoff here."

His face froze as he heard Dmitry. "Captain, we have received reports of two ships with breached hulls. We are having communications problems with them. The *Azov* is also off course by 20 degrees. What is your status?"

"We have a small breach." The radio crackled and went silent. "Lt. Commander Stepanov?" Mokotoff turned to the crewmen nearby. "Check our satellite communications systems. Get off autopilot to be safe. We will steer her ourselves." He looked back at the radio transmitter, calling to Dmitry a final time. "Damn. We lost contact." He slammed the receiver into its holder.

The chief mate cautiously reached for the controls. He was uncomfortable not using the autopilot in rough seas. "Captain, Viktor is reporting that Pavlov turned sick while patching the hull. Viktor is working on the patch but with Pavlov sick it will take longer."

"Send Pavlov to sick bay and get Krill down there to help fix that leak!"

The chief mate's face soured as he listened to Viktor. His head shot up. "Captain, his whole team has something wrong with them."

"Send them to sick bay. I'm on my way there."

Mokotoff snatched his raingear off the black painted metal hook. His hand slid on the wet rails as he climbed down the metal planks of the stairs, managing his way toward sick bay below. Pulling back the rain soaked hood of his rain gear, he struggled for breath. Panic set in as he entered sick bay. His crewman was encrusted in small boils. Fear etched across the captain's face. *Small pox? No, worse.* Memories of seeing this kind of illness during his military years led the captain to curse under his breath. He knew where it came from and how it got on his ship.

"Damn Yuri! Quarantine this man and others as well."

Pavlov screamed as pustulating boils rose up on his hemorrhaging skin. Mokotoff, backing out of sick bay, turned and ran.

"Turn this ship around!" he shouted as he entered the bridge, salt water dripping from his rain gear. His words fell on sick men. One by one, they felt the fever. Then the small bumps began. One of the crew members snapped; babbling, frantically pushing his way out, he stumbled and fell down the ladder leading to the captain's cabin.

"You." Mokotoff pointed to his chief mate. "Contain him with fire blankets. Don't touch him." He grabbed the small first aid kit off the shelf. Opening it, he threw the chief mate a pair of latex gloves that were neatly folded in the case. He slipped on a pair.

Within minutes, Mokotoff's hands began to hurt. Ripping off the medical gloves, he wrapped his throbbing fiery skin with clean rags, hoping to ease the pain. Moving to the ship's controls, he held his vomit down as he fought to keep his head clear.

"Even at full speed it's going to take us at least eighteen hours to get to the ship back into Russian waters and out of port range," he called out to his crew. "Try to stabilize that crewman to keep him alive." He looked down at the crewman writhing in pain.

The chief mate panicked. "Captain! Captain, I can't turn the ship by hand. Autopilot is jammed. All navigation satellite systems are down. We've lost control of the ship!"

Captain Mokotoff stepped back and raised his steeled eyes at the horrifying site before him. "We are all dead men," he said under his breath, watching his blood soak through the rags on his arms as his skin burst open with contaminated blood that dripped to the bridge floor. Grabbing a fresh rag, he tied it tight over the open wounds and cursed, "Damn Yuri! He was always a bad seed. Damn his brother for not listening to me when I told him not to give him access to the ship codes."

Mokotoff looked out through the rain-splattered windows. He hung his head in prayer, making peace with himself and God, asking for whatever a walking dead man asks of God. He pulled together the strength he would need to help his men.

"Give me the captain's log," he said after a moment. "Get on the flashers. Signal other ships, send an SOS and get the warning flags up." A crewman pulled the orange flag from its storage compartment. On the surface was a black disk next to a black square. The captain pulled out a red fluorescent marker. He drew a simple skull and crossbones over the flag's surface, writing the word "biohazard" beneath it in bold Russian print. "Hoist the warning flag. No one is to come aboard or get off. If we make it to U.S. waters, we may have a chance," stated the captain. "We will survive."

Mokotoff stood his ground at the bridge's helm. He took out an old radio and, with speed and competency, relayed Morse code messages to a rescue coordination center in New York and any ship, Russian or otherwise, in the mid-Atlantic. He prayed someone would hear them.

He tenderly glanced back at his crew. He pushed the radio to one side. He hid the farewell that was written behind in his eyes as his fingers snapped them to attention.

"Stop all the engines," he ordered the crew. "Our best chance now is to go with the currents. We should not be too far from land. We will hit U.S. waters in a few hours, more or less. We will be okay. Hang on, men."

With his closing words, the ship went adrift toward what he hoped would be safer waters, maybe an uninhabited island. The winds took control of his ship in a rocky sea. They prepared the ship to run aground. Finding land was now their only hope.

CHAPTER SEVEN

Day Two. 9:00 a.m. MSK. The Kremlin, Moscow.

"Damn!" Nikolai swore as Sergei entered the Presidential suite. The smell of vodka permeated his office.

"And who are you damning today?" Sergei asked. "I take it the American pathologist did not have good news for you? Americans never do with us." Sergei tapped his foot. "I haven't seen you drink this much in years."

Swirling his glass of vodka, Nikolai rubbed his throbbing temple with his free hand. Even in the constant pain of stress headaches he looked like a man of great power. The years had been good to him. Until today. Sergei noticed that Nikolai's neatly-combed hair was in sharp contrast with his bloodshot obsidian eyes.

"Did you get any sleep, Mr. President?" Sergei looked down, knowing the answer to the question he posed as Nikolai's friend, not his chief advisor. He gritted his teeth, discerning that an awful truth was hidden. He knew this feeling well and kept it to himself. He would know soon enough.

"No, General. Dr. Blake had no good news." Sergei waited studying, his President who was deep in thought. Nikolai rose and stepped forward. He leaned his strong frame against the burgundy-draped window of the presidential suite separated by a small vestibule from his main office and his private study. Nikolai started at the uncharacteristic stillness that hung over Red Square that morning, the emptiness in the day as it waked over Moscow. The quietness unsettled him. He strained to hear the muffled wheels of the morning traffic as he watched from his office. The strange morning mirrored his mood.

He needed answers. With pursed lips, he downed what remained of the clear liquid in his glass in one swallow. His fist tightened around the empty glass as his hand fell to his side, his mind drifting back to the grave site. He finally spoke. "Dr. Blake will be arriving shortly. She'll have her autopsy report, along with her initial site investigation."

"What could this American scientist find that ours can't?" Sergei's voice was harsh, his left hand rolled into a tight ball. "Are you really sure you can trust this woman not to make you, and Russia, look like a fool."

Nikolai turned sharply and glared into Sergei's weathered eyes. "Yes," he said without hesitation. "Sergei, if you remember, she and I met years ago and we've remained cordial since. Her uncle *is* the American Secretary of State, as well as an old and trusted friend. Dr. Blake can be relied on, too." He looked at the empty glass, inspecting it. "For now."

Sergei walked closer to Nikolai and placed his hand on his shoulder. "Just remember: old friends do not always remain your friend in these uncertain times."

Nikolai pursed his lips. "Wise words. But we have a problem and I need the Americans' assistance. If I have to sleep with an enemy, they are the ones I choose."

Sergei understood. "I see, Mr. President. What can I do to assist Dr. Blake?"

"It may be small pox. Glazkov was right. It's spreading fast. Faster than anyone could have imagined. We'll assist Dr. Blake with any precautions she has to take and act on all safety issues immediately. The contaminated areas were issued standard biological hazard procedures. Put all medical personal on high alert in St. Petersburg and Moscow with the same orders. And where is that devil Yuri? Damn. He is in charge of Dr. Blake's safety." Nikolai's gripped the empty glass and swung it up, mere inches from Sergei's face. "If he didn't have my father's blood running in his veins, he'd be assigned to run some isolated prison camp for the rest of his life. I do not understand him."

Sergei's faced tightened to conceal his bleak view of the situation. He was fully aware of how the Stepanovs felt about their half-brother. His eyes swiftly glanced to the left and returned to listen.

"My father took him in. My mother raised the bastard as her own, but he is not one of us. Blood or no blood, he is no Stepanov. I have no clue as to what goes on in his mind. But, he does take care of business, the kind we don't want the world to hear about. That, he is an expert at. You taught him well, my friend."

Sergei hid his wince. "Enough of Yuri. The virus, Mr. President?"

"I believe with the new procedures we can keep it quarantined in the infected sites. Our Russian team feels secure they have the virus under containment. As I mentioned, Dr. Blake does not seem so sure." Nikolai paused. "Make sure biohazard protective suits are issued to the military. You know who'll need them. Get on it immediately."

Sergei nodded. "I have some bad news, Mr. President. That's why I came to you this morning."

"Now what?"

"A fully armed helicopter was stolen at about the same time as the canisters turned up missing from the Siberian lab." Sergei's blood ran hot. He was not sure why they had wanted it, but he was sure he knew who had stolen the helicopter. "It was Pachen." He said no more.

Shock ran over Nikolai. Angry, he flung the empty glass to the hardwood floor. It shattered into a ring of broken fine crystal. Nikolai ignored the sound of glass crunching under his fine leather loafers as he paced back his desk. "And why am I just now being informed of the breach? Pachen is dead. Useless information. This is not like you, Sergei. You better have a better answer as to who has control of it."

Sergei rubbed the back of his neck. "I don't, Mr. President. It was an inside job. I will promise you, however, that I personally will handle the betrayal. The old way."

"The old way doesn't help me or Russia now." Nikolai pressed a single red button on his phone. "Put me in touch with President Brice. Request that Secretary Blake join our phone conference as well."

Sergei swung around and placed his hand over the speakerphone. "*Nyet, nyet.*" Nikolai brushed his hand away. "You're making a mistake, Nikolai."

Nikolai did not answer. Any other officer would have been reprimanded for such an action. Only Sergei was allowed to behave brashly. He had earned this right may times over. Still, friend or no friend, Nikolai knew Sergei was wrong.

Nikolai sat in the chair waiting for him and only him. It felt cold, icy, as he took his seat behind the Presidential desk. Settling in, Nikolai pushed his laptop to one side of the mahogany top. He picked up the secure line as it buzzed. "President Brice." Sergei silently sat in the chair closest to his President.

"President Stepanov," came a fixed voice over the com link. "Good news, I hope?" Brice asked.

"Never good news. Your Dr. Blake is uncertain how this virus is spreading." Nikolai scowled.

Brice tapped a pencil end on his own desk with the news. Sensing the distress from Brice's quietness, William chimed in. "William Blake here, President Brice, President Stepanov." The Secretary's trusted voice shot into the conversation. "We need to agree that a worldwide health watch must be issued by President Stepanov. I think it's best the U.S. stay in the background. I do not think it wise to risk worldwide panic by startling other leaders with the little information we have. My advice is to issue a warning following World Health Organization guidelines, but to keep facts and theories about how, where and by whom it may have been released between us and our countries' top security personnel. We are going to have to cooperate. That starts by letting Dr. Blake finish her job."

Sergei relaxed, understanding that Russia would be safe from the world's blame for now.

"Agreed. William, you have always been an honest man, one we, my government, can depend on," Nikolai said.

Brice firmly put Nikolai on notice. "President Stepanov, remember you're not out of the woods yet. If it turns out to be your bio-weapon, the U.S. will hold you and Russia accountable for the outbreak." Brice hung up without a goodbye.

William continued the conversation on a more personal level. "Nikolai, find out what it is. Use Elizabeth. If anyone can find out what it is, she can. I'll keep my direct line open to your government. We will talk more after I see how our President wants to proceed." William closed the conference call with confidence.

Nikolai hit the speaker button to end the call. He reached down to remove a Smith and Wesson 9mm from a small black satchel. He plucked a fresh cleaning cloth from the bottom of the same satchel. Carefully, he placed the 9mm on the polished desktop. Staring at it for a moment, it conjured up satisfying thoughts of his days in the secret police. He needed the distraction. Who would have thought his FBI counterparts would have presented him with a gift of thanks for his excellent marksmanship when he decided to retire from KGB covert operations? It was the one thing that kept him focused in rough times. The rumble in his temples lightened. There was nothing he could do but wait for more information. He allowed his mind to drift. He had left that life behind at Yeltsin's urgings to take up a more politically-focused career. But that would take money. Lots of money his family did not have then.

It was a stroke of genius when he bought up the old tainted Soviet oil land. Competitors claimed he would never clean up the abandoned land and make the oil wells profitable again. It was a big risk to put in all of the family's money. But it paid off. Big time. And now it could all be lost to a single act of bio-terrorism. He could not shake the vision of the grossly disfigured dead found on his land.

Nikolai leaned back deep into the chair. He closed his dark eyes. Images he sought to bury haunted him. Guilt weighed down on him as he thought of his wife and son, still safe and healthy, but trapped in the quarantine zone near his oil fields. "Sergei," he ordered, "check on my wife and son. See how much longer until they are cleared. They have both been vaccinated. I want them here in Moscow with me."

CHAPTER EIGHT

Day Two. 9:08 a.m. MSK. St Petersburg.

"My gratitude," muttered an old man in tattered clothing. He half-knelt, kissing Yuri's ring as he left his car. Yuri's driver pulled his gun and pointed it at the old man. Yuri emotionlessly took in what had become a familiar scene since he united the disjointed Russian mafia gang lords: a plea for a relative's life, in this case one he spared, or had barely spared. He pushed passed the old man, knocking him over. The ragged patron fell to the paper-littered street calling, "My gratitude! Thank you, thank you."

Yuri never glanced back.

He stood in front of his St. Petersburg laboratory, hidden among the commercial district on Moskovskoye Shosse as the Samson Meat Processing Factory. He turned and headed through the glass doors, past the bins of raw sausage, beef and fowl for sale. Yuri snatched a clean butcher's coat and put it on to cover his travel-rumpled suit. He liked his shirt clean, a ritual obsession. He entered a freight elevator. "Down," he ordered.

Misha, waiting inside the elevator car, silently complied. With jarring motions, they were carried downward to the basement. "Misha, have we moved our base of operations to the new facility in Western Siberian mountains? We need to be far away from the mass grave site. I do not want any clues to link me to it."

"We have a few more hours to complete the move." Finding Mikovich had its problems. Clever man."

Yuri's mouth twisted. "You found that traitor? Tell me we are back on schedule to move out of here, *da*? Misha, you are not going to disappoint me, are you?"

"Almost," Misha admitted. "We will meet your deadline with a few adjustments." He paused. "I have a shirt in the car for your meeting with your brother later today." Misha spoke carefully. He knew what words to say to soften any news that would enrage his boss. It was what kept him alive.

"Almost! More delays." The rusted elevator car squeaked and rattled as it touched down on the basement floor.

"We destroyed all records of our activities as you requested. Your orders to simultaneously contaminate key global water supply locations have been initiated. Navigational systems from our St. Petersburg stronghold have been transferred to the Ural Mount facility. No difficulty with the jamming signal during the transfer."

Yuri's twisted lips curved into a smile. "Good. The faster the chaos comes, the faster I can take control of the world with the sweeping promising of a cure." Yuri relaxed his shoulders. "What are the adjustments? And Mikovich?" Yuri asked.

"Finding Mikovich took more time than we expected. Getting information out of him about then new vaccines formula he insisted on producing before more mouse colonies died was a problem, too. He is telling us that none of the vaccines are working. See for yourself." Misha waved his hand towards an opaque glass barrier that separated the testing lab from the rest of the facility. "I think there might be some truth in what he said Boss. Today small bumps appeared on his arms, neck."

"Bullshit!" Yuri dismissed. "Was Mikovich's team kept away from him?" He peered through the glass at what was left of Mikovich. His body battered and blood-spattered. One eye remained; the other a hollow socket. "Can he still speak?"

"*Da*. He can use a touchpad, too. His left hand's still working."

"Good job."

Misha added, "You cannot take the whole team of scientists with us. They are already dragging behind your time table, collecting their equipment, notes." Misha paused, "Rubbish if you ask me. You have to pick, boss. Two, three, no more."

Yuri rubbed his morning stubble. "I only need one to take Mikovich's place. I'll finish Mikovich myself, and then see his assistant pathologist."

Misha nodded. Yuri's razor dropped into place. Yuri placed on hand on the unlocked opaque door, and pushed it open a crack. He turned to Misha and said, "Wait up top. Alert my men to be on standby." Yuri took a breath and let it out. "Make sure my whore is there with her fiddle and clean clothes."

A half-dead Mikovich raised his slumped head in terror at Yuri's voice. He gasped and hyperventilated as cold beads of sweet sweep across his blood cover forehead. He snapped. A strange calmness came over him as he heard Yuri enter the small poorly light room. He was finished and he knew it. He drew up what was left of his strength to face the Satan himself.

Misha returned to the freight elevator. Hitting speed dial on his cell, he spoke through his transmitter. "Sasha. Boss wants a new team of pathologists in Siberia when he arrives. Make it happen." Misha pulled the metal doors shut and rode up.

Blood seeped down Mikovich's nose as he sat hunched over the medical touchpad, heaving air into his punctured lung. His body was black with bruises, an ankle twisted at a 45-degree angle dangled. He said in a sarcastic, raspy tone, "So death has finally come to me. Welcome, Yuri."

Yuri's evil smile graced his face again. "Not yet, my friend. You need to give me the formula to this new vaccine you've been working on. Were you trying to steal away my bidders? Set yourself up as a rich man? *Nyet?*" Yuri pushed the touchpad closer.

Mikovich, mad with pain, managed to spit a blood clot onto Yuri's expensive leather loafers. "Friend? My ass. You are a dead man, Yuri, just as I am." A crazy man's laughter rang from Mikovich.

"I don't have time for your madness." Yuri slapped Mikovich's right hand on the lad table in front of him. He flipped his razor open and sliced the tip of his thumb off. Mikovich screamed.

"One by one, knuckle by knuckle, I will slice your fingers to stubs until you give me that formula." Yuri kicked Mikovich's broken ankle back in place.

Mikovich gasped. "It won't work I tell you."

"Have it your way." Yuri's hand wrapped around Mikovich's wrist. His razor cut through his knuckle.

"Yuri, just kill me!" He squealed in pain.

Another finger tip was sliced off and fell to the meat house's floor. Yuri said nothing through the cries of Mikovich. He placed his razor back on Mikovich's blood-oozing finger nub. He paused, the blade against the bone, letting the weight of the metal slowly slice the skin, through the muscles, nerves and into the joint. "I promise you, Mikovich, the next one will be even slower to slice off."

Sweat poured from Mikovich as his spirit slipped away. "OK. OK. Promise me – no harm to my family."

"I don't care about your family. I have you and you are what counts."

"You pig! Is this what you want?" He entered a four-letter code on the touchpad. The laptop's screen lit up with flashing data racing across it. "Here. All my failed attempts to stop the virus. Don't you know? It's a killer. No one else will be able to stop it in time. You kill me, you don't have a chance of living. Do you understand that?" Mikovich was sure he had been onto something before Misha found him.

"Yes," Yuri said calmly. He swiftly moved forward and pulled back Mikovich's head to expose his neck. Mikovich made a strangled noise of protest. "Death has come." Yuri's blade sliced across Mikovich's neck in one fluid motion. He tossed the dead man's body onto the table and left the room. Removing the blood-stained butcher's coat, he tossed it beside Mikovich's body.

Yuri strolled down the cold corridor of hanging beef hinds and entered a shielded metal door. He passed through a large sanitizing booth. A dry fine mist sprayed over him before he reached his private lab's glass door. The lab was small for a man with his ambitions, but well-suited for his plan. The white-coated scientists raced around seeing Yuri arrival, except one: Mikovich's assistant, Rurik. Yuri approached him.

"You are Rurik?" Yuri leaned toward several glass balls filled with a dense greenish gas.

"Yes, Stop!" Rurik pushed Yuri to one side.

Yuri staggered left. His razor dropped.

"Sorry! Sorry, you were about to break deadly chlorine gas storage balls. That would be one more problem the Boss would not like with Mikovich gone." Yuri pulled away. "You could have been killed." Rurik mistook him for just another mafia man.

"You know what Mikovich was working on?" Yuri continued, not bothering to introduce himself. His razor slipped back in place.

"Yes. I did most of the research on the mice colonies. Come see. All the colonies are infected except the small group we vaccinated first. Not sure why they are still alive..."

Yuri followed Rurik. He glanced around at the chaos of the scientists frantically packing up their research. They'll never finish the clean up, Yuri thought.

Rurik stopped at a small cage filled with six mice. "They're healthy," Yuri remarked, quickly examining the rodents.

"*Da*, they are fine. The blood work shows they are infected, but alive nonetheless. Mikovich was taking blood samples from them, hoping to find out why, so he could replicate the factor that was inhibiting the small pox virus."

Yuri looked around the lab. In cage after cage he saw hundreds of dead pox-covered mice. He began to realize that Mikovich was right: the virus was spreading much faster than anticipated. Anxious, Yuri wondered how much time he had left to sell the vaccine. He picked up the small cage of healthy mice and handed it to Rurik. "You are my new head scientist. Mikovich is dead. We're leaving. Only take the mice. Keep me informed about these vaccinated mice. I want to know if any of them die."

"Lt. Commander Nevsky?" Rurik asked. The frightened scientist suddenly realized who he had been talking to.

"*Da*. My men are waiting upstairs for you. I'll clean up. You have any other problems with the vaccinated mice?"

Making a presumption of Mikovich is dead, Rurik invented a quick lie. "Only that the dead vaccinated mice had to have compromised immune systems for the original vaccine not to work." He paused. "But I'm only an assistant. I'm not as knowledgeable as Professor Mikovich or any number of his colleagues. I respectfully request to be taken off the project. You need someone with more experience."

"*Nyet*." Yuri refused his request. "My basic expectation of the project's completion date has been moved up. Get the information from Misha."

Rurik remained silent with his suspicion that the vaccine was useless. "Do you have access to Dr. Mikovich's latest data?"

Yuri nodded. "I want you to begin the work he left off."

"*Da.*" Rurik determined to remain quiet if he was to save his own life using Yuri's resources. Holding the small cage to his chest, he hurried out the lab door.

Yuri waited calmly until Rurik and the mice had left before making his way back toward Rurik's workstation. He stopped at the table and carefully picked up a gas-filled glass ball. He made his way toward the exit, placing an emergency gas mask over his face. As he reached the doorway, he let the ball drop. He pressed the emergency hazard alarm to seal to door. He manually shut down the ventilation system with a press of a button as the scientists reacted to the yellow-green clouds drifting slowly toward them.

A wicked smile rose to his handsome face as he witnessed them fighting over the few gas masks left in the lab. One thin well built man pounded on the door, his lips plum–colored. A chair suddenly smashed against the safety glass, Yuri jumped back but it provided no escape for the trapped scientists. It would be a slow death by asphyxiation, Yuri knew, as the colors of human health drained from their faces.

Having had enough enjoyment, Yuri ran to the elevator and radioed Misha. "Burn this place to the ground. Make sure my contacts in the fire department find nothing left but ashes and animal bones. Not one single human body part. The mass grave was sloppy. The poor clean up has left the Americans snooping around longer than I had wanted. I'm heading for Moscow. I'll swing by the new lab when I am finished with Nikolai's new orders."

CHAPTER NINE

Day Three. 2:15 a.m. EST. Jackson Memorial Hospital. Miami, Florida.

"Incoming trauma, 12 minutes out," announced the desk clerk at the emergency room of Jackson Memorial Hospital.

"Where are they coming from?" Dr. John Astin, the attending physician, asked.

"US Coast Guard is bringing them in. A Russian oil tanker, the Dostoyny, ran aground," the desk clerk read from her emergency response computer screen.

"Where at?" Astin asked.

"Key Largo, in the coral reef preserve," the clerk responded.

"How many? What are we dealing with?"

In the background he heard a CNN news alert of an oil ship run aground, spilling black ooze into the ocean. A catastrophic number of dead oil-covered fish and birds were washing up on shore. All the crew members that were on board may be dead. "Breaking news," the announcer began. "A New York City hospital is now reporting multiple cases of an unknown illness. No information from the White House or CDC."

Adrenaline rushed through Astin's veins. He did not like dealing with international policies. His only concern was for the people under his care.

"Dr. Astin," the desk clerk called. "Emergency responders and paramedics are claiming all the victims are DOA except the captain and first mate. Military forensics is on-site. The first mate collapsed. Possible seizures."

"Are they stabilized?"

"Not sure. They sounded—"

The emergency room's double doors burst open. Two U.S. Coast guard paramedics crashed in, pushing along a comatose man strapped to a gurney, the apparent first mate. He was followed by Captain Mokotoff on a second gurney. His body was covered with oozing pox-like sores. A black log book was locked in his grip. Two nurses barely dodged the incoming stretcher. Dr. Astin turned to the desk clerk.

"Twelve minutes?" A half-annoyed smile was barely noticeable on his sun-tanned face. He turned and started to trot briskly toward the incoming trauma.

A young redheaded nurse followed, trying not to get in the way. "I'm right behind you, doctor!" she exclaimed.

"This is the first mate. Age 33. No known medical history. BP eighty over fifty-five. Pulse forty BPM. Unresponsive."

As the US Coast Guard paramedic rattled off the details, Astin looked down at the patient's blood- and vomit-stained sea jacket and blue jeans. He pulled a soaked brown leather boot off and scraped the handle of his reflex hammer across the bottom of one foot. "Positive Babinski. Nurse, check his eyes. He could have damage to the spinal cord in the thoracic or lumbar region, maybe damage to the pyramidal tract."

Penlight in hand, the doctor swished it across the patient's eyes, checking for pupil dilation as they continued to move down the hallway. "Pupils fixed," he announced swiftly.

The nurse leaned forward. "He's not breathing! No pulse. And look at the small lesions running down his neck." Confusion stretched its way across the attendant's face.

"Did you guys even bother to check for respiration?" Astin ignored the nurse's fearful comment. "Let's see if we can bring him back. Charge the defibrillator!" he shouted, pulling the gurney to a halt.

A paramedic said defensively, "He was breathing when we pulled him in, 30 seconds ago!"

"All defibrillators are in use."

Astin looked at the nurse. "I don't care! Someone get a cart. You bag him. I'll do compressions." At this point a half-dozen other people had gathered around, including two other nurses and a first year resident. The nurse grabbed a resuscitator mask from the supply cart.

The resident offered his hand to Astin, who grabbed it and swung up on top of the first mate. He straddled him nervously as he compressed the chest; the resident blew air into the patient's lungs with a compression bag. The emergency team began to move the gurney toward the trauma room.

"He's cyanotic," the nurse said. She grabbed a hand. "Getting cold, too. What about the lesions? Maybe an allergic reaction?"

From Astin's viewpoint, he saw the fear grow in his nurse's eyes. He glanced down at his patient's face. He was gagging. Foam had bubbled out of his mouth.

"He's choking on his tongue! It's swollen!" shouted the doctor.

"Wanna roll him?" the resident asked. They turned into Trauma One, finally coming to a halt on the sterile beige tile. There was a flurry of medical staff moving around him rapidly. The air was permeated by the scent of disinfectant solution.

The young nurse backed off, pulling the mask from over his mouth. Her eyes grew wide as Dr. Astin jumped off. "Scalpel." The nurse unwrapped an emergency surgical kit. Astin took the scalpel and slit his Russian's patient's stained shirt. Fear of the diagnosis took her breath away as the patient's chest was revealed, showing open pus-filled bumps, bleeding wounds and blackness where the skin tissue had already died.

"Those lesions look familiar," she gasped. "I've seen those in old medical books. Small pox. Or it could be some kind of plague." Her eyes darted between the other nurses. "I have to get out of here. I have to warn my family"

Dr. Astin grabbed the sleeve of her uniform quickly. "You can't leave." She shrugged his hand away and turned toward the trauma room doors. "It's too late. It's the risk we all knew we could face one day."

"We have been exposed!" the head nurse abruptly stated. She glanced at the other staff members bustling about the ER. "We have to tell them."

Panic overtook the young redheaded nurse. She ran from the trauma unit.

"Stop her! Quarantine this floor immediately. Call the CDC. Implement airborne precautions," Dr. Astin ordered. "Get a pair of long forceps, a laryngoscope and an ET tube. We've got to intubate. And start a line. CBC, blood gas, tox screen. I want to know if this is small pox." Astin shot up sharply, rolled his eyes over his team, and said, "Bioterrorism has hit our door here in south Florida, ladies and gentlemen. Get me a Chem-7 as well."

A nurse paled at his words, furiously scribbled down his orders. "Dr. Astin, are you ready to intubate?" She gestured to the endotracheal tube. "Is the tongue too swollen?"

"Either way we'll have a dead man if I don't get air in and hopefully he can tell us what happened on that ship."

Sweat dripped from Dr. Astin's brow. A nurse wiped it dry as the doctor slipped the tube into the man's trachea, reattaching the bag and resuming compressions. Without warning, blood splattered into the compression bag.

"Where is that blood coming from?" Dr. Astin demanded. He leaned over the patient to palpitate his abdomen. "My God, his stomach must have ruptured."

"How long before we are next?" the nurse wondered aloud. Fear filled her eyes.

"I don't know." Dr. Astin muffled a curse. "What could have caused this?" He squinted, examining the man's lesions more carefully. "The nurse was right. These look like small pox. But they're different. A new strain?" The doctor sprang into action. "See where we can get the small pox vaccination," he ordered, ripping off his bloodied trauma gown. "Check overseas hospitals, the world, damn it! Check with the CDC to get supplies. Give it to everyone who was born after 1947. Anyone older would have been inoculated."

The small red-headed nurse re-entered with the captain's log. "I pried it out of the Russian captain's hands. He said he knew who did this to him, that it's in here. But I don't know Russian. And he's dead."

"Put me in direct contact with the head of the CDC immediately. Maybe she has some answers." Dr. Astin turned back on the red-headed nurse. "Isolate that log in the sterilizing unit. We are going to need every bit of information we can get to know what the hell we are dealing with."

CHAPTER TEN

Day Three. 11:00 a.m. MSK. Kremlin Presidential office.

Elizabeth walked listlessly into the Presidential lobby. She paused before twisting the doorknob and pushing open the wood paneled door. The lack of sleep was taking its toll. "Damn high heels." She looked down to see an angry red ring where the shoe met her ankle. Brushing her loose strains of hair into place, she continued and walked in. She knew the virus would not wait for her to get some shut eye.

Elizabeth glanced at a linen flag in the Federation's colors of blue, white and red draped on a wall, shutting the door behind her. The scent of spice filled the lobby. Elizabeth was startled by the familiar scent. Her senses quickened; she inhaled the scent as if it were smelling salts. Glancing around she became keenly aware of how the Presidential suite had changed in fourteen years. Her mind flashed back to another time, another president and a much younger Nikolai Stepanov, then an FSB officer, but still smiling the same political pleasantries.

The memory was forgotten as quickly as the waft of spice awakened it. She noticed the technologically-advanced office was equal to that of her government. Walking up to the reception desk, a motion sensor automatically switched a beam of alarm lights behind her as she took a step closer.

"Your identification papers?" the clerk at the desk requested. It was a routine she was used to; she had been through at least three levels of security screenings just to reach this point.

Elizabeth pulled them from her suit pocket, handing them to the plainly dressed receptionist. She ignored the recently snapped photos of Nikolai's presidency that decorated the walls, making her way to his inner office. Her mind was on the newly discovered pathogen. It would have to be contained; the deaths it had and would cause would be in the thousands if Russia has no way to counter the virus.

She waited outside the entrance to his private office. His administrative assistant picked up the phone and announced, "Dr. Blake has arrived."

Nikolai responded, "Send her in."

She hung up the phone. "Dr. Blake, please follow me."

Nikolai's mind ran relentlessly as he stood by his desk, waiting for her report, drifting to who could have stolen the canisters. He anxiously moved a few steps toward a paneled wall. "They had to be very high up in the system to access the Siberian lab. Why would Pachen be connected? And to be able to keep the information secret for three days," he said out loud, as if hearing his own words would make it easier for the betrayal to sink in.

Listening to the door knob turn, his eyes turned to meet the sound. For the first time, he noticed the tiny particles of floating dust that swam in the thin security laser beam silently marking the hidden nerve center of his newly installed Intelligent Weapon Control System. He stared at the two large wood panels that the IWCS neatly hid behind. Nikolai hung his head in regret, gazing at the freshly cleaned carpet. Was he wrong in calling the Americans? He raised his eyes to meet his guest.

"President Stepanov, Dr. Blake." His assistant flatly introduced Elizabeth.

Nikolai shuffled past the window and picked up one of several cream-colored folders stacked neatly on one corner of his desk. He slipped it under his arm. "What have you to report, Dr. Blake?" He tossed a hard glance at his assistant. "And why aren't my pathology advisors here yet?" he grumbled, pacing past her. His mind, body was tense. There had been no word on his son or wife from Sergei; it weighed heavily on him.

"I'll check, Mr. President." The admin hurried out the door

"Well, Dr. Blake. What is it?" Nikolai urged. He strolled back to his mahogany desk.

"President Stepanov, this is a completely new virus. One we cannot rule out as a newly engineered strain. All of the international databanks I have reviewed, as well as the Russian databanks, have no match to the pox virus we're looking for. I'm not even sure that's what it is. Many symptoms suggest small pox, but it is behaving differently. The incubation period is just too fast, faster than any known virus period." She stood before his desk. She placed her medical bag on a chair next to it.

Nikolai raised one brow, "I take it you were informed about the stolen canisters. That it is an old strain of ours? Not a new one."

"It could be yours. If it is, then it's mutated. The databanks I checked included DNA references from the lab in Siberia. Even with a mutation it would have shown signs of the genetic family it came from. I have requested President Brice to inform our international team of this information. We need your team's information as well." She saw Nikolai turn edgy. She knew what he was feeling - the intense pressure, the unmistakable elusive haze that strikes knowing that the whole world was watching you. She said calmly, "They are the highest caliber scientists the world has to offer. I worked with all of them one time or another."

Agitated, Nikolai flatly said, "*Nyet*! I will not put my country in that kind of spotlight."

"It already is!" she reasoned. "I have always been straight with you. This medical team can be trusted. We need your approval Mr. President so both of our countries are on the same page."

Nikolai uncertain asked, "What about your report?"

"My autopsies were inconclusive as to the type of virus that caused the deaths. I do know that we have a killer virus on our hands and no known cure at this time. My recommendation is for your country to close all the borders in northwest Russia, quarantine St. Petersburg and the area east of St. Petersburg up to the Volga River. No one comes in and no one goes out. There is still much more investigation to do at the site. Your team is continuing as we speak."

"Quarantine St. Petersburg? I can't do that." Nikolai's hand went up in defiance.

"And why not?" Elizabeth was bewildered by the refusal. Her voice rang sharp.

Nikolai locked his eyes with her questioning ones. He thought for a minute, then spoke. "My wife and son are in St. Petersburg. There is a problem with their security team. We haven't heard any word on them as of this time. Last I spoke to them they were leaving St. Petersburg. That was over an hour ago. Then nothing." He had not meant to share that much information with her. He would deal with it as they dealt with other issues from the past.

Elizabeth's face softened. "I see." Crossing her arms, she leaned to the left. "I am sorry Mr. President. Still," she paused, "you are the Russian president. You do not need an American doctor to tell you to shut down your border regardless of your personal situation." She hated to say that, and to him of all people. A foggy feeling of déjà vu swept over her.

"No, I don't need to hear it. And coming from you, Elizabeth, doesn't make it any easier!" Nikolai's anger erupted. "We can't be having this conversation." He shook his head in puzzlement.

"Dr. Blake, Mr. President. Let's keep it formal," she corrected him. They had a certain trust between them, so she spoke the truth. Even if it was a truth he did not want to hear. "It has to be, Mr. President."

"Have it your way," he said. Nikolai forced himself to detach his emotions from her.

"Thank you, Mr. President. You haven't changed much," she added.

"Neither have you, *Elizabeth*." He emphasized her first name to make sure she knew who was in charge and that he damn well would call her anything he wanted to.

Elizabeth sighed. "I think we need to forget about our shared past, as difficult as it was. The focus is on your country's epidemic. Hundreds may already be infected, leading to not hundreds but thousands of deaths if we wait any longer." She shook her head. "You know you need to close those borders based on the initial forensic evidence." Elizabeth voice held an edge to it, "Do you suspect bioterrorism, Mr. President? I need to know, to expand the research to any hostile counties that may have altered your stolen virus."

"Bioterrorism." Nikolai paced around his desk. He sat on corner of his desk, his hands folded. "Elizabeth, get to the point. What has the U.S. government instructed you to present to me?"

Her arms fell to her sides as she smoothed down her gray Armani suit. Elizabeth shifted her weight and reached over his lap to the chair where her medical bag rested. "If I may?" She tugged it over his legs and placed on his desk, opening her medical bag, she pulled out her tech pad. "Would you like me to read it or would you like to see the report I plan to file with my government first, then yours?" She waited for Nikolai's response as he started at her outreached hand.

He sighed. "You right." He reached and picked up his phone. "Shut down the northwest borders inclusive of St. Petersburg up to the Volga River. Expand our current quaran-tine borders to include all area north of the site. And damn it, where are my wife and son?" Nikolai slammed the phone down. He reached out his hand. "I'll read for myself if you don't mind."

"I'm sorry. I hope your wife and son..." She stopped short of finishing. She handed over her report. "President Brice is en route to the United Nations. I am flying back to CDC headquarters to continue my research." She paused. "You know I'll have to give Brice a report of my findings first."

Nikolai ran his fingers over the touch pad as he began to read the report. "This is not good for my country." He looked at as a plea etched his face.

"No. I can't cover for your government. Nor would I, so don't even suggest it."

He raised his eyes from the pad. "I think you need to add Commander Ivan Stepanov to this American-Russian anti-bioterrorism team, along with your uncle, Secretary Blake. If my country is responsible and I have a traitor in my upper ranks, I'll have to be the one to deal with this, not just your CIA. Ivan is the best man for this work, Anton second, Dmitry back up." Nikolai responded.

"OK," she conceded. "I'll write in it to state that Ivan and Aton Stepanov, at the insistence of the Russian government, will join the lead search team for the bioterrorist. I not sure Brice will accept this condition. Let leave Dmitry as back up."

Nikolai nodded once and handed back her note pad. She slipped it back into her medical bag and clipped it shut. Nikolai stood. His eyes followed her as she gathered her things.

"Lt. Commander Nevsky will act as your Russian escort back to the United States. He will be here shortly. He will be my personal contact to keep me updated."

A buzz interrupted them. "Lt. Commander Nevsky has arrived."

Waiting in the lobby, Yuri cursed his step-brother under his breath. "Are you sure you can't get another officer to escort the American back?" he asked Ivan through the com link.

"No. What's your problem, Yuri? Those are direct orders from the President," Ivan said coldly as he signed off the com link.

Yuri wrote down a note and shoved it in his pocket. Aggravated, he snapped the pencil in two. He tossed the two halves on the admin's desk. Her brows rose, then lowered back to her work. Yuri walked to the door, stopping short. A large grin appeared. "This may work out for me," he mumbled to himself. He pulled out his cell and texted Misha. *Set up meeting with American Russian mafia leader. Will confirm time en route to U.S.*

Yuri straightened his black jacket, tie and clean white shirt. He felt time *was* on his side. He strolled into the President's office. "Mr. President. Dr. Blake," Yuri said.

"You received your orders?" Nikolai asked.

"Yes."

"Then get going and keep me updated as scheduled." Nikolai returned to his desk.

The admin pushed her way in. "Mr. President. News of your wife. General Serebrinsky is on line one, sir."

Nikolai snapped up the phone, half-forgetting who was in the room. "Where are they? Are they past the quarantine zone?" He stopped breathing. His eye glazed over as he gazed at nothing. He gently hung up the phone.

"Mr. President," Elizabeth spoke.

Yuri suppressed a grin at the blank look on Nikolai's face. He guessed the news was not good.

"Mr. President. Mr. President!" Elizabeth called again.

"Dr. Blake, we need to leave." Yuri pushed to get on with his business.

"You go ahead. I'll be there shortly," she stanchly said.

Yuri seized her arm. "Time to go. This is not your business." His voice, sharp like his razor, cut her. She was not about to let him bully her.

Nikolai finally exhaled and spoke. "Do as Dr. Blake requested, Lt. Commander Nevsky. Wait outside my door for her. Dr. Blake will be there shortly."

Yuri released her. "One minute and we then we have go, Mr. President." Yuri gave Nikolai a disapproving look. He was confused by

Nikolai's response. There was more to this woman than he first realized to have that kind of influence on his step-brother. He sent a message for Misha look into Elizabeth's past. He left to wait in the vestibule.

Nikolai turned to Elizabeth. "My wife and son are at the St. Petersburg Hospital. Their driver is dead. The whole FSB team assigned to them is infected. Is there anything you can you do for them? I can fly you up immediately. Will you go for my sake?"

Her frustration turned to helpless despair. She held back a tear. What she was about to tell him next sickened her. "I can't. I'm under orders to return immediately and I'm already violating that order by being late. What I can do is the same as if I were there or not by their side. Send any information you have on them to Eclipse. I don't have enough information to give you an answer. We'll start by treating the symptoms. Have your specialists follow standard small pox treatment. I'll double my efforts to find this strain." She paused before turning to leave. "Nikolai." He looked up at her. "If they've been vaccinated, they should make it. I'll keep a line of communications open with your specialist at St. Petersburg hospital. I'm sorry. That is the best I can do."

Nikolai looked down at the lush carpeted floor. A feeling of isolation came over him. Feeling the knot in his throat, he said, "I appreciate anything you can do, Elizabeth. They will, too."

Nikolai's words left a mark on her, a mark of determination to find this pathogen and stop it before it took more lives. She gave Nikolai a small smile of sympathy before she turned and walked out the door with a lump in her own throat. A hidden fear grew in her that this would become an epidemic that no country had ever seen or, worse, a pandemic no one could stop.

CHAPTER ELEVEN

Day Three. 5:00 p.m. China Standard Time. Dalian, China.

Droplets of oil splashed workers at northern China's biggest oil transit port as they hurried to unload the black cargo on board. A Russian tanker bearing the Stepanov company logo bobbed in the vacillating waters of the Pacific port. The blue-green ocean lapped at her three sides; the rusty dock hugged her anchored side as the sound of metal scraping her hull went unnoticed. The ship's replacement captain, Yuri's hired mafia thug, looked out the bridge's windows. From his view on the platforms, Dalian's skyscrapers etched the skyline of the mainland. The sky was clear blue. He watched one of two giant cranes robotically glide over the ship's cargo bay, taking in the contrast between nature's sea and man's metal design.

The loading ramp beside the large Russian tanker bustled with traffic. Watching the frenzied dockworkers, the captain smiled. His mission would be easy: his one goal was to poison China's capital and every village, town and junction between the port and Beijing. No one would question his orders.

He brushed a stray bit of lint from his shirt pocket. Raising his arm, the mafia-connected captain checked his watch. "Right on time." He glanced up at two of the crew members. "You two get out of here. See what all the noise on deck is about. Wrap up any loose paperwork with the yellows and tell the men this shipment is not to be delayed at any cost." His rash comments earned grins from his shipmates as they left the bridge.

Yuri's man dragged a simple cheap key ring from his pocket. He fiddled with it, keeping his eyes locked on the scene on the dock, until he found the small key it held. Looking down, he swiftly inserted it into the ship's black box system, deleting all records of the voyage. Slipping the key ring back into his pocket, the captain made his way toward the ship's navigation system. Opening the metal box encasing its hardware, he inserted a small microchip. The satellite jamming uplink was effective. All of the access codes required to intercept communication began downloading to Yuri's Siberian base camp. The captain re-coded the access panel and smashed the cover.

He glanced back at the exterior of the ship. The crew was preparing to unload the specified cargo crates. "Good. All is going according to plan."

On the platform, the dock foreman hit the computerized control pad to initiate the unloading of crude petroleum from the tanker. He kept an eye on the pressure gauges, calling out the readings to dock workers. Just another day monitoring the pump's hook up. The foreman did not break in his routine; he had done this a hundred times before. He had joked with his men he could do it in his sleep. But not today.

Stepanov crude oil filled one of several receptacles. Suddenly, oil began to spray from the connection, misting workers, barrels, rope-mesh cargo nets and ramps. Everything within range of the failed pump seal was quickly covered in a thinly transparent black slick.

"Shit!" the foreman cursed, lunging at the emergency shut-off control. Several Chinese crewmen ran toward the ship's dock, working to repair the leak, irritated by the Russians heckling them.

"Idiots! Didn't you check the pump seals?"

"Screw you, you damn Russian pigs!" one screamed back, putting the last clamp in place. The Dalian team prided themselves on perfection and the Russian shipmen knew it. The Russian's jabbed at them every time an opportunity presented itself.

The dock supervisor radioed to his dock manager. "Tell him to shut his mouth. He is to ignore their taunts. And get those Russian pigs to open a new ramp." He cut his own workers off before the war of words got ugly. "Let's get this oil off the tanker and send the shitty Russians on their way." He nodded up to the crane foreman to start the pumps again. The supervisor called out the basic Russian words needed for them to open the secondary ramp. He was not about to let them use language as a barrier to delay the unloading process.

"Kiss off. We don't take orders from Chinamen," one Russian worker muttered to another. He glanced back at the middle-aged Chinese man. "*Nyet, nyet.* It's broken."

The Chinese worker screamed. "You lie! You fucking Russians always lie. You clean up your own mess, then."

The insults stopped as the captain arrived at the site of the small spill. "Everyone back to work. It's the Russians' loss, you fools, if we delay delivery. We'll charge them for any delay in the delivery of the oil, as long as you get you asses in gear!" The dock workers nodded, chuckling in satisfaction at the money they could suck off this shipment.

The captain hurried to the off ramp. He wouldn't be delayed. His blood pressure had risen due to the flinging of insults. Stepping onto the off ramp, he slipped on the small slick of oil. "Shit!" He caught the handrail to steady himself. The Chinese workers laughed aloud. "Shut up, you bastards. Just you wait, you yellow scum!" he yelled. "Damn," he muttered. "Give me a rag."

A shipmate tossed him a few clean rags. Jumping over the small spill, he hurried off the ramp. He folded the last clean square handkerchief-style and shoved it in his back pocket. "Hey! Clean this up!" he ordered one of his Russian crewmen. He slipped away to a small tug boat that was waiting. He took a back seat along other seamen to hitch a ride to China's main land.

The ride was short. Exiting the tug boat, he calmly approached the customs agent at the gate, waving his passport.

"Where will you be staying?" the Russian-speaking customs agent asked in a monotone expression.

"I'm traveling to Beijing. Staying a few days. A little vacation." He opened his passport and handed his travel papers over to the guard.

The officer nodded and tossed the captain's duffel bag to the security scanners. The captain held his breath as a minuscule square object appeared in the lining of his bag. The screener let him pass. "You got gypped on this bag if you think it's real leather," the screener said. He let out his breath.

"It better be leather. I paid enough for it," he joked calmly. He picked up his bag with a smirk and continued quickly on his way.

The captain's mind was fixated on his mission. As he walked through the metal detector, alarms went off. The captain's face turned to stone as his heart thudded in his chest. The customs officer pulled him aside. The captain pulled up on a tarnished silver chain hidden under the collar of his uniform. A stainless steel vial dangled from it. Sealed inside was enough of the virus to poison all the water supplies in Beijing. "Sorry, I forgot to remove it." He carefully took it off, placing it on the table, and passed through the metal detectors once more. The customs officer waved him by. He grabbed the vial of death.

Pushing through the customs gates, Yuri's thug entered China's mainland. He tossed down his bag. Squatting over it, he cut a small slit along the edge of the leather trim and pulled out a thumbnail-size touch pad. He placed the plastic detonation device in his pants pocket. The captain stepped up to the busy street, hailing a cab. He glanced at his watch. The Stepanov ship should now be in the final stages of unloading. He grinned, exposing his yellow stained teeth. A dirty white sedan pulled up, a logo for a fake Chinese taxi company painted on the side. Opening the door, he tossed his bag inside and quickly climbed in.

"Let's go! Beijing's municipal water plant," the captain ordered the driver. The captain pulled out his cell phone. "Misha," he said quickly as his colleague picked up, "I'm on my way to Beijing. Tell Boss the plan is on schedule. Too bad he will miss the fireworks." He reached deep into his pants pocket. He hung up and hit the detonator as the car sped off.

Scores of explosions blasted up along the perimeter of the bow of the oil tanker. The ship's hull cracked open like an eggshell, spilling its cargo. Emergency alarms blared over the shipyard as workers feverishly rushed to pump oil from the tanker in order to control the spill. Sixty or more workers flocked to several other docked tankers, working quickly to shut them down as the destruction spread. Windblown sparks ignited two newly arrived ships. "Get away, get away!" screamed the dock manager.

The sound of the explosion fell on the ears of Yuri's henchman. They were felt several kilometers away, the henchman guessed. The Russian crewmembers on the tanker dashed from their normal posts, caught off guard as flames leapt up all around them.

"Where's the captain? Call him back!"

"Get the first mate!" a crew man called, stepping on deck from below.

"He must be dead. I saw him walking on the bow, and it's gone!" another crewman called.

"You!" the second mate called. He pointed to a crewman. "Get to the radio. Call Dmitry Stepanov! He's the one Stepanov who knows what to do with the Chinese. Let's get this fire out!"

A tall, muscular crewman swung a rope to the overhead crane and climbed up the rope, making his way over to the dock foreman's abandoned seat. No radio. He watched another crewman, his best friend, make his way from the stern. Flames ignited his clothes. He heard his screams of pain all the way up on his crane perch. He closed his eyes, unable to watch his shipmate running, his flaming hands over his face. Looking down at the scene from his perch, the crewman hung his head in shame, realizing he would be spared by the flames as he watched his comrades burn.

The dock foreman ran along the offshore docks, looking in desperation for the firefighters and fire boats. It was a futile effort. Glancing towards the main dock, he saw that the fire station was engulfed in red hot flames. A few of the firefighters' ships had been put out to sea. He turned left, then right. People ran in panic over the docks; men and women jumped and fled from the firestorm of ships, cargo and crates consumed with fire, their bodies ablaze. Others lay on the ground, dead. Human ash was swept high, intertwining with the oily black smoke of fatality.

"This is the Russians' fault!" the foreman cursed. He looked up and saw the Russian perched atop the crane. "Shit!" He ran to get to that one safe place, but never made it as the inferno stopped him inches before he reached the base of the crane. The heat scorched his skin. "Please, someone. Anyone! Help!" He fell to his knees. His lungs filled with smoke.

He turned sharply toward the sound of approaching firefighters who tossed him a fire escape hood. He slipped it on, taking deep breaths of fresh air from the attached breathing device. A fire blanket was tossed next. He looped his hands in the grips and tented himself. He felt the blast of heat race over him. Steadfastly, he waited for the fire to be snuffed out.

The ball of fire rolled past the tent then died in minutes as several firemen pushed through the small trail of flames that led to the foreman. Grabbing the worker, one fireman took off his hood and secured an oxygen mask to his face as two others dragged him out. The foreman lifted his head and saw a small round of flames contained at one end of the dock. His soot-covered face saw many other injured workers across the site. A fireboat pumped streams of chemicals, snuffing out the flames on the main dock.

A fireman rushed in and picked up the blanket as the foreman heard the medical evacuation helicopters arriving. Turning, he watched the head medical supervisor for the Dalian-based company step off one of the helicopters, his phone pressed hard to his ear.

"Tell the President I do not believe it was an accident." the supervisor said. "We have the flames contained to one side. Ships are still burning. It's ongoing." The medical supervisor listened, then answered. "No, we have nothing to tie to the Russians or a domestic terrorist. Security has opened up a case file. I'll wait for their arrival." He paused. "I gave orders to send what's left of the victims to the Beijing burn trauma unit. One Russian who escaped the fire is under surveillance. He was found, traumatized, in the crane control cab. He has an unknown rash on his arms. Could be hives, but the marks are too small. I'm sure it's nothing, but let's get him talking, see if we can find out more about how this fire may have started."

His voice stern in the medical supervisor's ear, the head of China's Ministry of Health asked, "Your final report to the news?"

"The families will have a hard time identifying their kin. The bodies are charred beyond recognition," the medical official continued. "I will have my next report to your office after I have examined the survivors. I can't offer the controlled news anymore than that."

The medical official hung up. Relieved, he headed for the triage stations. He ordered his paramedical team, "Get as many of them off this dock as possible. Take the ones who can be saved to hospitals. Leave the rest. Keep them comfortable. The medical facilities are already overloaded." He questioned, "Has anyone seen the Russian captain? Is he among the dead?"

The surviving Russian crewman spoke up. "He's gone. He left before the explosion. He had some work on the mainland. That's all I know. You can look for him there."

The medical supervisor's face twisted. "Call security. We have to find him."

A few hours away from the scorched docks, news on the radio finally told the story of the fiery explosion. Still sitting in the cab, the captain stripped off his uniform and tossed it in his bag. He pulled out credentials from the World Health Organization and attached them to his dress shirt. He glanced up at the young man, still boyish, glancing in his review mirror.

Listening to the news, the driver glanced in the mirror. "I think that may have been overkill."

"Shut up." Pulling out his phone, the captain texted Misha. *Ship destruction complete.* He slipped his phone back into its case. Rubbing the silver vial, he muttered to himself. "Drop. Drop. Drops into the water. Makes all the yellows go away." He spit on the car's well-worn carpet. He shut his eyes for the rest of the long drive into China's capital.

Waiting for Yuri's orders at the Siberian laboratory, Misha nervously paced the hallways. The captain in China was the last team member to check in. Finally, his cell phone beeped and news came via text message. Quickly scanning the message, Misha smiled and hit speed dial. Yuri answered.

"Boss, China's in place," Misha reported. "Last one. All targeted countries will be affected within 24 hours of distribution."

"Good. You have to take care of the new lab until I get there. Keep me posted on the progress of Mikovich's assistant. Keep an eye on him. I do not want him to bolt like Mikovich. And keep me posted on the progress of the spread of the virus. Make sure we have access to global communication links for when the time comes to offer the cure. I will not be disappointed."

"Yes, boss." Misha hung up. He headed for the laboratory to keep watch.

CHAPTER TWELVE

Day Three. 7:45 a.m. EST. The Eclipse.

Elizabeth stared anxiously at the dead corpse before her, the focus of her last autopsy. "Damn! How many more have to die before you give up your answers?" she asked the lifeless man before her. "MARY, run a body scan, stat!"

A flashing medical probe's sensor light ran over Elizabeth. "Heart rate elevated. Blood pressure 125 over 80. Brainwave activity -"

"Cancel last scan. No me! Once more over subject RUK002." The probe froze in mid-cycle. Elizabeth walked to it. Flipping open the glass cover, she checked its nano-circuitry. Snapping up the probe's calibrated neuro-link, she found specks of grayish powder on its neuro-connective audio plate.

"Dust!" She looked at the visual sensor of the probe. "Do you know where this came from?" She blew it clean.

"No, Dr. Blake," MARY responded. "There is no record in my memory bank. Thank you."

Elizabeth turned off the neuro-pen and clipped it to the collar of her green scrubs. Computers are not supposed to make mistakes, she thought to herself. She turned her attention, to the pox-covered cadaver in front of her, its torso sliced open from neck to groin, exposing what was left of the organs within. She was already under enough pressure to analyze any information she could from the victim. It only added to her frustration, dealing with the fact that these nano-computers were supposed to be infallible. Working against time to find this virus's DNA was taking a total on her normal good nature. She ordered, "Medical probe. Scan, please. Get it right this time and find a match in the data bank." Biting her lower lip, she stared at MARY's plasma screen, looking for a clue, any clue. "I don't understand. Why doesn't the virus's DNA match any of the Russian Cold War-engineered strains?"

The floating medical probe emitted a slight hum as it scanned the body of the deceased male from the mass grave site. "No life signs detected," hummed the probe.

"Of course not. I just did an autopsy on the man. What I need is confirmation of my autopsy DNA findings." She rolled her eyes at the bobbing probe. Despite her time as chief of surgery at George Washington Hospital, one of the country's most high-tech hospitals, she could not get used to the odorless, mirror-gray metal surrounding her. The Eclipse's medical system tapping into her own central nervous system felt like a violation of human ethics. She pushed her emotions aside.

"All tests confirmed to correspond with human-found data," the probe informed her.

"Great. He is confirmed dead. As anyone can see. And no DNA match." Weary, Elizabeth halted her examination. "MARY, shut the medical probe system off. I will handle the rest myself," she coolly said. The probe floated back to its shatter-proof case and switched to sleep mode. An optical glass door shut and locked it safely in place. The Eclipse was a technological vision come true but still had its bugs to work out, she thought.

The feeling of human compassion seemed lost in the purified air. The colored lights were the one thing that added vibrancy in the lab. Not that she minded the steroidal environment; she just needed more of a human presence on this trip. It was never easy dealing with the dead, but it became worse when the dead became an enigma.

To help, heal and serve in compassion: that was the reason she chose to be a doctor. Her uncle never really forgave her for refusing to go into the family business of politics. She smiled, remembering all William's tricks to persuade her to major in political science or law. But when she graduated at the head of her medical class, he was there to support her.

Slamming the Eclipse's morgue's cold storage door, Elizabeth could not release the habit of making sure the dead were dead before shutting them in for the night. Wearily, slipping on her headphone, her unspoken thoughts played over the speaker conference link. "Damn. Forgot to shut that off." Elizabeth was glad she was alone in the lab for that second. She moved closer to the data screen.

"MARY, run the diagnostic scan on the last two victims." Elizabeth's eyes swept over the hologram screen as she shut off the speaker link. The Eclipse was within hours of U.S. air space. In the passenger cabin was a man who had begun to make her uncertain of his intentions. He did not seem to have one compassionate cell in his body. Cold was an understatement, Elizabeth had learned as she spent more time with Yuri. "Is our guest, Lt. Commander Nevsky, secure and comfortable?"

"Yes. Current physiological status: his heart rate has risen above normal. I detect his skin temperature is elevated one degree above normal, suggesting he is tense or ill."

"Let's not play doctor, MARY. Those are all within normal limits. I just want to know if he is secure. I want to hold off giving any information to him until I run a few more tests." In reality, she was hoping to get a ten minute cat nap in before she had to deal with him.

MARY would not let her rest. "The commander has moved from his seat. His military escort behind him."

"Good! Well, let's hope he's enjoying the ride to the States alone if he is not pushing for a briefing at this point in the trip. I am not sure why he has not pushed for current information. Not a normal Russian characteristic. They are always in your face. Well, MARY, if I have some news to pass on to him, I'll let you know." Elizabeth was unsettled by her Russian contact on board; something ate at her gut. She knew she would have to keep her female intuition's warning signs to herself a little longer. At least she was in the lab while Yuri was confined to the passenger cabin. It gave her breathing room. Something was not right, regardless of Nikolai's trust in him.

"Dr. Blake, incoming message from CDC headquarters. Robert Yuan, Assistant Director, is on the line. There is an urgent request from the Chinese government. Shall I play it over your headset or on data screen two?"

"Headset will do," Elizabeth replied. "Thanks."

The assistant director's voice immediately rang over her headset. "Elizabeth, Robert here. I have some bad news. Stepanov's main oil tanker sank after several explosions while unloading oil in Dalian, China.

No one's claiming responsibility and now we've received news of pox-like symptoms appearing. You can draw a line all the way from Beijing to the Dalian shipping docks." Irritated by being left out of the information circle, Robert sharply criticized, "To add more to the case against the Russian government, which you can't share with me, we have reports from other countries with the same symptoms the Russian's health organization has described. Are you sure can't tell me anything? How about we play twenty questions on this pathogen and you can tell me if I'm correct."

Robert's smart ass comment annoyed her. "You have to be kidding, Robert. You know very well I can't tell you at this point why I went to Russia. Other than that they needed a pathologist."

"Elizabeth, I know the kind of damn secrets governments keep. Obviously there is something more to this outbreak. I was just handed a fax. Egypt, New Zealand, Africa and the United Kingdom have all contacted the World Health Organization claiming to have small pox-like symptoms. And something is going on in Miami."

"Robert, without letting you in on the specifics of what occurred in Russia I can tell you that I think we have a pandemic on our hands."

"Let's not take it that far yet," Robert warned her. "We have vaccines for small pox."

"Pox-like, not small pox," Elizabeth reminded him. She moved closer to the data screens. A keyboard moved into place as her thoughts focused on the task before her. "We can't rule out anything that might have started this disease."

He understood the many implications of her statement. "What can I do to help?" Robert's easygoing style turned stern and intense. This was big time trouble brewing.

"Just hold on for now," Elizabeth said. "MARY, link me up with the CDC international data bank and put it up on data screens two and three. Robert, send the new information."

"I am sending what information I have now," he confirmed.

Elizabeth rose from her chair and stood back to read the data flashing up on her screen. "Oh my god!" she said to herself, forgetting her headset for a moment. "Saudi Arabia is on the list? Well, we can rule them out."

"Rule out them for what?" Robert questioned.

Elizabeth's hand flew to her headset. She shook her head; she should tell him. He was her assistant director and would find out soon enough. "Bioterrorism is suspected. I thought maybe the Arabs... Iran? The groups the CDC is on constant yellow alert for." She paused, took a breath and let it out, thinking it could very well be the Russians. No, she shook the thought from her head. Not Nikolai. "We can't announce any findings without President's Brice's approval."

"Elizabeth, we have been friends for years and coworkers under some of the foreign outbreaks. Promise me you'll keep me in the loop even if you can't pass on sensitive information. I have to be in on this. Somebody has to watch your back."

"Of course," Elizabeth replied. "You're my top man on this pathogen." She frowned, knowing some personal issues would be out of bounds, even for Robert. Her hand reached forward. She pulled back. Her hands fell hard to her thighs as the Eclipse's secure link to MARY's systems superseded onboard data links and started before she reached the keyboard. "Damn telepathic machine," she murmured. "Robert, how soon can you have the CDC's main database linked?"

"Within the hour, maybe sooner."

"I need access in the next 15 minutes. The virus has a unique mechanism. The DNA acts like small pox, but examination shows that the victims die of a cause unrelated to the pox virus. I don't know the connection. If the small pox virus has mutated, it's mutated into something unknown to us at this point. We need to find the carrying mechanism, how it's spread. Air? Water? Blood? Time is something we do not have." She paused. "Robert, request that blood samples from reported victims in all of these nations be sent to the CDC to analyze via a computer scan immediately. Tell them to send several samples, from the first victim to the last one. I'll need to have Brice make a few calls to the heads of state. I will need the best of the best to assist from each of the international medical teams to get to the bottom of this."

"Doing it as we speak. Anything else?"

"Keep me updated. Any and all new outbreaks."

"I will, Liz," Robert confirmed.

"Thanks," she said. "Stay on the line. I'm going to call Secretary Blake." Elizabeth took a deep breath. "MARY, put me in touch with the U.S. Secretary of State," Elizabeth ordered.

Elizabeth paced between the screens, analyzing all the latest information on the direction and rate of the spread of the virus.

"Elizabeth." William's voice blared over the headset. "What do you have?"

She cut immediately to the situation at hand. "Robert Yuan is on the line with us. I'm sure you are aware of the other countries showing small pox out breaks."

"Yes. We have to go public with this regarding the Russian's stolen canister. Brice and President Stepanov will have to press the other world leaders to assist us as we take the lead to determine the virus."

"Whoa! What stolen canisters?" Robert cut in.

"I'll explain later, Robert. The virus may be from an old Cold War-engineered strain," advised Elizabeth.

"Now I see why you want the Chinese on this, too," Robert replied.

"That will take some doing. I know Russia and the U.S. agreed to lead an international team, but I'm not so sure other nations, primarily China, won't want to do it themselves. They will want to be on their own," William said.

"Fine, let them. The goal is to find a cure, through any means," Robert said.

"Before it comes to that, try calling Dr. Lee at Beijing University," Elizabeth suggested. "I remember working with him on the bird flu outbreak they had. Hard nose, no nonsense guy. He is one of top microbiologists in the country."

"I remember his name from reports," William replied. "I'll do what I can."

Elizabeth's voice grew solemn. "Uncle, the U.N. must immediately be notified and requested to get involved. With dozens of countries already struck by the virus, I fear a pandemic worse than any in history. I will send you the information needed to present."

There was no response from her uncle. She tapped her headset. "MARY, I lost contact."

MARY gave no response. Elizabeth's eyes caught the computer screens before her as the data turned to colored swirls.

"Elizabeth. Elizabeth!"

Elizabeth suddenly heard William on her headset. "Yes, uncle, I'm still here. I'm not sure what's happening. I'll try to send it again."

"Communications are off," MARY announced.

"MARY, satellite communication is down? Then fix it!"

"Yes, Dr. Blake. I believe William Blake is still on the line."

Elizabeth rolled her eyes at the computer. "Sorry, uncle. The sat com link is intermittently disrupting my signal. I'll resend the data to your office."

"Elizabeth, I am having systems problems, too. Keep trying to send all updated info."

"I will," she agreed. "Robert, change of plans. You have to head directly to New York for an emergency U.N. discussion on the outbreak. You need to brief Brice there. Good luck."

"I understand," Robert replied. "I've got the report - "

The communication link shut down. Ripping the head set from her ears, Elizabeth swore. "Damn!" She walked to the pilot's cabin door, knocked and then opened it.

"Boys, you have to take me to New York City for a U.N. meeting. Also, what is going on with the communications system?"

"Ma'am, it's the satellite links," the uniformed pilot replied. "We're flying this plane manually."

"Great!" she sighed.

"Ma'am, you'll need to have a seat," the pilot said. "We're going to have to step it up a few Mach's."

The co-pilot scanned several different radio frequencies. "Got one," he announced as he played with the touchpad scan system.

Elizabeth waited, watching.

"This is the Eclipse requesting approval for a new flight plan."

"This is the Marine Air Force Norfolk control tower. Where have you boys been? We lost communication with you and your course. We couldn't pick you up on the damn radar!"

The pilot smiled, "Well, at least we know we're still blind to roaming radar eyes even with satellites down. So, are we OK'd?"

Elizabeth anxiously commented, "It doesn't matter if they approve it. You have to get me to New York ASAP. Now that's an order!"

The pilot listened to the control tower. "We received our new flight orders, Dr. Blake. You can relax now."

"Relax?! We have no idea what we have on our hands, gentlemen. I suggest you get my ass over to the U.N., like yesterday! See what this plane can really do!" Slamming the door of the cockpit, she ordered, "MARY, get me data for all international blood samples from small pox victims in the last five years. I will also need the genocide data of the Kurds who were infected by Iraqi bio-weapons. Run it through the State Department. They should be accommodating. I also need any comparative data on the original DNA strain we have back at the CDC. Dust the files off and get it up and running."

Elizabeth rolled up her sleeves, straightened her single pleated trousers and sat. Putting on the head set, the screens danced with new data with each and every brainwave she threw at them. Her mind became one with the Eclipse's advanced nano-brain. Within seconds she had all the information exchanged. Stunned by the information transfusion, she closed her eyes to ward off a feeling of motion sickness, something she never had a single day of her life.

"Dr. Blake, prepare for landing," MARY announced.

"All guests prepare for landing." A second command came over the speakers.

Returning to his seat, Yuri tossed the opened ends of the seat belt over his lap.

"I suggest you secure them," the military escort said flatly.

"Why? This plane is an American plane. No worries." Yuri refused to snap the seat belt.

"Have it your way," the U.S. soldier said scruffily. He could care less if this man were secured in his seat or tossed about on a rough landing.

"A bit bumpy boys," Elizabeth commented of the landing at Gabreski Airport, New York.

The pilot and co-pilot smiled. "You said fast, Dr. Blake, not smooth."

She slapped shut the cover to her notebook and stashed it in her medical bag without comment. Without a touch, her seatbelt unhooked and slid back into place. This was one time she did not notice her thoughts in control of her surroundings. Rising, she hurried to the exit.

Elizabeth stepped off the Eclipse. The air was hot, humid, the sky cloudless. The smell of carbon monoxide hit her nostrils. She coughed. Yuri took a few steps behind her and said, "I'll meet you back at the hotel. We can exchange information then, Dr. Blake."

"I need you at the United Nation's briefing," she responded quickly. "That is why you're here, Lt. Commander Nevsky. Your president will want you to transmit my report back to him after I present it to the closed United Nations board."

Yuri gritted his teeth. Women did not speak to him this way. "Miss Blake, do not tell me what I must or must not do in regard to the duties assigned by my president. I'll see you tonight."

"It's Doctor Blake. Not 'miss' to you or anyone else on this case."

"Doctor." Yuri nodded and humored her. He hurried to the waiting sedan.

She shook her head in disbelief. She knew Nikolai should be told about this, but it would have to wait. She hurried to the waiting military escort. "I need to get to the U.N. headquarters. Check my bag at the Waldorf-Astoria and take Lt. Commander Nevsky with you."

"That will not be necessary," commented Yuri. "See, I have a car from the Russian embassy meeting me."

She turned around and noticed a black limousine with the Russian embassy flags halting to a stop. "Like I said, I'll see you at the hotel. I have to brief my president, too." Yuri jumped into the back seat of the limousine, shutting the door.

Shaking her head in disbelief, she turned back to her military escort. "Shall we go?"

"Yes, Dr. Blake." The escort shut the back door for her. Shuffling thoughts through her mind, and pulling out notes from her briefcase, she prepared to meet with Brice as they left the airport.

In the Russian-marked limo, Yuri turned on the speaker to talk to his driver. "Nice job getting the embassy to give you a car."

"Wasn't a problem, boss. Your brother gave orders to give you what you needed. I assumed that meant transportation, too." The driver laughed.

"Pick up Pinsky. We'll leave for Harlem after I check into the Astoria. Have him meet me there and inform Ivan back in Russia that I'm pulling Pinsky off his regular assignment. I sent a message via the embassy security line that I am onto something. Don't give him any other information. It will buy me some time I need to take care of business."

"Why take Pinsky? You can deal with Boris yourself. Don't mix the government into this."

"Shut up and do what I say. Boris is my problem. And as for the Americans, tonight is a night they will not forget for years to come." Yuri shut off the com link and retreated deep into the leather seat.

CHAPTER THIRTEEN

Day Three. 8:30 a.m. EST. United Nations Building. New York City.

Elizabeth stared out the tinted glass windows of the town car, viewing the usual crowd of street vendors, tourists in their cut-off shorts and logo-embossed I Love NY t-shirts, and all of New York City's "regular Joes" as her uncle called them, assembled along the streets, scurrying to get out of the unusually smoldering day.

She reached for her medical bag, pulling it closer as she watched the crowd entering the United Nations building. This prestigious group buzzing around the building's exterior was made up of finely dressed diplomats, ambassadors and top world leaders. Most of them hustled along with their security teams, compacting together, pressing toward the VIP entrance. She hung her head, tapping her medical bag in frustration. Her mind solidly focused on the bad news she would be presenting to President Brice. He would not take it well if she and her team could not find the cure. She glanced from the government officials back to the unaware New Yorkers crowding the sidewalks. Neither group's status would matter if she failed. She checked her watch. She was late.

The line of cars was not moving. "Let me out here," she said impatiently to the driver. "I can walk to the door faster than this." Elizabeth raised her hand to her lips to suppress a growing apprehension at briefing President Brice. What would his reaction be? He was a proactive president, even if it was unpopular. Nikolai, on the other hand, balanced that end. He would wait for all the facts before he committed to any political action. William would have to work his magic on the two opposite personalities, just like the old days. Her uncle had somehow always made peace between the two rivals. He would have to do it again to remove delays.

That remote thought of hers slipped away. The wheels skidded on the hot pavement as the limousine halted to a stop in front of the United Nation's V.I.P. checkpoint.

Elizabeth dug into her open purse, taking out a small perfume bottle to refresh her scent. "Well, let's get on with it, Liz," she said to herself. Tightening the cap, she dropped the perfume back into her purse and snapped it shut. Her patience was gone. She paused. Her hand froze on the door handle. A vision flooded her mind, conjuring up images of the mass grave site and Nikolai asking, "What killed my people?" Brice would have the same questions, but would be more demanding.

The illusion shattered as her phone beeped. She quickly pulled it out of her bag and read a text from her uncle saying he would be late, if he made it to the briefing at all. Her lips tightened in disappointment. She texted back quickly. Will send briefing report. Will include ISIDG satellite imagery from Digital Globe on mass grave. Having Robert send new imagery from new world outbreaks. She ended the text, feeling something more was on the way, more than the world was ready for. Elizabeth hoped she was wrong.

Her body rippled with a storm of emotions at the thought of the briefing. She knew it would have agendas she was not comfortable with. She had a strange feeling that Brice had offered her service not only because she was top pathologist and virologist in America, but because he knew of her Russian roots. That alone would weigh in favor of Nikolai trusting in her more so because he knew of her heritage. Even with that, Brice would never question her loyalty to her country. She was an American first and always. She reminded herself that both Presidents had requested to see her only because of her expertise. That was the reality of this meeting: to find what the hell was killing all those people. She dismissed the images of the past; she gathered her medical bag and opened the door.

Elizabeth's attention focused on the crowd before her as she stepped out of the backseat. "I'm with the CDC," she told the NYPD officer directing foot traffic. Elizabeth, feeling the uncommonly hot sun against her delicate skin, hurried past the crowd, toward the entrance. She glanced down at the cell phone still in her hand. "Let's see…" she mumbled under her breath. "Lt. Commander Nevsky is confirmed for this briefing. Hmm. Security Room 109. Meeting at 8:45 a.m. Let's hope he is there." Tossing the phone into her briefcase, Elizabeth entered the United Nations building.

"Have you heard of the small pox outbreak in Russia and now China, Dr. Blake?"

"What is America doing about our safe guarding our nation's health?"

"Is your uncle involved? We got no response from his office."

"Is President Brice involved? Is this another cover-up?" demanded a particularly cocky CNN reporter. "Damn!" Frustrated by delays caused by the media that was always present in hordes for these kinds of events, Elizabeth pushed past them, darting down the hallway and leaving unanswered questions in her wake. "No comment. You will have to ask the Secretary yourself. I'm a doctor, not a politician."

Her two-inch heels clicked on the tile floor as she passed the last security point. It was times like this that she did not like being the niece of the Secretary of State. Elizabeth picked up the pace, her silk stocking almost slipping from its garter straps. "Damn. Damn those journalists and their questions. They'll make the dead late."

She knocked on room 109, her face flushed. She tugged her light blue skirt smooth and quickly checked her stockings. How to explain why she was two minutes late for a presidential briefing raced in her mind. Brice was not the forgiving type.

Twisting the door knob, she pushed open the door. Elizabeth's apologetic face was swept clean. President Brice did not even look up to glance in her direction from behind the modest desk. She watched U.N. Secretary Quet as he sat uncomfortably on the small couch. Shutting the door behind her, she stepped into the musty room, wishing for a window to let out the damp odor. The odd choice to use this old office puzzled her. It was not fit for a President. Brice was covering something up.

She walked up to Brice. It was immediately clear that he was not happy. She acknowledged the two men. "Mr. President. Mr. Quet."

"Have a seat, Dr. Blake," Brice said flatly. She obeyed. His eyes focused on a current ISIS map of the latest viral outbreaks. "This does not speak well of you, Elizabeth." His eyes refocused on her. "I sent you over there to find out what this pathogen was and to contain it. Now I am informed that this disease has been appearing in other major countries." His voice was laced with a thin coat of sympathy and harshness at the same time.

Elizabeth sat up straight. She glanced over him briefly, taking in his mood, reading him as if he were a book. Brice looked menacing, decked out in a black pinstriped suit, expensive wing-tipped shoes, a white designer shirt and black tie with a gray diamond pattern adorning it. Even all dressed up, the Navy Seal in Brice never gave him a rest. He would demand no less of himself or his staff.

"To get to the point," she glanced at Quet, "we have to be proactive Mr. President. With rapid spread of the virus on a global level we need to treat this as we did SARS and the swine flu. I have to mention that the Russians believe we can contain it at the original site. However, as you can see, it appears we have a possible pandemic on our hands."

"Are you sure, Dr. Blake?" Quet asked, jumping forward from the couch. Nervousness surrounded him.

"I did say 'possible'." She had not realized that Quet was a bit of an alarmist.

"And what do you think we should do about this?" Quet snapped.

"Secretary Quet. Sit. Listen to what Dr. Blake has to say. The Russians are at the root of this, too."

Elizabeth continued. "For one thing, everyone, not just the U.N. will have to be proactive in making sure all countries are prepared for this virus if it cannot be stopped. This pandemic could be more severe than anything we've dealt with. Phase 5 within days."

Quet sat down and frowned. "Proactive. How?"

"First, let me brief you both." She swiftly snatched up her medical bag and pulled out tissue samples affixed to three glass microscope slides and small prototype nucleus Pip. "It has embedded RFID tag blockers." She handed it to Brice.

"What's this?"

Elizabeth looked surprised. "The Pip. It's from the high-tech system on the Eclipse, Mr. President, your space age lab in the sky I'm using. Funny how some of my biomed designs were used." She looked down slides. "The tissue samples are from my last autopsy found at the Russian mass grave site. They are virus-free. You can pass them on to the military to see if they can find something."

Brice frowned at the 30 by 10 by 2 computer interface connector. He took the glass slides and laid them on the desk.

"You look puzzled, Mr. President. It's a 3-in-1 device with an automatic storage retrieval system and medical analyzer. You can use it with any computer that has security code access to the Eclipse. It's my complete report and a mini lab. Just insert it into your computer and scan the slide. It pulls up everything you need to know about the virus." She paused to study him. "It allows you to access any files I'm currently working on at any time. The Pip's library keeps me in touch with our team of international scientist working on this case as well. With the RFID blocking systems, your data remains safe."

Brice waved to stop her explanation. He impatiently took the gizmo. "Fine." He tossed the high-tech paraphernalia to the side. Elizabeth saw it coming; Brice's probing analytical air set in. "I need to hear the report from your mouth. Not a machine. What is the virus? Is it Russian or American? Who set it free? And who are your choices for the international medical team? They have to be cleared by security immediately. Do you have any promising leads for a cure?"

Elizabeth was convinced the answers would be found in Moscow by reexamining the victims of the grave site. "I need to go back to Russia. The virus is still unknown. I do not believe it's a variant of small pox."

"But the Russians tell me it's a form that mimics its symptoms," Brice countered.

"It is possible that it's one of their engineered strains. It's appears to be Russian, based on Dr. Glazkov's report." Brice was on top of things as usual. Elizabeth crossed her legs. She leaned in. She listened with razor-sharp intelligence for what Brice would demand next.

"Glazkov?" Brice asked.

"Dr. Glazkov was the first noted pathologist called to the site. He confirmed he had seen a similar virus years before as young military medical student. It was engineered. This strain is not identical to the 1950 strain used during the Cold War. I cross-matched it 100 times over with this new one while flying back. I can't find the link. This is something new, faster, a real killer."

"I see." Brice stood up and began to pace the floor.

"We do not have any evidence on who, what or how the mass grave site was contaminated at this point. Bio-terrorism is suspected." Elizabeth turned her head and followed Brice's nervous pacing.

A small bead of sweat had formed on his brow. "Damn hot lights," he muttered.

"Bio-terrorism? Who? The Middle Eastern countries again?" Quet asked.

"We're not sure." Elizabeth rose, walked to window and closed the blinds. "I think the sun's a bit hot myself." She used it as an excuse to make Brice more comfortable with the news.

"Thank you," Brice offered. "Mr. Quet, I think she said it a nutshell. Does the United Nations have a plan to deal with this kind of illness on this level?"

"Yes."

"Then I suggest you put into action immediately. There is nothing more Dr. Blake or I can tell you at this time." Brice knew more and knew Elizabeth did, too. He did not like Quet, but he had to push to get the U.N. to implement their plan immediately. He was worried about politics; Elizabeth was more worried about the lives that would be lost without the U.N.'s help.

"I have a list. It's on the Pip I gave you. If you like, I can have my assistant fax it to your office," she offered both men.

Brice looked at the small object. "No, that will be fine." He nodded toward the strange black interface connector.

"I'll have the U.N. put out notices and implement health hazard warnings. We'll get our teams ready to send out medical assistance to those countries most in need."

"Thank you, Mr. Quet." Brice's face lightened with relief.

"The U.N. will keep you informed, Dr. Blake." Quet left the room.

Elizabeth walked over to face Brice as he turned. Stopping, Brice stood still. "And the cure? Tell me you have one."

"None," she said without flinching.

The air grew heavy. Brice raised a hand to his brow, wiping the sweat beads from his head. There was a rumble in the hallway and the door opened. William entered briskly.

"Finally, you're here," Brice said. "Dr. Blake tells me she has not found a cure. Mr. Secretary, it seems a small pathogen has taken control of our destiny."

William stood motionless. He had missed most of her briefing, but looking at Elizabeth's face he could tell it had not gone well. He searched the room for the missing guest.

"Where is the Russian Presidential Security escort?" William grilled. "President Stepanov was clear that he should be with you at all times."

Elizabeth was taken aback by her uncle's callousness. Something was wrong. He had to be carrying more bad news.

Her words held a touch of rebuke for Yuri. "It seems that Lt. Commander Nevsky believed it really didn't matter if he came at all. I see you are expecting the Russian ambassador as well." She pointed to the memo on Brice's desk.

"Yes." Brice turned the memo over. "But you already knew that." Brice winced.

"However, since I am here at the request of President Brice..." She stood firm in her convictions and addressed her uncle as the situation demanded. "Mr. Secretary, President Brice, explain what the Russian ambassador has to do with the medical team or the security team. Are the Russian's planning on dropping the ball in our laps without warning? We all know this virus has Russian roots. I will not have President Stepanov or my government playing politics and passing this off as my failure." Elizabeth tensed, preparing for a scuffle with these two powerful men. "You do both realize that the clock is ticking. Every minute more people are at risk of catching this pathogen. I will not be your fall guy, nor will I let innocent people die because of politics."

William pursed his lips. Damn, he was proud of her, despite her rejection of the family's traditional political careers. He would have to tell her one day. He knew how this battle would turn out. Elizabeth would not listen to any logic unless it would save lives, not just political face.

Elizabeth stepped closer to Brice. "Please excuse my forwardness. But I *do* mean to interrupt your meeting plans." Elizabeth pulled out her notepad. "I believe this file is for you, Mr. President. Security clearance confirmation and a schedule for my next meeting with President Stepanov. Here is the list of my team, Mr. President. All are high-level international scientists approved by and assigned to work under the CDC."

"You mean approved by you, as director of CDC?" He read the impressive list of names. "Do you speculate that clues may be found in databanks that the Russians have missed?"

"Yes." She looked at him pointedly. "I need this team to be approved by you, sir."

Brice glanced at her, then at the list. "OK, Dr. Blake, you have my approval. I want the virus stopped yesterday!" Brice made it clear there was no room for errors or delays. "Better to be proactive than wait for the Russians," he added.

"I assume President Stepanov will have to agree? And that it's my job to see he does? As an allied government, we do have an agreement with him." William crossed his arms.

"I think without the Russian representative present we have no choice. It's in our nation's security interests." Brice words were supportive.

"Mr. President, can assume my portion of this briefing is over? I'd like to get back to work," Elizabeth stated.

"Yes, but one more thing." Brice was stopped as the door opened and shut behind them. A secret service man entered.

"My apologies. I have Lt. Commander Nevsky requesting authorization to attend meeting."

Brice was beside himself at the arrogance of this man. "Now?! By all means let him in. I'm sure his president will deal with his tardiness."

Yuri walked in, shoving a small metal case into his pocket and carrying another larger one. He read the three pairs of eyes on him. "My apologies. There was breach of security. I was asked to assist."

"Well, welcome, Mr. Nevsky. But I am not interested in your excuses. Nor should you try to offer one for missing a meeting of such global importance." Brice refused to honor his rank. He could not show respect to any officer who failed in his duties. Yuri's late arrival was both a failure and an insult to him as the American President. A twinge of rage raced through him. Brice felt a strange dark chemistry between them. His eyes focused on Yuri.

Elizabeth stepped forward. She held out a file. "Here is the file on the autopsy of the bodies from the mass grave. I suggest you inform President Stepanov immediately." Her eyes focused on his. Yuri grabbed the files from her. Elizabeth coolly assessed his comment. "I do not believe your excuse." Elizabeth wrinkled her brow. "However, per your President's request, I think we have business to attend to, Lt. Commander." She paused. Yuri hit his chest and coughed deeply. "You should see someone about that." She pointed to his chest.

"Lt. Commander, can I arrange that phone call to President Stepanov now?" Brice's request was more of an order.

Yuri flipped the file open to the first page of photographs. His face remained unreadable as he scanned the photos of the victims. Yuri observed her reaction closely. He liked what he saw.

"Where are the bodies being kept?" William asked.

"On ice, I hope," Yuri said with a hidden grin. "President Brice, I appreciate your offer, however, I have my orders to follow."

Brice nodded. "I see he wants to keep it private."

"I would expect that. But what kind of information do you have to share with us?" William asked.

Elizabeth was surprised when he was given no answer by Yuri. "You will have to ask President Stepanov," Yuri replied.

Brice made a fist with one hand. He was not used to being denied information. Much less by the rank of a foreign diplomatic escort. "I will do just that, Lt. Commander," he replied tersely.

Elizabeth focused on the file. "Gentleman, the virus. We need to wrap this up. I have to get back to Russia." She looked pointedly at Yuri. "Please inform President Stepanov I need a day to collect more specimens from the original grave site. My initial investigations were limited." Elizabeth stepped toward the door. "President Brice. Mr. Secretary. With your approval, I'd like to get cleaned up, update my report and then return to Moscow as soon as possible." She glanced at Yuri then back to Brice. "Mr. President. I also included a small file on my escort's activities while with me. I'm sure it will be helpful when talking with President Stepanov."

Yuri tore back the cellophane wrapper and tapped out another cigarette. He did not light it. He let hang in the corner of his mouth thinking she was gutsy. Too gutsy.

"I want Robert in on this, too," Elizabeth continued. "He is one of our forensic experts."

Brice nodded. "You have my approval." Turning to William, he said, "Mr. Secretary, will you please make the arrangements?"

A strange feeling came over Yuri at the thought that she was the first woman ever able to keep him in check, and the first woman to challenge him to be on his guard around her. She should have been dead already. Stepping back, he sat in one of the maple chairs. He reached down into his pocket and took out a small travel chess game. He watched the three quietly talk amongst themselves. He picked up the white queen. Yuri struck the tip of a match against it, leaving a black carbon stripe on its side. Bringing the flame to his cigarette he lit it, inhaling deeply. He let out a large smoke ring, placing the chess piece in his pocket. He moved the black knight two spaces forward and one space sideways.

"Put that cigarette out. This meeting is adjourned," Brice said. Brice and William left.

"Are you coming?" Elizabeth asked Yuri as he inhaled again.

"I need to make a call," he replied.

"You are impossible! I'll meet you outside, Lt. Commander Nevsky." She eyed his cigarette. "You do know this is a non-smoking building, right?" The door slammed behind her.

Yuri pulled his phone from his belt clip. He pressed the number six. "Prince Adar," he acknowledged after hearing the familiar droning voice. He flicked some ash from the tip of his cigarette. The cooled cinders floated to the floor. "I have a favor to ask of you. It's in regard to Dr. Blake. Have Mus'ad watch her. I want to know all there is about her. She might become a problem. I have other duties I must attend to. I'm meeting with the head of the Russian mafia in New York. He needs to be taught a lesson on being too independent-minded. We will meet afterward at the pre-arranged location." Ending the call he punched two on his phone. "Commander Ivan Stepanov. This is Lt. Commander Nevsky. I have assigned a new man from our Embassy security staff to Dr. Blake for the night. I'm following a lead on the stolen canisters. I think I found the leak we are having trouble plugging."

"What is this leak again? No," Ivan replied. "*You* are in charge of her security. Those are the President orders. Send someone else."

"As you wish," Yuri confirmed. "And I'll transfer Dr. Blake's report as soon as I get back to the hotel." He wasn't about to let Ivan stop him. He hung up and considered how he would keep Ivan off his back until he finished his meeting.

Satisfied that he had his game plan under control, Yuri packed up, checked the time and extinguished his cigarette on the desktop.

CHAPTER FOURTEEN

Day Three. 10:00 p.m. EST. Harlem.

Yuri hated New York City in the summer, or anytime for that matter. He drove his partner, FSB Officer Pinsky, over the broken asphalt that heated the trash to a suffocating stench. He maneuvered past the dented cabs and double-parked box trucks, passing the slums.

"So this is the America they keep us from seeing," Pinsky commented on the deteriorated run-down buildings that decorated the streets of Harlem. Yuri pulled into an abandoned parking garage. He parked the car.

"Switch seats before they come." Yuri took the passenger side. "Wait for me before you do anything. There will be no American cops to worry about." He unlatched a biohazard case and took out a metal encased vial. He latched the case shut and shoved it back under the seat.

"What's that?"

"Top secret. Your clearance is not high enough, Pinsky."

"Bullshit. What does your step-brother have you doing?"

"Shut up or I'll leave you here to walk back to the Russian embassy."

Pinsky grew silent. He fidgeted in his seat, placing a hand on the black leather steering wheel.

Yuri smiled at Pinsky. He knew even New York's finest dreaded this place. He was sure the American Russian mafia leader, Boris, had paid them off to keep them from patrolling their beats tonight. Pinsky knew it, too. Yuri thrived on that kind of fear. He felt alive tonight. He waited patiently with his fellow FSB officer in the clammy darkness. Yuri opened his small metal box. A small magnetic chess set was visible inside the box, a game already in progress. White Russian marble and black onyx pieces, Pinsky noticed. Magnetic core. Expensive.

"What's that, Yuri? Never knew you played the game." Pinsky adjusted the seat a notch to accommodate his long legs. "Where do I get one like yours? I can play black while we wait."

"Forget it, Pinsky. One, you can't afford it. And two, it really won't matter after tonight. And three, the game's already in play." Yuri snickered. He moved a second pawn two spaces forward toward the white rook over his black knight.

Pinsky looked over and bitched, "Well, whoever you're playing is a dumb ass. His pawns will be dead with the next move."

"Exactly." Yuri snapped the case shut and placed it in his pocket. "They are here."

A blaring set of headlights pulled up behind them. A stocky man emerged from the passenger seat as several brash young men scrambled out of the back seat of the sedan, semiautomatic handguns aimed at the driver's seat of Yuri's car.

Yuri stepped out and signaled his partner to join him. Two gunmen retargeted. A red laser beam pinpointed Yuri's heart. The third gunman kept Pinsky in his sight.

"There's another. I can't make out what he is armed with," Pinsky whispered to Yuri.

"Don't worry. It will be over soon." Yuri replied. He nodded to the stocky man

"Boris. Good to see you." Yuri mentally counted how many men were with his acquaintance. He opened his jacket to show he had come unarmed. "See? As requested. No guns."

Boris waved a hand over his brow and let it drop. "I can't say the same about you, Yuri. You have an ugly new reputation to consider within the mafia," Boris replied. "I only agreed to this meeting out of respect for your brother Nikolai."

Yuri keenly sensed two other cars pulling up in the darkness. "I see you brought some friends with you." He spit on the ground. "You must be worried to bring so many of your men. My partner and I are not impressed." Yuri took a step closer to Boris.

"I hope you don't mind," Boris laughed. "What do I care about you two lousy FSB traitors?" Boris snapped his fingers. Four more men stepped out of the newly-arrived cars he waved to pull closer. "This is Bobby and his brother Catman." Boris introduced the top two Harlem drug dealers. "The other two are my Latino amigos, Raul and Goyo."

Yuri stood silent. He shifted his weight, observing the group of men before him. "These are my new partners," Boris continued. "In America, this is how it's done. Fast mergers against hostile takeovers from assholes like you." Boris observed Yuri as the crowd of men at his side grew larger. "I run my business on American soil. Not Russian dirt." Boris' face hardened. "I told you no. No mergers. You will not be boss on my turf."

"That's too bad, Boris," Yuri said. "I came with an even higher offer than the one you refused. It wasn't nice of you to send Alyssa back in that hat box. She was one of my best whores. I thought you'd like her. But you never did know how to treat the ladies." He glanced over Boris's shoulder to the men behind him. "Take my offer, Boris. It will save us both a lot of trouble. Ten million American dollars and a stake in the family stock, enough to buy you a castle back in Russia. I need you out of America tonight."

"You mean out of your way. Not interested. I have all the money and women any man could want. Now get out of here with your tail between your legs. Get out! Go back to Russia. We run this city. The Latinos run the city parks, the water filtration plants, the unions. They pay us to keep the illegals safe and working. You two cross me tonight and they'll slice you a million ways," Boris threatened.

Yuri reached for a cigarette from his shirt pocket. All the guns were immediately pointed at his large frame, aimed at his heart, head and anywhere else a clean shot would kill him. Yuri casually opened his jacket, revealing his cigarette pack. Boris waved his men down.

"You know you are outnumbered, Yuri. Say what you need to so I can go home to my women."

Yuri knew Boris was right. He had not planned on Boris being overly cautious. One group had to be taken out before he could get to Boris: the Blacks or the Latinos. The Latinos he could use. If they were not cooperative, they were already dead men. An evil grin formed across his face.

Yuri's eyes came to rest on Catman, a too thin, too tall, dark-skinned black man who nervously flinched at every imaginary sound. His drug addiction had already claimed his nervous system. He would be a vegetable within the year, Yuri thought.

Boris read Yuri's eyes and made the introduction. "Catman, my friend," Boris called to his man. "This is our Russian president's half-brother. A pig is the nicest word I can call Yuri."

"Don't you mean 'my nigger', Boris?" Yuri bellowed with a laugh. Their conversation froze at Yuri's well-aimed insult. Yuri had played his cards right: Catman was offended at the name calling.

"Who you calling a nigger?!" Catman shouted back. "I ain't no nigger. You white piece of Russian shit!" Catman jerked his switchblade out of his pocket. "See this?" The blade jutted up into the air. He waved it at Yuri, daring him to make another insult.

Yuri's face lit up with a wide-toothed grin when he saw Catman twist and turn the seven-inch gleaming steel blade. Just my luck, he thought. A knife fighter. Yuri shifted his weight to the left and balanced his large frame.

"Stop!" Boris demanded. "Yuri, I know you and your razor's reputation. Don't do this. A razor is no match to a seven-inch blade. I'd hate to explain to your brother why you are dead. Bah! More trouble for me than it's worth."

Yuri tossed his head back, flung out his arms and laughed a haunting laugh that would scare the dead. "Thanks for the warning Boris." Yuri fixed a gaze on Catman. "Well, nigger, you going to wag that sharp stick around or prove your point?" Yuri taunted as he knelt with one knee on the oil-stained garage floor. He pulled off his silk tie. Popping up his white linen collar, he exposed his pounding jugular vein and prodded, "Come on, Catman. Come get me, you skinny nigger. I have work to do. You're delaying my plans."

Pinsky stood still, nearly pissing in his pants. He was sure he'd be next. "Stop, Yuri!" Pinsky screamed, watching Catman's anger overtake him as Yuri ratcheted up his taunting.

"You shithead cracker!" Catman rushed toward Yuri in a heated rage. "I'm gonna slice you up like yesterday's lunchmeat!" Flipping the knife's leather grip in the palm of his hand, the blade extended, Catman raised his blade to deliver a lethal blow to Yuri's neck. The sweltering air stuck to his skin. His eyes bulging from his thin frame, he swooped down at Yuri.

"No, Catman! He's baiting you!" Bobby jumped forward to stop his brother. He missed. Boris grabbed Bobby's arm, dragging him back toward the cars. "Let me go!" Bobby screamed.

Catman lunged toward Yuri, but Yuri had the edge. He jumped up from his half-kneel. He had judged himself to be a good four inches taller than Catman, and that calculation paid off. He stood up; Catman stumbled downward franticly waving his knife at Yuri. "Shit. I'll cut you." Catman's knife swiped at the air, trying to slice any part of Yuri.

Yuri was fast, to Boris's surprise. He cringed, watching as Yuri trapped Catman's skinny neck between his large hands.

Snap-snap.

Catman collapsed.

"Damn it, Yuri! You shouldn't have killed him!" Boris screamed.

Catman lay shattered, as if his neck had been merely a toothpick easily snapped in two. His head mangled and twisted from his spine. "No more nigger!" Yuri snatched Catman's blade as it tumbled out of his lifeless hand.

"What the hell?" Boris screamed as Bobby broke free of Boris's grip. Catman's brother pulled out his .45 Magnum. Bobby's fingers lost their grip on the .45's trigger as he felt cold steel enter his chest. Bobby slowly looked down and saw his brother's blade jutting from his chest. Blood spurted from his chest. Yuri had flung the knife the instant Bobby's gun was raised.

"Call it reflex," Yuri said to Boris, watching Catman's brother tumble over onto a shaken Raul. He slipped to the cold concrete floor. Bobby's warm blood covered Raul's patent leather shoes. His gun lay unfired at his side. Things were happening fast, too fast for Pinsky. He was frozen, useless.

"Now!" Yuri shouted as he turned toward the mafia leader. At Yuri's command, Boris heard guns clicking, shifting, seeking a new mark: him. He was dazed by the betrayal of his most trusted men. Ripping the semiautomatic handgun out from under Catman's shirt, Yuri placed the barrel right between the confused eyes of a speechless Boris. "It seems I pay better than you." Yuri answered his silent question, then pulled the trigger.

A gush of blood spurted out of his head, splattering Goyo's shoes before it slowed to a trickle. A thud was heard as Boris fell backward, landing grotesquely twisted over Bobby's lifeless body.

Yuri twisted and swiftly pointed the gun at the Latinos, who dropped flat onto the chipped pavement. "You want to live, spics? I have some instructions for you and your wetback friends. Get up." The two Latinos swallowed hard, trying to slow their heart rates and breathing as they cautiously stood.

"What do you what us to do?" Raul asked, quivering.

"At midnight tonight, your people working in the water filtration plant will place a few drops of this oil in the water supply." He tossed a small vial to them. Goyo caught it in midair. "You're going to poison the city's water supply."

"*¡Que no, coño!*" Raul objected. "I have mouths to feed." He motioned for Goyo to toss the metal tube back to Yuri.

"Fine," Yuri replied. "Let me make this easier for you."

Pop! Pop! Raul fell to the ground. Goyo, shaken at the image of his friend's brain splattered on the garage floor, took a few steps back. He searched for a way to escape. There was none. Boris's remaining men focused their guns on a quivering Goyo.

"What about me?" Goyo questioned. Rattled, he took a stand. "If I'm going to die, I'll die here. Not by poison."

Yuri tossed his gun to one of Boris's old men. They were his now. "I have an antidote for your people. But you really don't have any choice. If it's not you, it will be someone else. You'll either cooperate or you'll die and so will your family." He brushed oily dirt from the sleeve of his jacket. Goyo was silent. Yuri gave him a chance to think over his options, and then said, "Fine. When your kids are dying, tell them it's your fault." Yuri walked toward his car.

"Wait," Goyo called. "OK. I'll do it. Where's the antidote?"

"Poison first. My men will take care of you once you complete your assignment. Fyodr, go with him. Cover his tracks. Make sure he gets home tonight."

A small black sedan came into sight on the ramp below, leading up to their location in the garage. Yuri was startled. "Pinsky, who is that?" Both men knew no one knew they were here. Pinsky shrugged his shoulders and looked away. "It's Ivan," Yuri realized. "Damn Ivan. He sent someone." He turned on his radio transmitter. "Lt. Commander Nevsky here. I have an update."

Ivan's voice rumbled over the communication link. "What the hell is going on, Nevsky?! Why did you turn your FSB link off? You are in direct violation. I sent Oleski to find you. He'll be at your location any minute. You have been called back to Russia immediately."

Yuri franticly tried to think of a way out. "I got the leak, commander. Inside job. He knew how to cut off communications."

"The leak? Who? We need him alive," Ivan pressed.

Pinsky strolled over to Bobby's dead body. Yuri glanced down at the man kneeling over the body, stripping the dead man of his drugs and wallet. "*Da*, I found the leak. It's Officer Pinsky."

Pinsky looked up abruptly and stared, unable to believe his ears. He stood, dropping the cocaine bag he had stripped from Bobby's corpse. "I'm not going to let you get away with this. I'll tell Ivan everything. How you poisoned the oil ships and now the water supply systems. You'll do more than rot in jail!" exclaimed Pinsky. His hand raced for his com link. "Ivan will hear it all."

"Commander Stepanov. I'm not the leak. It's—"

"Too late." Yuri's eye's narrowed. "Time to die, Pinsky!" Yuri's favorite weapon dropped from its hiding place in his sleeve. Grabbing a fistful of Pinsky's hair, he yanked his head backward, exposing his throat. Pinsky's terror-filled eyes sought out Yuri's evil glare as the edge of the razor slid across his throat. Pinsky gasped for air, gurgling as he looked up at Yuri. He fell dead at Yuri's feet.

"Yuri, report! Get Pinsky back on the line," Ivan ordered.

"Pinsky is dead. It was me or him," Yuri answered. He turned off the link. "You, spic, go with my man before that sedan parks." Goyo ran behind the concrete columns and the two made their way out. Boris' men scattered, their cars racing away just as the FSB sedan pulled up. Yuri dropped down to mourn Pinsky and slipped his blade back into its place. He mumbled in a hidden mockery, "Why, Pinsky, did you do this?"

Russian security stepped out. "What the hell is going on here, Lt. Commander?" Oleski demanded. He heard Yuri's words over his fellow FSB officer. His hand was red with Pinsky's blood.

"I do not know why he did it," Yuri offered, his voice resigned. "Pinsky was working with Boris. They tried to kill me." He pointed to the two dead black men. "Pinsky's men scattered when we showed up.

He was after the drugs. Hooked up with the Latinos, too. I had to kill him. I had no choice."

"I don't believe you, Yuri. Pinsky was clean and clear at the Embassy. I guess we'll have to wait on your debriefing," Oleski replied. "There's a matter of national security. You have been assigned to immediately escort Dr. Blake to Moscow. The virus has spread beyond the quarantine area. You have less than twenty minutes to get her on a plane to the Kremlin. Orders from President Stepanov." The officer looked around the scene. "We'll clean this up."

Yuri signaled in affirmation as he stepped back to his car. Checking that his biocase was secured, he sped off, vanishing from the bloody scene grinning.

CHAPTER FIFTEEN

Day Three. 11:46 p.m. EST. The Waldorf-Astoria.

Flashing green diplomatic sirens blared in the hazy night air of New York City as speed limits were broken. Yuri ignored a cab driver's insults as he ran another red light. An angry motorist's horn added to the clatter of the night. Beads of sweat formed on his forehead.

Yuri, absorbed with the spoiled state of his affairs, found himself fumbling for his droning FSB communication link. He slid the link over his ear.

"Where the hell are you, Yuri?" Ivan's voice bit into Yuri's ear. "You were to remain in continuous contact with Moscow."

"Stuck in traffic."

"With Dr. Blake?" Ivan asked in expectation.

"No." Yuri's lips tightened.

"No!" Ivan heatedly exploded.

"I am on my way to pick up Dr. Blake as we speak. Inform the President that she'll be in Moscow within the hour." Yuri held back a foul-mouthed comment and coolly added, "Ivan, I need a MiG. Pull some strings to get the approval from the Americans to land it at JFK."

"Are you crazy? We don't have a MiG in the area. Why the hell would I authorize one for anyone if we did, much less you?"

"That's crap, Ivan. We both know. Even the American's know a Russian Fighter jet is always within 30 minutes of Washington on maneuvers. Divert it to New York," Yuri pushed Ivan. "I'll file the new flight plan upon its arrival."

"What for? You both are required to be in Moscow."

Yuri frowned at the grim news. "I have a new lead on who stole the canisters. Pinsky gave it up. His last words."

Ivan suspicion's nagged at him. "You're bullshitting me, Yuri. We all knew Pinsky was a coke head, not a traitor. He didn't have enough clearance to even know the contents of the canisters, let alone get near them."

Yuri swept passed a broken down Yellow cab. His clammy fingers gripped the steering wheel and yanked it hard to the left, missing the drunken cab driver. He was irritated by Ivan's questions.

"Well, he was the source," Yuri insisted impatiently. "I do not have time for these questions now. Are you going to authorize the MiG?"

"Lt. Commander Nevsky, if I say you have time for my questions, you Stepanov bastard, then you do!"

Yuri would get his own Jet if Ivan denied him his transportation. He hated to be reminded of his half-blooded secret connection to the Stepanov family. He hated even more that Ivan outranked him. Ivan, who never shied away from reminding him of his lowly family status. "Nikolai may honor our father's request to watch over you, but you'll always be a bastard to the rest of the family." Ivan pounded the family's shame into him every chance he had. Ivan's death would be almost as pleasant as Nikolai's when the time came. A cruel laugh floated out of him.

"What are you laughing at? You're insane, Yuri!"

Yuri stifled his malicious feelings. He slammed on the brakes, stopping short of ramming the Hummer waiting at a traffic light. "Ivan, I gave you my report. I stand by it. I think Nikolai is more concerned with the arrival of Dr. Blake in Moscow than our brotherly 'love'," Yuri said.

Ivan disliked being wrong. He rarely was. It ate at his gut. But he also knew that if Yuri's information was correct he'd need that MiG. Ivan paused, then casually said, "I'll see about the MiG. Follow orders and get Dr. Blake to Moscow as originally scheduled." Ivan cut off his com link.

Yuri clutched the steering wheel with angry fists. "Damn Ivan. Damn Dmitry, Anton, all of those son of a bitch Stepanov brothers." He'd have to wait to see if he got his MiG or not.

Yuri eyes cut to the left, looking for a way around the Hummer. "Shit." There was none. Yuri let go of the wheel and whipped out his chess set. He made two moves: the white rook took the black bishop, and the black knight took the white rook. Snapping the metal tin shut, he shoveled it in his pocket. He hit a speed dial number on his cell phone. "Adar, we have a problem," Yuri said.

"Mine or yours?" Adar asked smugly.

Yuri wasn't in the mood for his cocky answer. "Nikolai wants Dr. Blake in Moscow tonight. Our time table has changed. The release of the virus in New York's water supply will be completed tonight. Everything else moves up six hours. Tell Mus'ad. I'll need that second payment from him within the hour. Put the money in my Swiss bank account. One more thing: make sure Mus'ad gets me in and out of Syria fast when were done with the exchange of the empty virus vials." Yuri hung up. "Fuck. This is the last delay," he ranted. His control was dangerously slipping away. He honked at the Hummer in front of him. A "fuck-you" finger salute flew from the Hummer's driver's window. "Forget this American ass."

Backing up from the Hummer, Yuri spied an open alleyway. He turned right and hit the gas pedal. He sped through the back alleys of New York, finally turning onto Park Avenue he pulled up to the 47-story Waldorf-Astoria. Tossing the keys to the valet, he told him to park it. He placed a crisp $50 bill in the valet's hand. "I'm expecting a car from the Russian Embassy shortly. I'll be out within fifteen minutes. Have the door open when you see me coming." The valet nodded.

"Crap. Now what?" Yuri muttered, seeing an agitated Prince Adar waiting for him in the Astoria lush lobby. He walked toward the Prince.

"It was not very polite of you to hang up!" The Syrian quarreled, grabbing Yuri's shoulder. "Where is the antidote vial you promised us? And what the hell is this request for the second payment *before* we get the antidote?" Adar demanded.

Yuri swatted his hand away. "Do not touch me." Adar tooka breath and stepped back, glancing at Yuri's blood-stained shirt. "I had to move my lab," Yuri said. "Come, ride the elevator with me. We'll talk there. Not here, you fool." Yuri noticed sweat pouring heavily from the Syrian's brow. "You look pale. Sick?" Yuri cocked a half-grin. They walked, stopping short of the elevator doors.

"No. It's damn hot in here!" Adar snapped.

"But you live in a fucking desert," Yuri joked. "This should feel like home."

"This is not home." Adar stared at the opening elevator doors.

The two men stepped onto the elevator. Yuri blocked a hotel guest from entering, pushing the button to close the doors. "International security," he told the middle-aged man. The mirrored doors shut tight.

Yuri slid his key card to gain access to the Waldorf's secure floors. The two men rode up. "I lost my head pathologist. Employed a new one. His price is twice as high. Our move to Western Siberia was an added expense."

Adar glared at him, not knowing whether to believe him. "Did you lose Mikovich or kill him?"

"Does it matter?" Yuri asked. He glanced both ways, making sure no one was listening in.

Adar picked up on his anxiety. "We are not paying for your murders, only the stolen antidote vials. I hope his death was easy." He bowed his head a half-second out of respect for the dead man. Yuri remained silent. "And this new pathologist. Who is he?"

"You do not need that information."

Yuri's attempts to hide his growing frustrations were failing. Adar felt it. If Yuri had a weakness, Adar would test it. With no top pathologist, Yuri could never be sure of the virility of the vials. Mus'ad could use that information to Syria's advantage if it were true. Adar turned quickly to dispute Yuri's claims. "We'll see if Mus'ad thinks you're lying. And we don't care about your costs." He pulled out his cell to send a rapid text message to his brother. "I can't imagine Mus'ad is very happy, Yuri. You promised to meet us in Syria with the antidote yesterday."

"So that is why you're here, Adar. To collect." Yuri gritted his teeth and fumbled with his jacket. "You have to wait. I have Presidential orders to return Dr. Blake to Moscow tonight. I have to keep Nikolai happy for now. You know that!" Yuri's razor slipped into his hand. "Or, we can end it here."

Adar took a step back in the elevator. He inhaled the stale air, glancing at the blood on Yuri's shirt, his razor in hand. He looked him squarely in the eyes. Death was in Yuri's eyes. "Put your razor away." He tried to calm Yuri. "You are being careless. Nikolai will have your head if he finds out before we are done. Whether I'm dead or not, we are partners. Give me the antidote vials and we'll postpone the meeting." Yuri's hand began to rise. He placed his razor hard against his palm and fingers for a swift slice. "Wait." Adar's phone vibrated in his hand. He glanced down at the sound. "It's Mus'ad." The phone call saved his life.

Yuri dropped his blade hand. His razor slipped back into its hiding place.

Adar smiled, reading his brother's words.

Yuri felt a strange twinge go up his right leg, seeing that smile. It was a warning. He clasped Adar's arm. "Have you contaminated the Syrian-Iranian oil trucking route? You are not keeping your half of the bargain, *partner.*"

Prince Adar looked at Yuri's hand, then jerked his arm away. "Did you take us for fools? We knew the kind of man we were dealing with. We have insurance. The vials first."

"Insurance?" Yuri asked.

"Yes. Give me the antidote tonight. We are going to settle up tonight," Adar pushed, wiping dripping sweat from his brow.

"Don't play with me, Adar," Yuri warned.

"Ah, you're not in charge. As of this moment, we are. It's been confirmed. My men have your new so called pathologist. He is Mikovich's assistant!"

"You lying bag of shit! Misha would never let that happen," Yuri responded.

"Call him. I can assure you Misha is busy at the moment, looking for your pathologist as we speak. He will die if you don't give me the antidote. Nikolai will pay us highly for this information, I have no doubt. And I do not think there will be a trial in Russia for you. Just a hanging. You will never make it back. Your step-brothers would be chomping at the bit for this information. Did you really think we would poison our entire homeland? Go ahead. Call Misha." Adar mocked Yuri.

Yuri abruptly smacked the emergency stop button on the elevator. The car jolted to a halt. Yuri cut the alarm off as he pulled out his cell phone. He hit Misha's number on speed dial. The only response was a mechanical screech in his ear. Yuri screamed in pain and ripped the com link from his ear. The ear piece hit the tiled floor of the elevator. "Shit!" His hand rubbed his ear. "Damn you, Adar. You used the jamming codes I gave you!" He snarled. "You lie, Adar! You and 100 of your men could not get past my growing mafia army." He tilted his head. Yuri's gaze fixed on Adar said, "But I can't prove it." Yuri snapped up his receiver from the floor and placed the ear piece back in place. He hit the elevator's start button and the car continued its ascent.

Adar opened his hand in demand. "The final three vials of the antidote, please. The new world will not be yours, Yuri, but ours. Only those worthy of Allah will receive it."

"As long as they pay and keep paying, you mean," Yuri growled.

Adar nodded. "I think my people would rather have their lives in our hands than yours."

The elevator stopped on Elizabeth's floor. The doors opened with a chime. Freshly vacuumed carpet lay before them. The scent covered the stale air of the elevator.

"Wait here," Yuri replied. "Keep the doors open. Dr. Blake will be joining us for the ride down and *our* vials." Yuri felt the double cross like the sting of a hornet. He had not counted on Adar betraying him so soon. Truthfully, he did not care whether the new pathologist lived or died. But he did care that Nikolai would stop at nothing to get his revenge and Nikolai would be a formidable enemy. He knew Nikolai would step back and use old Soviet ways. General Serebrinsky would take care of business and keep the President's hands clean. A single shard of memory flashed in his mind. Yuri had seen firsthand what Sergei was capable of. He was Yuri's greatest mentor and more. Sergei made it a science to get information out of a person and still keep them alive. His would be a long slow death if caught too soon. There was one difference: Sergei knew when to stop. Yuri did not.

"Ah, I should have known Dr. Blake was how you planned to smuggle it out through U.S. customs. She could be useful to me, if the virus becomes a problem," Adar mused.

She will be dead before you touch her, Yuri silently said to himself. "Give me five minutes and you will have the vial," Yuri began. "That is, as long as I receive confirmation that the oil is contaminated and my money is safe. I will keep the other two vials, to ensure the return of my pathologist, if you do have him." Yuri would not give the vials up so easily.

Adar smugly said, "Three minutes and three vials. You'll have your confirmation after I see the vials."

Yuri paced down the impeccable hotel hallway. His shoes were silent on the French art deco carpet. Her room was a short way up from the elevators. He swiped the stolen master key card and pushed open the door of Elizabeth's hotel room. Her floral sent strongly unnerved him from the moment the heavy door swung open. She was slipping a blouse over her lacy white bra.

"Close the door." Her words were sharp. "It's bad enough you didn't knock, much less leering at me half-dressed, Lt. Commander Nevsky.

"You knew?"

"I can smell your brand of smoke in the air," she said in disgust.

He slammed the door with the palm of his hand rather than smack her cheek. He fought to control a violent fit of temper rising inside of him. First Ivan, then Adar, now her. He stepped toward her. Elizabeth was startled when his heavy, calloused hand clutched her delicate upper arm. Without a word of warning, he said, "We're going now." He jolted her to his side.

"Ouch!" she cried out, ripping her arm away and turned around swiftly. Her eyes burned with heated abhorrence. "What the...?" She rubbed her arm in shock. "Keep your hands off me. I don't care if you're a top Russian, U.S. or any other security officer. Don't touch me like that again!"

His fisted hand fell to his side. "My apologies." Yuri had lost control of himself for a brief second and that second could have exposed him. "The small pox is spreading faster in my country," Yuri offered an explanation. "I am under orders from President Stepanov. He requires your presence immediately." Yuri hated the feeling of being trapped in a box with no escape route. Adar on one side, Nikolai on another, and her and the Americans surrounding him. He jerked his neck tie open for air. A faint red ring had appeared.

Yuri glanced impatiently at the clock as Elizabeth slipped on her black pumps. She was taking too long to get ready. He brushed his sandy brown hair back in place. "Come."

The command was layered in his thick Russian accent. Elizabeth turned at the sound of his coarse male voice. Anger bubbled up in her until her prickly eyes focused on the blood on his suit. "You're bleeding. What happened?"

Yuri looked down to see a small cut across his chest. Catman didn't miss, he thought to himself. He didn't answer her.

"Take off your shirt. Looking at the blood on your shirt, you might need stitches." She hurried into the bathroom and grabbed a towel. She called out, "Can you get my medical bag from the side table?"

"No time for you to play doctor," Yuri snarled back. He searched the room; his eyes fixed on her medical bag. He paused, realization lightened his mood. "Or maybe we do," he corrected himself.

A familiar vibration was felt at her hip. "Now what?" Elizabeth said aloud, snapping up her cell phone from her clip. Glancing at the screen, she saw the CDC's number. She answered it. "Robert. What do you have?"

"The U.S. Coast Guard called in a request for the CDC to investigate and report on an oil tanker run aground in the Florida reefs."

Elizabeth raised an eyebrow. "And?"

"It's a Russian oil tanker," Robert continued. "From the Stepanov's company. It could be connected. It's been on the news. And, as usual, I'm sure you have been too busy to keep up with news you consider unimportant to the CDC."

Elizabeth ignored his comment. "I understand. Thanks. But it is a matter for the Coast Guard. As for the news reports, we have no comment. Pass it off to the Coast Guard PR person. It's their jurisdiction."

"It had a biohazard flag posted," Robert added

"Understood. However, at this point I do not see the connection with what my team is working on. Oil is a biohazard on its own. It appears the captain of the tanker was following procedures by raising the flag. Let's wait for more information to come in. I have to keep working on finding the DNA to this unknown pathogen. Keep me posted. Send any news to the Eclipse. I am flying to Moscow within the hour."

"Elizabeth, wait. There is more. Watch this." Robert transmitted the lasted news briefing to her phone.

Her face dropped as she watched. Her voice lowered, she said, "You have got to be kidding. The international news is claiming one third of the world's been infected as of this time. Who authorized that bit of information?"

"The U.S. Health Department issued a statement based on incomplete data."

"Of course. They would have to jump the gun without checking with the CDC. And with Brice sitting on this unknown virus with the Russians, my hands are tied." She sighed. "Keep the media at bay and the citizen's at peace, Robert." She ended the call.

She called out to Yuri, "Do you know if any Stepanov oil tankers were on their way to Florida?"

Standing in the center of the suite, Yuri was carefully rummaging through her medical bag. "No." He pulled out four penicillin vials from a smaller bag inside. He quickly removed their label and exchanged them for the metal antidote vials in his pocket. "How the hell did the *Dostoyny* wind up in Florida Keys Gulf waters?" he wondered. The ship was not meant to stray that far south.

Her words, "one third of the world's been infected," had surprised him. *If Mikovich was correct and it's spreading that fast, I have made a timing error.* He shook the thought from his head. *No. No. No.* Yuri denied the facts. He told himself that the antidote would be all that more valuable. She was wrong. She had to be wrong. She was just a woman.

"I said take your shirt off," Elizabeth said, reentering the room, visibly upset. "What are you doing in my medical bag?"

"Looking for an antiseptic," Yuri said. He removed his hand from inside, empty. The other slipped the vials in his pocket.

She reached for her medical bag. "How did you get cut? You need stitches."

"Sorry, Dr. Blake. Those stitches will have to wait. Time's up." Yuri's large hand seized her wrist. Yuri ignored Elizabeth's protest. The small suturing kit fell to the carpeted floor. He snatched her medical bag from the palm of her hand. "We will send for your luggage."

Uncertain of the man who had her in his control, she said nothing as they both headed to the open elevator door. Elizabeth was critical to see Prince Adar waiting. The elevator doors closed.

"Confirmation," Yuri's only word to the Syrian.

Adar passed him his cell phone. Yuri glanced down at the silent live video feed. A small group of Adar's men stood outside an open valve of the newly finished Iranian-Syrian pipeline. Yuri clicked on views similar scenes at Middle Eastern water filtration plants and oil refineries.

Elizabeth could not make out the images on the screen. She leaned left to right, then right to lean left, trying to get a glimpse of the small screen. "Confirmation of what?" she demanded. "What was the video of?"

Adar shot Yuri a look of demand. Snapping the phone shut, Yuri handed it back to Adar. Yuri pulled Elizabeth closer to him. He pressed her body against the wall. "Russian business. Stay out of it."

She felt his threat. Adar stood behind Yuri. "Let her be." Yuri's other hand slipped the penicillin-filled vials into Adar's open hand.

"Get off me!" Elizabeth yelled. The palms of her hands shoved hard against his chest. "What is on the video?"

"Please, Dr. Blake. You need to calm down. I agree that Lt. Commander Nevsky has behaved poorly, but," Adar replied slowly, his diplomatic voice ringing, "I'm sure you understand. It's the property of the Syrian government."

She shook her head in amazement, putting the facts together. "President Stepanov will hear about this tape, and your threat to me, as will President Brice!" she informed Yuri. She turned to Adar. "If the Syrians are responsible for this act of terrorism -" Interrupting herself, she reached for her Pip com link and entered a number to reach her uncle. She twitched as a sharp pitch rang in her ear. "Ohhhh!" She shot an icy glance at Yuri, then at Adar. "Who's blocking the system?" Yuri stepped to the other side of the elevator. His breath was heavy.

Adar spoke. "There is no reason for you to be alarmed, Dr. Blake. Why do you American's always blame us? I believe it's your country. We are in America, after all. Our phones are having the same problems." He offered his to Elizabeth. "You're welcome to try."

She pushed his phone away. "I will get to the bottom of this. I promise you that. No one is to interfere with my investigation." She turned to Yuri. "I am demanding another Russian escort!"

"I'm sorry, Dr. Blake," Yuri said through gritted teeth. "You are stuck with me for the moment." The elevator doors flew open. Yuri waved his hand for her to hurry along as Adar traveled off to the left.

"Don't keep us waiting, Yuri," Adar called back. "I leave for Syria immediately." Adar hurried away, his hand grasping his stomach.

"Us? Syria?" Elizabeth looked hard at her escort as they rushed to exit the Astoria. "You're mixed up in this, aren't you?

"No," Yuri coldly answered her.

"How do you play into this mass grave site?"

"It's none of your business. It's Russian governmental business," Yuri harshly spoke.

Both quickly passed through the hotel's doors. The valet opened the back door of the Russian Embassy's black sedan. The door slammed shut. "Hurry. John F. Kennedy International Airport, back lot," Yuri ordered.

Shortly into their ride, Elizabeth's Pip flashed. Robert was fast with data. She answered her phone.

"You should have the test comparisons in a few moments."

"Thanks, Robert." Elizabeth ended the call and checked the incoming information. None of the scientists had found anything to link the virus to Russia's missing strain. The rest of the ride was silent.

Arriving at the airport, Yuri ushered Elizabeth out of the backseat. She managed to snatch her medical bag before he did. Bypassing the security checks, customs guards and luggage carts, they hurried to the back hanger, seeing the vehicle they were approaching, she dug in her heels. "You have got to be kidding!" she protested loudly. "We are not flying in that."

Before them sat a Russian MiG fighter jet.

Ivan came through, Yuri thought to himself. He dropped his diplomacy. "You got your wish, Dr. Blake. I won't be your escort back to Moscow. Your jet lab will get you there even faster than Russia can clear it for landing."

"You're not coming with me?" Elizabeth said, surprised. She could not believe what she was hearing. President Stepanov would want Yuri's presence on board to send him immediate updates.

"I will meet you in Moscow," Yuri responded callously, walking toward the planes.

The pilot of the MiG snapped open the latch and pulled the hood back. He jumped out with a large duffle bag. "Lt. Commander Nevsky?" the Russian pilot asked.

"Yes?" Yuri replied.

"You have my plane. Your flight suit is in here." He tossed the camouflage-colored bag to Yuri's feet.

"Take good care of it. I'll see you back in Russia." The MiG pilot turned to Dr. Blake. "Dr. Elizabeth Blake?" She nodded. "The Russian Government sends its greetings and apologizes for any inconvenience you may have concerned with this transition. A new FSB team will be waiting for your arrival. I am to fly with you back to Russia. Here are my clearance papers." He spoke to her in clear English. The pilot walked past them, toward the terminal holding the Eclipse, without even a glance back.

"This is not President Stepanov's orders. He would never do this. Brice would never do this. Yuri, what are you up to?" she asked

Yuri pulled a green flight suit from the duffel bag. "You'd better hurry," he warned Elizabeth, pointing toward the Eclipse on the runway. "Your new escort is way ahead of you."

"You've not heard the last of this, Lt. Commander," she said. Shaking her head, Elizabeth hurried to the Eclipse.

Yuri pulled on his flight suit. Adar had been lying about everything. He felt it in his bones.

On board the Eclipse, Elizabeth set to work immediately. Strapping herself in, she slipped on her headset. The virus was a priority; she would deal with Yuri's attitude later. "MARY," she greeted the computer. "Secure our new Russian guest and verify his clearance. Run a scan on him then get me any international updated data from our team. Put me in contact with Secretary Blake."

"Yes, Dr. Blake."

It was after midnight on the U.S. east coast. The moon was full and pierced the night sky. Glancing out the window, she watched the MiG's tail lights taxi down the runway to take off. She softly said, "Our turn next." As she felt sensations of the Eclipse's lift off, she turned her attention to the latest holographic images displayed before her.

CHAPTER SIXTEEN

Day Four. 12:05 p.m. MSK. Building 14, The Kremlin.

Nikolai wearily strolled into the Presidential office draped in the Federation's colors of blue, white and red linen, shutting the heavy door behind him. A motion sensor automatically switched on the lights. He preferred this more technologically-advanced office over the ceremonial office at the Grand Kremlin Palace. It was the heart of his new government. He had spent billions to update its outdated Soviet systems. With his son and wife trapped in the quarantine zone, he had taken up residence in the private study off his main office. There was no point in going back to the Presidential family quarters without them.

Nikolai walked over to a small panel that looked like a large domino. He pressed a black button. Mahogany paneled walls slipped into side grooves along the edges of the information center. He focused his attention on the six exposed television screens, each with its own version of global news.

"Prince Adar of Syria was found dead after his private jet crashed in New York's Hudson Bay," a news announcer began as the top left screen came to life. "The prince and his crew of three were found to have contracted the same pox virus that has appeared in hospitals internationally. This just in: We're trying to confirm that an oil tanker has run aground off the southern U.S. coast. The name and location of the wreck have not been released."

Nikolai shut off the screens. His mind ran relentlessly over who could have stolen the canisters. No radical group had claimed responsibility. Nikolai pressed the intercom button on the phone. "Is Sergei on his way? Check with Dmitry. See if we are missing any more tankers or if it belongs to another Russian company. One lost in China is bad enough."

"Yes, Mr. President. He should arrive in a few minutes," his administrative assistant answered.

"Any news on my wife and son?"

"No. The hourly report stated no improvement. I'm sorry, Mr. President."

"Thank you." Nikolai hung up, agitated. He was hoping to hear good news. He paced a few steps, his mind tense, racing. How could the thieves have gotten so close as to slit the throat of the one remaining Siberian guard? If he hadn't known better he might have suspected his old friend; the sliced throat was Sergei's signature at one time. This slit was different, not Sergei's handiwork. It was designed to let the victim die painfully, slowly, bleeding from the vocal chords rather than the jugular. A killer's mark. He slapped his hand on his trousers and exhaled harshly. It had to be one of his top ranking people. "There has to be a traitor in my office. Damn," he swore. "Who?" He could not be certain, certain of anything. "If there is a traitor, what is he waiting for?" Nikolai's chest grew heavy. "If they are using my office as a pawn..." His head dipped in anguish. He would not let the terrorist break him, even if it cost him the presidency. "This massacre can't be tolerated. My people, my son, my wife... They will not lose their lives because of my inaction."

His hand curled into a fist. A piece of him died. His eyes grew dark as they glassed over vengefully. Nikolai reached down in the pits of the shadowy side every man possesses, for this was where he needed to draw his strength from. Political protocol would have to wait. He did not have far to dig to find the old KGB bloodline that ran in his veins. For him it lay closer than most men, hidden under his polished manner. Trust would not be so easy for him, he thought as his blood turned hot.

A vow flew from his lips. "If my son or my wife dies, the terrorists will pay. And pay hard. Presidency or no presidency," he said without a hint of weakness. He glanced at the photo of his military unit. "As a soldier there were rules to play by. With these terrorists, there are no rules." He cursed under his breath.

Nikolai sat the newly-commissioned mahogany desk he had ordered for his term. His head began to ache. He shifted again, searching through his memory for anything to help prepare him for the worst. Agitated, he rose from his seat and paced the room once again.

He paused before the mahogany bookshelves stocked with rare books, his own private collection. Glancing up, he plucked out War and Peace. He thumbed through the worn pages. He must have read it a hundred times. It was complex enough to drag his mind away from his responsibilities and take him to Tolstoy's time. It was the only book that gave his mind the escape he needed. Oddly, it was also the one book he had shared with Elizabeth, fourteen years ago when he was assigned as her guide.

He had fought that assignment. He thought it was beneath his qualifications as an FSB officer. He was the last one who wanted to spy on the new American ambassador's young niece. Little had he known that they would become his strongest allies. Nikolai relaxed for a moment, for the first time since the news of the grave site. Still, doubt plagued him. He put the old vision aside.

His steps slowed briefly. Nikolai slammed the novel onto the presidential desk. He dropped into his chair. He eyed the stack of papers on his desk and pushed it to one side. He leaned back and looked at the digital clock staring back at him as if to warn him that time was not on his side. Nikolai brooded over the clock's display. "Yuri should have been here by now. His stop in Damascus was not authorized. More time lost due to his wild behavior." He grew more apprehensive of Yuri's actions each day.

Reaching down, Nikolai opened a single side drawer and pulled out Elizabeth's dossier. He regretfully said to himself, "I shouldn't have flown her here." Annoyed, Nikolai placed her file on his desk alongside the stack of papers. He cracked the old brown leather cover of Tolstoy's work, flipping the pages, not really reading them, hoping to find any random passage that would flush the demands on his mind as he waited. Fate would not allow it as an old snapshot of a young Elizabeth fell into his lap.

Nikolai lifted the old photograph up and ran his fingers over the yellowed and ragged edges. Tapping it, he was flustered that this woman had entered his life again. He had to trust the Americans. He closed his dark ebony eyes and recaptured the ethereal images of their youth. Young smiles had filled the room at their first introduction. It felt as if had been yesterday. An instant rapport had formed between them. She, an overly inquisitive post-adolescent interested only in old books and his job. He, a hardcore undercover FSB agent who once found solace in her eyes. "Are you a spy?" she had asked him once, point blank.

He frowned. He glanced at her dossier. She was not so innocent now. He flipped the photo into the darkness of the desk drawer and slammed it shut. He had enough to worry about without that old memory. His people, the family, the shipyards, even himself, since the international news was politically hanging him for the environmental repercussions of his ship's oil spill in China. If the Florida tanker was his, there might be no chance of recovery for his political or business career.

Nikolai heard the sound of his office door opening. "Finally!" he exclaimed, anger in his voice. "You're here." His voice held relief and distress.

Sergei trudged in, reading his President's concern. "Dr. Blake and Yuri are both over Moscow air space. I received and approved Dr. Blake's request to expand the quarantine area a few moments ago. My apologies if I acted without your clearance. With Glazkov dead, I—"

"Glazkov is dead?" Nikolai asked, surprised.

"The virus. I asked Dr. Peter Petruc from Moscow Central to step in."

"And Yuri?" Nikolai sighed.

"Yuri is another issue. He stopped in Syria, as you know. I okayed his fight plan after it was filed. Dr. Blake should be landing shortly. She stopped in London for fueling. I assigned Ivan to pick them up at Zhukovsky Airport. He's taking your brothers as added security." He paused. "I'm requesting to hold off on implementing any disciplinary action against Yuri at this time. He reported that he learned important information on who stole the canisters. It looks like Mus'ad had a hand in it."

"What about Adar? Was he involved?" Nikolai pressed. "And is the oil tanker off the U.S. coast one of mine?"

"Yes, it was the *Dostoyny*. Dmitry confirmed it. We do not have any more news on the tanker at this point. President Brice was made aware of it. As for Adar, he was dead before the crash. Secretary Blake told me. The Americans are keeping it under wraps, away from their news hogs. They do not want to start a panic in their country. I do not blame them.

According to Secretary Blake, both Adar and his pilot died of a type of small pox." Sergei gritted his teeth.

"Our virus? On American soil? This is not good." Nikolai slammed shut the rare copy of the novel and tossed it aside. "Who else knows? Why didn't Yuri inform me personally as ordered? I handpicked him at your recommendation as an escort – and undercover agent – for Dr. Blake. And now we are connected to Syria. It's a political disaster!"

Nikolai's temper was erupting. Sergei knew Nikolai held him personally responsible. "Mr. President, Yuri gained information that is creditable. You can rest assured."

Nikolai leaned back in his chair. "Did he? Tell me more. If Mus'ad fills in the vacuum created by his brother's death, we are all in trouble. Mus'ad has too many ties to radical leaders in Iran. You and I both know his only goal is to make Syria a world power."

"Yes, I agree, Mr. President." Both men were worried.

"What does Yuri have?" Nikolai asked.

"Yuri claims he has proof that Adar's men were involved in the Soviet lab breach, connecting the dotted line to the bio-terrorist attacks."

"I do not like this independent streak Yuri has developed," Nikolai said, annoyed. He glanced up at Sergei and added, "However, I can't deny that's the best news I've heard so far. "If Yuri is correct, we can get this to the press. President Brice and I can make a joint statement of condemnation." Nikolai relaxed. "Bastard or not, Yuri seems to have come through."

"Mr. President, I wouldn't relax yet. Your office isn't untarnished in all this," Sergei said. "You need to see this." He reopened the mahogany panels of the information center. "CNN is broadcasting that Russia is suspected of using your oil tankers in an act of biological warfare. It's become more than an issue of environmental cleanliness." The screens came back to life, the sound muted as Sergei explained the newest developments. "They're reporting that small pox killed the crew of the *Dostoyny*. The AP is delivering the message that China is claiming the same. The BBC is reporting Yuri's trip to Damascus. Interpol has linked his stop there with your position and your relationship to him. They have created a conspiracy theory accusing you of wanting to overthrow democracy and reinstate communism."

Nikolai's fist came down hard on his desk. The old novel vibrated against the wood. "What the hell is going on? Get President Brice on the line now. Reach President Chang after I talk to Brice."

"Yes, Mr. President, immediately." Sergei picked up a secure line to make the calls. He watched Nikolai's expression. Desperation appeared to drain the life from his face as he listened to the horrific news being played all over the world. He stared with disbelief as the global news broadcasts poured in.

"Total human extinction is hours away we are told. Over 100,000 dead in the port area and in the city of Beijing. Riots have begun in the streets. Shops robbed, public buildings destroyed. A frenzied crowd armed with knives, clubs and firearms is attacking anyone who tries to stop them from fleeing the city filled with sickness," a newscaster announced. "Tiananmen Square is littered with dead. No one has been spared. Women, elderly and children lie among them."

Nikolai felt cramps in his stomach. He listened to the U.S. report of hundreds of cases of small pox-like virus claiming lives in Florida, and of New York City shutting down its city limits. "Unknown small pox-like symptoms are appearing in hospitals in regions across the world," the reporter summarized. "All this the day after Russian President Stepanov's oil tanker crashed in Florida. Is there a connection?"

"All commercial jet liners have been grounded after several crashes in France, England, Spain, the United States and the latest near the Great Barrier Reef. Transportation systems are shutting down worldwide to stop the spread of this unknown virus."

A fourth newscaster drew Nikolai's attention. "It is worth noting that Russia has not reported any such illness. Why? Why, President Stepanov?"

Nikolai grew tight-lipped hearing the accusation and fear in the young woman's voice. A mixture of political anger and astonishment coursed through his veins as he took the receiver from Sergei.

"President Brice, President Stepanov here."

"I assume you have seen the news, President Stepanov?" Brice's voice boomed over the phone. "We tried to keep Adar's death quiet, but there is more. He alone could not have spread the virus throughout New York this quickly."

"Yes, I have seen the broadcasts."

"Your country has contaminated my coastal waters and the Russian crew brought the virus onto the mainland. What are you going to do about it? Was this some kind of biological warfare dispersed on your country's part? Did you ask for my help to cover you own tracks?" Brice demanded. "I'm demanding that Dr. Blake return to the States immediately."

Nikolai's anger stirred at the accusation. "Brice, I understand it was one of my private ships that was involved in the incident on your shores. But don't push me. We have a fragile alliance! We agreed to share any new information that may help solve this problem. I have some but I need Dr. Blake here in Russia, too. This is a common enemy."

"What have you got?" Brice's temper went unchecked. "Your news better be good." His voice held a reminder that they were of equal rank in the political world. Short on diplomacy, he pushed for answers he knew Nikolai would not be willing to give him so easily. Their counties had been at an uneasy truce since before they both took office.

Nikolai bridled his words at the fit of American machismo tossed at him. "At this time, we have intelligence reports to confirm that the Syrian brothers, Adar and Mus'ad, are suspects in the stolen biological weapon," Nikolai responded truthfully.

"That's why your FSB officer was in Syria."

"Yes. He is following a lead. I learned this moments ago." Nikolai twisted the order of facts.

Brice coolly said, "Ok, Nikolai. You have Dr. Blake's services. If she comes up empty-handed, I'm calling her back immediately." Brice continued, "I have something for you. Your captain kept a log. We have recently received it. CIA translators are working on it as we speak."

Nikolai's ears sharpened. He sat forward in anticipation. "You have the captain's log? Good, good." He motioned Sergei to listen in. He would not have Brice holding the trump card in this alliance. Nikolai offered, "May I suggest that, out of our nation's friendship and keeping in mind the U.N. vote you need to support your government's embargo on Iran this week, we'll keep the contents of that log between us for now?"

"Touché, Nikolai. I almost forgot you can play political hardball with the best of them." Brice added calmly, "When Dr. Blake finishes that last autopsy I will have her send her report in duplicate to us both. Time is critical." Brice added, "One more thing. I'm sure she is aware of what has transpired back home in the States." Brice took in a deep breath and exhaled to make sure his counterpart understood. "Nikolai, I need her back immediately after she finishes her investigation. There is no negotiation on this."

"I am expecting her at Moscow Central within the hour," Nikolai offered. "I'll forward a message informing her of our chat. Since we are both being upfront, I have approved her request to reexamine the findings of the autopsy of the only guard found at our storage facility. It is my understanding that she needs to compare his DNA and others of the mass grave site with the international teams' samples." Coolly Nikolai added, "I'm sure we can piece this puzzle together with Dr. Blake's help." The two men could not exchange their goodbyes fast enough as they both hung up.

Nikolai wrote down some notes. "Brice will not keep his word on Dr. Blake if the infection is spreading rapidly in the States, too. Sergei, notify Elizabeth en route that we need her findings on the guard and emergency autopsies immediately upon completion. I'll deal with Brice. She will be ordered to provide the results to him first. I do not want Brice sitting on them. Take her directly to her living quarters to drop off her bags, then directly to Moscow Central Hospital's morgue. Have our top team prepare the bodies for her arrival. I want Dr. Petruc on it. He is trustworthy and will keep me informed, unlike Yuri." Nikolai looked up from his notes abruptly. "Sergei, we know we can't deny there are traitors among us any longer. With death spreading faster than we imagined, we can't afford to play it safe. Find them."

Sergei pressed his lips together tightly. He silently understood he was cleared to use any method to stop the terrorist. He reached into his pocket and felt an old friend he had carried with him for years, a habit from his former life as a Soviet interrogator: his razor.

CHAPTER SEVENTEEN

Day Four. 1:12 p.m. MSK. Zhukovsky Airport.

Elizabeth was herded into a dingy aircraft hangar that held a pristine black Mercedes parked out of the public eye. Two Russian presidential flags adorned the Mercedes' hood. The early warm moist summer air left droplets of dew on her skin. She squinted to see two military commanders exiting from the Mercedes and approaching her as if they had a claim to her.

Dmitry. Ivan. Nikolai would send his top personal security officers to meet her. She frowned. "Gentlemen, time is short," she said as they reached her. "Let's get going." Elizabeth raised a hand over her face to shield herself from debris kicked up by a MiG landing near the Eclipse.

Yuri's face soured taking in the sight of his half-brothers and Elizabeth upon landing. He was not expecting any high ranking officers to meet her, much less Ivan and Dmitry. "More delays." This would ruin his plans to escort Elizabeth and her medical bag to his mafia office. He had a special death for her. "Shit," he swore out loud. He needed the swapped vials in her bag by tonight. Adar had already caused him one delay; he could not afford another. Nervousness nearly cracked his icy core. He quickly slammed the latch to open the top of the MiG. "Wait! I'm here!" Yuri shouted, leaping out of the fighter jet. He broke into a run to catch them.

Dmitry nodded toward Yuri's call. Ivan was visibly upset with their half-brother. Their bodies tightened and they kept walking, entering a small tin-roofed five-car garage. Yuri slowed his pace to match Ivan's as he arrived at the taller man's side. Ivan snarled, "You're late!"

"Nyet. You are here. I am here. That means I am not late." Yuri formed a cocky smile.

"Wipe that shit-eating grin off your face. You are lucky General Serebrinsky told us about your latest news. You are also discharged from…" Ivan paused and glanced at Elizabeth, who was listening intensely to the two men. Ivan wanted the pleasure of saying "from all duties" but instead finished his sentence, "Escorting Dr. Blake. We'll be in charge of her security."

Elizabeth raised a brow at the men before her. This was big news. She remembered all too clearly how the Stepanov brothers worked. It seemed as if they could read each other's minds as one functional unit. "I assume the death toll has risen more rapidly at the grave site area than Glazkov's last report stated."

"You will have to ask President Stepanov about any new data."

"What about Glazkov?" Her stomach tightened. If he was dead, they were not about to tell her. Nor would she push. She'd find out soon enough.

Ivan hustled her toward one of the presidential motorcade cars. The click of Dmitry opening the back door echoed through the metal building.

"Dmitry, take the doctor's bags," Ivan ordered.

Yuri tensed as Dmitry reached for her medical bag. Beads of sweat formed on his brow.

Dmitry clutched her medical bag from the back seat. Elizabeth forcefully jerked her medical bag out of his hand. She pulled the black leather bag tight to her chest. She declared in uncompromising Russian, "That will not be necessary. I had critical medical supplies sent to me before I left New York. I prefer they stay under my personal care. Do you understand, commander?" She tilted her head in defiance.

Dmitry's brows rose. Elizabeth's voice had smacked him in the face with her bold move. He let his hand slip to his side. He made a sharp nod to Ivan. "I guess we will let the doctor carry her own bag for now." Keeping with their new orders, to provide her with security that would not interfere with her investigation, he let this brazen woman have her way.

Yuri took notice of the brashness. Elizabeth tightened her grip on her medical bag. She brought it in closer to her side. It troubled her to have them there. Anton in the driver's seat, the rest surrounding her. She felt trapped. Her cool gaze ran over the intimidating six-foot plus men. Something raised a red flag in her. It didn't bother her that Nikolai's hand-picked security officers were all Stepanovs. It was Yuri who was the odd man out in this group. *Why is he here?* He should be court-martialed for how he behaved, her mind screamed. With her sharp perception she studied Yuri a second longer than she should have. His tall frame fit in, but his eyes and face were different, her forensic trained eye noticed. He somehow belonged to that clan. She was sure of it.

Agitated, Yuri lost his cool. "Come on! Get her in the car and let's go before any more problems delay us." Her stare was unsettling. It unnerved him.

Ivan shot a look at Yuri, noticing his clammy appearance. His skin was blotchy. Ivan opted to rebuke him in private later. "What's wrong with you?" he asked. "I've never seen you sick. You look like shit." Ivan's words held a tone of suspicion. The mass grave site came to the forefront of his mind.

Yuri tapped a cigarette from his pack. "Nothing is wrong. I just flew a MiG out of Syria and I haven't had a cigarette since before the flight." He wiped his forehead with the back of his hand. "I just need a smoke." He turned to Dmitry, tapping a second cigarette out of his pack. "Want one?"

Dmitry held up is hand. "Not interested."

Yuri shook the cigarette back into the box. He slipped the half-empty pack back in his pocket.

"What are your orders?" Yuri asked walking to the rear of the Mercedes.

Elizabeth observed the interaction of Nikolai's men. Of all of them, Yuri was the one she needed to know the most about. She pulled out the Pip uplink, accessing the Eclipse's codes. She entered in only one request to MARY, asking her to retrieve any new information on Lt. Commander Nevsky. She slipped the Pip link into her pocket.

"Adar had the same symptoms in New York as we were leaving the Astoria," she said, interrupting the men's conversation. "Yuri may have the virus. I'll need to take him to the Eclipse for a blood test."

"*Nyet*," Yuri forcefully said

"Are you crazy?" She was astonished by his disregard for life and turned to Ivan for help. "If Yuri is infected—"

"Then we're all infected," Ivan asserted. Elizabeth deduced there would be no help from this team. "Dr. Blake, you have an appointment with President Stepanov. You will not keep him waiting." Ivan looked at Yuri with disgust. He ordered, "Put your smoke back in the pack. You'll have to wait until we get to the Kremlin."

Yuri flicked the unlit cigarette from between his lips and slipped it back in the pack. "So this is more than official business."

Ivan snapped at his lack of discipline. "Keep your insubordinate comments to yourself. Dr. Blake is our priority. We can remove your rank immediately if you keep this up." Yuri had become more brazen with each tick of the clock. Ivan walked to the front passenger door and stood, gauging Yuri. "Get in, Officer Nevsky. You've been stripped of your Lt. Commander rank as of this moment." Ivan couldn't let Yuri go undisciplined. He would deal with Sergei later.

With Ivan's action, Yuri was made fully aware that family blood would not come in the way of the President's directive concerning Dr. Elizabeth Blake. It would be hard to kill her. She would have extra security. He had to back off for now. The vials of antidote in her medical bag were too important to lose. Unzipping his flight suit, he clenched his teeth. He had always hated the Stepanov powerhouse. If only his whore of a mother and her lover had not bargained with Joseph Stepanov. She should have told him the truth before she died in that hole Tula, Yuri thought. *I would not have been his "obligation," his "charity son."* He spit on the ground before he opened the trunk. His eyes were fixed on Elizabeth's medical bag. He briefly glanced up and caught Ivan staring at him. An eerie smile came over Yuri. In less than 24 hours, the world would be his. The Stepanovs would be dead. Yuri stepped out of his flight suit, picked it up and tossed it in the open trunk.

"Dr. Blake." Ivan reached into his inside suit pocket, exposing a holstered Makarov PMM and pulled out two identification cards. "These are your new security clearance tags. General Serebrinsky advised that you will be watched more carefully. You're an important guest."

Yuri did not like the sound of that statement. He was aggravated; it would put yet another kink in his plan. He mentally pitted his plan against the general's. Sergei would move her to a new location. One he would not have access to. He would have to find another way to get her alone.

Irritated, Elizabeth exclaimed, "I don't care whether your general is watching me or not. I must get back to working on the investigation site and keep the flow of information between my global team on going." She glanced impatiently at her watch as she was funneled into the back seat. Yuri slipped into the other side. Dmitry jumped in across from Elizabeth and Yuri. Anton at the driver's wheel barely waited for Ivan to shut the front passenger door before he hit the gas pedal and raced down the back roads of Zhukovsky Airport.

Elizabeth leaned forward, placing her hand on Ivan's shoulder. "Ivan, take me to Moscow Central. I need to re-examine the exhumed corpses immediately."

"*Nyet*," Ivan replied. "I told you. You will keep your appointment with President Stepanov. Those are my orders."

Before Elizabeth had a chance to complain, there was a vibration in her pocket. Lifting the small Pip device, she pressed the com link in her ear. "Hello, this is Dr. Blake. Robert?"

Yuri leaned closer. She glared at his obvious ease dropping. Damn him, she thought. Well, they might as well find out what new information had come in, she reasoned. They would know soon enough anyway from Nikolai. "What do you have?" she asked Robert.

"Elizabeth, we have big problems back here in the States. The virus has spread into all of South Florida and is in New York City. We've contained it in New York."

"Do you know the source? Who from the state offices is monitoring it? Brice is going to call me back, isn't he?"

Yuri felt unnerved for the first time. The antidote vials couldn't leave Russia.

"No known source, and CDC standards and reps are in place," Robert replied.

Elizabeth shook her head. "No known cause? Robert, I need you to get to Florida and find out if the oil tanker is the source. You have to take my place and cover until I get back. As for New York City, send Dr. Chase. Shut down the borders. Up the CDC's alert to phase four effective immediately. Robert, exactly how quickly is it spreading?"

Yuri was agitated as he continued to listen in on Elizabeth's conversation.

"All of Miami? And the Keys, too? This is more deadly than either of us can imagine. Put more of our resources on it. More manpower."

Yuri leaned back and reached into his pocket. He nervously fumbled with his metal chess set, uncertain who would be the winner of his little game. He stared out the window, maintaining an aloof appearance as his mind raced. *It is spreading too fast. Am I losing control?* He glanced at her medical bag. Dismayed, he lowered his arm and let the freshly sharpened razor drop into his palm. He'd make his move on her medical bag and vials now, he thought. He would take her hostage, kill her later. Ivan wouldn't shoot him if she was his shield. Yuri turned his empty eyes in her direction. He felt pushed to take this dangerous risk to regain control. Her medical bag was his only thought.

Pulling the Pip com link from her ear, Elizabeth bent forward to speak to Ivan. She stopped short, listening to the car radio broadcast announcing an explosion at Moscow's Sheremetyevo International Airport. "Now what?" she bluntly asked

Yuri looked at his watch. Right on time. Yuri relaxed. He was back in the driver seat. Soon Moscow would be infected.

"An explosion!" Elizabeth was startled. Ivan sat in silence as he shut the radio off. He listened hard for any instructions over his radio ear piece. Yuri slipped his razor back in place. There would be another time.

Impatient, Elizabeth tried to reason with her escorts. "Is this another bioterrorist attack? You need to quarantine the area and I need a forensics team at Sheremetyevo to gather as much evidence as possible." Silence was all she heard. Ivan ignored her questions. Letting her temper get the best of her, Elizabeth raised her voice. "I need to know what is going on! Don't you realize how serious this is?"

"Feel free to contact whoever you need to back in America," Dmitry finally responded. "But we will follow our order. And that is to take you directly to the Kremlin."

This was not the kind of support she'd expected when she started the investigation. Flopping back into her seat, she pulled out her Pip to check for new reports. The news was staggering. They had a pandemic, the likes of which no history books had ever known, and she was stuck in the back seat of a car.

CHAPTER EIGHTEEN

Day Four. 2:00 p.m. MSK. Moscow city limits.

Moscow had changed over the years she had been gone. The eclectic mix of ten-story Soviet-style apartment buildings and newer westernized housing developments was a constant reminder of Lenin's failed dream of a socialist world. The changing times were also seen in the modern department stores like Global USA popping up. Elizabeth thought of how they contrasted with the 1800s-era state department store, GUM, which took up most of the eastern side of the Red Square with its elaborate neo-Russian façade.

Her tiredness was turning into exhaustion. She longed for a shower to wash away the traces of jet fuel that lingered on her skin and hair. Elizabeth struggled to keep her eyes open as the Mercedes drove over the Moscow River. She squinted at the early morning rays that lit the waters like soft waves of glimmering patina. If only life could be that glimmering, she thought. Leaning forward to peer out the window, she saw the Kremlin Towers appear in her sight. Elizabeth's blood ran cool as more of the Russian fortress became visible sitting high on its hill above the river. Bleakness overcame her as they passed through an ominous Kremlin gate. The towers, embraced by the red stone walls that surrounded the complex, unsettled her. She winced as odd feelings overtook her. "Russia's mythic refuge," she whispered. She knew even its foreboding walls would not be able to keep out the deadly virus. Elizabeth realized for the first time that the global powerhouses were becoming fragile glass houses that would be swept away by an unseen enemy. Even this fortress; the old war-torn Kremlin was not unlike Washington D.C. in its fate. The virus would be their downfall, theirs and every other nation's capital if nothing was found soon.

Shaking off the ice cold sense of this harsh reality, she blamed her oversensitive mind on a lack of sleep. Focus, she told herself.

The custom-made Mercedes slowly pulled up to the Grand Palace. Elizabeth questioned, "Why are we stopping here?

Ivan draped one arm over the black leather seat and said, "Relax, Dr. Blake." Ivan turned his attention to Dmitry and radioed in their location. "We are clear." The Mercedes proceeded toward the State Place.

Elizabeth pressed closer to the glass as she stared out the window. The car rolled to a stop and Ivan swung open the door. Elizabeth slowly stepped out onto the hard cold pavement, clutching her medical bag. She tightened her resolve. The breeze cooled her irritated skin. She felt hot, hotter than normal.

Scrutinizing Yuri stepping out of the back seat, she noticed his flushed skin. His symptoms were worsening. She had to try again. "Before we go any further I insist that I examine Officer Nevsky. I think he has been infected."

"I've been vaccinated. That's impossible," Yuri protested. "We've all been vaccinated more than once for this and any other pathogen we might encounter in our line of work."

Ivan replied, "Dr. Blake, Lt. Commander Nevsky is correct. We have all had been medically cleared. We don't have time to waste. Are you sure he's been infected?"

"We don't know what this virus is, much less if the vaccinations you've had actually prevent it," she replied.

"You're not sure?" Ivan repeated.

Irritated, Elizabeth looked at him quizzically. "No, but –"

"Then we'll have *our* doctors examine at him after his report." Ivan looked Yuri. "General Serebrinsky has requested an immediate debriefing in his office. He will meet you in there. You will receive further instructions from him."

"I can't do that. My orders were to take my information to the President personally," Yuri belligerently demanded. His concern was to make sure Mus'ad would not implicate him as the bio-terrorist before he convinced Nikolai it was the Syrian brothers.

"Your assignment was completed. One more outburst like that, Officer, and you'll find yourself guarding ice floes in the northernmost part of Siberia," Ivan warned. "What is wrong with you?"

"Nothing." Yuri reached for his pack of cigarettes. "I am on my way." He gave one last possessive stare at Elizabeth's medical bag. Glancing at her, he whispered within an inch of her ear, "I'll see you later."

Elizabeth was stunned. "I don't think so." Her chin lifted up as she adjusted her wrinkled clothing as best she could before turning to follow her new escorts.

Yuri leered at her brash ways as he reached into his pocket for the small chess set. Opening the case, he moved black rook to capture white bishop. *She is my queen to play.* Yuri pulled the black-streaked chess piece from his pocket. He placed the white queen back on her square. *Too bad they put you in the game.* His mind began to plan his next move. He cynically grinned. He tossed the small box on the dashboard then hopped back into the sedan and headed for Building 14. Pulling out his cell, he called Misha.

"Where you been, boss? Who jammed the calls?"

"Don't worry about it. I've taken care of it. Adar is dead. Mus'ad is taking his place."

"Boss, you gotta get back here to the lab. It's all wrong. The vaccinations Pachen provided us are ineffective. Your medical guy claims it's only slowing down the infection."

Yuri stifled an impulse to call Misha a liar. It was the first time he was worried. "Get me that damn Mikovich's assistant, Rurik. Put him on the phone."

"Boss, he's dead. His team of scientists is dead or dying, too. Yuri, you're left with no pathologist. All your men, you know, the mafia army you built to take over..." Misha paused. "Most are to succumbing to the virus. Boss, you have to do something. Our men are dying rapidly. We have no place to store the bodies. We filled one storage room already."

"You're wrong!" Yuri gritted his teeth, trying to collect himself as rage bubbled up inside him. "Misha, I have one more task to get out of the way. You have to wait. I'll be there as soon as I can." He ended the call and hit the dashboard with his fist. He let the razor drop from his sleeve and slashed the fine leather seat of the sedan in a fit of anger.

"We just need another shot of the antidote. Damn American bitch." He would have to send an inside man to her room. He grabbed his security badge. "You will have to come in handy one last time." His dark side kicked in. He looked and acted nonchalant, but he was on full-blown red alert, his veins pulsing. He calmed himself as he pulled into a vacant parking space in front of Building 14. Glaring at the side mirror, he caught a glimpse of Elizabeth walking swiftly toward Building 14's V.I.P. entrance, Ivan and Dmitry close to her side. He had no doubt they were heading to Nikolai's office first. "First the Syrian, then you, Dr. Blake." Stepping out of the sedan, Yuri called to get their attention. "I am checking in with security."

Elizabeth glanced at Yuri. Ivan pushed her on. Dmitry waved Yuri to go on as they proceeded through two metal detectors and a body wave scanner. She stopped to notice a small, unusual rash on the wrist of the guard before being pushed on. The guard's skin tone was a pale yellow. Looking at the other guards and government staff, she noticed all wore that same sick, pale yellow skin tone.

Ivan put his hand on her back and guided her to the left. Dmitry pushed open a set of gold ornate double doors and before her eyes loomed four hundred years of Russian history. She wondered how much longer that history would stand against the spreading virus.

Elizabeth arrived at Nikolai's working residence. Ivan and Dmitry walked toward the heavy mahogany doors, passing the President's assistant at her desk.

"Wait, Commanders!" she protested, jolting from her chair. "You can't go in right now! He left instructions to wait on…" She pressed her body between Dmitry and the doors.

"And I have my orders," Dmitry said nudged her to one side.

Elizabeth stared for a moment at the ornate doors flanked by two armed guards. "Why don't you listen to her? I am sure there is a reason he wanted us to wait." Ivan and Dmitry opening the door, ignoring them both.

Elizabeth hesitantly followed the commanders past the unfamiliar Russian president's threshold only to be sweep up by sounds of an intense exchange between Nikolai and the chief of staff of the Mariinsky Hospital in St. Petersburg. Their voices scraped over each other. Nikolai was deep into exchange of heated words; their unannounced arrival slipped past him. She stood quietly, waiting for some kind of acknowledgement. None came.

"You can't be serious. You're lying!" Nikolai screamed furiously at the phone as he paced behind his desk.

Sergei and Yuri walked in and heard the final exchange as the presidential family's doctor attempted to offer help. "I'm sorry, sir. If I can do—"

"No!" Nikolai slammed his hand on the phone to disconnect the call. He balled up his hands and placed them over his eyes. "No, no, no."

Sergei caught the President's ear. "I'm not certain who was on the other end of that call or what was told to you, but Mr. President, you might have waited to hear what else he might have to say."

Nikolai pulled his hands away from his face, his eyes holding back a wall of grief. "Get out. All of you, get out." Elizabeth turned toward the door. "Not you!"

Nikolai's voice resonated with a tone she was familiar with in her line of work. "Oh, no," she whispered to herself.

"Dr. Blake stays." His mind was over worked on how to save his people from the deadly virus was at a breaking point.

Sergei grimaced. His gut reaction told him who was on the phone. "We will be back to debrief Dr. Blake once you are finished with her." The FSB officers left the room.

Elizabeth turned to face him. She stood fixed to the floor. She knew. He didn't have to say it, but he did.

"My wife is dead. The virus. My son's on life support. He'll be dead before I get to see him again. I want your report. Is there anything in there that can save him?"

Her tired muscles tightened around her chest. She grasped at the kind of horrific outcome a biological weapon of this magnitude will have on the innocent people of world. How many more would die? Her lungs drew in a hard breath. She felt like she was drowning in air. Dealing with loss was the hardest part of her job. Harder with him, because they had shared a brief history. She tried to remain detached. She failed and placed her hand on him. "No, if you are asking for a cure, we don't have one yet. I'm sorry for your loss. If the team of doctors is treating your son as I instructed, your son has a high chance of holding on until we find a cure. Hold onto that thought, Nikolai. I can send Mariinsky Hospital the new data we have been experimenting with to slow viral progression. It may buy time until we find the real cure."

He placed his hand over hers and nodded in false hope. He turned his back. Her hand fell away. Anger swelled up in him, a president, a man was not to show weakness.

"We can still beat this, Nikolai. With both our countries working hard, we'll beat this together." Her voice was strong. He almost believed her. "Trust me. Let me do my job before more die."

Her job. He was brought back to the severity of the situation. "I need your current report. What resources do you want?" he requested. He regained his composure while he silently vowed retribution.

"It is essential for me to perform the remaining autopsies immediately. I understand the bodies are still at Moscow Clinical Hospital morgue. It will save time if I start there. The grave site has given up all the information I can use at this time."

Turning back to face Elizabeth, for the first time he saw the softer young lady he had known before. "Thank you for you kind words," he said. "You know President Brice is not going to like this. He wants you back in America."

"I know. But I can't justify the travel time and the virus started in Russia. The answers are here to stopping it. I have the best team, the best equipment and the best assistants working around the clock. If I have to be back in America, the Eclipse will take me there in under two hours. That buys us enough time for me to re-examine the original victims."

He looked at the growing dark circles under her eyes. He said, "You need to rest first. I'll have my assistant make the arrangements. You will be no good to anyone without a brief break." Nikolai's hand gently swept her cheek. "You know, that's all I wanted to do for my wife and son. Touch them one last time." He frowned. "Thanks for being their stand in."

Elizabeth took his hand and squeezed it once. She saw a look of determination found his grieving eyes. "Nikolai, I will perform the remaining autopsies first. There is no time. I'll rest later."

CHAPTER NINETEEN

Day Four. 4:00 p.m. MSK. Moscow Central Clinical Hospital.

"Are there any restrictions on the autopsy permits?" Elizabeth asked the technician as she passed through a set of metal doors with the large biohazard signs posted. She was relieved to see that the morgue was adjacent to the hospital. "How many have you completed?" She was not sure if any of the victims would turn up new clues before her meeting that evening with Nikolai. The only way to find out was to go into the body cavity and look for herself.

Dr. Peter Petruc, her appointed liaison, opened the door leading a long ceramic-tiled tunnel made for several gurneys to pass through. "Morning, Dr. Blake. We have been anxiously awaiting you. Dr. Lee from China has forwarded new information to the team."

"That's great. So you are the head coroner, Dr. Petruc?" she asked as she scanned the slim blond man with tired eyes in his green surgical scrubs. She shook his hand and noticed that although his face was coarse from working long hours in the hospital his hands were steady and youthful as a new surgeon's. They walked down the triple-wide hallway toward the security doors at the end.

"No," Dr. Petruc responded. "I am the Chief of Staff. But I am serving as chief medical examiner for you as requested by President's office. I can assure you I am more than qualified." He handed her a standard disposable water-impermeable medical garb. She slipped it over her clothes. Wrapping her hair in a secure bun, she covered it with the same medi-cap provided. She had never realized how long it took prep until this race for the virus when seconds counted. She donned the double-lined gloves and surgical mask. At least the surgical mask made the strong odor of formaldehyde fixative easier to live with. It was one smell she could never get used to. Elizabeth stopped and mentally took note of the various disposable supplies stacked at the entrance to the morgue.

Dr. Petruc suited up in his protective gear. He commented, "I've read your file. Impressive."

"Thank you for your vote of confidence," she responded. She handed him a file outlining the procedures. "We're adding two new members to the forensics team. Dr. Nari Shakar in toxicology and Dr. P. D. Chromley as a forensic anthropologist. Dr. Shakar will be conducting the research from her lab. Dr. Chromley will be taking my place and re-visiting the mass grave for further excavation. I want to see who or what is buried deeper than the layers we sifted through."

Dr. Petruc raised his brow as Elizabeth.

"I'll need your government approval to send the three main tissue and blood samples from the unknown guard, the victim # 11 you worked on and victim #27, a female we'll be doing today to Dr. Shakar's lab in London," Elizabeth continued. "I need the turnaround time within an hour."

Dr. Petruc nodded. "Dr. Burov will be acting as the diener. The victims are prepared for your to examination, all in accordance with the World Health Organization standards."

Although the WHO was in sync with the CDC, Elizabeth felt she needed to personally take the search for the virus's DNA a step further. "Dr. Petruc, I would like these added biohazard preventatives set up." She gestured to the file. "You are aware how different countries interpret the procedural methods listed for a normal flu, and this is far from the flu."

"Dr. Blake, are you trying to insult me? If you are, you've succeeded."

Elizabeth immediately reassured him. "Not at all, Dr. Petruc. I just have to be sure. We do not want to take the risk of any contamination skewing the report."

Petruc put on his face shield and used his key card to unlock the entrance of the inner morgue. "Understood. It only takes a few minutes for Dr. Burov to set up." The door beeped and opened.

They entered the examination room and the diener added her biohazard updates. The room was large in size, off white and tiled. It had adequate overhead lighting. Elizabeth approached two stationary dissection slabs and a moveable cadaver hoist placed off to one side.

The diener rolled in the dictation equipment on a stainless steel table covered in plastic. The stainless steel plating held the body of a young female. She switched on the dictation mic. "Elizabeth Blake, set to work. The body of victim #27 is that of white female. Height: five feet six inches. Weight: one hundred twenty-two pounds. Hair: blond. Eyes: blue. Victim #27 measures 26 based on her cranium and dental pattern. What did the forensic odontologist's report say?" She glanced at Dr. Petruc.

"He concurred."

"Her skin is still moist," Elizabeth continued. "Skin tone off yellow in color." She studied the skin lesions that appeared to be small pox. Elizabeth noticed that a Virchow method evisceration had been done. That is not good, she thought.

"Where are the organs? I hope kept on ice," she questioned Petruc as she examined the corpse.

"Yes. We have them in the refrigeration system over there." He pointed to a large metal cooling unit.

"Are they intact?"

Petruc hesitated. His lips tightened.

"Are they intact? You and I both know that any organs involved in a disease process should be kept intact."

Walking around to the corpse's feet, he said in frustration, "No, not all of the organs. We stopped at the heart, lungs and liver. Some organs seemed as if they had somehow, well, burst inside. The stomach ruptured, apparently due to excessive body fluid. It appeared that blood was trapped in its lining to the point that it, well, exploded."

Elizabeth shot him a look of confusion. "That doesn't sound like small pox. Or a viral infection." Elizabeth continued her investigation. "I see a backflow of blood in her nasal passages and esophagus. Her teeth are stained with blood. What a horrible way to die after suffering from the lesions. Bleeding to death." Elizabeth clicked the slabs to regulation height to avoid needless strain on her back as she stood on the epoxy-sealed floor.

Petruc walked over to the neat line of cabinets as he removed a key from his pocket. He unlocked the microbiological supplies cabinet, revealing bone saws and scalpels, all sharpened and clean. He pulled medical twine for the closure stitches off the shelf.

Elizabeth moved the whiteboard and charts nearer to the organ scale for convenience. "Doctor, I'd like to keep the disinfected water pumps and aspirators handy. Even though the waste goes to biohazard treatment, I'm not sure we should wash any debris down the drain until we know what we are dealing with." He nodded in agreement.

Elizabeth felt comfortable as she continued the autopsy. As she worked on the cadaver, she was glad the air conditioning was running. Although the primary exhaust system was old, it was sufficient to enable total aeration of the formaldehyde fixative. The ventilation hoods rattled as it sucked out the odor of decay. Elizabeth took the scalpel and made a secondary cut into what was once the stomach area.

Petruc offered, "We first thought it might be related to hemorrhagic fever. Then symptoms of a small pox virus showed up alongside the Ebola symptoms. We are at a loss. With this strain, it's impossible to say."

"Have you formally named the strain?" Elizabeth asked.

"No," he said.

"Since we are not sure what we working with, I think we should leave it coded as SV121R. I have never seen this kind of damage to a human before. And so quickly. I need to look at it under the microscope. I'm not sure it's a true small pox. It may turn out to be a different biological agent from your country."

"Or yours," Dr. Petruc added.

"I doubt it. We do not have missing viral canisters. Look for any new virus your government may have engineered that would cause this type of blood loss. We will keep looking at the small pox data as well. I'll need more thorough records for all the old Cold War agents."

"Hold on, Dr. Blake," Dr. Petruc replied. "That is a request I do not have the authority to grant. It will have to be approved by President Stepanov office."

"We don't have time for political protocols!" Her face hardened. She pointed the scalpel toward the corpse. "Are you willing to go through red tape so more people can end up like her? You are a doctor and you're obligated to stop this virus, government or no government. Do you think you can find a way to obtain them?"

Petruc stepped away. He looked at what was left of the organs of the female victim.

"Every second you think about it, we are losing lives. I need you to cross the line!" Elizabeth pushed.

"Okay, I have my loyalties," he said with a hardness. "But you are correct." He paused. "It will be hard to get them." His lips tightened. He confirmed, "I have a few contacts left in the military. What exactly are you looking for?"

"I need the actual formula used to engineer the original stolen virus and the next batch they made after it. If I can get a DNA match, then your country should have an antiviral agent on file as well. It is the only way to ensure an accurate forensic evaluation and that my diagnostic will be valid from a pathologist's point of view." She paused, laying her scalpel down. "In truth, this will also protect both of our countries from pointing fingers."

Petruc listened to the weight of her words. "The diener will finish up with you. You'll get what you need."

"Thank you. Send the records to the Eclipse via the CDC. Robert, my assistant, will know what to do. After I have concluded my tests, I will be making arrangements to return to America."

"I'll send the information as soon as I have it confirmed," Petruc replied. Turning he swiped his key card to exit the morgue's examination room.

Elizabeth leaned over the corpse, removing body tissue out of the way to continue her examination. "Look at the color of the gastrointestinal tract." She used the foot pedal and overhead mic to dictate her findings. "There's a reddish gastric mucosa. This leads me to the conclusion that the agent was admitted orally. Possible the skin pores." She asked, "Would you concur? Have you examined the stomach contents?"

"Yes," the diener replied. "We found water with a high sulfur content and a few pollutants, mostly industrial com-pounds that can get into the water systems. Even the small amount of unrefined oil did not surprise us given the area the body was found. But this puts a twist on it. The lungs were stained, too. It hinted at the potential of an inhaled agent as the cause of death."

Elizabeth said, "Maybe both. Let's finish up with her. One of the bodies I saw had bullet wounds. Was a full autopsy done on that corpse? I'd like to see that report as soon as possible."

The diener responded, "I will get it ready."

"Thank you. I have to report to President Stepanov now. Send the report to the CDC. Robert will make sure I get it." The diener nodded and unlocked the door so Elizabeth could exit.

She walked few steps beyond the lab, passing through a disinfectant mist. Her mind raced with the new findings. She entered the adjoining dressing room that housed the medical staff's lockers and showers. She would be late to meet Nikolai if she didn't hurry.

She passed a nurse gathering her items. The woman looked pale. Elizabeth undressed and jumped in the shower for a routine scrub and scour with iodophor soap. She was worried as potential left over germs washed down the drain. That nurse was on her mind. Something was wrong.

As she returned to the locker room she noticed the nurse cleaning her hands. Scanning her forearm, she saw that the skin held tiny raised bumps not unlike the ones she had seen on victims at the grave site.

Elizabeth asked, "How long have you had those?"

"Had what?" The nurse looked up.

Elizabeth pointed to her arm. "Those red bumps."

The nurse pushed up both sleeves and stared. "They're new. I didn't have them when I finished up my shift."

"Who were you taking care of last?"

"An American, a Marine. A guard at the Embassy. Tall. Blue eyes. He was bleeding from his nose. The color of blood was abnormal. We were able to stop it. Temporarily at least."

Elizabeth twinged. "Blue eyes?" She knew of one Marine at the Embassy: her cousin, Jason Blake. "What was his name?" she asked. "Was it Jason? Jason Blake?" Dread ran through her body.

"I don't remember," the nurse said weakly. "We have so many sick coming in."

"You have to take me to him!"

"I am off duty," her voice muffled. "Ask the triage nurse." The nurse struggled to keep her balance.

Elizabeth ripped protective gloves from the wall mounted stainless steel box and strapped on an outdated M65 mask over her face. She grabbed the small blond nurse's arm to steady her. "Have you had a small pox vaccination?"

"Yes." She frowned at Elizabeth. "Why?"

Elizabeth could only answer, "You were notified of a viral outbreak. It is possible that a new strain of small pox is the cause." The nurse's eyes grew wide. "Take me to the American Marine. This whole hospital may be compromised if he has this virus. We have to get you on an antiviral IV immediately."

They quickly made their way to the hospital's emergency room. Elizabeth thought back to Yuri's unconventional way of dealing with her and Prince Adar conversation in New York. Pulling out her Pip link, she requested, "MARY, get me Secretary Blake."

"Yes, Dr. Blake," MARY responded.

Damn, she thought. If the hospitals were compromised by Adar being a carrier for the virus, then this and all of the U.S. Embassies, no, every governmental Embassy, must be considered compromised. Elizabeth's heart raced at the realization of how bad it really was. *How can you shut down the world? Do we even have a chance at stopping this virus?*

"I'm sorry, Dr. Blake." MARY broke into her thoughts. "We are offline again. I have picked up several unauthorized signals emitting from Western Siberia. Two international communications stations are online. Their systems are running on emergency systems only. All international satellite communication systems are not responding."

Elizabeth could not image how much worse it could get. She ordered, "Keep trying to make contact, MARY, until you reach someone at the State Department who can get a message to him."

Stripping off the ear piece, Elizabeth took a deep breath; an unearthly fear came over her, a fear for all of mankind. One word came to mind. "Extinction! Just like that," she exclaimed as she snapped her fingers in the air. The nurse stumbled and fell to one knee. "Come on," Elizabeth said to the nurse. "A few more steps to go. We can't give up." The emergency room doors slammed behind them leaving her with that crushing realization. That realization would force her to push harder to find the elusive cure for this virus.

CHAPTER TWENTY

Day Four. 9:15 p.m. MSK. Moscow Central Clinical Hospital.

It was a war zone, but a different kind of war. Elizabeth could not believe the chaos in the halls of the hospital crowded by victims of the plague. Was it the same back home? Had this epidemic spread in the States and how badly? She had to find out.

Elizabeth settled the ailing nurse in at triage. She heard a troubled technician calling the morgue to pick up two body bags. "We don't have any more room to keep them here," the technician screamed at the other technician alongside him as he slammed down the phone. "Shit. The morgue is at capacity and they're telling me I have to find a place to store them."

"Get a refrigerated truck. The new bodies need to be sent outside of the city," another tech ordered, walking past them. There were not enough medical personnel to take care of all the sick and injured. The pungent smell of sickness rose in the hallways. Death was everywhere. Age did not matter. Everyone was at risk. Nurses, firemen, police, all strong men, lay with their faces white with death near a pregnant woman whose hand was clenched in rigor mortis over her unborn baby. Stacks of body bags off to the side waited to be stuffed.

Hardening herself at the vision before her, Elizabeth turned to the triage nurse, and asked, "What room is the injured American Marine in?" She was determined not to let that happen to him.

The nurse jadedly said, "Room? You have to be joking! Look along the hallways. He is probably on a gurney somewhere." Elizabeth's temper snapped. Taking the sign-in clipboard off the desk Elizabeth signed her name under the column for physicians on duty. Shoving it back to the nurse, she said, "I am Dr. Blake. I will start with the American Marine. Any issues?" Her words held a challenge. She would not take no for an answer.

A weary Dr. Petruc walked past the crowded nurses' station. He was irritated as he overheard their exchange. Pushing past several people and picking up the clipboard and asked, "What's the problem?" He gave a forced smile to Elizabeth and initialed over her name.

"I need to treat the America Marine you have admitted. He may provide additional clues," Elizabeth answered.

The Chief of Staff pursed his lip and ordered the nurse, "Please treat her with the same respect you treat me." He handed the clipboard to the disconcerted nurse. "Dr. Blake, please follow me. I'll take you to the Marine. In the mean time, my assistant is uploading the data you requested. It should be completed as we speak."

"Tell me of the American soldier?" she requested.

"He and several others were on their way back to America but were caught in an explosion at the train station. He is the only one who survived. I'm not sure we can do much more for him. We are short a few surgeons. Two of our best called in sick." Petruc stopped abruptly, staring at her. "As you can see, we need the extra hands in the emergency room. I'll see who I can reassign if you need the help. There will be no tour of the facilities. Forgive me." He grabbed a sealed surgical uniform and passed it to her. "You'll have to wing it."

"Just take me to him. I suspect he has been infected with the virus. At this point there is no need for formalities. Thank you for your help, Dr. Petruc." Trading her suit for new scrubs, she placed a stethoscope around her neck and prepared for the worst. She asked, "Exactly how many patients are being treated?" Elizabeth followed Dr. Petruc down the hallway.

"We don't have enough rooms for the incoming casualties," Petruc explained. "As you saw, the halls have become makeshift triage centers. I am afraid we're not going to make it. And what we discovered with that last autopsy... God help us!"

"With communications so sporadic I'm concerned about how this epidemic has spread in the States. I have to leave as soon as I complete my task here," Elizabeth explained. Petruc nodded, affirming he could not count on her to help him with the chaos they had before them. Elizabeth transmitted a single order to MARY to provide continuous updates from her team.

Entering the hospital room, Elizabeth approached the first bed and drew the curtain back to find a semiconscious young man. His face was turned away. She became grim at the sight of a large piece of metal jutting out from his thigh. Elizabeth gently lifted his face toward hers.

She struggled for breath with a pain she had not felt in years. Elizabeth always treasured the intricacies and the enigmas of life and death that went along with her job, but she was not so hardened to the lost of humanity. And now it struck home. Her family. She felt wobbly, overwhelmed with all that had happened. Her hand fell on the heart monitoring system as she looked for support. Humans were fragile after all. She lost her usual solid composure. "Not this." Her worst fear was realized. Grief-stricken, she took in a deep breath to fill her empty lungs.

As her breathing steadied, it started to register that she was the only one who would try to save him. She made her way back to his side. "Jason. Jason Blake!" She cupped his face in her hand." Elizabeth studied the young man laid out before her. She saw he had the same dark hair, the same brow and the same long lips his mother had. Only the eyes, those blue eyes, were different. They were William's, his father's. "You were supposed to be back home two days ago." No response. Skin pale. Adrenaline flooded her veins. Bloodied and heavily bruised, his face was chalky white. She had to act fast as the pool of blood staining the sheets left her horrified. "I can't believe they left you like this," she whispered to herself. "I'll do whatever I can to have you back on home soil, Jason," she promised.

Working quickly, she stopped the slow bleeding and started a morphine drip. She pressed her fingers against his wrist, checking his vital signs. *Rapid, thready pulse.* "Jason, talk to me. It's Elizabeth. I'm here to help." The young man, waking and restless, tugged at her scrub sleeve. She removed his hand and placed it back on the bed. Opening his half-closed eyelids wider to check his pupils, she noticed his pale blue eyes did not shift toward her. It was if her uncle's eyes were staring back at her. Elizabeth's stomach knotted. The listlessness was not a good sign. She checked the morphine drip line. "Stay with me, Jason." She placed the stethoscope in her ears. Glancing at the wound, concerned about the loss of blood, she put thoughts of her family's shock out of her mind.

Elizabeth suddenly a felt strange sensation, as if she knew the odds were against him. Pulling down his hospital gown, she saw the lesions. "Not this, Jason. The virus. Not you, too." His chest was covered in the oddly familiar pox she had examined at the morgue earlier. She instantly washed the area with disinfectant and placed a clear shield over his chest and pulled tight her face mask. She wondered if all this protection was worth it and not just some comforting ritual to keep her and the rest of the medical staff's minds at ease. They were all infected. She knew. Petruc knew. They all knew. She fought the hopelessness that overcame her. Time was the new enemy that added to an already uncontrollable micro-army of this death-minded viral strain.

Placing the stethoscope over his heart, she listened. "Jason, you're still beating strong. I have to take a risk, "We can't lose you."

Elizabeth reexamined his leg, looking up at him with gentleness and strength only her eyes could give him. "Sorry. I have bad news. It's surgery for you." She calming told herself, "We'll have to deal with the virus afterward. Are you up for it, Jason?"

Jason reached for her with barely opened his eyes. He forced a gaze on her. "Tell my father..." He pushed one arm up and started to move off the hospital bed.

"No, don't move. We can't have any of your bravado here. You're not going anywhere but to surgery." She ordered an anti-viral medication to be given.

Jason fell back onto the bed. Drugged, his breath grew shallow. With a strained breath, he murmured, "Better you to doctor me up than anyone else. If I don't make it..." He closed his eyes with those last words as the morphine running through his blood took full effect.

Sliding the green curtain back, she motioned to two nurses checking charts. "Finish the preparations. I want him in surgery stat! Bump whoever you can. I need an operating room free at once." She called out orders to them, moving toward the hallway. "I'll be in the scrub room!" Rushing away from Jason's bedside, a human wall blocked her.

"Out of my way," she ordered. Elizabeth was not prepared to walk smack into Dmitry. He towered over her. She asked, "Why are you here?

"I was ordered to escort you to the President immediately." Dmitry reached up to his radio earpiece. "Yes, Ivan, I have Dr. Blake with me." Elizabeth paused at the implication of his response. Taking a step back from him, she said, "No, no, no. This is not happening. I have an emergency surgery. An American Marine." Elizabeth's hand rose to her hip. The smell of blood, sickness and death in the hallway became stronger. It called to her.

A brow rose at her challenge. Dmitry studied her a moment. "Commander. There is a problem. We will be delayed." He closed his com link. Straightening his jacket, Dmitry said, "You are under special protection by order of the Russian Federation. I am your new escort and will be under the care of the FSB for the remainder of your investigation."

"We don't have time for these political games." As she coolly looked at him, she added, "Inform the President that my cousin, the son of Secretary of State Blake, is dying in his country and no one had better stop me from saving his life. I need to get *that* message to my uncle." Elizabeth defiantly unclipped her cell phone and dialed. Dmitry allowed her phone call.

"No answer," she said. Her anxious blue eyes landed on Dmitry. She could only leave a voicemail message and pray he would get it soon. "Uncle William, this is Elizabeth. I have news about Jason. He was injured in an explosion and I suspect he is infected as well. I'll be his surgeon. I'll give you an update when he is in recovery or whenever I can."

Dmitry reached out to end her phone call. She stepped back out of reach. "When I have completed the surgical procedures, get me the hell out of here and back home on American soil! I am taking Jason with me on the Eclipse as well. Clear him!" She clicked it off and slipped the phone back into its holder.

"First, you will report to President Stepanov," Dmitry warned as she moved away from him.

Elizabeth was flustered as she made her way to the operating room. Elizabeth passed several doctors in the hallways without a word. Arriving at the surgery ward, scrubbing in, her mind focused on saving Jason's life, if she could. She would try her best. Her elbow pushed open the doors to the surgical room. She asked, "What are his vitals?"

"BP 100 over 70. Respiration normal. Heart rate 95," the nurse replied.

Elizabeth read the vitals monitor. "Strong enough. Scalpel." The nurses placed it in her palm. Taking one last glance at Jason's face, she noticed a few new pox lesions had appeared on his cheekbones. "It will be OK," she whispered. A false hope. She looked at the clock. 10:15 p.m. She made the first incision in a race against time to save him.

Fifteen minutes into the surgery, the American Marine, the Blake family heir, her cousin, died.

Tears rolled down her face. Elizabeth ripped off her mask, making her way to the bathroom. For the first time in all her years as a doctor, she vomited up her grief. Catching her breath, she moved to the sinks, splashing water over her face and rinsing out her mouth.

As she left, she found Dmitry waiting for her in the hall outside. "Tell Nikolai." The political formality was of little importance to her now. "Tell him Jason Blake is dead. We can leave within the hour, after I take forensic samples. The tissues and blood samples from him may provide a new lead to the virus." The words stuck in her throat. *Tissues.* She felt like vomiting again. But she knew what she had to do as she replaced her mask and headed back to the surgical room.

CHAPTER TWENTY-ONE

Day Four. 11:35 p.m. MSK. Russian Presidential suite.

The Presidential suite's soundproof windows could not keep out the sirens of ambulances leaving Red Square. Nikolai wrapped his robe around himself, giving the deep blue belt a tight tug. He had paced another sleepless night away, unable to rest his mind or body at the horrors of his country and the homegrown terrorist he could not point a finger at. The dangerous circle of deceit in his office gave him no peace as the spreading virus spun out of control.

Deep circles rimmed his eyes. It had been almost 4:00 a.m. before he retired. His leather slippers stepped silently as each foot hit the carpeted floor of his suite. Nikolai could not remove the dark images of what had taken control of his land from his mind. This tiny germ had killed his wife and was holding his son's life on the brink. The news of William Blake's son's death added to it. With her cousin's death, Nikolai questioned Elizabeth's ability to finish her investigation. Thoughts of her and the altered life they would be forced to share raised concerns for him.

A knock at the door came. Sergei's gravelly voice announced, "Mr. President. I have some urgent news."

The door cracked opened before Nikolai could respond. "What is it now come in, come in!" Nikolai said, turning to face the door as it opened fully.

"All commuter lines into Moscow have been completely shut down as of 9:05 a.m.," Sergei said, his face stern. "At 8:45 a.m. a massive train collision took place. The conductors were found dead at the controls. They ran red lights, ramming into each other's commuter train. Freight is still running."

Nikolai frowned. He knew there was more. "What else is wrong? I see it on your face. It's not like you to hesitate."

"Mr. President, Russia's main military communication systems have been compromised. This terrorist has taken control of the public communications systems, too."

"Can we fix the disruptions?" Nikolai asked.

"Communications are at a halt nationwide," Sergei replied. "No one's healthy enough to operate the computers."

"All communications?"

"No. We still have communication with President Brice and with several of Dr. Blake's international team members. Your last orders to update to the new security link with the Americans are unaffected. I do not think they know we put new codes in place after Dr. Blake's first arrival."

"I see. Does this give us any better idea who is responsible?"

"We have confirmation the Russian mafia had a hand in this. Dmitry's inside source confirmed that before he turned up dead in the Volga River."

"Do we know which splinter group?" Nikolai continued. "The leader? Can we confirm, then, that the terrorist is Russian?"

Sergei paused. He knew more than he could say. He had to be sure before he would tell his president, his friend who was like a son to him.

"Out with it Sergei," Nikolai demanded. "What is the problem?"

The general shook his head. "The mafia is no longer a collection of splinter groups. One man is in charge of what is now a global army at his command." Sergei's lips shut tightly. His gut told him Yuri was involved, but he couldn't confirm it.

"You know more." Nikolai waved a finger at Sergei. After all the years they'd worked with each other they had a knack for understanding each other's unspoken thoughts.

"I can't confirm it, but, my instincts tell me one or more of our FSB officers has been passing along information to this leader and the Syrians."

"Mus'ad and one of my own men?" Nikolai turned his back to Sergei. "And what about Dr. Blake? Has her safety been compromised? What is her location? We need the Americans on our side right now."

"Dr. Blake's arrival is expected shortly," Sergei informed him. "We don't expect to get any additional information until later tonight. I made arrangements for Dr. Blake to stay in Building 14's V.I.P. guest suite before she returns back to America after her briefing with you. It will be the safest place for her if she is a target. We can keep an eye on her."

Nikolai reached for his white shirt and said, "Give me a minute, general. I'll meet her in the guest room. It will save time. If you can get through to her, inform her I need all her findings, speculative and hard evidence." He slipped into his dressing room where rows of nearly entirely white and blue shirts hung beside ties to match and professional, creased suit pants. He slipped off his robe and placed it on the valet hook.

"Please give my regrets to Dr. Blake and Secretary Blake." Nikolai's words were emotionless. He pushed aside the mourning for his own recent loss. A kind of numbness set in. The calm before the storm.

Sergei watched him. He wondered when the powerhouse of yet untapped strength that defined Nikolai Stepanov as an unconventional leader would break loose. "Consider it done, Mr. President. Take your time. I'll notify you of their arrival."

Nikolai slipped into his perfectly pressed shirt. Grateful for the offer of reprieve, Nikolai added, "That will not be necessary. Send an FSB officer to meet Dr. Blake and post a guard at her door."

Sergei said, "As you wish." Nikolai nodded. "I have orders waiting for Dmitry to report to you when you are finished."

"What was Dmitry's last report?" Nikolai asked.

"He stated increased hospital admittance. They are far over their capacity. The morgue is overflowing with dead."

"That is not good," Nikolai commented.

"As with everything else this virus has thrown at us, they're asking what the government will do to ease the burden," Sergei continued. "The media has stopped asking what this is and where it came from. If our own people find out it's ours - and they will - you, Mr. President, will be the target of every angry countryman we have. I have to request that we prepare the secure area and move you there."

"Not yet," Nikolai huffed, looking at his watch. He wasn't ready to admit defeat. "How much longer before she arrives?"

Sergei's com link vibrated. He pressed the link closer to his ear. "Da! Good." He nodded approval at the news. "They have arrived. Dmitry is on his way to my office. Dr. Blake will be in her suite shortly."

"Let's go." Nikolai pulled tight the knot he had carefully woven in his Privado tie. "Keep a lid on any new information until I speak with Dr. Blake. No further comments from this office until I know what we are dealing with." Feeling the pressure, slipping on his suit jacket, Nikolai headed for her suite.

"It seems I will have to accompany you, Mr. President," Sergei said as they stepped into an empty hallway. "I do not know where your bodyguards went to." He frowned. "It's odd. I do not like it. It's the virus. It has taken several men out, but they were here when I first arrived. I'll call for back up. We'll wait."

"No waiting. You will have to do, Sergei, my friend." Nikolai and Sergei made their way down the flight of stairs and several corridors to her door. Arriving at her door, he commented, "No one posted here either."

Sergei offered, "We will wait for a team to arrive before I can allow you enter..."

Nikolai finished Sergei's sentence. "We are going in. I doubt Dr. Blake will harm me. Damn! This is the Kremlin. And find me the name of this new mafia boss." Screams bellowed into the hallway, echoing past the door.

"Get out! Get out of here now! Get your hands off my medical bag!" Elizabeth's voice pierced Nikolai's ears.

"Elizabeth!" Nikolai twisted the doorknob. "Locked," he growled.

"Let go of me you, bastard! Give back my bag!" they heard her shout. A crash of broken glass sounded. A blow of flesh on flesh led to a fearful silence. Pulling the doorknob harder, they heard the sound of shoes dragging across the marble tile on the other side pushed Nikolai over the edge. "Open it now!" he ordered.

Sergei unholstered his gun and pushed Nikolai to one side. "Stay down, Mr. President." Sergei aimed and fired at the locked doorknob. It split apart. Sergei cautiously entered.

Nikolai snatched up Sergei's spare gun from his back belt as he warily followed him into the room. They moved in old KGB fashion as they swept the room. A downed velvet drape caught Sergei's eyes. Wind blew in through an open window. Sergei leaned out the window and looked down. He saw the intruder's escape route: A broken window one floor below with its drapery rod half-hanging out the open window. "He's below us."

"Sergei, check the suite out," Nikolai ordered, moving from the entrance door to the half-open double door leading to the bedroom. Peering around the door frame he found a dazed Elizabeth on the floor, clutching her medical bag. "She's in the bedroom. I am going in. Get some men up here. Sweep the second floor."

"I am on it." Sergei activated his com link. "Ivan, we've had a break-in. Dr. Blake's suite. The suspect is one of ours. And God damn it, where are the President's bodyguards?!"

"They're dead," Ivan replied. "I am on it! I lost contact with Yuri. He might be among the murdered FSB unit." Ivan continued, "New FSB officers are on their way to the sweep the building for unapproved visitors. We are in lockdown mode for Building 14."

Sergei replied. "The President is with me and he is armed."

"Dmitry is within 30 seconds of you," Ivan said.

"Recheck the window, Sergei," Nikolai said. "I'll get the rest of the room."

"I got it covered, Mr. President," Dmitry entered the room

Keeping an eye out for the intruder, Nikolai said, "Dmitry, check the bathroom. The closet."

Dmitry swept the bedroom. He called, "The bedroom is clear. Nikolai, secure Dr. Blake. I'll cover the door."

Nikolai slipped Sergei's gun into the back of his trousers and called, "Elizabeth?" Nikolai's footsteps echoed on the marble floor of Elizabeth's suite.

Sergei and Dmitry listened as they did a second swept of the rooms. "I suggest you call her by her formal name," Dmitry advised. "The room may be compromised."

Nikolai frowned. Dmitry was correct. "Damn it! Then check for bugs." Pissed off, he said, "I do not think the intruder wanted to eavesdrop." He realized he had fallen into a habit of crossing political boundaries with her. It was something neither expected they would have to deal with again.

"Nikolai?" Elizabeth asked, opening her eyes. Her cheek was red from the intruder's strike. Her body was sore. Answers raced in her head to fill in the question "why?" She needed to use logic, analysis and facts, to regain her equilibrium. She didn't find any. Elizabeth pushed her medical bag aside and reached for Nikolai. She embraced him tightly as if she was sinking into quicksand and he was her only rope. Diplomatic protocol slipped away as basic human survival instincts took over.

Nikolai felt a familiar old rush. He once again dangerously crossed lines with her. He felt they were the only ones who understood each other in the chaos of the world.

Sweeping back her messed hair from her face, she looked at him. "Do you who that man was? How did he get in here? He would have killed me if he hadn't heard the gunshot. He was armed with some kind of specialized razor blade. After he struck me, he ripped my medical bag open. He pulled out some penicillin vials. As if that would help stop the virus." The last line was meant in mockery.

Nikolai pulled Elizabeth up, holding her close to his chest. He needed her calm. It was crucial a clear response came from her. "Was it one of my men?" he asked. "You've seen them, worked with them. You know what to look for."

She thought a moment as her head rested on his chest. "Yes. No. Yes. He was, but he said this was mafia business and he couldn't let me live. Said the contents of my medical bag were vital to the new boss's plan. He struck me when I refused to give it to him." She lifted her head off his chest and said, "He was my FSB escort to this room. He claimed Yuri was dismissed when I arrived." Elizabeth's mind was racing, disjointed.

"It was Yuri's replacement? If he is not one of the murdered FSB team, then he is in on this. His recent lifestyle is too rich for what the government pays him. We have to prove it." Nikolai burned with fury at Yuri. He felt Elizabeth shaking. He offered, "He's gone. There is no one at the window. I need you to pull yourself together."

Elizabeth nodded, taking a few deep breaths, struggling to calm her nerves.

"Dmitry," Nikolai called to his brother. "We have a suspect. An FSB officer who had 10 years of service. And, like she said, he was her escort to this room." His face turned back to Elizabeth. "We'll find him."

She nodded, stepping back from Nikolai. She stumbled. He grabbed her arm, steadying her. "Sit." Nikolai looked at the edge of the bed.

"I am OK," she reassured him. Moving toward the bed, her shoe tapped against a small object on the floor. She stopped. He held out a hand to guide her. "Wait," she said. Her other hand went to her forehead, pushing loose locks of hair out of her eyes as she peered downwards. "Look, he dropped something. A medical tube."

Nikolai tossed the open black medical bag onto her bed. Stooping down, he took his white linen handkerchief from his pocket and carefully picked up a metal vial. With one clean move he stepped to the nightstand and pulled the chain on the bedside lamp. He held the vial under the strong glow of light, reading the Russian code words.

Elizabeth stood next to him. "A clue?"

"Sergei, over here," he called quickly. Sergei stepped toward him and examined the vial. They both looked at Elizabeth. Nikolai's eyes turned hard, dark. Sergei saw he was losing his polished control at the discovery of this evidence. He stepped between Elizabeth and Nikolai.

"Why was this in your possession?" Nikolai snapped as the ramifications of the vial fell upon him, desperate to find anyone to blame for this pandemic. "I could wring your neck over this!"

"What are you talking about?" she asked in disbelief.

Sergei aimed his gun. "Don't move," he warned her. He nodded to Dmitry. "Send up a team of guards. We have a terrorist suspect: Dr. Blake."

Elizabeth was jolted. All political protocol went out the window with those words. "You have got to be kidding! Nikolai, you are not thinking rationally. If you believe that, we lose the one chance we have to find the virus code and cure!" Elizabeth said to defend herself. "Why would I, how in the world could I, have someone, no less a FSB officer, break into your government suites and pretend to steal penicillin?" She stood her ground, hearing the cock of Sergei's gun. "Go ahead, shoot me! Then explain that to President Brice and my uncle." She threw her hands up in the air as if to signal surrender.

Nikolai fought an internal war of logic and rage. Moving toward her, he pushed Sergei out of the way. He tried to explain his actions. "The vial is one of ours, Elizabeth. It is the stolen biological agent off the Siberian site." He paused, "Can you tell me what the hell you are doing with it?" His face was red with wrath.

"Don't take the tone with me! It's not one of the vials I normally carry," she replied, infuriated. She placed her hand on his arm and shook it to make her point. "I don't know where it came from." She saw that Nikolai was not listening. He was too set on seeing her as his scapegoat.

"You said he stole, tried to steal, medical tubes from your bag. You must have had this all along. And you didn't tell me! *Me* of all people. You would betray what we shared to get back at me?" He pushed her away. "Damn! Are you mixed up in this? You knew all this time. You had this on you?"

Elizabeth shook her head, unable to believe the turn of events. "I've been working my ass off, the whole team has, trying to save your country and the rest of the world. You can't honestly believe I'm with the bioterrorist!" She paused. "Or could you? Don't make this about me and you! What happened all those years ago had been settled. It has been a long time. You played the same blame game with me fourteen years ago. Why in the world would you bring that up in my face under these circumstances?"

Nikolai went silent. He forced himself to listen.

"I betrayed you?" she continued. "Funny. I seem to remember you telling my uncle that the morning he found us in bed was nothing. Very different words than the ones you used to get me in that bed. I never once told anyone about our secret. Not even my uncle, who, I may remind you, saved your ass from jail or worse. Treason!"

Nikolai's blood coursed through his veins at her lack of tact. "Looks like our secret is out finally. And it was nothing." He waved his hand at Dmitry and Sergei, who were bewildered by her outburst. Nikolai cursed under his breath. "Damn you! It's too late. Too late for everything."

"Damn me? Damn you, Nikolai. It *was* really only eight months of nothingness," Elizabeth said in desolation.

"Eight months!" Dmitry said, astonished his brother had kept the affair that long with no one suspecting.

"It helped to be the best of the FSB," was Nikolai's only response to his brother. He rubbed the five o'clock shadow claiming his chin as he paced back to her. He pushed Sergei's gun arm down and glanced at her. Seeing the disbelief painted on both of his men's faces was enough of a wakeup call to put an end to it. He never intended for it to turn personal. His lips pursed. His face was taut as he took in the reality of the situation. She was right. Overwrought and restrained, he had to admit that.

"I see your point. I agree. Let's not bring up the past. We've suffered too many losses of loved ones. We have a killer virus to stop. Sergei, call off the guards. She's not the terrorist."

"No, let's bring up the past. As far as I'm concerned, she is a terrorist suspect," Sergei replied. "I am not about to let this go. How could you not tell me this for all these years? Now I understand why you hesitated to bring her on board. Nikolai, you told me it was just a young American tourist who caught your eye. Not Secretary Blake's niece? That is why her uncle gave up his ambassadorship, and why he didn't press charges as an ambassador. Not even a demand for a public apology at the time. You two are good. He even fooled me. I knew he was covering for someone. Never would have thought it was for you and her." Sergei pointed a finger toward Elizabeth.

"Enough," Nikolai said. "The issue is closed." Nikolai felt there was little else he could do but try to repair the damage. "She is the best pathologist and we need her and her team's knowledge. Our own team failed! Have they found anything useful? No. We have to leave it to the Americans to lead the war on this pandemic now. And I do..." He paused. He looked at her one more time and oddly saw his own reflection in her eyes, a reflection of those eight shared months. "Trust her. No more questions. Find out who the real traitor is. Yuri has to be tied to this. If he is alive, call him in. I don't care where he is. Get him in my office immediately. Do not let him know he is under suspicion." Nikolai turned to a dispirited Elizabeth. "Can you get back to work?" She nodded.

"Mr. President?" Sergei's gravelly voice hung in the air. "Under the circumstances, I cannot allow Dr. Blake to leave. Whether you trust her or not isn't the issue. Lines have been crossed. Both of you are in danger. And, until we can prove otherwise, she is now a suspect as well as Yuri. They were together."

Nikolai swung around fiercely. "Someone may have used her to get to me." Unsettled, he picked up the linen covered vial. "With this." His hand grew tight around the vial. "General, it's the missing vial from the Siberian storage facility. And the only person I can think of is Yuri. He had clearance to the facility. Access to the family oil fields. I need proof."

"We can't be sure of that," Sergei offered. "It has a Russian biological code on it, but we can't be sure of the source. The vial may have held nothing."

"I am sure," Nikolai said without reservation. "I'll let you decide for yourself."

Sergei was unsure what could be going on. How had the vial come into her possession? Dr. Blake had cleared the toughest security checks he gave for anyone. Pushing a chair aside, he slipped his gun into the inside of his jacket. "Dmitry, guard the door."

"Yes, general."

"Send up a forensics team to see if they can turn up a positive ID," he continued.

Dmitry called the orders in and received a message from another officer. "They found a FSB officer on the floor below. Dead. Whoever was waiting for him below left with no trace. Guards are here."

"How can that be? No trace in the Kremlin?" Sergei wondered. "Get on it." Dmitry shut the suite's door with his foot as he left. The newly-arrived bodyguard took his place.

Elizabeth looked up. Worry was replacing anger. Nikolai had taken on a yellow skin tone as they talked. A few sweat beads had now formed on his brow. "How long have you been sick?" she asked softly. "You're showing minor symptoms, Nikolai. Stage one of the SV121R virus."

Nikolai ignored her question. He chalked his feverish sweat up to finding the vial in Elizabeth's room. He was losing his patience. Exasperated, he shoved the handkerchief-covered vial into Sergei's palm. "Make sure I am correct."

Sergei glanced down at it. Taking his glasses from his shirt pocket, he held it up to the yellow haze of the chandelier, twisting and turning it carefully.

Nikolai thrust his hands into his trousers' side pockets and paced the floor.

"*Da, da*. This is one of the vials that are missing," Sergei said. "As for Dr. Blake having the vial in her room, I don't have an answer." He turned to her. "You are under house arrest." He was broken, angry at what he still believed to be her betrayal of his president.

"Wait, general. Let's see if we can get a print off of this first. No one should jump to conclusions at this point."

Nikolai's words of reason struck Sergei, but he could not give up so easily. There was too much coincidence. "She was in New York at the same time as Adar and Yuri. And the virus. People around them have been getting sicker. She has been exposed as well."

"Yes, Mr. President," Elizabeth argued. "But it doesn't explain the oil ships being contaminated. That had to be an inside job. I can help. Let me do my job. I'll fly back to my staff and see what next move would be best for the investigation. I need to see what the Florida tanker turned up. I'll send a team member to China. See if they picked up anything," Elizabeth concluded.

Nikolai refocused on the reason she was there: her report. "What did you find at the hospital? Tell me what you learned," he asked.

Shaking her head, she gathered the last of her stable emotions, she replied, "I understand. Jason's tissues samples may prove to be the key to finding the DNA of SV121R. His autopsy revealed that victims, like himself, died of internal bleeding due to ruptured organs. Stomach and liver are the first to tear. No known cure for this kind of internal bleeding." She paused. Raising a hand to wipe a small drop of sweat from her brow, she continued, "I do not believe it is a true small pox based on Jason's tissue samples. My autopsy confirmed some kind of mutation we are not aware of. It is premature for the time being to say what exactly it is or is not. Add the fact that communications have been disrupted, sporadic at best. Less information has been getting through. If it will help, Robert, the CDC assistant director, informed me prior to my arrival that the virus is spreading in the States at an uncontrolled rate. I was ordering small pox inoculations to begin nationwide. I suggest you order the same inoculations. I was talking to Robert when I came into the room." She rubbed her sore shoulder. "When my escort grabbed my bag..." Her eyes widened. "It's clearer to me now. He was sent to retrieve vials. Not steal new ones. He kept asking me for the penicillin vials. I assumed he thought I had a cure already, or he didn't understand that penicillin would not work. We struggled. He dragged me onto the bed, threatened what he planned to do to me. I hurled a few water glasses from the side table at him. One hit him in the face. That was when I grabbed my bag. He must have heard your voice, Nikolai. He hit me and left with whatever vials he could get. He must have dropped the empty vial then."

Dmitry opened the door. "General, your com link? St. Petersburg has been trying to contact the President."

Nikolai stood silent for a moment. He wanted to suppress his feelings of what he knew was coming by the look on his brother's face. "It's my son? He's dead?"

Even the general didn't know how to answer him. He nodded his head in confirmation.

"God. No!" It was the last straw. Nikolai felt weak in his knees. His fist pounded on the side of his pant leg. He grabbed Elizabeth and pulled her to him, chest to chest. She gazed up at this powerful broken man's face. His grip was strangling the blood flow into her arm. Hesitantly, she reached her hand out. He snatched in midair and brought it to his face. He held it tight.

He spoke with primal determination. "Find the cure, Elizabeth. You can have anything you need. I failed on my promise fourteen years ago. I will not now. Find the cure to the virus that took the life of my wife and child."

She held her own feelings of those long gone days in check. Drawing in a breath, she reminded Nikolai of who she was. "My team will find a cure." She spoke with confidence void of past emotions.

Nikolai nodded, knowing old feelings had resurfaced to test their will. He dropped the urge to tell her how he really felt all those years ago. It served no purpose.

Dropping her hand, Nikolai walked over to Sergei. "None of my prior personal relationship with Dr. Blake is anyone's business. Including yours. Understand?" Nikolai coolly added, "As for this vial, what do you suggest, general?"

Sergei stood down, showing his disappointment. "I understand my orders," he said simply.

"I have a suggestion," Elizabeth offered. "I'd like to return to the Eclipse to test for any potential DNA inside the vial, or fingerprints on its exterior."

"No. I do not approve." Sergei paced, worried his involvement with Pachen and how his ex-contemporary came to acquire the Ka- 25 chopper would be discovered. "I demand to oversee the vial investigation."

"You demand!" Nikolai reprimanded.

"Yes. It is Russia's responsibly, not the Americans."

"No. You're wrong," Elizabeth, ticked off, protested. "You really are a suspicious old warrior. This is the world's problem. You do realize that the whole world's infrastructure is beginning to fail, don't you? All major airports and transportation systems are shutting down. Even your own metro rail system is off line. The Eclipse is the only airship that doesn't need any infrastructure to operate. Let me take the vial on board. I can find what we need if there is something to be found."

Sergei measured her anger. She was too well-informed for him to argue. He decided then and there she would not be granted permission to leave Russia. He'd ground all flights in and out of Moscow. She was a political threat to his President. He took his job to protect him very seriously, regardless of whether Nikolai felt safe. Whatever she could do on that fancy plane or in any of Moscow's laboratories would have to do for Dr. Blake. He kept his intentions silent.

Wiping the sweat away with his sleeve, Nikolai said, "Do it. She's right. All political games must be put aside."

Sergei was not happy. He gripped the vial more tightly, carefully and secretly wiping the outside clean with the white handkerchief before handing the empty vial to Elizabeth.

"I want to know the results as soon as she finds them. Find out who she was with at all times during Yuri's New York escort assignment." Nikolai paused. "And call my aide to send a pitcher of cold water to my office. Have them check the air. It's hot in here." Nikolai was filled with a new conflicting storm that raged within him. His mind raced from the death of his wife and son, and with thoughts of his former lover, Elizabeth, now his only chance at putting an end to this pandemic. How did he get to this point? he asked himself. He wanted nothing more than to punch a wall and release his tensions. He didn't.

Nikolai left her suite and slammed the door. He hurried to his office to see what information his team had found on her attacker. He flicked on the lights in his office. His blood was bursting in his temples. It thumped like a base drum. His head ache grew when he suddenly had the horrible realization that whether Elizabeth could find the viral strain or not, some kind of bad dream was becoming a reality. More people were going to die because of the small vial he had found in her room, and not some, but millions. And it was his fault. Whole cities would be decimated by one drop of that liquid his country had made. Guilt, shame and helplessness shadowed him as he stood alone in his office, unable to move in either direction, a world leader with no answers, no hope and no way to stop death from coming.

CHAPTER TWENTY-TWO

Day Five. 1:00 a.m. EST. Office of the Secretary of State. Washington, DC.

"What do you mean you haven't heard from her?" inquired William as he slammed his fist on his desk. The speakerphone echoed as he handed written orders to his assistant.

"Unexpected issues concerning Dr. Blake have come to our government's attention," William's Moscow counterpart said flatly.

"Your government is in violation of international protocol. I suggest you contact President Stepanov and find her. Dr. Blake was instructed to report in the moment she arrived in Moscow. That was hours ago! I expect your office to get back to me within thirty minutes or there will be difficulty between our two countries," William countered.

"The Russian government doesn't like threats, Mr. Secretary," the Russian official replied. "However, I will see what I can do."

"It wasn't a threat. It was a statement of fact. Our countries agreed to work together. I suggest your government start holding up to your end of the agreement." Pushing the off button, William ended the conversation with his Russian counterpart without as much as a goodbye.

"Mr. Secretary. President Brice is on the line."

"Damn. Now what?" William wondered aloud. He changed handsets and hit the security link-up. "Mr. President?"

"Mr. Secretary. Have you any news from Dr. Blake's team? Communications systems are failing over the globe. Any updates from Dr. Blake on the Florida epidemic?"

"President Brice, the last update that reached the CDC before losing contact with Dr. Blake was not good. Our suspicion is that non-government sources are interfering with all international communications in and out of Russia. I can't even get through to President Stepanov."

"Additional terrorists taking advantage of the chaos? I hope not. Tell me what you have so far," Brice pushed.

"According to Dr. Blake, we are dealing with a rapid spread of a plague like the world hasn't seen since the Middle Ages." William sighed. "There are rumors that Dr. Blake is trapped in Moscow. Those rumors fuel my fear that it's not Syria, but that the bioterrorist is Russian. I'm guessing the terrorist targeted Dr. Blake to make it look as if we betrayed the Russian government."

"Hold on, Mr. Secretary," Brice said. "I'm getting a call from Jackson Memorial. I'm putting you on the line. Listen in." There was a click as the third party was connected to the call. "Dr. Robert Yuan? President Brice here. Secretary Blake is on the line as well."

The assistant CDC director replied, "Mr. President. Mr. Secretary. As of thirty minutes ago, I was able to make contact with the Eclipse. Dr. Blake left orders we were able to attain from the onboard computer, MARY. We intercepted a telecommunication transmission that stated the Russians refused her flight clearance. We have had no contact with her since she arrived at Building 14. The orders she left were that all of Florida be quarantined. That quarantining effort has taken effect immediately." Robert paused. "I can tell you this: people are caught in the grips of fear. Miami and all major South Florida cities are rioting. I am with a military escort leaving the area as we speak. Florida is a dead zone. The CDC feels we've contained the virus to this state as of 12:55. The reservists are in place. A mandatory inoculation program was started for all medical personnel a few hours ago at Dr. Blake's request. We are doing an inventory of the small pox vaccine." Robert's voice hardened. "Some people are going to have to go without, Mr. President. We just don't have enough." His voice trailed off in despair.

"That will be all, Dr. Yuan." Brice hung up. "William, you heard that? They're holding her. Why?"

"The rumors must be true. They suspect her," William said.

"Contact the Russian ambassador in D.C. and I'll make a call to Stepanov directly. Damn him," Brice said. "Either way, I am demanding Elizabeth Blake's immediate return."

"I'm glad we're in sync on the message to send," William said,

"Meet me at in the Oval office within the hour. The Joint Chiefs of Staff will be joining us." Brice hung up.

William called his assistant into his office. "Make arrangements for

Dr. Yuan at the CDC to call me after he clears the quarantine zone. I need more information about Dr. Blake's last message and what is being done to contain the epidemic in New York. Also, get me an update on the oil tanker clean up. When I talk to that son-of-a-bitch Russian foreign minister again, I will need the information that they are holding her confirmed." he stated, anxiously making his point. His assistant scurried out of his office, taking a seat at her desk. She made the calls.

Impatient, William did not want to wait the thirty minutes for the Russians to get back to him. He paced the floor, restlessly, his hands tied against the fact his niece was under their control. American's next generation of stealth aero-technology was also on their soil and they'd had no contact from any U.S. official in Moscow in hours. His instincts were on red alert. Unlike Brice, his deep concern for the safety of his niece cut him like a twisting knife inside. It was personal for him. "God, if Nikolai's playing a game with her life…again…" His words trailed off.

"Mr. Secretary, the Russian ambassador is waiting for you, as you requested.

"Send him in," William responded to his assistant.

The Russian ambassador entered the spacious office. "Secretary Blake."

Their visits were always cordial and friendly. Not today. "Sit down, Mr. Ambassador." William's blood pumped hard in his temple. His temper was barely held in check. The ambassador took up his guard. "You were summoned here to provide answers to the recent breakdown in diplomatic relations with your government. Where is our U.S. medical envoy, Dr. Blake? She did not report in at the appointed time. Is she being treated as a diplomatic hostage? I remember the negotiations we had to deal with when I served as ambassador. Don't play with me. We've been friends for too long. I hope your country has not failed to recognize her status of diplomatic immunity. That would put both counties in a dangerous position." William's tall, lean frame towered over the sitting ambassador who looked as if he had visited one too many pubs. "Is she being held because of the SV121R virus? To cover up your country's screw up?"

The ambassador's face went white. He had never heard William this agitated; he took umbrage at his accusations. He hesitated before answering. "I haven't any idea what you are talking about." Truthfully, he did not. The rumor that Dr. Blake was arrested had never left Moscow.

"Mr. Ambassador, don't play me for a fool! You were made aware of Dr. Blake's travel arrangements and of one of your country's oil carriers contaminating our waters and cities. Come on! It's been all over the news."

The ambassador squirmed. Tugging at his collar, he replied, "I'm sorry. I only know about as much as the news." The ambassador jumped up. His eye caught a red and white flicker outside the Secretary's window.

"Get down, Mr. Secretary!" He lunged forward, tackling William to the floor. The window panes shattered with a crash. Tiny pieces of glass littered his office. The wing of a Learjet clipped the window before crashing into the street below.

The men rose quickly, before they had time to fully recover, and rushed to the remains of the window, hearing screams from below. William's pale blue eyes held a startled silver cast as he gazed at the avenue outside the building. A FedEx jet liner littered the Potomac River with debris. A commercial jet liner followed suit within seconds. William knew it was a heroic last minute maneuver by the pilot to save lives by crashing in the river. More jets were falling out of the sky like rain drops.

The Russian ambassador raised his hand to his mouth in shock. "What the hell is going on?" Both men watched cars stop in the middle of the road, drivers and passengers bellowing, sick and dying, vomit and blood pouring from their mouths. Families on tour of their capitol collapsed where they stood, clutching their bellies in pain. Their children and babies lay crying in strollers with no one to help.

"Thank God," William said aloud, hearing emergency sirens beginning to bellow in the streets as an army of officers arrived below. Shock over took the men as they gazed at the tragic scene being played out before them.

The door burst open. Three secret service men arrived. "Mr. Secretary! We have to go immediately! Mr. Ambassador, we have to ask you to leave now. You'll be provided an escort out of the building. Your car is waiting for you," a sandy-haired security officer instructed.

William snatched his laptop, briefcase and satellite phone. He was hurried off by the security team ushering him out the open door. William called back, "Ambassador, get President Stepanov to contact me directly. Use my emergency numbers. Tell him Liz must make contact with me this morning. You have my direct number. I need answers!" The ambassador nodded.

William was whisked down the emergency staircase to an awaiting State Department sedan that took him to a nearby helicopter. Hopping into the side door of the chopper, he was greeted by the White House attaché. Taking a seat, William placed his laptop on the seat beside him. He asked, "What is going on?"

The attaché words were electro-charged. "Chaos, Mr. Secretary. We're being taken to the Cheyenne Mountain facility."

"Old NORAD!" William exclaimed. "Why? There was no notification of incoming hostile action. No missiles. Just a damn bug."

"President Brice is on his way to Peterson AFB. He'll explain more. I am to tell you that Dr. Blake is under the care of the Russian government for the next four hours. It appears the location she is at will not allow direct communication access to her. She tested an empty Cold-War dated medical vial that was located. It was confirmed to be from the Russian stock pile. We were unable to receive the results on the vial. Communications were broken off before we received her report. We are trying to redirect the other international team members in expectation that she can provide the any further results to them. England may be our best chance to contact her."

"Do we know the reason for the loss of communications?" William asked.

"There are two, sir. We suspect communications operators have been infected and can no longer perform their tasks. Also, someone is jamming us. Out of Siberia."

"They're jamming our frequency? Damn that Nikolai! What is he up to? She has to be somewhere in the State Palace. Get a man inside there. I know we have an agent on premise." William paused, then asked, "Have you heard anything about my son Jason? He was to leave Moscow about the same time Dr. Blake arrived."

"No, sir."

"What else? This is going to be one long flight to NORAD," William complained,

"I am to pass this information along to you at President Brice's request. He informed President Stepanov personally and insisted she be returned to the U.S." The attaché flipped through some notes. "Once we arrive you will be given direct video links for any questions you have."

"Are you sure there's nothing on Jason? Damn."

"No information on Jason Blake," the attaché repeated.

William asked, "Why NORAD?"

"It's a plague, sir. It's shown up in DC, not just one or two cases, but as a large scale epidemic. Within the last thirty minutes. We have begun to set up military MASH units close to the city, as close as we can, to tend to the sick. We can't let them back into the city."

"You mean you set up death camps outside the city? I'm not stupid. There are plenty of hospitals, schools and emergency medical centers to use. Plus other warehouse facilities. We shouldn't need to use tented MASH units."

"The units are for," the attaché paused and coughed, "the overflow of infected casualties we expect."

"Oh, bull shit. You mean there's no one to provide healthcare. And this is our solution? To count the dead as they leave our cities."

"No, Mr. Secretary. We are just trying to keep the capitol closed off. We are protecting the governmental infrastructure. Congress has been asked to stay in session to address the needs. President Brice, the Joint Chiefs of Staff and you were moved out. We have to give the image that we are in charge of the crisis and working on it. As you know, China, Russia and the Middle East were hit hard."

"The Middle East, too?"

"They asked for our help. We provided them with our CDC standards and advised them to tell people to stay home, make a safe house, tape up the windows and drink bottled water. The Emergency Alert System is up and running the message throughout the U.S. The virus was in the oil supply of the Russian tanker and now it's in the water. The Russian ship's log points a finger at the Syrians, too."

"Adar poisoned his own country? This is unbelievable."

"The journal ties to Prince Adar and FSB officer who name is distorted. Other information was half-written. Water-stained letters, poor Russian grammar. Like a little child wrote it."

"You mean a dying captain trying to give us a clue."

"The translators can't make it out. All we got was that someone is a bastard son of someone in charge of this terrorist act. It's a dead-end lead."

William said, "Don't tell the Russians that. At least not now. So it's a waterborne virus? We can purify the water? Yes?"

He shook his head. "According to Dr. Blake's last autopsy report and a testing of antiviral agents, nothing kills it. Not chlorine or other major disinfecting agents. It feeds on the antiviral agents. What we don't know is if it's also airborne. Dr. Blake would be able to tell us that if she was here. We also found it in New York City water filtration plants. We had them shut down. We have a water shortage in the city. The bad news is that our office and Stanford's biological labs both came up empty-handed."

"Great. What do you know?"

"Only that Dr. Blake has a theory that it's not the small pox virus."

William paused, clenched his hand into a fist and added, "Time is not on our side. Have all your reports ready for Elizabeth. I want updated copies of every change you find sent to me at NORAD."

"Yes sir!" He nodded. "This is all the information I was able obtain for you." He handed a file to William.

"I'm sure you have told me enough. I'll look at it when we get to Colorado Springs." It had been less than half a day and already containment camps were springing up. What was next? William's lips tensed. He tapped the co-pilot to switch seats. William, an ex-Air Force general and Black Hawk pilot, could fly the chopper himself. The men switched seats. William strapped in. He placed the co-pilot's radio transmission helmet on. "Command Central. Secretary Blake here. Patch me in to President Brice. Get Russian airspace clearance for one of our F15s. Have it ready, fueled and in position for me at NORAD. Tell the Russians that if they don't provide clearance, I'm coming personally with or without permission. And it will not be friendly or alone if they don't grant access."

William was not making an empty threat. He guessed Brice would be on his side. If the plague were unstoppable, there would be no one able to fly or maintain order. Based on the small amount of information received, the world was on the brink of anarchy. Elizabeth and Nikolai held the key. His graves and her skills were keys to the solution.

"After we drop you off, you should be at NORAD within two hours," the co-pilot said. "A jet is waiting for you." William looked at the approaching tarmac and nodded.

The chopper's landing was hard and fast. Military escorts waited on the edge of the landing platform. William grabbed his laptop and folders. He hopped out of the helicopter.

"Mr. Secretary, this way." The men waved him over to a staircase leading to a government–owned 10-passenger jet. William hurried up the stairs and settled in. The men followed behind him and closed the jet's door. His seatbelt on, William asked, "How long before I can make contact with President Brice?"

One officer replied, "Five minutes, Mr. Secretary."

William settled in his seat. "Not fast enough. Now get this God damn plane out of Washington's Airspace."

"We will have the President on the line in three minutes, sir." The officer acknowledged his orders. The plan took a hard angle. William felt the G-force push him against his seat. A few seconds later, they leveled off and he heard, "Mr. Secretary, President Brice is on the line for you. We had to reroute security links to older satellite codes. May not be as secure as you'd like," he warned.

William unbelted his seatbelt and made his way to the communications system. "Mr. President, did you get in touch with Moscow? When can we get Elizabeth back? You and I both know she's the only one who will get this bug under control. Who else in the world is working on containing this?"

"Mr. Secretary. I spoke to President Stepanov. There was brief misunderstanding on who was the real terrorist, as he explained it."

"Misunderstanding?" William asked impatiently.

"Yes. William, she's on her way home. They confirmed it is a stolen Russian Cold War-era virus that may have mutated over the years."

"How did they come to acknowledge that? Not like the Russians."

"Dr. Blake found an old empty vial that gave clues as to its origin. However, the vial is useless. She said it was clean. We have an idea that Adar was an accomplice. Need to prove it." Brice's voice weakened.

"I see." William hung his head. Brice's voice was weakening at each call. He assumed the worst fate for his President. He kept it to himself. "Then tell me about this plague and Adar's link to it. I'll get on it. Which countries do I need to call? I suggest China first, then India. The Brits will go along with what we say. Regardless if the Middle East is infected, Syria has to be made accountable along with President Stepanov's government if Adar did this."

CHAPTER TWENTY-THREE

Day Five. 5:35 a.m. Yekaterinburg Time (YEK). Siberian lab hideout. Perm.

A wide, high-powered security beam passed over Yuri. He emerged from a six-inch Plexiglas containment unit. Knots of frustration made his back ache.

"Boss. The men are dying more rapidly." Misha's tone divulged his level of discouragement.

The Siberian hideout was an isolated laboratory carved out of the side of a mountain, set up to deal with this particular pathological agent. The brightly lit lab was exactly as Yuri had requested. Yuri stared at the vacant laboratory. It was fitted with the best histology technology available on the black market. And no one was running it. Misha stood alone in the empty lab in his sweat stained shirt. He wiped his chin with his pushed-up sleeve.

"How many men have we lost to the virus?" Yuri asked.

"Over half of your St. Petersburg's team. It's like that in every sector."

"And my team of scientists?"

"Dead. All of them," Misha cautiously said.

"So, darkness had fallen on us as well. Get the rest of my men vaccinated." Yuri pulled out the stolen antiviral agents and tossed them to Misha. He noticed small red blotches on Misha's outstretched arm as he took the useless serum. "Do we at least have an MD alive on my team?"

"One. He is in the infirmary with Mus'ad."

"Mus'ad's here? Why did you let him in?"

"It wasn't like we could stop him. He brought extra men. Demanded an audience with you. He was fuckin' mad you weren't here. We settled him down. His men are dying quickly, too."

"Is he sick?" Yuri pressed.

"Not that we can tell."

Yuri looked around the vacant lab. "Give yourself another shot of the vaccine and see what else my doctor can give you for those red marks. I need you all. I lost my top two bodyguards on the trip in. I need another pathologist. Who is left? We have the antiviral serum in our possession. If Adar hadn't pulled that trick, my men still would be alive."

"Want me to get rid of the bodies, boss?" Misha scratched his head, trying to think of how to break more bad news to him. He did not want to draw on his enmity and wrath. He was loyal as a dog to his master and respected him for his intelligence and articulate manner, darkly evil as it was.

"No. I pushed their corpses out of the chopper myself. Autopilot went on the fritz just before I got here. I had to land it myself."

Misha studied Yuri's temperament. The man was deadly cold. He glanced at the vial in his hand. Misha delivered a defeated sigh. "Boss. This antivirus serum is bad. It's not working right. Mikovich's assistant is dead, even with an attempt to duplicate Mikovich's antivirus batch from old records. We already gave it to the men."

"You lie, Misha!" Yuri drew a fist to strike him.

Misha's had flew up in attempt to reason with Yuri. "Boss, stop. I have an idea. You need a pathologist? Why not use the American female your brother brought in? Sergei didn't approve her flight out of Russia."

"Why is the old man denying her return? Something must have happened. She knows something."

"She's a suspect. He thinks she's helping the terrorist out. She's grounded in Moscow."

Yuri was delighted that the old general had inadvertently helped him. "Good. Easier for us to find her and remove her from them. I need her to make the antiviral serum for me." Yuri released his fist. His eyes ran over Misha. He did not display the advanced telltale virus symptoms – the physical weakness, blistering, open lesions and nose bleeds. Something was keeping the virus at bay, at least for now.

He glanced at a chess set across the room. A game was already in play. He moved across the laboratory and removed two pieces. He wrote a note on a white slip of paper. Yuri wrapped the chess pieces and secured them with a thin rubber band he pulled from a supply drawer. "Can you go back to Moscow?"

"No," Misha said honestly. "They know my face. I'd be putting you at risk because there are too few mafia men left in Moscow able to protect any of us. We have one or two left on the inside. We discovered a U.S. mole, too. He's being held in a safe house outside Losiny Ostrov National Park. Mus'ad's men discovered him after a prearranged meeting to exchange information with the mole. He was looking for information on Dr. Blake."

"And what you did you find out?"

"What I mentioned before. Nikolai suspects you. The mole was as able to get a message out to the Americans before Mus'ad met him. We don't know anymore. He's not talking."

"Then kill him. Don't waste time on him." He grabbed Misha's wrist and pushed his shirt sleeve higher. "You seem to be OK. This rash is not the worst of it."

The laboratory alarms suddenly blared, interrupting the eerie silence of the empty room. Both men pulled their guns.

"Yuri! Where are the original antivirus vials?" a familiar voice demanded. Yuri watched Mus'ad and his men approach the entrance to the lab. As they crossed an invisible security laser beam, two bulletproof glass doors slammed down from the ceiling, trapping them into a Plexiglas cage.

Yuri lowered his gun. "Mus'ad. Welcome to my lab."

"Let me out!" Mus'ad's voice held a tone of anger. "You betrayed us. Your plans have all turned to bullshit. We need a pathologist and not just a boy running this place."

"You are right, my friend," Yuri admitted.

Mus'ad spit on the sanitized floor of his cage. "I'm not your friend. But you still need me, Yuri, so let me out. We did what you asked. All those precious scientists have either been assassinated by us or killed by that virus you unleashed. But my people are dying faster every hour. I need that antivirus formula and you need me to get you a new pathologist. Your best option is Dr. Blake. She has become a valuable asset to you."

"I already have something in mind on that end," Yuri conceded. "She is literally life and death for us." Yuri walked over to the Plexiglas door. He spoke as if he were a man who had nothing to lose. "I need the American's jet lab. Can you get both?"

Yuri was a model of arrogance, ruthless and self-indulgent. It was as if he were a creature from Hell, or its master, Mus'ad thought. He had no choice. "Yes, I'll have my men work on acquiring them. With this extra work, I get that antiviral serum first. If I want to keep my men loyal, I need something for them to believe in."

Yuri saw how deeply his plan was flawed with Mus'ad's demand. Unless he forced Elizabeth to develop a cure for him, any vaccine would be useless at this point. If he had recognized the real power of the stolen bio-agent, he would never have lost control over the pathogen's spread. "Damn Mikovich was right." Yuri hated the thought that Mikovich was smiling at him from the Hell he had sent him to. How ironic that he would die from his own hand, that his own quest for power would be his downfall.

He snapped at Mus'ad. "If you get me Dr. Blake and that flying lab in the next 24 hours, you can have the antiviral serum. I'll hold on to the original formula. Gentlemen, I need your guns unloaded. Dump them in the security door. Misha, secure the area," Yuri ordered.

Misha moved to a small control panel. He pressed a sequence code. A small Plexiglas box dropped from the ceiling. Mus'ad's men bitterly tossed their guns into the box.

"They will be returned after you leave Siberian airspace."

Mus'ad lip twitched. The door to his prison opened. He walked out and stopped a short of Yuri.

Yuri signaled Misha to hand the vials back to him. He faced Mus'ad again. "One more thing." He handed Mus'ad a paper wrapped chess pieces. "Get these to Nikolai. I have a little surprise for my brother."

"Get it to him yourself," Mus'ad replied, glaring. "My only agreement is to pick up Dr. Blake and the American's jet lab."

"Add this to the list, too, if you want the serum. I don't have enough men in place to draw him out of that fortress he is protected by. Also, my brothers will nail me if I lay one foot in Moscow. I can deal with one of them, but if two or all of my step-brothers find me, you will not see a cent for the cure."

Mus'ad took a cheap shot. "So you are scared of the Stepanov clan. I seemed to have an alliance with the wrong Stepanov."

Yuri seized Mus'ad throat and flung him against one of the dissection tables. Mus'ad groaned as the back of his head hit hard on the stainless steel table. He struggled as Yuri's blade took off half his beard. "Nevsky! I am not and will never be a Stepanov."

Misha hauled up his semi-automatic gun, aiming it toward Mus'ad's two bodyguards, hitting the security door controls to contain the remaining Syrians.

"I'll skin you alive, Mus'ad!" Yuri threatened. "Layer by layer, starting with your tongue if I ever hear you say that again. You Syrian pig! My brothers are weak, but they outnumber me three to one. It's better to divide and conquer one by one. That is why I am in charge of the operation and you take orders from me!"

"Come on, boss. Let him up. Mus'ad's got your message. We need him. Remember the agreement? Your plan? Keep to it," Misha pleaded, watching Yuri squeeze a deep red ring around the Syrian's neck. "Let him go!"

Yuri froze. He ordered, "Misha, get a couple of our snipers in Moscow. In case Mus'ad can't come through on his agreement." He slowly released his grip on Mus'ad. His blade still in his hand, he backed away.

Mus'ad coughed for air. The color returned to his pale face as blood flooded back into it. He sat up and stared at Yuri. "You are fuckin' crazy!"

Yuri ignored the insult. "Mus'ad, you will put the final piece of my plan in action. As for our agreement..." He tossed one blue-striped antivirus vial to Mus'ad. The Syrian caught it as his lungs continued to fill with air. "One for you and one for me. That's all that remains of the original antiviral formula."

"And what is this last piece of your plan? It seems your plan has already failed."

Yuri raised his gun, placing the barrel to Mus'ad's forehead. "You are ballsy. I can kill you and your men here or let the virus eat your men away like it is doing to me and my army. Why do you continue to challenge me, you ass?"

Mus'ad pulled back and coolly said, "Put your gun away. Our deal has not changed from day one. And I'll be your delivery boy for Nikolai."

Yuri lowered his gun and swung around. He pressed forward to his chess game and moved a black pawn one spaced forward. White pawn captured black pawn and opened up white king to black knight.

Turning back to Mus'ad, he said, "That note I gave you should draw Nikolai out and away from Dr. Blake. You are on your own once inside Moscow. I can't give you any back up."

"I don't need any." Mus'ad rubbed his neck and ran his hand over the remains of his beard, feeling the depth of the offense. He became fixated on how he would make Yuri pay for the insult.

Yuri replied. "Bring her to the Trans-Siberian train station at Irkutsk. Send the jet ahead to this lab site. I'll be waiting for her. Misha, get Mus'ad and his men on the chopper. Fly him to a mile outside the Moscow city limits."

Yuri glanced back at the chess game once more. He picked up the black queen and moved her four spaces. "Check," he said to himself.

CHAPTER TWENTY-FOUR

Day Five. 11:00 a.m. Mountain Time (MST). NORAD Cheyenne Mountain Directorate. Colorado Springs.

"I can't understand why I'm required to be here and not at the President's side." William cursed as they hit a half-filled pothole. "Take it easy on this road." His hand grasped the Jeep's roll bar more tightly. Needle-like tingles stabbed at his white fingertips as his grip held firm. The driver did not yield to the Secretary's request.

William complained in frustration. "The President should be here during this kind of emergency. He should not be at Peterson Air Force Base. Damn it! That's why we still keep this antiquated facility operational." The driver held a steady hand on the steering wheel, riding through the one-third mile tunnel to the pair of nuclear attack-proof 25-ton steel blast doors that led to the underground complex. A cold sweat ran over his back. It was a familiar sweat, a sweat he had felt every time he went into combat. Something was not right.

He gritted his teeth. William had never liked being underground. It was unnatural to him. That was why he chose to be a jet pilot when it was his turn to serve his country. He drew upon old memories of free flying the old F-101 jet fighter during the time he spent in oversea. He hated sitting like a toad in a hole, waiting for something to happen. It was not his style. He had spent enough time behind enemy lines to know how not to be a sitting duck. Yet that was how he felt as the granite walls of the tunnel closed in on him.

William was not much happier as the North Portal entrance appeared. The blast doors led to the 4.5-acre grid of scraped out granite chambers and tunnels. William, irritated, barked, "Get on with it." He waited, crossing his arms across his chest, as the driver received clearance and the huge blast doors slowly swung open. He hopped out, grabbing his case. "That will be all for now. I know my way from here."

Making his way through the steel doors, he walked the metal walls of the tunnels that connected 15 buildings. He was reminded what the metal walls were for: to block electromagnetic pulses. He mumbled under his breath, "Elizabeth will never get a hold of me down here." The wall was the only way at that time to protect the government staff against nuclear fallout, biological and chemical warfare, but it also sealed out the rest of humanity.

William headed for the Air and Space Operations Center, ASOC. Entering the center, he found General Patrick McShane, commander of the North American Aerospace Defense Command and U.S. Northern Command Lt. Samantha Bouvae, watching a moving hologram tracing a three-dimensional map displayed on the data wall. William, impressed, commented, "I see you have redecorated since I was last here."

"So you haven't seen our new toy, Mr. Secretary?" General McShane asked. McShane turned to Lt. Bouvae. "Ask the damn computer how much time before California is a dead zone." William heard the familiar bleeps and blips of the multi-million dollar interactive database with its flashing rainbow of lights. The female voice named off the cities, times, wind direction, paths of incoming and outgoing jets.

William studied the interactive world map. It was hard to believe how far spread and fatal the epidemic had become. Frowning as he took a step closer, he saw Moscow was for the most part spared. Why, he wondered. St. Petersburg popped up on the map in red. Blue lines traced possible routes of contamination. Cities already considered dead were marked in black; Peking, Miami and New York were all black dots. Damascus oil pipelines were etched in black.

"Mr. Secretary," General McShane said. "Let me introduce you to Lt. Bouvae. The lieutenant has been instrumental in design and data input for ASOC. This will enable us to protect America from aerial attack by those who seek to take advantage of this epidemic. Which brings me to this point: has your niece found out anything?"

"No, damn it. The Russians have her under lock and key."

"The Russians?" McShane questioned. "Well, then you haven't heard."

"Heard what?"

"We received a message here from your office before it was shut down," McShane continued. "It came from your niece, Dr. Blake."

"Why in the hell didn't you tell me that first! Where is it?"

McShane waved over a low-ranking officer and passed instructions along. "It will arrive shortly. We have more pressing news, however. President Brice requested a secure live satellite feed roundtable conference as soon as you arrived. Everyone is waiting, Mr. Secretary. This way."

William was led into the mission panel's conference room. General Green, the U.S. Secretary of Defense, was outlining the strategic maneuvers to protect the main land. "We know this was an act of bio-terrorism so grossly underestimated that we must be on the offense and not the defense." General Green did not show traces of the consternation he was feeling on the inside.

William quickly took his seat, worried that this had all the signs of a war meeting and not one on stopping the bio-agent. Perhaps he should have expected this from Brice's top military advisors. Even though Brice was an upstanding man, he would not hesitate to use military action even while using the great minds that were available for this very kind of threat.

"We are monitoring all Russian jet bombers, subs, foot traffic at this time as well. We have made progress in the recovery efforts in New York, Miami and south Florida. The cities have been placed under military curfew and are restricted areas. Anyone left in those zones are on their own. No one can leave or go into these areas. Even Washington has fallen."

William sarcastically interrupted, "'Fallen? You mean it's filled with the living dead and rotting corpses we can't contain. Am I correct? What you are telling us, General Green, is these cities are dead. Not fallen! How bad has the military suffered? Can we still defend ourselves? I see Afghanistan and Pakistan have not been affected. The Saudis, Egypt and North Africa are starting to show evidence of SV121R. Thank God that none of those countries have weapons significant enough to really damage us if they blame us and retaliate. I am concerned that Iran has not even been touched. Iran and Syria have to be in bed together."

The Assistant to the Secretary of Defense swiftly barged into the room. "I have the President on the line." A large plasma screen lowered from the ceiling.

The video screen flashed a pulsing light once, then twice before the screen displayed President Brice standing. He was clearly distressed.

"Ladies, Gentlemen, I have some bad news. Ninety-five percent of our congressional representatives have succumbed to the bio-agent in some form. The virus has contaminated the entire eastern seaboard. Every one of our most strategic Air Force bases along the Atlantic cost is closed and under ridged security restriction. The only positive light is that all of the soldiers have not shown symptoms of the virus at this time. The CDC has found nothing at this time. The Atlanta headquarters is shut down and inoperable. Eclipse is providing the mobile international headquarters for the operation. I have cleared it to operate in conjunction with the CDC." Brice hesitated, then added, "The problem is that the Russian's have it. It's grounded in Moscow as I speak. We have contact with Eclipse through MARY." Brice's voice hovered a moment before he flatly stated, "That is not the worst of it. It is with great sorrow I have to report the deaths of our Vice President and Senate majority leader." He wiped away large sweat drops with his handkerchief as he gave his executive order. "I am appointing William Blake as our country's acting Vice President. The remaining Congressmen have already voted and approved the nomination. I have with me at Peterson Command Center the last of two Supreme Court Justices and the Chief Justice. She will do the swearing in." The participants at the roundtable discussion scrambled to understand the implications of the President's words.

William leaned forward. He understood all too well what had just been announced. His stomached tightened. "What you are saying, Mr. President, is that we have only a shell of a government left to function. Who and how many are really left?" The recycled air that pumped through the ventilation system added a raspy dryness to his voice. William did not agree that this was the correct course of action. He was not prepared to take that office. He commented, "With the plague racing across our nation as fast as it are you suggesting a 'one-man rule?' That can be put in place in no time at all." He needed to be sure this was not Brice playing with the political rules instead of Commander-in-Chief. "Mr. President. As you know, I have defended the war powers of the President. This is also not the first time our country has needed to defend itself, but we are not at war with an adversary but a pandemic. This unknown virus is for our best scientists to deal with efficiently. Give them the chance, the tools and, my God, the freedom to peacefully search for the cure."

"Unknown. Mr. Secretary, that is the problem. This Russian-engineered small pox strain moves so fast that in hours, days, maybe a week there will be no United States of America or a world as we know it for that matter. As you read in the reports, all livestock is affected, water, air, anything that comes in contact with it dies or is contaminated. Will we survive? I do not have an answer. But what I do know is that we have to protect what is left from contamination. The CDC assistant director's report estimates that on day nine of this outbreak we will be on the verge of extinction, if not before then. That's four days from now. I have ordered more safe houses be opened. This is all I can do."

William pressured Brice. "Mr. President. That is exactly why it's necessary to strongly persuade the Russian government to release Dr. Blake." The tension dropped as William spoke. "I'm waiting on a message from her. Mr. President, with her leading it, the international team we have put together *will* get a handle on this. In addition, I'm sure there are others in this government who disagree with this approach. I know Supreme Court Judge Sorral would."

"Sorral died an hour ago. William. There is no one left to run the government except a handful of our highest elected officials. They are good people. I understand your point. But your country needs you. I need you." The President hung his head. Remorseful, he said, "I just been handed a messages that two more senators have died of viral complications. We have chaos, murder in the streets and rampant crime. We have wild and domesticated animals running amok, not just humans." Without a blink, Brice announced, "Martial Law has been put into effect. Have you been able to glimpse what the media is broad-casting, William? Turn on the news. People across our country who haven't been exposed are taking up illegal arms to protect what they have and will kill anyone who they see as a trespasser. Anarchy is beginning to take hold. To stop it, I need you to take your oath while we can still broadcast it live to everywhere in our nation that we can reach and to those abroad. Our people need to hear and see that even with Washington lifeless, they still have a President and a Vice President along with enough of Congress and the Supreme Court to function and have control of our defenses. I shouldn't have to remind you that as long as our Constitution lives, we need to live by it. And you're part of that process."

William suffered through the debate. He knew Brice was right about getting a message of hope to the people. But William would not be pushed that easily, not with Elizabeth trapped in Moscow. He reluctantly agreed to Brice's request. "I will accept the nomination," William paused, "but I want your promise that you will do everything in your power to bring Dr. Blake back to American soil." He went on defending his policy against the virus. "Give her the best team of scientists, the best equipment and no double standard rules to follow so she *can* find a cure. Complete freedom and funding. No less. You and I both know my reputation as a war hero and my international political influence will greatly help you control the emerging chaos, and that more than any other reason it is why you nominated me. It's definitely not my good looks." William stood abruptly with his hands placed firmly on the table in front of him.

The door creaked open and a senior leader of the North American Defense Command came in, handing William a note marked urgent. "This just arrived, sir, from Moscow."

He opened the sealed note. He looked down at the unencrypted message and read two lines. William's gut wrenched. He took a long hard swallow. He eyes glassed over with a resolve Brice had never seen in William. "Mr. President, do we have a deal? Jason Blake, my son, has died in Russia. His death was due to the virus." The room hung in repressed shock with the disclosure. William continued, "The international team of specialist must be given the chance to solve this. This biological *attack* cannot be stopped by guns, missiles and backdoor politics. We, the leaders, owe that to our people." William words were tough in the wake of grief he held. His throat filled with knots of pain as he waited for Brice to respond.

"You have your deal. Talk to McShane on our CIA contacts in Russia," Brice replied. "We are transferring to a live public broadcast feed via our last international operational satellite. Chief Justice, will you do the honor of swearing in our new Vice President?"

The Chief Justice wasted little time in giving the oath of office to William. As she finished, she disappeared from the screen as quickly as she had appeared.

"Congratulations, Mr. Vice President," Brice offered. "Citizens, with our Vice President in place you can lay your concerns aside. It was a shock to many for our nation to endure this evil attack with no less than a coward's weapon: a plague. It important for you to know we are working endlessly on find a cure. Dr. Elizabeth Blake, the head of our CDC, is working with not only with the Russian government, but a highly specialist team of scientists to determine the source of the virus and a cure. I can think of no better person than Dr. Blake to provide the answers we seek. Thank you, America. God Bless."

President Brice signed off. The live satellite feed ended. The screen went blank.

"That's it? That is a tall order for Elizabeth to live up to," William huffed. "Well, that's what he thinks. We had a deal about getting Elizabeth out of the hands of the Russians." He glanced at General McShane. He seemed like a man he could work with. If necessary, they would become fast friends.

"I have to agree with the President's plan to put the nation at ease," McShane replied. "I see it as an added benefit for us. It will be good for morale under these circumstances."

"You think so?" William added sarcastically, stepping out from behind the podium. "Look around you." The room was humming alive with computer systems working overtime, interactive maps, holograms and attachés all franticly working to maintain communications with the outside world as, one by one, global communications systems began to fail. There was no one to operate them. Support systems ran unchecked. The world was coming to a halt. William muttered, "We will be back in the stone age soon."

He worried for the safety of his family outside NORAD. He wondered if he would even have a wife to go home to after all this. He still had Elizabeth. At least he knew she was still alive.

William looked up and saw a military attaché waiting for him. His hands held several recently arrived intelligence reports. "Well, what is it boy? What do you have for me?" William pulled out his pipe and placed it in the crook of his mouth. The young military attaché handed him a file marked Top Secret.

William's blood pumped. He held onto a thread of optimism and steadied himself for the worst as his eyes focused on the message.

McShane stood near. He reached for a pencil on top of the computer console and nodded for a pad of lineless paper. He asked, "Can I be of service, Mr. Vice President?"

"Our mole in the Russian presidential office sent this. It concerns Dr. Blake. It was reported she is under suspicion of aiding the bioterrorist. The Russians found what they claim to be one of their missing vials in her suite." William lost his temper. "Damn that Nikolai! First he keeps vital information from us on how deep his family involvement is with the mass grave site and then he has Elizabeth fly off to Russia. He ignores my phone calls and holds her as a political hostage, all to protect his own government's ass! The evidence is stacking up against him and his country," William fumed.

"With this new information I suggest we call in the remaining members of the Joint Chiefs of Staff," McShane said. "We need to move from DEFCON 3 to DEFCON 2. We can provide enough evidence that the Russians are hostile toward us."

"If I understand correctly, we don't have anyone left to contact. We would have to inform the President and he would have to approve the move to DEFCON 2," William said. He added, "I question if it's the Russian President. Looking these files over, I feel someone else is playing games. I have a better idea." William grabbed McShane's arm. "Let's go where it's less noisy. I need this to be a private conversation."

They approached the entrance of a dusty unused security chamber that dated back to the 1960s. McShane punched in the code on an old keypunch lock. "In here. Nobody uses this area much anymore."

William walked into the stale room and removed a linen dust cover. He sat at one end of a long conference table. McShane chose the seat to his right. Placing his pencil and paper on the table, he asked, "What's on your mind, Mr. Vice President?"

"I want to assign a Special Ops mission to go back into New York City and find out what happened."

"What is your plan?"

"I need a unit to go into the Waldorf and get the hotel security recordings. My gut tells me Prince Adar had something to do with this.

He was close to the Russian's escort. There may be something on those tapes to clear Elizabeth.

McShane wrote a single name on the pad of paper. He passed it to William.

Glancing down, William smiled and nodded in understanding. "Harrison. Special Operations Officer Harrison. I remember him. A wildcat of a man. Get on it, McShane."

McShane noted the base Harrison was currently stationed at. "Mr. Vice President, it's time for me to leave." McShane walked out the door but not before saying, "We'll do what we can, Mr. Vice President, but take a moment for yourself. I know how close you were to your son."

McShane wasted no time in putting William's plan into action.

CHAPTER TWENTY-FIVE

Day Five. Dusk. New York City.

Harrison sucked in deeply from the O2 mask pressed hard against his face. The smell of rotting corpses and burning human flesh tainted the air. The odor was too much even for his special face gear to filter. He held tight to the rappel line as it dropped from the recon helicopter.

His whole frame quaked with fatigue. His muscles were pushed to the limits. This was the fifth drop and final drop he had made into the disease-filled city. New York was finished as a Metropolitan area. Each time he hit the ground, he had to fight off the walking dead to keep them for stealing his oxygen mask, goggles, guns, or anything else they could get their hands on.

Food was in scarce supply. The streets were littered with carcasses of what were once beloved pets. He sidestepped the mice, birds and beagle-sized city rats decomposing in the gutters. Some had died from the virus; others had been skinned by the hungry and cooked over trash fires. Their bones and carnage were scattered in the streets. Human bodies were piled high in Times Square. More carcasses, both wrapped and unwrapped, were tossed on a makeshift open-air cremator by those left behind in the living hell trying to contain the spread of viral plague.

Harrison's eyes swept upward, scanning those in the safe houses looking on from their crudely sealed, duct-taped plastic covered windows. Too fearful to step out, they watched him calling, banging the glass windows for help. What they once knew as life had deteriorated into the worst primal state of humankind. He kept moving.

Harrison figured most of those living in the safe houses would not outlive the ones in the streets by much if they did not find a cure soon. He estimated they had only a 30 day supply of food and water before they would be forced to leave their sterile prisons. He cringed, knowing it would take longer than 30 days to clean up a city of this size, if there would even be anyone left to clean it up.

He was no optimist. He knew what he and everyone else were facing. He had experienced unbelievable horrors similar to these in Iraq. It did not matter if it was cutaneous manifestations, hemorrhagic fever, mycotoxins, pox viruses, plague or melioidosis. They all led to one thing: a painful, hideous death that made victims scream out to be shot just to end their suffering. He quaked, remembering a small baby girl's death as her mother held her head in a bucket of water to end her pain. The young mother begged him, then a private in the army, to shoot her. He almost did fire the mercy shot. Now he carried that guilty scar deep inside him, knowing that he could have shortened her suffering. "I should have pulled the trigger. At least she wouldn't have suffered."

That snapshot in his mind of that young mother's screams of agony continuously haunted him. That was why he had accepted the mission, risking his own life to go into New York City's dead zone. He could not bear for that kind of nightmare to play out again, not on his home soil.

Harrison's attention turned as he heard the rustle of trash in the streets. They were coming for him. He had to move fast. He jumped over a decomposing police officer lying next to his patrol horse, legs rigid with rigor mortis. Harrison kicked over the saddle bag and peered in it. There was nothing. *Damn.* They even stripped the horse's gear, Harrison thought as he moved fast, asking the same repetitive questions to himself. *How in hell did the virus start?* The first two drops had turned up nothing. The poisoning of the water filtration plant was confirmed on drop three. Now the question remained: Who released it?

Harrison raised his gun with the laser target up and armed as he swept the gray dusk air for anyone or anything that might stop him. He had one more visit to make: the Waldorf-Astoria. His orders to retrieve hotel security tapes and any other information that would provide the necessary intelligence to find those responsible for this and clear Dr. Elizabeth Blake of any thoughts of treason were critical to his mission.

Damn Russians, he swore. Damn Syrians. He'd have to find Prince Adar's guest room to be searched and fingerprinted as well. Hopefully the information was not corrupted and they'd see who the Prince may have been with those last hours of his life.

Harrison had held a great respect for William Blake ever since he came to his hospital bed after Harrison took a bullet for his sergeant. He had not hesitated to help the man now and had jumped at the chance to help after watching the Secretary be sworn in as Vice President. Harrison was one of the handful of special ops personnel trained for this type of mission. This would be his final mission, he thought as he entered the Waldorf-Astoria.

It looked and smelled like the medieval black plagues he had learned about in history class. Bodies were wrapped in the posh hotel sheets, bound with fine cords from the drapery that no longer hung in front of the once crystal clear windows. It appeared there was no life in the lobby except for the wind blowing dust through the broken glass doors. He saw the broken locks of the Waldorf-Astoria's main entrance. They had not held out the rioters for long. The scene looked deserted, but Harrison knew better. He knew those eyes were watching him. This mission was going to be more dangerous than he expected. He moaned inside. Instinctively, he knew he needed to find an alternate exit route. If he came through here again he would be outnumbered by the savages that were once upstanding New Yorkers.

Catching a glimpse of movement near the security doors he ran to the lobby desk and jumped on the counter. He fired at three men. Their faces nearly shocked him as he noticed the oozing pox covering them. They all scattered except for one man who still possessed enormous upper-body strength, considering his sickly condition. The sore-covered man grabbed and flung a fine wooden chair at him.

Harrison dropped to the ground. The one thing no professional soldier should ever let happen to him happened: he lost his gun. The weapon fell next to him, tumbling beyond his reach. "Shit!" he said as the big man's eyes fell on his semiautomatic submachine gun and then on him. He knew he was a goner if this man got hold of him. Time was not on his side. He had to complete his mission before dark or his team unit would have to leave him there to his fate. The pilot had orders to pull off as soon as night hit. He jumped to his feet and left his gun untouched. He had no time to pull his pistol out as the pus-covered Neanderthal went for a single cross punch to the jaw. Harrison sidestepped it and connected a knuckled punch to his torso.

As the man howled in pain, Harrison sprang at him. Butting his head into his adversary's chest he heard what he wanted to hear: the man's expulsion of breath. Harrison swept his right foot into the man's ankles. The attacker took a bone-crunching fall on the marble tile. Before the man hit the ground Harrison had snatched up his gun and fired at two disease-covered young men who began to rush him.

With racing, skillful movements, Harrison yanked out a tear gas canister and pulled the pin. Tossing it in the direction from where others had begun to surface, he tugged once to adjust his camouflage jacket and combat vest. He looked around and found the security room doors. Without a single breath of uncertainty, he rammed the door open.

Time was of the essence since tear gas would soon fill the room. Glad for his oxygen mask, he started his search. As he searched the office files he found what he was looking for: the CCTV recordings of who went in and out of the place. He pressed the button, releasing the disc from the HD DVR security system. He slipped the disc into his pocket. Harrison reviewed the disc storage rack as he started to run his finger down the dates and floor numbers. "Floor 42, that's it." He plucked those off the shelf and stuffed the storage cases into his combat bag.

Harrison's intuition was burning. He knew they were coming for him. He heard at least 30 of them hollering. Maybe more. He checked his time. "Crap. I'll never make it back to the pickup point." He radioed ahead. "I'm running late at the Waldorf. It seems I have a few hungry mutants to deal with. Meet me at the hotel. Drop a tag line for the discs. It looks like I am staying for the party."

Without waiting for an answer, Harrison pushed the dead security guard draped over the emergency console onto the floor. He engaged the emergency generator override button. The audible emergency notification system started sounding and the emergency lights started to flicker. He ran over to the elevator bank and pried open one of the service elevator doors. He slipped in the elevator just as the door gave way. He pushed the button for the VIP floor as he opened the top hatch and climbed out, perching himself on top of the elevator cab. With any luck he hoped to get to the floor before the mutants figured out how to shut down the generators.

Luck was not on his side. The elevator ground to a halt. "Blast them! How in the hell did they figure out how to shut that off so fast?" Looking up the elevator shaft he noticed it was a short two floor ascent to reach the VIP floor. He pulled a powered hoist off his belt and hooked it on the cables, holding his bag against his side as the hoist pulled him up to the 42nd floor.

Harrison immediately found the backside elevator door release latch and opened the doors. With his burning muscles, he gave it all he had and swung through the doors, rolling to a stop on the floor. Hopping up, Harrison made his way cautiously through the hallway, sweeping his gun, looking for any movement with his trained eyes. After completing a detailed sweep he found that there was no one else on the floor.

He radioed his team. "I'm on the 42nd floor. I'm going into room 4211 now. Bring the chopper. I'll hand the discs off to you. Then get the hell out of here!"

Harrison pulled from his gear a master lock card specially made for this mission and swiped it through the electronic door reader. He pulled out a battery-operated power unit the size of a deck of cards to provide temporary power to the reader and electronic door lock. Zapping the electronic lock, the green light lit up. Entering the room, Harrison wedged the door open with a crystal ash tray he snatched from a small table near the door. He glanced down the hallway, looking for the fire exit door. He immediately noticed that the stairway was exit only and could not be opened from the other side. He was secure.

He rolled out a fingerprint kit and dusted the handles of room 4211 for prints. Nothing. He dusted the door. Nothing. *Shit. God, give me something... anything!* Harrison's keen sense picked up the sickening odor. The odor was coming, maybe from a half a floor down. The rotting flesh of the mob wafted through the halls and passed through his mask.

Shutting the door and locking it, he dusted the back of the door. His luck changed. There was a full handprint. He taped over the black powdered print and lifted it. Placing it carefully in a waterproof case, he stored it with the security discs.

As he dropped his combat bag on the floor next to the sofa and knelt down, he hit the jackpot. Out of the corner of his eye he saw sitting under the sofa an empty vial with Russian codes etched on one side.

Bingo. He took out a special plastic bag and dropped the vial in it before securing it with the other findings in the bag. Patting it, he said aloud, "All I need now is to get you out of this city of death. One way or another."

Harrison heard the cries of the sick coming. He pulled two tear gas canisters from his combat belt and laid them on top of the glass coffee table. Standing up and taking a step backward, he aimed his submachine gun at the window and blasted it open. Radioing, he inquired, "What is your ETA?"

"Harrison, we're here."

"Send a rope and hook down for the mission bag. Forget me. Not enough time."

A squeal poured over his earpiece. He hit his helmet twice to knock out the static. What the hell was that? He keyed the radio. "Repeat?" Harrison could not hear what his team leader's orders were. "Oh, great. What are they using to jam my signal?" he muttered as the door suddenly took a hit from some kind of axe. The blade withdrew and another gouged the door. Harrison turned on his night vision gear. The light of dusk was gone. Night had fallen. His deep blue eyes grew razor sharp. Adrenaline rushed through his body.

"Hey, fellas, they're using a damn fire axe to cut down the frickin' door. Get the hook down now! Where the hell are you?" With some relief, Harrison heard the whirl of helicopter blades. He hurried to the window, but he saw no rope drop.

"Drop the rope. Drop the rope, damn it! They're almost through the door." Harrison thought fast. He bulldozed the suite's sofa against the door and wedged it in to delay his inevitable fate. Backing toward the window, he glanced back into the darkness. No rope. He glanced down the street. It would be a long fall, but he had to jump.

Harrison began to sweat rivers under his combat fatigues. He clipped the mission bag to his vest alongside several AA battery-sized self-detonation devices. If the bag pulled on the activated devices on the way down it would be possible to lose a hand or more. His combat vest would keep the bag safe for only so long. A team member would be able to disarm the recovered bag, but would have to get to it before dawn. He yelled over the radio. "You better call in backup and retrieve my body when this is over. I just armed myself. You won't find the mission bag after daylight. The scavengers will get it. Pour in the tear gas and rain the rubber bullets on the crowd. I hate to think I died for nothing." He placed his finger on the trigger. "Guys, I'll take out as many of them as can before they get me."

The door splintered open and the wedge failed as a rush of deformed bloody, oozing, sore-covered mob poured in the luxury suite. "I failed," he said into his radio microphone.

"No, you didn't! Jump, Harrison!" His team leader hung outside the window, suspended on a hoist line, waiting to catch him. "Jump!"

Harrison turned and leaped for his team leader. The mob struggled to topple over the makeshift barricade. With one arm hanging onto his team leader and his legs wrapped around him, Harrison fired two single shots at the tear gas canisters. He grinned as they exploded. Harrison had made it. He used his gun to give a salute goodbye to the gagging mob as he and his team leader were hoisted up to the safety of the helicopter.

Once on board, Harrison carefully unarmed the detonation devices. "Gee, Harrison, you scare me sometimes. Did you think it was necessary to arm yourself for hotel security discs?" the team leader inquired.

Harrison could not explain his feelings. He coolly said, "Yes." As he unzipped the pouch attached to his camouflage vest, he asked, "What's our method of contact with command?" He pulled out the security records.

"We have an encryptor on board that goes directly to NORAD. The fanciest email I have seen in awhile. It's the latest and has total breakaway security safeguards."

"Here then. Send these recordings direct feed to Vice President Blake as ordered. You have the pass codes?"

"Yeah, Harrison." Within seconds the images on the recordings were transmitted securely. The helicopter banked right and flew toward home base, clearing the restricted area.

The team leader said, "Harrison, Vice President Blake is on the line."

Harrison removed his mask and rubbed his hand over his damp hair. He picked up the two way radio and responded. "Mr. Vice President, sir. Special Ops Harrison here."

"Officer Harrison. Benny, you did an amazing mission. With what we've seen on the feed line, you have just given us the terrorist who caused this. It's enough to clear Dr. Blake's name. Thank you. There is recognition and a medal in this somewhere. Did you find anything else?"

"Yes, sir, a handprint and a vial labeled in Russian. Sir, if I may say so, it looks like an antivirus label. I've seen enough in the war to recognize the labeling, sir."

"Really. Harrison, you have been a great service to your country. I have to get you to NORAD. Get cleaned up and get those items here as fast as you can."

"Yes, sir," Harrison said.

The team leader warned, "Be careful, Harrison. They want to sign you up again. I would bet your next assignment would be worse than this. You almost didn't make it out this time." Harrison half-laughed as he began to remove his bio-suit. "Hey, Harrison. You need to check that out with the medics." His team leader pointed to the side of his neck. "It looks like a pox mark starting up."

Harrison tugged his collar open. He looked at the reflection in the window. "It's only a bug bite. It looks like we all got bit up tonight." He nodded to the pilot's uncovered neck and glanced to his team leader's wrist.

The team leader rubbed his wrist. "We had all better go to the medic after this. You'll have to put your trip to NORAD on hold."

"What are you worried about, Sarg? We all had our 'dog shots'," he joked. "We just got bit up tonight by the mosquitoes."

"There have been a few guys from our unit on sick leave."

Harrison confidently said, "It's a bite. Look: no pus, no inflamed skin. That's how it starts and we shouldn't even get the common cold with all vaccines they pour into us."

"OK," the team leader conceded. "But have it checked out anyway before you arrive at NORAD. After you see the medics, I'll sign off on your assignment."

Harrison smiled as he packed up some gear, winking at his leader saying, "Nice to be in demand. Well, let's not keep the Vice President waiting." Benny breathed a little easier as the memory of the young mother replayed in his mind for what seemed like the millionth time. One day he would shake that off, and with every mission he came closer.

CHAPTER TWENTY-SIX

Day Five. 8:30 p.m. MST. NORAD.

William was awakened by pounding on his door. Sleep, when he could find it, had been fitful. His dreams turned into nightmares. His sanity was held hostage by the real life nightmares being played out across the world. The sanitized dry odor of the non-aromatic carbon-filtered recycled air in the confines of NORAD made William long to be out in the fresh air. How fresh was the outside now? He did not know. The pandemic had begun its move toward America's heartland.

Another set of pounding echoed in his room. William's usual patience dissipated into frustration.

William hauled himself out of bed and appeared at the door. He cracked it open to find an agitated General McShane. He pushed open the door and passed William, walking into his drab military quarters. "Your man Harrison just arrived at NORAD. Unfortunately, he and his team didn't clear security. They are quarantined in a temporary sick bay outside. I'm afraid NORAD may have been compromised. We scanned them and found it the Russian strain. They kept the men out but not the information."

"I ordered any evidence sent to me ASAP," William said, biting back his guilt at exposing the soldiers to the virus.

"The screeners took their time," McShane said. "We were able to analyze the intelligence Harrison retrieved. It was a storehouse of information. We linked the captain's log from the Dostoyny with the fingerprints he found. The Waldorf's camera and security recordings gave us what we suspected. We can confirm it: the Russians and the Syrians are behind this. What we can't figure out is why Mus'ad's men were last seen moving toward Moscow. It's possible that President Stepanov had prior knowledge of this."

William guessed, "More likely Mus'ad is after some kind of

bargaining chip. I have known President Stepanov for a long time. I don't believe he had anything to do with this after reading the security files." He pulled his tobacco-free pipe from his robe pocket and gripped it between his teeth. "Tell me more." He paced over to McShane.

"Your gut was right. The Adar was part of this. That we know. We also have uncovered evidence that your niece was used to get the vials out of the U.S."

"Elizabeth a pawn." William cursed. "By whom?"

"President Stepanov's step-brother, FSB Officer Yuri Nevsky. He was her escort." McShane paused. "It's a strong lead, but we can't we prove it to the Russians or Syrian governments."

"Hold onto the information until you hear from me," William reasoned.

"Okay. The intelligence we obtained from the recordings tells us Yuri had plans to put the vials on the arms black market. We know Mus'ad has taken over Adar's followers in recent days, and he's even more dangerous than Adar was. The payment procedure was pieced together from conversations between Adar and Yuri caught by the tap placed on the Waldorf's phone system by hotel security. Unofficially, of course." McShane sat in a wooden chair at a small writing table. His fingers tapped the desktop. Frowning, he said, "The only problem is we can't get a fingerprint set from Nevsky due to his security level. The Russians made sure no one even has historical record of his prints."

William paced over. "They have to be somewhere. We have our special operations prints secured. They have to have theirs somewhere."

"Yes, probably, but for now we can't confirm if they are his prints on the door," McShane said.

"I want to see the intelligence with my own eyes. Does the President know about this?" William asked.

"The President knows."

"If he knew then why didn't he inform me?" The general did not reply. "What is it, McShane?"

McShane let his hand drop to his side while running the other over his clean shaven face. He said, choosing his words carefully, "I do not have encouraging news about President Brice's health, Mr. Vice President."

William frowned and blandly asked, "What is the White House concealing now?"

"It's presumed that President Brice is showing signs of the SV121R virus in its third stages."

William barely caught his pipe as it fell from his open mouth. "Can he still act as Commander-in-Chief?"

"Yes, but not for long. He may have only a day, maybe 48 hours before the virus manifests itself fully. We have all our best doctors working on it. Take this bit of information and prepare yourself, Mr. Vice President. You *will* become President if a cure is not found within the next 12 hours. After that, if we lose our military defense capabilities, anarchy will win. This is exactly what this Yuri wants. Then he can step in and take over with his men." McShane continued, "I need to ask you if you have had any symptoms."

"No, which it sounds like is a damn good thing," William bluntly said. "If that's the case, get me all the latest intelligence we have on Yuri Nevsky and the SV121R virus. Dead ends, leads, everything. Call President Stepanov. If you can't reach him... Who do we have over there? CIA? Special Ops? FBI? Anyone who could get to Stepanov himself if we had to?"

McShane nodded. "I like your thinking, Mr. Vice President. But, it will compromise our agent." McShane dialed out codes on his com link. His nervous fingers continued to rap on the desktop.

William hurried to his bedroom, showered and dressed. Buttoning his suit jacket, he walked over to McShane. "Anything?"

"Nothing!" McShane announced. "The Russian government has basically shut down. They are in the same state we are."

"Damn. What are our options?"

"We have two operatives. One is CIA who I don't think can get to Stepanov quick enough. The other is a long time mole in the Russian central government. If we use her and blow her cover, she's a dead woman," McShane responded.

"Any other options?" William inquired.

"No." McShane was worried.

"Do it!" William felt at odds giving that order, but saw no other option.

"I anticipated your answer and our informant in Moscow is on notice as back up if our CIA operative cannot make contact. I need your approval for military force if this fails."

William put an understanding hand on his shoulder. "McShane, if we don't do this, we'll all be dead soon enough. You have my approval. Send our Russian contact everything we have on Adar, Mus'ad and Yuri immediately and get it to President Stepanov with a message to contact me on my secure private line immediately after he receives the information. We will need Elizabeth cleared."

CHAPTER TWENTY-SEVEN

Day Six. 6:05 p.m. MSK. Moscow Central Clinical Hospital - Laboratory.

Elizabeth sat bent over a digital microscope linked to NORAD's bioterrorism systems. What was left of Russia's elite scientists worked alongside her. The room was secure in the basement of the hospital. It was an isolated laboratory created to deal with pathological agents. It was soundproof, fireproof, dustproof. It was also escape-proof, as Russian soldiers armed with semi-automatic weapons watched them.

"Damn that General Serebrinsky. He will not listen to reason. I can't believe he went over Nikolai's orders." She turned to Petruc. "Have you found a way for me to talk to NORAD?"

"Shh! I'm working on it," Petruc said. His eyes caught those of an old soldier as he glanced up. "You look sick. If I don't get my computer link soon, you'll all be dead. Your families, too." The soldier squirmed but said nothing.

Elizabeth turned back to the records on the table before them, flipping through years of old Cold War data, translating cryptic biological weapons codes. A tall, skinny man in his 40s ran countless blood samples at the centrifuge. The various hums, bleeps and whirs of pathology equipment filled the room. The background noises were familiar to her.

Staring at the monitor's flashes of genetic material, Elizabeth better than anyone else understood how important it was to ascertain the identity of this virus. It would give her and her team the best chance to stop the SV121R virus. If they did not find a cure, all that would be left was a planet filled with contaminated water, soil and air. She was working the last of her adrenaline to keep moving. The past days had been grueling. The team of five remaining at the Russian lab had agreed to stay up 24 hours with three-hour nap intervals. She had lost contact with three of her team members abroad and presumed they were dead. If she could at least get a hold of Robert, she could pass on new information. But even he was impossible to reach.

Dr. Petruc walked over and handed her a cup of coffee. "You don't look good, Dr. Blake. Your face is flushed and you're starting to sweat. I'm worried that you are showing symptoms of the first stage. You have been infected."

"We are all infected," she commented as he walked back to his station.

Elizabeth rubbed her strained, blood-shot eyes and sipped the cold black coffee in her mug. "What do we have here?" she asked herself. She placed the cup back down. She scanned the electron microscope image of the single DNA strand, searching for what the closest cousin might be. It did not match up to or even behave as a small pox virus should. It behaved somewhat more like a bacterial infection than a virus. Elizabeth sat back in unexpected skepticism when a rainbow colored DNA helix dancing under her microscope appeared. "This can't be correct." She stood quickly. "Dr. Petruc, I need that link now! Come look! See the identical pattern between Jason's tissue and this one?"

Petruc studied the screen. He ripped off his glasses. "I see it. I never would have thought this to be possible." He turned to the officer in charge. "Get the Americans at NORAD on the line! Notify President Stepanov! We may have a lead."

The soldier tapped into any Russian private computer link still operational to reach NORAD. "We have NORAD," another soldier announced a moment later.

Elizabeth froze the screen and spoke over the com link to her counterpart at NORAD. "Where did this DNA come from? Robert sent this to me just after our last call."

"The Russian oil tanker's captain," the NORAD medical officer acknowledged.

"I need the autopsy records of the Russian oil tanker captain. And send me the breakdown data of the oil on that ship," Elizabeth demanded.

"Why the oil specimen?" boomed the voice of their intercom link with NORAD.

"Do it. I have a hunch I need to play out. It's highly theoretical at this point. I need more proof. There may be a connection to oil! I need the image broken down more. This one doesn't fit into standard viral definition. This is too complex. It looks as if it's a new viral host pattern. A mutation or a new life form. I use the term 'life form' loosely, mind you. How soon can you do that? I need the image to be taken to the highest electron magnification. I also want images sent of oil-eating bacteria used on oil spills. The ones from Spain, Alaska and lab-created images. High to low magnifications."

"Elizabeth, this is William. What's on your mind, girl?"

William's voice was a pleasant shock to hear over the intercom. "Uncle! How long have you been listening? It's so good to hear you. We tried to get through. I'm sorry about Jason."

"Elizabeth, it's okay. Jason would understand. I need you to focus on what kind of killer bug we have here. Have you found anything? The virus has made every major city here and most of the free world a dead zone. Air traffic has come to a standstill. The only airplanes flying are the declining military air force and private jets owners who can still fly. The United States has grinded to a halt. What's left of public communication services has been reduced to old handheld radios and CBs. A few internet sites are still up and running on automatic. All this high-tech equipment and we can't use the damn stuff. Public transportation is gone. We are under Marshall Law. They are an angry bunch, with people stealing whatever they can to eat. Groups are banding together. There are warnings posted that they will shoot to kill anyone who trespasses. It's chaos." William vented his frustration. "The NORAD facilities and a few bases are still operational but I'm not sure how long they will be. When they go, Elizabeth, we won't be able to help you anymore. You will be on your own, sweetheart." William's voice faded with words.

The lab door buzzed a few times before Elizabeth realized a morgue technician had entered with skin tissue specimens from the grave victims.

"What is your hunch?" William pressed.

"I can't say until I get the images and reexamine a few specimens. I need those bacteria images as soon as possible," Elizabeth said.

"Well, then get them to her now!" Elizabeth heard William bark out his demands in the background. "You'll receive them in couple of minutes. I haven't been able to reach Nikolai. Have you heard from him?" William questioned.

"No. When I left him, he was still searching for leads."

"I see," William said.

"We have identified the terrorist. That information should have been received by President Stepanov as we speak," William cautiously added.

"Who?" The soldiers made it known they were listening in. She glanced around. "Never mind. Later. I have company."

"Damn them." William held back his more caustic remarks and refocused. "One more thing. You were right. The terrorist dumped the virus in key cities' water supply. Not sure how the crashed tanker fit in. Maybe a decoy."

"Hold on, a few of the images are coming through." Elizabeth slid her digital notepad closer. She wrote a few notes. Her mind dug deep, studying the makeup of the cell on the monitor. "When I have something more, I'll get back to you, uncle."

"Nonsense. Just play out your hunch."

Sudden concern for Nikolai's health crossed her mind as she continued to work. Maybe she should have said something to him and not let him push his sweating off as nothing. Nikolai was beginning to show symptoms. Stage one.

"Dr. Blake. Dr. Blake."

Elizabeth shook off her trance. She turned to the assistant. "Put it by the tray next to the specimen scope. Thanks." As the assistant waited, Elizabeth placed each sample under the high power magnifying lens.

Inspecting the tissue, she pushed the silver tray away. "These are no good. I need recent specimens and fresh blood samples. Where are the soil samples for the grave site? Bring the water samples, too."

What kind of new organism is it, she wondered. We know the water supply systems have been contaminated. But what about natural resources? I bet that is how it is spreading so fast, by entering wells and springs, even puddles or trapped rain. Elizabeth's mind was filled with a list of possible variations of the genetic makeup of the bio-agent as the assistant left. Her medical bag was at her side.

All of the hundreds of samples turned up the same pattern. The blood smears showed they were not within normal limits but the ranges did not show anything unusual. The skin was unusual. It was almost absent, as if it was eaten off. The victims seemed to have bled externally first and then internally after the pox sores opened. The one odd result was the autopsy on Jason and the victim from the mass grave site with the bullet. The sample showed some kind of natural anti-agent. If she could isolate it...

The gunshot victim was the only victim who had lived on the polluted grounds all his life. "Polluted with what?" She turned to her keyboard and typed up the last soil testing survey. "Yes, there it is. Oh my God, we were looking for the incorrect pathogen. It's not just small pox."

"Elizabeth, what do you have?" William boomed over the intercom.

"We have discovered a new type of bacteriophage."

"Bacteriophage? In layman's terms, doctor!"

"Listen. The soil is full of oil-eating bacteria. The host."

"The host? What the hell does that have to do with the engineered Soviet virus?"

"This bacterium is the smallest known bacterium that eats oil. The virus has mutated along with it, attached itself to the bacteria to multiply," Elizabeth rambled. "The killer is twofold. It is a genetically-altered small pox virus, the original bio-weapon. But now that virus has attached itself to an oil-eating bacterium and is spreading with it. And human skin tissue has oil in it. Granted our oil glands are not crude, but this bacterium doesn't seem fussy." Elizabeth waved to gather her team over to the monitor. She entered formulas and genetic codes as she explained, "Stage one is the bacterium that allows the host SV121R virus to enter the body cavity and take over the blood clotting agents."

"What are you talking about? Elizabeth, simplify please," William pleaded.

"The oil-eating bacteria are an antibiotic-resistant strain that literally eat flesh, human and otherwise. Once the host gets it inside, the mutated pox virus multiplies and adheres to human cells, resulting in pox symptoms along with the skin literally being eaten alive by the host bacteria. Once the pair enters the digestive tract, the altered virus takes over."

"If it's bacteria, we can kill it!" William exclaimed.

"Hold on, uncle. If we kill the bacteria, we still leave the viral host. It's a parasite, this one, and it would move quickly to find another host. It's not that easy. We need a vaccine, a cure. Antibacterial solutions may ease the symptoms of those in the early stages of infection, but they might die anyway. The miracle we need is an antiviral drug that treats this superbug as if it were a parasite. Kill the DNA, we kill the bug. I do not know if we have the time or the knowledge of how to kill the viral host and bacteria at the same time, except..." She paused, knowing what she had to say would be a death sentence for hundreds of key global cities.

"Damn it, Elizabeth. What do we do to stop its spread until you and your team find a cure?!" William shouted.

"It's like the old cholera epidemics. Heat kills, cold slows the growth. Cryo-chambers will help and from that point we can create a vaccine to stop the mutating host on others. My hunch is it started with the Cold War lab and test grounds, and then mutated in the abandoned oil fields that Nikolai's family bought up. Sure, they cleaned up the land, but the host organisms were still in the soil and water supplies, mutating over the years until the right bacterial host presented itself. I'm sure I can prove it when I get the samples. It was the water that carried the bio-agent everywhere: to homes, rivers, all the world's water systems. But the lubricants, the greases and oils, even lightweight oils used in buildings and factories to keep machinery working, provided the 'food' for the bacteria to feed on, to keep itself alive. One drop of contaminated oil in water would be all it would take to carry the disease. The contaminated oil that spilled from the Russian tanker in the ocean was enough to spread it along the eastern coast line. I'm not sure we can purify the waters. We have to protect whatever uncontaminated water supplies we have now."

"With the resources we have, that will be next to impossible. Then what? Last a few days, weeks for a few people? We can't put everyone in a cryo-chamber. Do you know what you are saying?" William quickly responded.

The locked double-sealed door burst open. The alarm cut short as Sergei and his security team burst in. "Dr. Blake, we are moving you back to your Eclipse. This lab is closing."

She stated, "I can't leave. Not yet. I think I found out how the virus works and how to stop it from spreading or at least slow it down."

"Take what information you can and I will send Dr. Petruc and his assistant with you."

"No. I want to speak to President Stepanov immediately." She crossed her arms.

"No," Sergei's gravelly voice stated.

"Look, you suspicious old man. People are dying and you're worried about me being a terrorist. Tell him! This is not the Soviet Union anymore, so stop behaving like it is!"

William hesitated to let Sergei know he was on the conference call, but realized it was in Elizabeth's best interest. "General Serebrinsky, we sent word to your President that we've identified the terrorist," he stated, knowing the general would recognize his voice.

"Who gave you permission to set up a com link?" Sergei glanced at his men.

"Stop it!" Elizabeth argued. "This is not about Russian security. This is about people's lives."

Sergei bit back harsh words. "You're right. What do you have, Mr. Secretary?"

"He's one of your men. That's all I can say. You know that, general. So call President Stepanov. You know me as well as he does. I am not playing a game with the life of my niece or the people of the world."

Sergei found himself in an unendurable mind game of Russian roulette with one of his men as a suspect and the Americans pushing. He walked toward Elizabeth. "I'll make the call. But keep it short."

"I'll let your President decide on the length of the call," she spat back.

Sergei ignored her as his phone connected. "President Stepanov. I have Dr. Blake under my security."

"Security?" Nikolai asked. "She was to be back in America hours ago. Why is she still here?"

"I'll explain in your office," Sergei replied.

"Put her on."

"Nikolai," Elizabeth began immediately, dropping all pretenses of formality. "We believe we have found the pathogen and how to slow it until we develop a cure."

"Great news. What do I have to do?" Nikolai was relieved.

"Burn Moscow."

The phone dropped from Nikolai's hand. He stepped away from his desk. He carefully picked up the receiver and placed it back to his ear. Cynically, he burst out, "No. I can't do that. This is the heart of Russia. No."

"Nikolai, listen!" Elizabeth forced her voice to be calm. "You need to understand." Her heart broke to be the one to tell him. "Burn Moscow and save Russia. Save Moscow and the whole world dies. You have no choice." She waited for him to grasp her words.

"Damn it, Elizabeth. You know I have no choice but to save this city."

William remained quietly shocked as he listened over the communication line, knowing that Moscow was not the only city that would have to be burned. Washington, DC, New York, Miami. My God, he thought, it would be nearly the whole eastern coastline.

"Bacteria in water and oils are host to a virus that travels in the oil-contaminated water." Nikolai was rooted in place. "You need to burn Moscow to stop the spread. Without a host, the virus is dormant. Burn the oil off. That takes away its food and buys us time to study it and create a vaccine. That is why the anti-viral agent will not work with the mutated host. It just slows the process down. There is no known agent to kill it. We have to find one."

Standing in his office, Nikolai turned toward the windows and questioned, "Are you sure about this?"

"Yes. I need more time."

"How much time?"

"A couple of hours," she softly replied.

William spoke, "Nikolai, William here. Our scientists have confirmed what Elizabeth just sent us."

"Uncle, you have to tell President Brice that all of the east coast has to be burned. All the buildings."

William, in a low unsettled voice, said, "It's spreading quickly here, Liz. Brice died a few hours ago. We kept it undercover. I'm the last one in the chain that is in charge. Elizabeth, I have symptoms of the super bug. Do what you can and hurry. I have a special operations team on standby to pull you out whether or not I am able to give the order. You have no more than 36 hours to find a cure and deliver it."

"Less than 36 hours to burn your capitol and cities?" Nikolai said. "Moscow will burn. You have two hours before we start. Do what you can, gather what you need. We will be moving to the Novograd facilities." Nikolai sat for a final time in the leather chair behind his heavy mahogany desk. "If you're wrong, Dr. Blake..."

"I am not," she countered.

"We'll see. Please return General Serebrinksy's phone." Elizabeth passed the phone back to the general. An angry Nikolai addressed him. "How dare you override me! Get back to this office immediately. She is free to go anywhere she pleases and if you disobey my orders again, you'll find a cold grave in Siberian waste land."

"Yes, Mr. President. The Americans identified..." Sergei shook his phone as static overtook the call. "Shit. The server is out." He tossed the phone to one of his men. "Find another server or get me the old two way radios. I need to find out who the American's ID'd. Start handing the radios out."

Elizabeth understood the impact of what Nikolai had said. "We have one hour to gather information from this lab and move it to the Eclipse," she told her team. "We have to make sure we're out of the area before he starts the controlled burn." She franticly hurried to review the new images appearing on her screen.

CHAPTER TWENTY-EIGHT

Day Six. 7:26 p.m. MSK. The Kremlin.

"Commander, you can't go in there!" the Presidential secretary yelled, scurrying in front of the thick bullet proof doors.

Ignoring the secretary, Dmitry pushed her to one side and barged into the Presidential office, slapping a thick manila envelope on Nikolai's desk. A serious mood settled over him. "You need to review this at once. The Americans sent it. This is a code red security issue." Dmitry's voice was razor-sharp.

Nikolai observed the bulky envelope. Pushing his laptop aside, suspiciously glancing toward Dmitry, he asked, "Where did you get this?"

"The CIA. With communication systems failing, they sent it in with one of their agents on her way to see you before she was stopped." Dmitry's jaw clenched; his eyes narrowed. "A CIA agent we had contact with before and an American infiltrator who was linked to this office gave their lives to get you this information."

"What happened?"

"The CIA agent took a .22 caliber bullet to the head trying to pass this off to one of our undercover men."

Nikolai's anger erupted in a fury. "Why wasn't Sergei aware of this? This is his area of expertise. This is twice he failed me. And to have a spy among our senior ranks?"

"The American operative in your office was good. I can vouch for that. It was a surprise to me."

"Who was it?"

"An assistant aide." Dmitry paused, bitterness etched on his face. "You were right about traitors in your office. How many?" Nikolai's lips tightened. Dmitry shoved the envelope closer to Nikolai. "Your answers are in there. Nikolai, take warning. The intelligence is very damaging," Dmitry cautioned.

Nikolai looked up at his brother oddly. He peeled back the sealed flap and removed the contents. He was sickened as he scanned the material, stunned by the name repeated throughout the report: Yuri Nevsky. "That bastard! I'm such a fool to have taken him under our family's protection!"

"It gets worse," Dmitry continued. "Yuri is not only the breach of security. The American intelligence shows he's the one, boss, who united the Russian mafia fragments."

"Do we know how long he has had his association with the mafia? Damn it!" Nikolai read the list of names of the assassinated scientists and heads of major international health organizations. "He has been planning this for years. And we missed it. Not one clue. Or they were covered up. By whom?" Nikolai felt the scandal in his bones. The number of medical personnel who had been murdered or succumb to the virus was astonishing. He groaned in silence, realizing there were not enough pathologists, biochemists, or even simple doctors left alive to manage this pandemic and its aftereffects. He smacked the file against his leg in disbelief. The Cold War bio-weapon engineers would have been very satisfied, knowing a single drop of a biological warfare agent designed for that very purpose: to wipe out the global population without shooting a single bullet, had worked.

Nikolai's adrenaline coursed in his veins. The same super powers that had failed to monitor the infectious pathogens on the false belief that the treatment would be as simple as antiviral agents would now be taken down by a tiny bug. The "caretakers" of the world, figure heads, watch-dog groups and presidents, had all dropped the ball.

Nikolai turned and faced Dmitry. He tapped the envelope against the palm of his hand. "Elizabeth was right. Moscow must burn. We have to evacuate the city immediately. Have my motorcar on standby and ready." He paused. "No one is to know about the contents of this envelope except family and Sergei at this time. If this has been going on for as long as I think..." Nikolai paused. "Dmitry, this photo of Yuri and General Pachen is from the same day the general was murdered. And this one was six months ago at the United Nations with Adar. Yuri has been busy taking over all the gang leaders since then. With Adar dead we need to find out who the other high stake players are. Mus'ad, his jihad-crazy brother, will be deadly to deal with." Putting a hand on Dmitry's shoulder, Nikolai called up an ironclad will. "You did the right thing to keep this a private matter between us. When Ivan arrives, tell him I need to know if Dr. Blake has arrived at the American jet lab. If not, get Anton to get her there immediately. She has to go back to America. She'll be better protected there. I can't promise her safety with the FSB compromised this way. With Yuri missing, he and his men could be anywhere."

"I'll check with Sergei. My guess is she's still at the Moscow Clinic with the few hours you gave her," Dmitry offered.

Nikolai nodded in acknowledgement. He handed Dmitry one of the photos from the file, showing Yuri with Adar, passing off the bio-agent vials in the elevator of the Waldorf-Astoria. "Make sure you get a copy of this to that blasted Adar's brother. Send a message he'll understand. He will be held responsible for the death of my son and wife. I want him to know that I know what they've done, and that I am coming for him not as President, but as a father and husband." Nikolai pulled open the side drawer of his desk. Removing his Smith and Wesson, he placed the gun and holster on his desk. "Root out his followers in the Federation. I want them to talk." Nikolai clenched his fist. "Offer money. If that doesn't work, use Sergei's interrogation methods."

Dmitry was uncertain. "We picked up a radio transmission to Yuri. Yuri made a stop before he came. We think he's in Moscow or arriving shortly. It looks like Yuri is using a train to smuggle Mus'ad and the remaining vials out of the country, but the American evidence is sketchy as to which train."

Nikolai walked over to the panel on the wall and pushed the control button. Monitor screens and a map of Russia appeared. Two monitor screens only buzzed. Nikolai huffed. "It looks as if two more news stations are off the air." He studied the screen showing Moscow's transit systems. Green, red, blue and yellow dotted lights moved about on the screen. They represented trains, buses, planes, boats, all the major public and private business transportation systems. "Find that terrorist," Nikolai replied. "Sergei will have to do a heavier investigation into the possibility of who else could be working with Yuri. Get him back here immediately. Anton can escort Dr. Blake and what's left of the team from the Moscow

Clinic. I want Yuri's associates in custody and neutralized immediately. Tear the place up, all of the Kremlin, if need be, to secure this office."

"Even with all the information, the chances of finding Yuri are slim," Dmitry pointed out. "We will need the Americans' help and more. Most of the European Union has broken up. They're all trying to contain the virus, which they blame you for." Dmitry was a realistic man. "It's not friendly beyond Russian borders. You are damned by the rest of the world."

Nikolai shot a hard look at his brother. "Get on it. I'm placing a call to William Blake. We will need them if Mus'ad plans a hostile attack against us."

A troublesome uncertainty washed over Dmitry as he watched Nikolai pick up the secure satellite phone to contact the U.S. Secretary of State. He took a deep breath and focused on the duties at hand.

"President Stepanov!" an exasperated William said upon hearing Nikolai's voice. "Finally. Where the hell is Elizabeth? She was to contact me on her arrival at the Eclipse."

Nikolai frowned. "You should have heard from her. Anton will be with her. Sergei is being called back."

"Nikolai, something is not right."

"Secretary Blake—"

"It's President Blake," William interrupted. Nikolai frowned. "Haven't you been updated? Our President and Vice President have succumbed to your virus. Judges. High-ranking military officials. Computer techs and other critical personnel. Nikolai, we are operating on a skeleton government here, maybe less. I contacted the United Nations to step in and change some of their policies. I suggest you do the same. My statements will be plastered all over the international news agencies that are still operational."

"President Brice is dead?" Nikolai shivered as he absorbed the news.

William ignored his reaction. "Nikolai, we're done playing with your damn red tape. I demand Elizabeth's immediate return. Have you seen the intelligence?"

"Yes," Nikolai grunted out.

"Yuri is your problem. The plague is everyone's. I'll help you where I can, but my concern, my country's concern, is stopping this pandemic.

That means securing Elizabeth here in the U.S. where she will have the resources she needs to do what she can. She shouldn't have been in Russia this long in the first place." William stated the facts bluntly.

Nikolai heard William's anger. He did not like it, nor was he convinced that he agreed with William's decision to influence the United Nations without Russia taking the lead on it. "President Blake..."

The title stuck in his throat. William his political equal now, their political relationship totally changed. Nikolai drew a breath. Dead air filled the void as neither man spoke.

"William," Nikolai's voice rang in. Calmly, he said, "You're right. But this is a not a good point. Listen. The engineered virus is ours. I cannot deny that. But Yuri acted on his own. As for Elizabeth, it still makes sense for her to work with us to find the cure, given the fact that most of the international team is dead. Dr. Petruc is our best and they have been working closely since she first arrived at Moscow Central. At this point, he knows more about the virus than anyone except her. I understand that you want her back. So take him back to America with her. If they work together, I believe she and Dr. Petruc can create the antiviral agent to stop this. You need us as much as we need you."

William's sound political wisdom kicked in. "You have always been a straight talker. That is what I liked about you Nikolai. I agree. Keeping this alliance strong is the only hope to stop this global disaster. We have to pool our resources together to learn more about how this virus works. If Elizabeth is right, she has to figure out the antivirus."

Nikolai, concerned, said, "Yuri is planning to put the vials on the black market tomorrow night. He is trying to get Mus'ad out of Moscow. We're not sure why he's here." Nikolai said nothing of his fear that Elizabeth could be a target.

"There are very few rules to go by now." William spoke up. "Nikolai, what information do you have on Mus'ad and Yuri's men?"

Nikolai swore softly at the worsening situation. "Just that Mus'ad's men are on the move into Moscow."

"Then they are after Elizabeth?" William was no fool.

"I have a team on Mus'ad's men. They will find them. Elizabeth will be safe." He paused. "If I find anything new, I'll get it to you one way or another."

Nikolai hung up the satellite phone. Total silence imprisoned him. He heard no sounds. He smelled no odors. He saw only a lone vision of his late wife, his dead son and Elizabeth, appearing in a mist-like swirl standing among the dead. Shaking off the vision, he looked at his brother. "Dmitry, send all the information we have on Yuri to the attention of President Blake. Fingerprints, personnel files, whatever they ask for." Dmitry nodded. As Nikolai flicked on several more lights in his office, Ivan impatiently entered.

"Where is she?" Nikolai demanded as Ivan arrived with bloodshot eyes, half-asleep and puzzled. "William, I mean, President Blake, informed me they haven't been in contact with her."

"Dr. Blake is still at Moscow Central. She and Dr. Petruc are waiting for several new pathologists to arrive. The last of Russia's top bacteriologists is with them and alive. Anton is escorting the team."

Nikolai, perplexed, asked, "With the latest news, has the security team with Anton been cleared?"

Ivan was confused. "Anton is assigned to her. We moved up a few FSB officers. We are cleared," he flatly replied.

"The new FSB officers haven't been cleared with Sergei, myself, or you personally?" Nikolai exploded. "Ivan. You haven't been informed. Yuri is our terrorist! The Americans found out."

Ivan was taken back. "You are kidding. I was at the hospital when I was given orders to return to the Kremlin."

"By whom?" Nikolai demanded.

"Your office. Maria, your assistant. She radioed your orders."

Nikolai heart pulsed. He marched to the doorway, flinging open the heavy wooden door. The desk on the other side was abandoned. "Damn it," he swore, letting go of the door. "Her background check was cleared by Yuri. Dmitry, send out an order to find her. I want her back!"

"Find who?" Anton pushed past the door as it was closing. He tossed a small package to Ivan.

"What are you doing here?" Nikolai asked, perplexed. "Where is Dr. Blake?"

"She's still at the hospital. Orders from your office said-"

"They were not my orders!" Nikolai stole a small glance at the computer screen monitoring transportation. "What's Yuri's plan? He's not only after Mus'ad." Nikolai turned to face his brothers. "This is serious if you are all here," he said as he briefly scanned them.

His brothers sat in chairs surrounding his desk. Anton's face was grim as he looked up from behind Nikolai's desk while Ivan unwrapped the bundle.

"It's from Yuri," Ivan said. He held up a chess piece: a white queen. "Where is that chess set you have around here?" he asked Nikolai. Dmitry walked over to a small mahogany chest. He opened the door and pulled out a chess board. "That's it. Give it here."

Ivan placed the chess board on the desktop, noting the locations marked on the sheet of note paper the white queen had been wrapped in, and setting the board appropriately. Following the sheet's notation, Ivan moved a white queen across the small chess board toward the black king. "Check!" Ivan said.

Nikolai gave him a look of puzzlement. "What the hell are you doing, Ivan?"

"That is your message from Yuri," Ivan explained. "To him, this is all a game. He sent instructions to set this board with four pieces: a black knight, a white pawn, the white king and the white queen. It said to place the queen on square C5, two moves away from the king. What I can't figure out is why the black knight and the pawn are together on H8." He frowned. "This is useless."

Nikolai, aware of Yuri's torturous games as a youth, warned, "He is letting us know what his next move is. Take this message seriously. He has the vials, the new pawn in his game, and he coming for Elizabeth."

"And you," Ivan added.

The door opened. "Mr. President, what's going on?" Sergei asked, entering with an air of confusion. "Why did you order me to Sheremetyevo International Airport? There's nothing there. All the flights are grounded."

"I didn't," Nikolai replied. "You were the only one to check on that order. Sergei. Look here." He pointed to the chess board. Nikolai stared at the game pieces. "There has to be some correlation. Find out what the squares mean. Places, locations, times. Ivan, get our best cryptographers on this. Tell them to keep it simple. He's playing with us. Yuri wants us to find him."

Sergei glanced at Ivan and said, "You don't need the cryptographers."

Dmitry rocked his chair forward and clicked the remote. "It is a grid map!" A map of Russia and its territories popped up on the screen. He pulled over Nikolai's laptop, superimposing a chess board. "It's a map. A4 is Moscow. You and Dr. Blake are here. E2 is a lot of territory without a major city, but Irkutsk is one area to look at. Yuri's given us a clue. But we need more facts, more information, to find the specific location. When we find it, then you will know where Mus'ad will meet up with Yuri. As for the white queen, he's letting you know he's coming for Dr. Blake in Moscow."

"And the white king? The piece not on any square?"

Dmitry pushed the king over. "Dead. Yuri plans to assassinate you. Bold son of a bitch."

"He's a madman!" Nikolai paced the floor.

Sergei adjusted his shirt collar, taking a seat next to Ivan. A dead silence held the air. Anton said, "Well, I for one will not let this happen." The rest of the team agreed.

Ivan noticed Anton's wrist was red, flushed. "Anton, have that looked at. Are you alright?"

"I am fine. Just hurry up and let's find Mus'ad and Yuri," Anton snapped back.

Nikolai walked over to Anton, grabbing his wrist. "How long have you had this? You didn't think to inform us?"

"It started an hour ago, just after I visited the water plant explosion site." He paused. "I'm not leaving. You need me. If I'm going to die anyway, let it be trying to save us, brother."

Nikolai inwardly cringed. Shaking his head, he said, "I understand, but I will not lose any of my brothers to this disease. All right Anton. Make sure Elizabeth gets out of Moscow. Bombs fall in two hours."

Anton grabbed an extra gun from Ivan. Walking out, Anton turned to glance over to his brothers. "Stepanovs. I'll see you later when we're done. At the old place."

His brother's nodded hopeless. "Sure, Anton. The old tavern in Rostov. We'll have a vodka waiting for you," Dmitry said. Anton shut the door.

Nikolai turned to Sergei. "There is one more thing to attend to."

With a look of solemn resolution, he pulled his wedding ring from his hand. He tossed the gold band to Dmitry. "Gather any other gold, silver and gems we have and secure them. Paper money will be worthless soon."

Dmitry nodded. "No problem."

Sergei frowned. "You are fully aware this may all be a trap. He is baiting you, Mr. President."

Nikolai shuffled his feet and hung his head. "I have to chance it. We have been compromised and by midnight we will know if Moscow stands or falls. If the fires don't contain the virus and it runs its full course, there will be no country left for me to be President of." Nikolai steamed as he pulled off his suit jacket. A raging fire erupted inside of him as he snatched the Smith and Wesson off his desk and slipped it into the holster. Nikolai's patience was being chipped away second by second. "I don't want to alarm Yuri. I don't want him to know our plans. Keep security on a tight leash." Giving a curt nod to Ivan, he asked, "What time will Elizabeth's jet take off?" He felt an overwhelming urge of control taking a hold of him.

Ivan shrugged his shoulders. "No time posted to leave, only arrival." He watched Nikolai hastily put his jacket back on over his gun, pacing back and forth. "Anton and Elizabeth should evacuate the hospital 45 minutes from now." Ivan walked over to Dmitry, reading his fact sheets.

"Wait. There is a train heading toward Anadyr," Sergei replied. "Mus'ad may be on that train or one heading toward the Chechen rebel towns. Not the private jet. I feel, Mr. President, that Mus'ad may be on the train and Yuri on the plane. Your step-brother has always liked fast transportation."

Nikolai picked up the white queen. "I see your point Sergei. I want Yuri arrested. We'll go to the airport. If I were him, I'd want to get her out of Russia fast. A jet would do it. Send a motorcade as a decoy to the train station with Special Forces. If Mus'ad and his men are there to assassinate me, then we'll beat him at his own game. If Sergei is correct that Yuri is using the private jet to get in or out of Moscow with Dr. Blake, we'll have both sites covered."

Ivan said, "We have to leave immediately if you intend on intercepting Mus'ad."

Nikolai ordered coldly, "Bring around the car."

CHAPTER TWENTY-NINE

Day Six. 8:45 p.m. MSK. Moscow Central Clinical Hospital.

The Russian pathologist brought the magnification higher. He carefully fine-tuned the lens. Puzzled, he entered the small laboratory examination room. "I may have found something useful, Dr. Blake. The DNA of the oil-eating bacteria is the same as the ones found at the mass grave site and at the Western Siberian Lab testing grounds."

"Are you sure? That could be the link I was looking for. Let me have a look." Elizabeth rose. Feeling her knees weaken, Elizabeth grew pale. Her spirits faded as she fell toward a nearby chair. The pathologist's hands circled her waist and set her down into the chair. He took her pulse. "Dr. Petruc, come take a look at Dr. Blake. She is ill."

"I am fine."

"No, you are not," Dr. Petruc scolded. He checked her skin for inflammations and signs of the virus. There were none. He found two small injection sites on her forearm. "And what are these, Dr. Blake?" he asked, turning her forearm up.

"We are running out of time. I had to be a test subject. The mice all died from the initial dose. The upside to this experiment is that the bacteria they were exposed to are dead, too. I need more time to confirm if the viral component was affected. There are two assistants who willingly volunteered to test the serum, too. They are in the bathroom puking. They seem no less healthy than before."

"What did you inject?" the pathologist asked, watching Dr. Petruc examine her.

"A prototype antimicrobial compound, part nucleoside reverse transcriptase inhibitor, part synthetic nucleoside analogue. The NRTIs should help the body break down the prototype into chemicals that will stop the second phase of the virus from infecting healthy cells. The analogue will help speed up and decrease pain in the body from cells that have already been infected. It has to end this pan-epidemic. I have no idea what the effect of it will be on infected animals. What we need next is a viricide. I jotted down a few base chemicals that might work. I'm sorry to say that fire, heat incineration, is still the only definite killer of the viral composite that I've found so far." She held out a small bottle filled with a brown liquid. "I don't know if the mechanism of action will work. I'm not even sure if this virus is a true bacteriophage. Either way, even if this is ineffective on the virus, it should stop the host bacteria. That's half the battle." She sat motionless waiting for a wave of nausea to fade. A few seconds later she continued. "Doctors, the side effects are unpleasant but manageable. I guessed at the maximum dosage a human of my weight could handle before it would become toxic. The mice had too little mass to adjust the calculations."

"What did you use?"

"Chemical and plant compounds toxic to us and this bacteria strain." Strength slowly returned to her limbs.

"Do you need anything?" He asked, seeing the color return to her face.

"No. Just help me forward this formula. It needs adjustments. This is the only bottle I have. I need the team to create a way to mass produce the antiviral component and administer it to the masses as an inhalant. Can you do that?"

He turned to Dr. Petruc and nodded. "Dr. Petruc, with your permission, I'll follow up on this and leave you to finish coordinating the evacuation. You know this hospital better than anyone."

"Sounds good," Dr. Petruc confirmed. "Let me know if she degrades." The pathologist gave Elizabeth a concerned look and went back to work. Elizabeth slowly rose, grabbing the arm of her chair to steady herself. She sank back into the chair. His medical skills instinctively acted. "Elizabeth, if you're having an adverse reaction, we need to know."

She waved him off. "It's passing. I can monitor it."

"How long have you been feeling this way?" he pressed.

"An hour."

Agitated, he tapped his foot, steadying her as she tried to rise again. "You should have told one of us as soon as you decided to inject yourself."

She grimly smiled. "Too busy working. The first steps are completed. Just get me some water. Sit down and take a look under the microscope and you'll understand."

Dr. Petruc handed her a bottle of water. Curiously, he sat next to her chair, peering into the lens. "The bacteria are still alive in this tissue sample."

"Its DNA is identical to the bacteria in the water and soil samples I have."

"Where did they come from?"

"The victims of the mass grave."

"Of course. Water. We have a confirmation on how it gets into the body," Dr. Petruc theorized. "I see what's been on your mind. The body is made up of approximately 70% water and natural oils, the perfect breeding ground for something like this. It overpopulates the digestive tracts good flora, flushes it out of the body. Then the virus moves in and attacks the lining of the internal organs. If the person can't fight off first stages of the attack, the organs develop pox, they swell and they burst."

Elizabeth carefully stored the prototype antimicrobial and several syringes in her medical bag. She gave a quick look at him and said, "You understand then. The prototype will work."

"Or kill you," He scolded.

"I would be dead already if that were the case," she boldly shot back. "I have to have a fresh specimen. A scraping from one of the hospital patients should give me the host."

"Yes, good idea. But you're out of time. President's Stepanov's man is already waiting for you," he said.

"Then we have to buy some more time. We need to get to the Eclipse. I'll drop you off at the Novograd facility and head home," Elizabeth declared. "Work on this angle. I'm not sure how bad it is at NORAD." She turned to her computer. "I am sending all the information there. Tell your team that if they can get to a cold site it will slow the rate of replication, buy them some time. Keep in contact with me by satellite phone. They should have image sending and receiving capabilities. If you find any breakthrough send it to my cell phone, too. Some communication towers are still operating." Her mind raced. She grasped his hands tightly and pulled herself up. She paused as the examination room door opened.

Anton walked in. Elizabeth almost did not recognize him. A few years younger than her, she remembered him as a clumsy adolescent whose voice still cracked when he spoke during her days with Nikolai. "Dr. Blake, it's time to go," Anton's deep throaty voice commanded.

"Wait." Elizabeth scribbled some notes and handed them to Dr. Petruc.

"We're not waiting," Anton interrupted. "There has been an evacuation in place for the last hour. Most have already left the city. The military unit is already packing up this area. We have an order to evacuate you and your equipment in the next 30 minutes. You're leaving now, Dr. Blake. The others will gather their notes and the equipment, and join you soon."

Elizabeth felt panic rise within her. "It can't be time yet." She dropped her hand and started to unbutton her medical jacket.

Anton took her arm and grabbed her medical bag. "This way, Dr. Blake."

Anton scanned his key card at the door.

"Wait." Elizabeth pulled two surgical masks from a box, laying her white coat on the table. "Wear this."

Anton slipped the mask in his pocket. "Too late for this," he announced. Several buzzes later, they dashed through the hospital. The hallways were littered with body bags and staff too sick to move. He pushed her through the smell of the dying to the entrance. Outside the sky was changing to gray storm clouds.

"Where is the car?" Anton wondered, looking at the empty curb. "It was here when I went in." He dabbed at his forehead. Sweat poured from his brow.

Stepping onto the curb, Elizabeth said, "Anton, stop." Pulling her mask below her chin, she lowered his glove-covered hand from his forehead. "I can't leave you like this. I need ten seconds." Anton looked on as she pulled the bottle and syringe from her bag and prepared an injection of the prototype antimicrobial. "This may kill you, too, but I can't just watch you die without trying anything."

"No time." Anton scanned for the Mercedes.

Elizabeth ripped his glove off. Running a finger down the back of his hand, she found his basilic vein. She injected him.

"Ouch!" He jerked his hand away. "Elizabeth, what the hell?! That hurt worse than getting all those military shots in the ass."

"That is still Dr. Blake to you, Anton Stepanov. Look, here it comes now." A black government limousine rolled to a stop several feet short of the hospital entrance.

"Why are they stopping there?" Anton complained, slipping the glove back over his hand. "Why is the secondary Mercedes here to meet us?"

Dropping the bottle and capped syringe into her medical bag, Elizabeth hurried to the passenger door. Anton hesitated. "Come on, Anton. Let's go."

"Stop! Don't get in!" Anton suddenly shouted. "The flags are wrong." The diplomatic flags' ragged edges were a clear sign they were old. They would never be on any Presidential motorcar. They should have been destroyed.

Elizabeth hesitated. "Flags?"

"Move away from the motorcar." Anton pulled his pistol out. Elizabeth backed away. She knew it was her misfortune as the front door swung open and blocked her path.

A scared-faced wiry blond man stepped out and ordered, "Get inside." He pulled the trigger on his semi-automatic weapon.

Anton hit the ground to dodge the blanket of bullets. "Elizabeth, get down!" Anton yelled. "Shit! Shit, I can't get a shot off. He is mafia! What is going on here?" His words muffled by the concrete sidewalk.

Before she could step back, shots rang out around her. An instant later, another man jumped from the driver's side and jerked the back passenger door open. Elizabeth felt a large hand encircle her arm from the back seat and tug her toward it. She stiffened as the blond man grabbed her midriff. She held onto the metal door frame and shouted, "Anton!"

Elizabeth's screams forced Anton's hand. He pushed himself to his feet and rushed the motorcar, reaching for the silver door handle. His body stiffened within inches of the handle. A cold gun barrel pressed to his temple and held him there as he heard the gun cock. Out of the corner of his eye he caught the image of half-bearded Mus'ad at the other end of the pistol. "Shit. Nikolai is not going to like this." Anton snapped. A wave of rage sweep through him. His stomach knotted as he watched them haul Elizabeth into the backseat. He shook as he heard the door slam shut.

Mus'ad took two steps backwards and pushed Anton hard to the cement. "Lay down. No need for heroics." He kicked Anton's gun away. "Anton, Anton." Mus'ad taunted. "You were the only one I liked out of the Stepanov brothers. Smart, very resourceful. Fast on your feet. Look at you now." He dug his heal into Anton's gloved hand. The glove ripped. Anton refused to groan in pain. Mus'ad saw blood seep through the ripped glove and drip around his inflamed wrist. He lifted his foot and placed it next to Anton's face. "I could ask you to plead for your life, you infidel. However, it looks like the bio-agent will be taking care of you. From what your step-brother said, it's a very painful death. Still, to make sure you don't get in my way and warn Nikolai..." Mus'ad pulled the trigger.

Anton jerked as he felt the sharp sting of the bullet entering his left leg. Gritting his teeth, he held still. Mus'ad pulled the com link from Anton's ear and stuck it in his own pocket. With one last kick, he growled, "See you in Hell. I will give this to Yuri when I turn over Dr. Blake to him. I am sure he would like to listen in on Nikolai's plans."

Feelings of powerlessness stabbed at Anton as he lay on the dirty gray sidewalk.

"Where are you taking her, you bastard? Flying back to your shithole of a country?" He pressed Mus'ad, trying to force out any information he might gain and pass on before the bombs drop on Moscow. He didn't like it, but it was best for now that they would take her out of the city.

Mus'ad quickly slipped into the backseat, wordless. The motorcar sped off. Anton sat up and pulled his tie from his neck. He tightened the fabric around his bleeding leg. "It's going to be a long way back," he said to himself. He hopped up and steadied himself as he edged toward a corpse who lay untouched near the hospital doors. He checked the dead body. Pulling old mobile phone from its clip, he pressed the buttons to contact headquarters. Curses fell from his mouth as an automatic message notified him the towers were out temporarily out of service. Anton tossed the obsolete cell phone aside.

"Damn it, where the hell did the military backup go?" He checked the time on his watch. Fifteen minutes before the vacuum bombs hit. "Oh, Jesus. Now what to do?" He hit the automatic door button and pulled himself up on the hospital's entrance railing. His leg writhing in pain, glancing back, he saw the taillights of the Mercedes fading out of sight. Anton began working his way back to the hospital laboratory.

The time read 9:35 p.m. on the dashboard as Elizabeth's body hit the leather seat hard. Her mouth went dry as the door lock snapped shut behind her. Steadying herself, she brushed her hair out of her eyes and sat to face her abductors. Heavy smoked filled the motorcar and stung her eyes, robbing her of air. She blinked at the men across for her. "I must be having a hallucination."

She could not hide her shock at seeing Mus'ad and a man she did not recognize wearing a conductor's uniform under his jacket, cigars pinched between the conductor's lips. Mus'ad laughed at her as she coughed, her lungs burning from the smoke. The tainted air left her lungs in a rush. She boldly asked, "Where are you taking me?" Her heart pounded wildly in her chest as she tried to make sense of her kidnapping.

"To Yuri. But first he will have to pay back all the money we gave him and more for your pathology services," said Mus'ad. The odd man crushed his cigar in the ashtray, blowing a final stream of smoke circles toward her.

"You are crazy," Elizabeth replied, drawing back into her seat. Mus'ad raised his hand in warning to slap her face at the remark. Her eyes filled with a new, deeper panic.

Instead, his hand dropped and lowered his cutting gaze to her breasts. "I do not think Yuri will mind if I check out the goods first." He slipped his hand over her skirt-covered thighs.

Mus'ad's violating stare stung at her skin. It left Elizabeth cold. She pushed his had away and gently crossed her arms. "So much for your sacred righteousness," she scoffed at. Mus'ad grinned. She struggled to calm herself, emotionlessly watching her kidnappers, searching for any opportunity to escape. She bit the inside of her lip to keep her panic in check. She knew she had to gain control over fear if she were to survive they can use against her.

"Are you vaccinated?" she asked abruptly.

"Vaccinated? Everyone's been vaccinated. Yuri's small pox vaccination works," Mus'ad replied.

"Are you sure about that?" She pointed to the young mafia man beside her with a flushed face. "He's been vaccinated?"

The man's attention was drawn immediately. "Adar was right. He said Yuri would fail," the young man shot out.

"Shut up! Adar is dead. Yuri is not. Who is the failure?" Mus'ad picked up on his dissatisfaction with Yuri. "You want something? What is it?" Mus'ad asked.

The man leaned forward in his seat. Mus'ad was right. He wanted more than his cut.

The young mafia hired hand demanded, "I almost died getting this car off Kremlin property. Not to mention the train Yuri wanted. I was almost caught twice!"

"It is what you were paid to do?" Mus'ad said.

"I want more money. If I don't get it, we will end it. You hear?" He opened his jacket to reveal several sticks of explosives strapped to his chest.

Elizabeth pulled her medical bag onto her lap and reached for the door handle. Mus'ad struck her hand. She pulled it back. He looked at the nicely rigged bomb jacket and calmly questioned, "You would blow us and yourself up for more money?" He let out a laugh. "I like you. You are okay. Let's work this out." Mus'ad reached over. He patted the young man's shoulder.

"I want a half a million now. My life may not be worth it, but hers is. Half a million or I push the detonator," the young man nervously demanded.

Turning to Elizabeth, Mus'ad eyed her antique necklace. "What an unusual necklace. Old Russia. Faberge? Those are real diamonds. A few carats guessing by their size." Her spine tingled at his pretentious voice. "It was a gift?" Elizabeth ignored him. Mus'ad ripped her precious golden heirloom from her neck.

Elizabeth raised her hand to her neck feeling for the missing necklace. Her heart broke. It had been her grandmother's. Her eyes flicked up in anger as Mus'ad back and tossed it to the young mafia operative. The man snatched the heirloom in midair.

Mus'ad's said, "That's worth more than any funds I could arrange for you later. Take it and leave or you will be dead before you have a chance to blow up anyone." He hit a button. The door swung opened on the moving car. "This is your exit." He shoved the young man from the car. He was amused by the sound of a small explosion as the car continued on its path. He pressed another button and the door slammed shut.

Elizabeth's felt disgust. She forced herself to focus on escape. The motorcar pulled off onto a small country dirt road a few miles outside the city limits. "Foolish woman," Mus'ad muttered under his breath. "Get your medical bag. We're almost at the Zhukovsky Airport."

"Why?" she asked.

Mus'ad's voice was cut short as the car rolled to stop. "Your ride has ended, Dr. Blake. You will not be going home, but to the Siberia mountains. Yuri is waiting for you, but, first I collect my money."

CHAPTER THIRTY

Day Six. 10:06 p.m. MSK. Zhukovsky Airport.

Boarding the Eclipse, Elizabeth stared at her only exit long after the lift door was shut. There was no time left to spend on lingering thoughts of escape. Her captives had her and the Eclipse under their control.

She promptly turned and walked to the communication panel. The normally sanitized smell of Eclipse was infused with contaminated sweat and rotting flesh as they made their way through the small corridor reaching the secured flight laboratory entrance. She gazed at Yuri's men's faces. She felt they had no more than two hours to live.

She pressed her fingertip against the access panel. "MARY, shut down security."

"I am sorry. I cannot comply due to alert status. Hostile intruders are detected," the computer replied. "Medical alert. The intruders' pulse rates are up. Fever. Scanning... All are infected with the SRV121 virus."

One kidnapper jabbed the point of his semiautomatic weapon deep in her rib. Elizabeth stood more upright. "MARY, inform the pilots we have hostiles. We are all infected. Clear us. If I don't get to the lab we will not have a way to work on a cure." She kept silent about the prototype serum in her bag, not sure if that was what they were after. She was not about to give it to Yuri's men.

"I detect an unidentified compound in your blood, Dr. Blake," MARY announced as she began running the scans.

Agitated by the delay, the gunman dug his weapon deeper into her rib. "MARY," Elizabeth said more sternly. "Code 024. Voice recognition 224. I personally provide clearance."

"Clearance approved." Elizabeth was relieved the temporary override code she programmed back in the States still worked.

Yuri's mafia men had found it just too simple to hijack the Eclipse. "We are in, Mus'ad," the gunman said into his com link. "But it's not right. Too easy." He wheezed. Elizabeth guessed he was in stage 4. The final stage. His lungs were filling with blood. She was torn, unsure whether to be a doctor and save his life or protect the serum for those left behind. Her mind was swiftly made up by the sound of Mus'ad's tormenting voice.

"Shut up! Think, you Russian puppets. With the virus killing off the military, few are left to provide adequate security. The virus left the American jet vulnerable to infiltrators like us. Yuri's plan is going well. Secure the captain of the ship. I'm leaving to meet up with Yuri at his Siberian Lab."

The sick gunman grabbed Elizabeth's arm. "Where is the cockpit? The captain's flight chair?" He spoke in Russian. He knew she understood him and understood him well.

"I see Yuri mentioned I speak your language. How unfortunate for me." She tried to delay his entrance into the cockpit, reasoning that the other gunman would soon be dead. That would give them the advantage: the captain, the co-pilot and herself against the remaining mafia man.

He smacked her with the back of his hand. Elizabeth stumbled to the floor. A series of red flashing lights began.

"No, MARY! It is an order." MARY stopped the defense procedures, deactivating the laser weapon. Elizabeth knew MARY would have fired as soon as the gunman was close enough, and she couldn't take the chance of the other gunman shooting a hole in the living nano-skin of the Eclipse. She pulled herself up and steadied herself. "This way."

Walking deep into the Eclipse, they entered the lab and saw the cock pit door open. The captain and his co-pilot hands' were already raised, having been notified by MARY.

"Good," the gunman said while the other kidnappers flocked the cabin door. "Get us up in the air, captain."

"I don't speak Russian," the frustrated captain said in English.

He nodded to his sick partner. "Translate." The gunman was breathing heavily. Small droplets of blood had formed on the inside of his nostrils.

Elizabeth translated for him. "He wants you to take her up." She turned to the six-foot mafia man. "Where to?"

"West Siberia mountain range. Input the coordinates I will give you when we are out of Moscow air space."

The captain glanced at the fuel gauge. "We don't have enough fuel." He tapped on the LCD readout to show the mafia men.

Elizabeth quickly translated. She knew he was trying to delay the take off. The plane's hydrogen fuel cells were in working order and would provide more than enough energy.

"Looks like we have at least enough to get us out of Moscow," the gunman replied. "And this plane can land anywhere with its wing design."

Frowning, Elizabeth quickly overrode the captain's order, not bothering to re-state the gunman's words. "MARY, get ready for takeoff. Code 666." The captain gritted his teeth, hearing her command. He and the co-pilot took their seats as Elizabeth and the gunmen strapped themselves in inside the passenger cabin.

With a vertical lift off complete, they were in flight in seconds. A soft collection of hums, beeps, and buzzing drifted out of the open door of the cockpit as Elizabeth sank deeper into her seat with an unearthly premonition they were not going to make it back home. She was watching the life drain from one kidnapper. As the plane leveled off, Elizabeth unfastened her seat belt, looking for her telekinetic head set.

"Put it back on." The gunman pointed his firearm toward the black flight harness. His body was edgy as he cocked his semiautomatic weapon.

Elizabeth plucked up the small headset. "Do you mind if I listen to music? After all, where the hell can I go?"

He pulled his gun away from her face, allowing her nerves to calm. The ruse to regain control of Eclipse was risky but she had no time to worry about the risk. The enormous speed of the Eclipse meant it covered a lot of land quickly. They were already nearing the plains of Western Siberia.

She slipped on the telekinetic headset. Elizabeth mentally ordered MARY to silently activate emergency procedures to return to the United States. She closed her eyes to focus on that one thought. The last thing she needed was the cabin door opening or her thoughts being broadcast over the conference link. She hoped MARY would lock that down.

Crossing her fingers, she clutched her medical bag tighter with the other hand.

The short, stocky intruder walked over to Elizabeth. Her eyes locked on him. His walk was unsteady. The smell of rotten flesh deepened as he leaned over her. A half-smile flashed across his face as he reached out with his pus-covered hand, hoping to pull off her headset. "What are you listening to? I want to hear."

"Mozart!" she quickly replied. She pushed him away as blood sputtered from his mouth. Her concentration shattered, and the telekinetic system reacted. The worst happened. The lab table began to slip out. Cabinets opened, revealing emergency medical equipment and the audio conference mode played her thoughts aloud.

"What the shit is going on?" The sick gunman fired round after round toward the lab equipment.

"No!" Elizabeth protested. "It's just medical equipment!" Two bullets pierced the nano-skin of the ship. The sound of outside air rushing in filled the cabin. Oxygen masks dropped from hidden locations as the sick gunman dropped to the floor, heaving up bloody green foam from his mouth. Jerking in an epileptic fit, he died. His partner grabbed for the oxygen mask but was swept and slammed into a wall as his gun accidentally shot off a few rounds into the open cockpit.

"Fuck!" the captain screamed as the bullets rang into the open cabin, exploding lights on the control panel. He glanced over and saw his copilot shot in his neck and head, slumped over in his seat. The captain pressed frantically on the control panel, sending the Eclipse to a lower altitude.

Elizabeth reached up and snatched an oxygen mask. She breathed in deeply again and again until the plane reached a lower altitude.

The captain snapped off his seat belt. Setting the Eclipse to auto-pilot, he pulled his automatic hand gun from an inconspicuous location and fired several rounds into the hijacker. The hijacker slumped over as his chest was riddled with bullets. The captain stepped over him and pointed his gun at the other mafia man crumpled on the floor. He checked the pulse on the bile- and blood-stained dead man. "He's gone." Elizabeth nodded, still pressing the oxygen mask to her face.

Pulling open the metal latches of an overhead bin, he ripped out a parachute. "Put this on. We're in trouble. Damn hijackers shot up the main flight computer system. It's shutting down the back up hydrogen fuel cells."

The captain rushed back into the cabin as Elizabeth dropped the mask and began to put on the parachute pack. He pulled open the main flight console and entered a system code into its core. "Come on. Come on! Kick in!" the captain screamed at the panel. The console flashed and the fuel gauges displayed new levels. "That's it!"

He rushed back out the passenger area. "I was able to regain control. I'm going to try and land this crippled plane by hand. If I can't, I'll input a flight path landing just short of the Siberian mountain range."

Oxygen started pumping into the cabin as the nano-skin self started to heal from its bullet holes. Elizabeth looked at the captain. His nose had started to bleed. Stage three. She tugged to make sure her chute pack was securely in place.

A sudden beeping filled the cabin. "That's the fuel cells again!" the captain shouted. He glanced at their altitude. They would hit the ground in less than three minutes if he didn't get more fuel to the engines. He re-entered the code with a silent prayer and pulled out a small black bag secured by Velcro to the console panel. He walked briskly toward Elizabeth.

"This is going to hurt." Before she could say anything, he had grabbed her arm and stabbed a needle into her bicep.

"Ouch! What the hell was that?" She jerked her arm back roughly.

"A GPS microchip so they can find you. You need to parachute immediately. Recovering the plane is impossible. I'll fly her to an unpopulated area. It's the best I can do."

Elizabeth panicked. "No! You have to keep this plane flying. I have the prototype serum. I have to get back to America."

Unfaltering, he grabbed her wrist and pulled her toward the lift door. He shoved her medical bag in her other hand. "Impossible. Hold on to your bag, Dr. Blake. Count to ten and pull the cord." He raised one palm up and lightly touched her shoulder. "It's going to be okay." Before she could protest, he pushed her out the hatch door.

Suppressing a scream as she felt herself falling through the air, Elizabeth focused on counting. She opened her eyes and said, "Ten." She pulled the rip cord. She moaned at being jerked upward as the bright yellow parachute with an American flag on each panel filled with air.

Great, she thought. *No one is going to miss this color chute.* She glanced up to find the Eclipse. It wasn't there. She looked down and her heart stopped as she shielded her eyes from the blast of the Eclipse exploding into an open field. Black metal debris was tossed high into the air. A wall of smoke, jet fuel and ash blinded her.

Fury overtook panic as she took a breath of clean air after passing through the smoke cloud. Helplessly, she floated down to an open grassy field crammed with fully-armed non-military personnel. She groaned, crying in pain as her knees hit the ground. Her medical bag was tossed to the side on impact.

Elizabeth immediately found herself surrounded by a team of Yuri's mafia men.

"Get that yellow monstrosity out of sight," Misha ordered, coming to the front of the group. Two men stepped forward and began cutting offer her parachute pack. "Welcome, Dr. Blake. I am Misha. It's a pleasure to finally meet you."

Elizabeth glared at him silently, remaining on the ground, brushing off her grass-stained knees.

"Come on, get up. You're coming with me." He handed her medical bag to her as the two men pulled her to her feet. "There is a road up ahead."

Their footsteps thundered on the hard pavement as the dampness of the night air hit her. Misha guided her to an unmarked black Volvo hidden in the darkness. Seething, she tried to slip away from Misha's clasp. A door swung open in her path. She looked around. There was nowhere to go as Yuri stepped out of the Volvo.

"You have surpassed my expectations for a woman, Dr. Blake. I'm sure you will be honored to assist me with developing a cure for this..." Yuri's lips tightened and turned downward; he still refused to admit his great error. "This plague."

"Honored? I don't think so." She stared at him defiantly.

Yuri grabbed her arm. "If I didn't need your mind for the cure..." His eyes flickered with the fires of Hell.

She held her breath at his implied message. Yuri shoved her into the backseat of the Volvo. Sheer black fright swept through her. She began to shake as fearful images played in her mind.

The ride was short, too short. Elizabeth soon found herself shoved out of the Volvo and onto a train platform. In the distance, she heard Russian fighter jets howl overhead. Within minutes Moscow would be in flames. The sound of the impact of the vacuum bombs was so loud it vibrated everyone and everything, even at that distance.

"It's begun." She grabbed her medical bag close to chest, horrified when Yuri did not even flinch as the flames shot up into the gray sky in the distance.

"Are the cases on board?" Yuri questioned as he pushed past several men with signs of the pox on their hands and wrists, dragging Elizabeth toward the train. "Take my bag and get it settled into the passenger car for the ride to Tyumen. Dr. Blake stays with me."

In the last ten minutes of the car ride to the train Elizabeth had watched Yuri's face swell. His lips and eyelids were raised with tiny pustules. The skin on his hands was raw. She did not know how long he would last. "I can help you, Yuri," she offered as he rubbed his crusted eyelid. She did not dare tell him she carried the possible cure with her. She would not give him that power to hold against the world. She used caution in her words. "You don't—"

"Shut up. You will find a way to stop the cursed virus for me," he snapped. "We just have to take care of something first." Even in his refusal, it was the first time he had admitted he was at a disadvantage. Yuri turned to another man. "Do you have the detonator set?"

The short young man with an olive complexion responded. "I have everything." He looked at Elizabeth. The young man, irritated by the sight of a strange woman, questioned, "Who the hell is she? I don't think having her here is a good idea, Yuri."

"She's my new pathologist," Yuri replied with a cold stare.

"What the hell do you need this pathologist for? You've got the cure. Right?" his hired man questioned. "The plan has not changed! We blow up the train in Tyumen, destroy all the oil wells and half of Russia so you can have sole ownership of what's left as the last surviving heir to the Stepanov oil company, then we're off to Irkutsk with the money, the antidote and no government to stop us." He brushes his hands, said factually, "And that's that."

Yuri lunged forward, seizing the young man's throat. "I paid you enough to keep your thoughts to yourself. Shut up!" Yuri shoved him away. "Get on the fucking train." He noticed Elizabeth's attention on his man as she was pushed to board the train. "Don't get any ideas, my dear. He is a hired hand. He is in it for the money, not for you."

"You arrogant ass. Your hired help is infected! He'll be lucky if he makes the trip to Tyumen. And who else on board is infected? Everyone, I am sure of it. Would it make any difference to you if I told you the SV121R virus you so stupidly unleashed has mutated into a bacteriophage. Your antidote is-"

He yanked her arm hard. Her words fell off. "Did you just call me stupid? You pompous bitch. I can kill you, cure or no cure. And, no, it makes no difference to me." Before Elizabeth could get off another protest, he pulled her toward him as they began to board the train. Yuri nodded at his man to follow up the rust pitted steps.

Elizabeth stumbled. She became tangled in the gray metal step. "Wait! My foot." She pulled against Yuri's grasp.

"Hurry! I don't give a damn about your foot, just get it out. You're becoming more trouble than I need. We can always cut it off. I just need your brain." He cursed at her.

The man wrapped his hand around her ankle to release it. Elizabeth gave a shallow smile briefly to thank him. Yuri, enraged at his act, pulled his gun out and fired a single shot into the man's forehead. Elizabeth struggled for breath as the man fell to the ground. He had no warning of his fate. Would hers be the same? The fleeting though struck her.

Shivering at the thought of what future events may be, she was pulled through the corridors of several train cars. The train was outfitted with a mixture of freight cars and passenger cars. Yuri pushed her past the doorway as they finally reached the caboose, revealing three shiny, lead lined metallic cases.

Elizabeth recognized the construction specs. "My, God, you found a way to link up a biological binary explosive device! This is no ordinary dirty bomb. You made a bio-weapon IED. And you have packed way too much explosives into it. You really are going to take out half of Russia." Her voice cut the silence.

"Do you not know what shut up means?" His voice held an edge of steel. His hand gave her a shove. She was thrown against the wood-paneled walls as the train jarred forward toward its destination, knocking the air out of her. She filled her lungs with air. Steadying herself, adrenaline began to pump through her. She knew she had to do something to stop him. She lifted her eyes to meet his icy gaze in an act of defiance. Her deep blue eyes narrowed and hardened. "I will stop you," she brazenly stated.

"Go ahead and try, woman." He had no time for her superficial threats. Elizabeth watched the two men unpack, laying the last silver case down next to the others and opening them. Her eyes widened as she made out the tiny sophisticated digital system no bigger than a ballpoint pen lying within.

Yuri knelt over the first case. "Misha, set the timer."

"How much time do we need?" Misha asked.

"Enough time for us to get a safe distance before it hits Tyumen."

Misha moved to the second case. "We have a problem with this one. It is damaged. It will take time to rewire it."

Yuri coldly demanded, "Leave it for later. Calibrate and set the timer on the other one. We'll worry about arming the third when the train gets a few miles down the track. It's taking too long already."

Elizabeth waited. It didn't help as the bruises started to throb in pain along her lower spine and legs. She gathered what was left of her self-control, remembering the microchip embedded in her shoulder. She had faith someone was picking up GPS locations somewhere in the world. Her face blank and unreadable, she leaned back against the panels.

Yuri glanced at her. Watching her, her expression led him to a false believe she had accepted her fate. "Good girl. You're finally learning to come to terms with what is." Yuri's mind slipped away from his hostage and focused on arming the toxic explosives.

Elizabeth carefully looked around for escape routes. As she peered down the corridors of the train she could see clear through at least the next five train cars, one a passenger car.

Yuri finished with the first case and removed his satellite phone from the belt clip. Elizabeth raised a brow, viewing the colors displayed on his phone. The icons were unusual, flashing across the small screen. He entered a code into the phone and asked, "Misha, see if the timer is set and my codes match." The arming of the bombs seemed to be all that mattered to Yuri.

Her eyes fixed onto the digital read out: 120 minutes and counting down. The phone is the trigger! Of course, it works easily with the IED bombs. They are using sound to detonate it.

Misha moved to the duffle bag near Elizabeth's feet and pulled out four two-and-a-half-foot pipes. He called to Yuri, "We have to hook them together here and here, to stabilize the bombs' movements after we jump the train. Or the train's vibration may set them off too soon."

Yuri nodded, noticing that the train had slowed. "Here, I'll do that. Go see what the problem is. Tell him to pick up the speed, but don't spook the conductor. I had a hard time finding one left to operate the engines. He thinks we're smuggling medical contraband into the city. He's only been paid to pick us up and get us to the city. Hurry up. I'll arm the last case."

Misha left without giving a single look to Elizabeth. Yuri grabbed the pipes and began attaching them. He picked up two of the side-frame pipes, leaving one on the ground.

Swiftly, Elizabeth lifted the two foot pipe and swung hard and fast. Yuri caught her out of the corner of his eye. Her swing missed him as he leaned away. He fell awkwardly on his side.

"You bitch." He fumbled to his feet. His hand sought his gun but was forced to swing out to hold his balance as jerky movements of the train threw him backwards on the floor. "Damn train," he hollered. Elizabeth braced herself and swung again. She made her mark, cracking him on the side of his head as he stood. Yuri fell to his knees before collapsing. His body was weakened from the virus. He lay motionless.

The pipe fell from her hands as she scanned his body for life uncertain how badly she had injured him. Stepping over him, Elizabeth stepped over him, ripping his phone from its case and worked her way through the train cars. Her body moved with the rhythm of the train. She prayed Yuri's phone still had international satellite service. She moved fast. She waddled forward with the train's movements, grabbing onto anything that would help her balance. She dialed the only emergency number she could count on: her uncle. After two rings, she heard, "William Blake."

"It's Elizabeth. I need help. Do you hear me? Are you there, uncle?"

Breathless, Elizabeth raced through the third passenger car, holding the phone to her ear. Passing through the doorway, she found the fourth car filled with pigs and feed troughs. "Of all things, pigs!" she mumbled to herself. She sighed in relief, hearing her uncle's voice cut through the silence on the phone.

"Elizabeth, I am putting you on speaker phone. Where are you calling from? I don't know how much longer we'll have communications." William concealed his turmoil over her safety. "We're on the move to our Fairbanks research base in Alaska. NORAD was quarantined after we left. Your idea bought us time. The cold is slowing the growth of the bacteriophage. We're manufacturing the serum now on the Alaska base. It works, Liz! Our team confirmed it!"

Relief swelled in her at her uncle's words. The antiviral compound worked. If they could administer it quickly enough, there was still hope. She had to get to safety, to oversee the administration. Robert wasn't trained for this. Elizabeth shouted over the squeals of the penned pigs. "I'm on a train. There are three binary explosive devices on board. Two are calibrated to go off when we arrive at the Tyumen station with the virus. The third I am not sure about. ETA in maybe two hours. Call Nikolai. Tell him he has to stop this train no matter what the cost." The train jerked and she fell to the ground, nearly dropping the phone as it tumbled out her hands. She scooped it back up. "Uncle?" she placed the phone back to her ear.

"What the hell is going on? IEDs? How? Trains? Liz? I'm sending a team for you. Can you give me your location?" William was filled with dread.

Pulling herself up, holding onto the side of a pen, she steeled her voice. "We're on a freight train headed for Tyumen. There is a GPS tracking chip embedded in my shoulder. The Eclipse's captain injected it. Find the signal, you'll find me." She waited but heard nothing. She repeated, "Did you hear that? Two are armed for detonation." Squeezing by the animal pens, holding her medical bag overhead, she made her way to the next open doorway. Shouting over the clanging of the train wheels as they rolled over the tracks on a deadly course, she bellowed, "I don't know how much time I have left, uncle."

A dark wave rolled over her from behind. Yuri's voice radiated above the clanging. "Bitch! I see you! I am coming for you!"

Panic began to set in. She desperately searched for an exit. Nowhere to go. She took a deep breath and said with finality, "Send my coordinates to Nikolai. He is closer. You should be able to get my GPS reading dead or alive as long as the signal holds." She made it clear, "Uncle, tell Nikolai to not let Yuri use me to his advantage. I'm expendable now that you have the formula." Resigned to her fate, she disconnected the call and looked around the train car. "There has to be a way off," Elizabeth groaned, passing through a fourth boxcar. She glanced over her shoulder and saw in one dim corner an animal groomer's pen with clean hay, tools and brushes. A rusty iron bar ran along the wooden panel boxcar wall above the tools. "Animal hitches," she mumbled to herself.

Her eyes focused on the set of groomer's tools. She buried Yuri's phone deep in a trough of animal grain that lined one pen. If she was going to die, she would give Yuri hell first. Moving toward the tools, she grabbed a smallest of brushes that matched the size of Yuri's phone. She set out to use the brush as a decoy. Elizabeth glanced back and saw Yuri's broad body slowing him down as he made his way between the narrow walkway of the passenger car, still far enough away not to make out the grooming brush, or so she hoped. Holding up the fake phone, she waved it at him. A glimpse was all he had.

"Not the phone! The detonator!" Yuri screamed.

Straddling the doorway between boxcars, the wind stung her face. Her long hair whipped around. She raised the bogus phone back quickly waving it in his direction. "Say goodbye to it!" she called out to Yuri before tossing the decoy into the black night air.

Yuri raged. "You really did it." He said in disbelief. "You killed my plans! Even if I had another I am out of time." Vile, horrible, revolting images flickered in his head. Images that the devil himself could not even conjure up as to how he would deal with her. In a voice from another world, he said, "I'm coming for you, bitch." Yuri's voice echoed through the open doors of the moving train cars.

Elizabeth's heart stopped for a second. There was no time to think. She had to move. He was coming for her. She swept her eyes around the freight car to another corner filled with bundles of mottled hay stacked neatly to the ceiling. "No exit," she sighed. Opposite the bales of stacked hay were several small crates, lined three to four deep against the paneling. "Useless." Her mind raced. "No place to hide."

She placed her medical bag in the animal bin. She covered it with hay and tossed an old blanket over the pen's wooden gate. Elizabeth made a vow that if Yuri would get her, he would not get her formula. She turned and scanned the area again. Panic set in as her eyes focused on her only two exits: an unlatched cargo side door from which she could feel the sting of the night air and the other, an old rusty train door leading forward to more boxcars.

She peered out the open cargo door. Elizabeth hurried to the last closed door. She yanked it open. "This has to be a way out." She told herself. What was before her eyes siphoned the blood from her. Elizabeth nearly screamed at the sight of a long, metalized flatbed. Her escape route was a dead end. She cursed. Elizabeth's choice was made for her in that moment. "I have to jump," she said aloud. She focused on keeping her bruised body and fragile control intact.

Stepping away from the door, she made her way to the open cargo hatch. The hot and sticky wind stung her face. A mean storm was brewing. Her long hair tangled in the wind from the open door while she judged the train's speed. She had no time to determine that if speed was even slow enough to safely jump toward the grass-covered ground passing before her. She pushed off only to be hauled back. She felt a wicked grip on her messed hair and screamed as her body fell backwards, tossed like a ragdoll to the boxcar floor.

Yuri stood over her. His temple bleeding from her strike, his face contorted in evil thoughts of revenge. She would not die easily.

CHAPTER THIRTY-ONE

Day Six. 10:35 p.m. MSK. Sheremetyevo Airport.

Lightning flashed outside the Sheremetyevo Airport as a storm approached. Inside the Mercedes, Nikolai felt trapped as he gave the order to burn Moscow. Ivan was silent in the driver's seat.

Nikolai was frustrated. He grabbed a pair of new tan leather gloves from the box that lay at his side. He was showing symptoms of the virus. He hoped Anton had secured Elizabeth. At least she would be safe. He doubted he would make it to the Novograd facility.

The front passenger door opened. "I found this on the pilot seat of the private jet. The plane is abandoned." Dmitry tossed Nikolai a note wrapped around a black king and white queen as he sat next to Ivan.

"Yuri has her. It's a trap. Get us out of here!" Nikolai shouted. Ivan hit the gas pedal as a fuel truck rolled up in front of them. Dmitry broke out his semiautomatic gun.

Three men from the truck fired at the Mercedes. Ivan threw the gear shift into reverse, spinning 180 degrees and accelerating through a locked chain link fence along a runway. It was close enough to feel the heat as the tanker exploded.

"Did you see who they were?" Nikolai yelled.

"Looks like Mus'ad's men," Dmitry replied.

"Damn Mus'ad helping Yuri." Nikolai slammed his hand into the head rest in front of him. "Could you tell if Mus'ad is with them?"

"I didn't see him," Ivan replied.

The airfield was suddenly dead. No planes, no sounds, not even a cricket chirp was heard. Nikolai flipped open several compartments loaded with small arms. "Find out where Anton and Elizabeth are. I want to make sure there aren't any more tricks," he demanded.

The car phone rang. "What the hell?" Nikolai asked, looking at the dash. They never used it. "I thought I ordered the car phones to be disconnected months ago."

Ivan just shrugged his shoulders. Dmitry picked up the unsecured line. Ivan found his way back onto the main road. "Commander Stepanov," Dmitry said with uncertainty.

"Mus'ad has Dr. Blake."

Dmitry's mind registered his little brother's raspy voice. "Anton?"

"She was kidnapped from the hospital in a stolen Presidential motorcar," Anton said. His breathing raspy, sick to his stomach, his body fixed to the floor in pain. The hospital landline, knocked off the information desk, hung by his side.

"Yuri has her." Dmitry announced Anton's news to Nikolai. "He stole one of the Presidential fleet." A disturbed glare appeared on his face.

Nikolai reached into the front seat. "Give me the phone, Dmitry." Dmitry passed it off.

"Anton, where are you?" Nikolai asked.

Anton straightened his shoulders against the side of the information center, rubbing his wrists, and repeated over the static, "Dr. Blake was taken from the hospital entrance approximately twenty minutes ago. They headed east. My guess is they plan to steal the American jet lab. It was the direction they were heading."

"I said, where are you?" Nikolai repeated impatiently.

He heard a grim laugh over the other end. "In Moscow, of course." Anton hit the security panel, locking the blast doors of the hospital lab.

Nikolai hear the scrapping of the blast doors. "Get out. I cannot rescind my ordered for the vacuum bombs to be dropped. You have fifteen minutes tops to get out."

"Nikolai, her last words were to get to you." Anton paused. "There's no point in trying to get out. I am a dead man. I've been shot, my skin is inflamed and I'm coughing up blood. Do me a favor. When you see Yuri, before you kill him, shoot both legs." Anton's breath faded with him. He passed out on the sterile tile floor as the blast doors sealed him in.

"Anton? Anton!" Nikolai shook his head and handed the receiver back to Dmitry. "We lost him." Anton's news swept across Nikolai. "Dmitry, give me your transmitter." His hand urgently rose to press the small link fitted in his ear. "General Serebrinsky. President Stepanov here."

"Moscow code One, this is Moscow code Two."

Nikolai's voice deepened. "General Serebrinsky."

"Code two here."

"Anton is trapped in the city. Yuri has kidnapped Elizabeth and a Presidential car is missing." Nikolai swore under his breath. He continued, "Dmitry, get a fix on the last location of the stolen car. Sergei, find out who requested it." He shrugged off his suit coat, loosened the knot and tore off his tie, placing the garments on the seat. Rolling up his sleeves, he ordered, "Find them."

Dmitry was quick, spotting a stationary bleep on the GPS tracker. "We have it. The car is not far from here. A few minutes."

"Good, get going. Be stealth about it. We can't be sure how many of Yuri's men we'll have to deal with. It's just us now." He nodded to his remaining brothers.

Dmitry pressed a few buttons to pull up the map of the city and outlying area. Nikolai twisted toward Dmitry. "Get me any operational secure satellite link. I need to speak to President Blake."

"We have him on the line," Dmitry said a moment later. He passed the com link to Nikolai.

"What's going on, Nikolai?" William asked immediately. "How could you let Elizabeth be kidnapped from under your nose? If they find out she has the prototype serum on her, she's a dead woman. And you're responsible!"

"How did you know?" Nikolai asked, surprised, bypassing his accusation. "Has Yuri been in contact with you? We're going after her."

"No, Elizabeth contacted us."

Nikolai stunned, asked, "She is still alive?"

"Yes. We have a way to track her," William continued.

"Track her? How?" Nikolai asked with anticipation.

"An encrypted tracking chip was injected into her before we lost contact with the Eclipse."

Nikolai wiped a bead of sweat from his brow and with a forced calm voice said, "How soon can you relay that information?"

"Give us a few minutes. We've lost NORAD. We are heading to Alaska. Nikolai, her prototype formula works. We've confirmed it and been in touch with what's left of her pathology team. We're working on mass production techniques now, double checking the formula doesn't degrade."

"I'll get our scientists once they're at the Novograd facility to prepare any updates to the last formula she sent," Nikolai replied.

"As for Liz..." William paused, then said in a somber voice, "Nikolai, with or without your approval, I have a special ops team going in to extract her." William paused, "And kill those responsible."

"I understand. We'll do whatever we can to coordinate with you. We should be able to get to the area first. Moscow will go up in flames in minutes."

William heard sorrow in the other man's voice, a sorrow he felt reflected in his own words. "I've ordered that every city from New York to Miami be burned. The west coast is gone, too. I don't know how long we'll be able to keep in touch, Nikolai. Even with the formula for a cure, we're not sure how long it will take to make enough of it to save the rest of our cities, or if that's even possible. We'll be in touch."

With nothing more to say, Nikolai hung up. "How close are we?" His eyes shifted from one commander to another.

"We're approaching the dirt road now. I see no cars." Dmitry looked through his binoculars. "Stop. Let me look around."

Dmitry stepped out of the car and carefully swept the area, walking up ahead of the car. "There it is. They abandoned it further up. Ivan, drive up," he called over the com link. "I have something."

Ivan slowly pulled up to where Dmitry was stooped over a half-charred upper body. Nikolai slipped out from the back of the Mercedes, his gun at his side. "What do you have?"

Dmitry carefully searched what he could of the remains. "It looks as if he blew himself up. Mus'ad must have back tracked to this location. I see a second set of wheels and several Jeep tire marks."

"This is getting us nowhere." Nikolai seethed with frustration.

"Wait." Dmitry hurried over to a dismembered arm. Clutched in the fisted hand was a necklace.

Nikolai pulled out a pocket knife and cut the charred flesh away from the necklace. He recognized it instantly. "She was here. This is her grandmother's necklace, a family heirloom." He slipped the necklace into his pants pocket. "What's this way?" He pointed in the direction of the tire tracks.

"Zhukovsky Airport to the north. Trains to the west."

"Let's go. We'll have to wait on William. See if he has any luck." Nikolai started walking toward the Mercedes.

"Wait." Dmitry ripped a union badge and some partially blackened fabric from the corpse. "He was wearing a uniform. "A conductor's uniform. I have the station number."

"Find the train!" Nikolai ordered. Dmitry jumped in the car. Nikolai followed and ordered, "Have the Presidential helicopter sent to Zhukovsky Airport. Ivan, you're taking over flying duties when it lands. We'll meet up with Sergei there. We're not out of luck yet."

CHAPTER THIRTY-TWO

Day Six. 10:59 p.m. MSK. Zhukovsky Airport.

Dark storm clouds rolled in. Urgency swept across the men as the sky thundered. Nikolai waited for Sergei's arrival in the chopper. The portable satellite phone rang. Ivan answered and swept a glance at Nikolai. "President Blake is on the line."

Nikolai reached for the phone. "Mr. President. Do you have a fix on Elizabeth?" His eyebrows rose as he listened to William.

Dmitry swung open the passenger door and stepped out. Sergei's landing was ugly. He stepped out of the pilot's seat. He grumbled, walking towards the Mercedes. "Nice landing old man," Dmitry teased.

"What's going on?" Sergei tossed his gear to his feet and ignored the half-hearted jest Dmitry always made before a dangerous mission.

"President Blake's on the phone," Ivan informed him.

"She's where? Bio-bombs heading toward Tyumen? That's our country's oil and gas center. So he plans to leave us barren with no way to rebuild. As if the virus alone wouldn't do that." Nikolai made a slight gesture to Sergei. "President Blake, I am placing General Serebrinsky on the line with us. He will need all of the information you have."

Sergei requested, "Mr. President, can we arrange an exchange of information over our temporary satellite link? It is secure. Still operational. For how long, I don't know."

"Then let's make the exchange quickly," William ordered. Sergei nodded to Ivan to prepare to receive William's data.

Nikolai's hand clenched into a fist. He was anxious to find out and stop Yuri's plan. "Ivan, are you ready to pick up the information?" Ivan gave an affirmative nod. "We have the GPS link," Nikolai said a moment later. "I'll be back with you as soon as we find her."

"I have two F-35 Lightning IIs on standby," William offered. "I'll be in touch."

Nikolai hung up the phone with a slight curse under his breath. "Ivan, how far ahead are they?"

Ivan replied, "There is only one train that is in that area, but the times from the station information we have are incorrect."

"Do what you can."

Ivan shut his laptop. All four doors swung open. Nikolai and his FSB specialty team stepped out, fully armed.

Fixing his eyes on the horizon, Dmitry walked toward the helipad. "The sky is getting darker," he commented to Ivan. "I remember the last time I flew with you in this type of weather. I couldn't get a clean shot off. Can you hold it steady?"

Ivan shrugged off his brother's comment as they neared the chopper. "Yes. A thunderstorm is nothing. Jump in, Dmitry." Ivan opened the door to the pilot's seat. "Don't forget the AK-97. We'll need it if Yuri and his men are wearing body armor. You should use the new model, Dmitry. You have been attached to that old AK-74 for years," Ivan commented as he put the submachine guns in the back of the open chopper. Nikolai took the co-pilot seat.

Dmitry walked around the chopper to Nikolai. "Here, don't forget this. You better remember how to use it," Dmitry taunted Nikolai as he tossed a semiautomatic pistol to him. Nikolai snatched the gun in mid-air and checked it. Dmitry slipped into the backseat behind the pilot seat and secured the portable GPS unit.

Sergei was the last to reach the chopper. Nikolai whirled his finger around in motion. The movement of the propellers blew up a whirlwind of dust. He yelled over the noise of the blades in a voice of authority. "Sergei, jump in. We don't have much time left." Sergei quickly found his place next to Dmitry. They heard the rotors above. The drumming changed pitch as the chopper picked up its passengers and banked right.

Sitting back, Nikolai checked his Smith and Wesson and shoved it into his side holster. It was his good luck piece. With one sweeping move, he placed the semiautomatic pistol into the back waistband of his pants and pointed forward, looking at Ivan. Ivan complied.

A moment later Dmitry candidly announced, "We have success, Mr. President. I have a fix on the coordinates the Americans sent," Dmitry informed him. "I recommend sending in two SU-34 fighter bombers to take out the train tracks at this location." He pointed to the GPS screen. "The train will reach that location in approximately fifteen minutes. Our ETA gives us nine and a half minutes before it derails. Sergei and I can defuse the detonation system once on board."

Nikolai nodded. "Do what you must." The chopper flew through the threatening, stormy sky. Nikolai shifted uneasily. Impatient, he remarked, "Kick it up, Ivan!"

"We are at top speed."

Nikolai, anxious, said, "Then take it down lower. I want to see the train when we intercept it."

The helicopter skimmed over the rolling contour of the Russian landscape. They flew north and west above a line of dense dark green forest, before they hit a clearing. "There!" Dmitry called out, pointing to the worn steel train track.

"Just tracks. No train. Good," Nikolai said as the land opened up to reveal the tops of scattered farms and open fields. He turned to Dmitry, watching the flickering equipment. A half dozen glowing lights all fixed on the same point. "What do we have?"

The electronic beep from the GPS came in faster as they flew closer to the given coordinates. "We are presently locked on to the American GPS signal. The train is moving slow. That works in our favor. Ivan, I'm sending you the new coordinates. They change as the train's traveling speed changes," Dmitry called out.

Nikolai's nerves tensed up. They were getting close. "Send in the fighter bombers. Target the tracks where we planned."

Sergei sent the order. The helicopter banked, heading east over the well-worn tracks. They passed a small town and a stream then dropped lower to assess how far the train was from their location. Ivan pointed at the first sight of Mus'ad and his men in combat gear moving along the train rails. "It looks like we will get there before they do, Nikolai. My guess is they are going after Yuri to get Dr. Blake for themselves."

"Have the jets take Mus'ad out. We are not equipped to deal with them."

Nikolai shouted into his radio helmet above the humming of the chopper's blades. "Ivan, the train! There!" Ivan nodded in confirmation. Nikolai felt helpless. There was nothing he could do but watch. It was bleak knowing that in a few minutes the engineer would either refuse or be unable to stop the train in time. His only prayer for Elizabeth's survival would be if the train did not fully derail. "Hold on," Nikolai muttered aloud. He motioned to Ivan. "Land this thing immediately!"

"That is a negative," Ivan replied. "There is nowhere to put her down." He pointed ahead to a curve in the track. "That's the soonest I can set the chopper down."

Nikolai shot an alarmed stare at Ivan. He looked down, spotting a head of black hair barely visible outside of a boxcar. His heart halted as he saw Elizabeth begin to push off.

"No!" Nikolai shouted. A sick feeling hit his stomach as Elizabeth was abruptly snapped back. He watched. Yuri dragged her backward by the wind-tangled locks of her dark hair.

Nikolai's face flushed red with an unmatched rage toward Yuri. "Ivan, get me as close as possible to that open cargo door!" He reached for his semiautomatic pistol, pulling it out of his waistband.

Ivan tilted his head toward Nikolai. "You only have a 30-meter range if you want to hit him." The transmitter helmets hummed with his words.

"Can you get me that close? Dmitry, can you get him?"

Dmitry chimed in. "I don't have a clear shot at him. Nikolai, you have to take it."

"Give me Ivan's rifle." Nikolai placed his semiautomatic pistol at his feet and loaded the 30-round magazine into the submachine rifle. "Dmitry, if I miss, you take a shot anytime Elizabeth is clear. Shoot over me or through me if you have to. Ivan, get me close enough to fire a few shots off to let our sick bastard know we are here."

Dmitry took his loaded AK-74 rifle, tapping Sergei. "Switch seats with me." Both men moved. Nikolai strapped himself in. The chopper's bay door opened to allow a clean shot. Nikolai perched himself near the open door.

The chopper swung away right and approached the cargo door. Nikolai aimed the automatic rifle, firing off two rounds. Hitting the metal door, it rang out. The sound provided the distraction he needed. "I think I have his attention." He fired another round.

The chopper sailed in and dropped further down. "Nikolai. This is as close as I dare." Ivan flanked the open boxcar. "Let's see if this will scare the hell out of the bastard," Ivan's deep voice chimed. The chopper blades were almost deafening.

Inside the train car, Yuri held tight to Elizabeth, scanning for the chopper's location. He fixed a piercing stare on her. "You did this! I don't know how you did it. You warned them somehow!" Yuri shouted at her above the noise of the helicopter blades. Inflamed, he pulled her to her feet, screaming, "Listen, you bitch. I don't care if they know. It's too late to stop me. The virus is doing the job all my men couldn't do in destroying Russia and the Stepanov's. Your filthy American countrymen will all succumb. It's over. I win, even in death." A wicked smile rose on his face. "But I won't die before you do." He dragged her toward the motley hay bundles.

Elizabeth struggled for her life. She jabbed her elbow into his rib cage. She picked up a small fallen iron hitch at her feet and smacked him hard on his hand with the metal ring. Yuri cried out from the intense pain. Her hair became free from his grasp. She pulled herself away from him. He snarled, rubbing the skin to get feeling back in his hand. Elizabeth ran for the open cargo door.

"No you don't." Yuri lunged for her and clamped his pus-covered hand on her waist. He pulled her toward him easily and flung her down on the loose and scattered straw. "They can't stop the bombs. They can't have you. I'm a dead man. But you and I are going to have a last round, bitch for all my trouble."

He knelt over her. Elizabeth struck at him with open palms, struggling to move her battered legs.

"That's what you think, bastard!" she screamed. Elizabeth watched the Presidential helicopter drop and flank the cargo door.

Bullets flew through the cargo door, one past Yuri's ear. Another hit the boxcar floor, pitting it near his feet. Yuri twisted toward the sound of submachine gun fire. He rolled away behind the boxcar panel. His reflex was to recoil. Nikolai took aim from the chopper. Ivan kept it dangerously close to the open boxcar door.

"Steady, Ivan!" Nikolai called. "I need all the shots to count."

Yuri drew his semiautomatic weapon. "I don't care how or when I kill you, Nikolai, but I will kill you. All of you!" he shouted to his step-brothers as he jumped in front of the open cargo door and fired.

Terror swelled in Elizabeth. Nikolai was in Yuri's gun sight. Shots fired off.

"Oh, no you don't!" Raising one battered leg, she pushed at Yuri's backside. He tumbled forward. His gun shot missed. Ivan whisked the chopper up, jarring his passengers. The chopper dropped back out of range.

Yuri regained his footing. He faced her, his gun pointed at her. His eyes blazed with hatred. "Where do you want it? The head or the heart?"

She closed her eyes tight and let out what was to be her last scream.

Nikolai reloaded, hoping to get another shot off before the train derailed. "Hold on!" Ivan called, pointing to the track ahead. Two SU-34 bombers thundered low past the train before them. Ivan swiftly pulled the chopper out of harm's way, banking right and up. Nikolai glanced behind them to see a spectacle of lights as the track exploded. They watched the erupting pillars of blinding red flames take out the tracks, feeling the heat of the explosion. He cleared the chopper just as the debris scattered in the air.

Curses fell from Nikolai's lips as the smoke cleared away. He could not stop the train. It was seconds away from the blown tracks.

Yuri put pressure on the trigger. His bullet never left its chamber as he was thrown out of the boxcar's open cargo door as the car crashed forward, into the flatbed. Elizabeth held tight to the animal hitch on the wall behind her. The train tipped off its track, scattering boxes and hay everywhere. She felt another roll and hit. The slamming of the train cars sent Elizabeth tumbling. Scraping her already swollen knees against the boxcar floor, she steadied herself, bracing for another roll that never came.

CHAPTER THIRTY-THREE

Day Six. 11:45 p.m. MSK. Derailed Trans-Siberian Train.

Nikolai ignored the crackling of electricity as he pulled his semi-automatic rifle back to his side. He saw Yuri tumble from the train as the engine slammed into the blown tracks. The train careened out of control and the trailing boxcars slammed one into another, smashing through the wooden walls. He watched the pillars of fire simmer down to small scattered flames along where there had once been tracks. The rest of the tracks lay still, twisted and burnt.

Nikolai's heart stopped. Scanning the wreckage illuminated by the helicopter's search light, he recognized the bodies of an engineer and several of Yuri's men tossed like broken sticks in the field. The train lay in a tangled heap of metal. He did not see Elizabeth among the scattered.

"Set it down!" Nikolai commanded. "She has to be alive."

Ivan shook his head in pain. The chopper banked left sharply nearly knocking Nikolai off his seat.

"Damn it, Ivan! What's wrong? I said, set it down now!" Nikolai ordered.

"My hands are on fire." He bit his lip to hold back the pain. "Dmitry, take the controls," Ivan said. Dmitry climbed over. Ivan barely held the controls steady as Dmitry took hold, his own body feverish. Ivan's brow was flush and droplets of sweat had formed. "I'm sorry." He slid over to where Dmitry had sat and pulled off one flight glove, exposing his bloody raw flesh. "Give me a minute to fight this thing off."

Dmitry leveled the chopper off, setting it down on a grassy wildflower flat. "Ivan, stay with the chopper. We'll be back for you." Even as he spoke, Nikolai was unsure if any of them would make it out. His own skin was beginning to burn; more pox marks were appearing on his back and chest. He forced himself to go on.

Hopping off the chopper, the men hurried toward the wreckage.

Nikolai steeled his composure as they approached the accident site. Twisted smoke rose from the crumpled metal that had once been the front cars. His mind raced in agony. Nikolai worked his way toward the damaged remains of the boxcar where he had last seen Elizabeth. Climbing inside, he franticly removed crates, tossing aside hay and other debris. He called her name and heard no answer. Pushing aside several tumbled hay bales, he found Elizabeth, half-conscious, crumpled in a corner of the car.

"Elizabeth." He knelt by her side and turned her soiled face toward his own. "Here, over here!" he shouted. Dmitry and Sergei hurried closer.

Elizabeth slumped into his arms, shivering. "Nikolai? My bag. Get my bag." A dry, cracked, faded voice came from her. Coughing, she spoke urgently, "You need to get to the IEDs. They're armed. If the train wreck didn't detonate them, something will. They were counting down for two hours, but I don't know if that's when they're set to go off. Three of them, in the last car...cell phone in the feed trough..."

Nikolai nodded to Dmitry and Sergei. "We'll find the bombs. Dmitry, go see what you can do. Sergei, keep a watch outside."

Nikolai helped Elizabeth raise her shoulders slowly. She winced in pain. Placing a hand under her left arm, he pulled her up. Sitting her down, he let her lean against his muscled torso. Taking his handkerchief from his pocket, he dabbed the blood from the corners of her lip.

She could hardly speak as he checked for wounds and broken bones. Elizabeth tried to pull herself up, holding her left wrist. "I need my bag." Straightening herself, she used the wall for support. "It's here." She sifted through the fallen hay covering the floor of the car. Nikolai franticly joined her. He tossed one bundle of hay, then another.

"There." She pointed to a small black leather handle. They tugged and pulled away the old animal blankets. She pulled her bag from the pile and brushed it off. She glimpsed back at Nikolai to find the color drained from his inflamed skin as he leaned against a wall for support. The virus was claiming his strength.

Elizabeth moved toward him as he stumbled to his knees. She took his arms and settled him against the bales of hay. "How bad are you, Nikolai?" She felt his pulse. "We have to get you out of here."

"I don't think so." A cold chilling voice rang out from nowhere.

A sudden fear ran up Elizabeth's spine like needles. She would have known that voice anywhere. She slowly lifted her eyes away from Nikolai.

A scraped-up Yuri stepped through the smashed door that led from the flatbed. He pointed his gun at Nikolai. "I am not so easy to get rid of. No one will send me off this time. Not to the orphanage, not to Tula, not to anywhere, Nikolai."

Elizabeth stared at Yuri in disbelief. The virus had taken greater hold of him in those few minutes they thought he was dead. His face was covered with agonizing pox. His hand was wrapped in fabric torn from his shirt. "I will not die first. I intend to take you to hell with me, Nikolai! Then that bitch next to you!" He pointed his gun at Elizabeth. "It's all your fault. Like my mother. You're just like her. You left me to die as she did in Tula. But death and I are old friends."

Yuri's talk was that of a crazed man. Elizabeth shifted closer to Nikolai, kneeling beside him.

"Don't worry about Dmitry," Yuri taunted. "He made a run for it, like a spooked rabbit in the brush. One shot to the back, he was easy to dispose of."

Nikolai tightened his lips. He did not respond. He slowly reached for his Smith and Wesson. He knew he had only one shot before Yuri would kill him. Both were expert marksmen.

"Would you like to watch, Nikolai? While I murder your old lover in front of you?"

Nikolai mind fixed. One clean shot was all he needed. His mind raced. Yuri let out a sick laugh.

"Put your gun down, Yuri!" a familiar gravelly voice said.

Yuri stiffened as he heard Sergei. The general stepped through the door behind him. Sergei's weapon was aimed.

"I cannot let you do this anymore. If I had known what you planned all along, I never would have given Pachen the chopper or access to the old lab. You lied to me, Yuri!" Sergei bellowed. "You said you wanted the old vaccines, not the viruses. It was to buy your way out of debt with the mafia. No! I realized too late it was to *buy* the mafia. I am a foolish old man to have believed you. To have taken care of you. You are a bad seed like your mother."

"Sergei, you?" Nikolai felt the sting of betrayal. "You were part of this?"

"Forgive me," Sergei said remorsefully.

Nikolai snapped, "For some, there is no forgiveness." Elizabeth moved closer to his side.

A small droplet of blood fell from Yuri's nose. He wiped it with his sleeve. He dropped his gun to his side. "You never told him, did you, old man?" He looked at Nikolai. "That is why he kept me on as a FSB officer. My mother was not only your father's whore, but his, too." He tipped his head toward Sergei as the accusations continue to fall.

Nikolai's face blanked. He looked at his old friend. "I don't understand. Yuri is your son? You kept it quiet all these years. Sergei, you were family to us, a best friend to my father and to me!" he yelled.

"You don't need to understand, Nikolai," Yuri continued. "Your father treated me like one of his, but not because I was his son. It was a favor. To my father and their whore." Yuri delighted in tormenting Nikolai with the ugly truth. "No blood between us."

Nikolai bit his lip hard. It bled, a drop falling to the boxcar floor. He would kill him.

"Sergei's the real traitor. He has helped me along. How else do you think I could get access to so much information about you, the oil fields, clearance for jets, everything that will be all mine after I blow up the Tyumen oil fields? Thanks to your father's adoption I'll be the last living family member to inherit all the Stepanov's wealth. What more do I need to build my empire? It is unfortunate *she* had to become involved," Yuri said, glaring at Elizabeth.

Sergei tried to explain as he stepped closer to Yuri. His gun was aimed at his illegitimate son. "Nikolai, I could not tell you. My wife was sick. I had no way to care for him. Your father knew. We struck a bargain and he took Yuri in for me. Fed him, raised him like his own. Your father was supposed to tell you before he died. I don't know why he never did. But then I couldn't either."

Nikolai and Elizabeth watched as cold darkness seeped into Yuri's face, turning it to stone. Hatred lived in his blood. He hated everyone he had ever known. As he gazed at Elizabeth, revenge took over his soul.

"That's enough of your sentiments, old man. It ends here." he said coldly. "Your usefulness is over, father."

With a twist to the right, Yuri raised his gun, pushing the tip against Sergei's chest. He pulled the trigger.

Nikolai fumbled for his gun. "Stop!" he screamed as one pointblank bullet ripped through Sergei's heart. The general slumped to the ground.

In less than a second, it was over. Sergei was dead. Nikolai fought to maintain his self-control. He watched in disbelief as his best friend's blood spilled out from his chest cavity, pooling on the hay-scattered boxcar floor, staining it a deep crimson. A mix of emotions ran through him.

Elizabeth's breathing was becoming ragged, her ribs aching. She must have a cracked rib, maybe two, she self-diagnosed. There was nothing she could do for Sergei. She looked at the rear door. She could make a run for it. She glanced toward Nikolai. His eyes said no. Her eyes dropped down to his waist and she noticed the gun in his hand, shielded from Yuri's view by her own body. If she moved, the gun would be exposed to Yuri and it would be all over.

Catching the message in Nikolai eyes, she read his thoughts. She shifted slightly to the right, closer to him. Nikolai raised a hand over his lips. He let out a cough. She understood what she had to do. It was the first time she would have to take a life rather than save it. Her scraped-up hand wrapped around the cold metal of the gun handle. She turned her head and glanced at the door behind Yuri, taking in a breath.

"I wouldn't make a run for it, Dr. Blake." Yuri smiled a sickly grin, guessing her thoughts. He pointed his gun at Nikolai. "I said don't move, Dr. Blake. It would be unwise."

She froze in place as his words hung in the air. Yuri tightened his grip on his gun. His gray, embittered eyes went lifeless and cold. "It's between just us now, Nikolai." He reached one infected hand into his pocket and tossed a black knight onto the ground in front of Nikolai. "Checkmate."

Elizabeth's eyes slowly rose and locked on Nikolai's coal black eyes telling her to make it count. She had six bullets, but just one chance before Yuri would react. In his mind, he rebuffed, "Not yet." Ignoring the chess piece, Nikolai remained silent.

Yuri acidly said , "*Do svidaniya*, Nikolai." Yuri pointed the weapon toward him and squeezed the trigger.

"Now!" Nikolai lunged to his left. Elizabeth twisted her body, raising his Smith and Wesson. She found Yuri's face. She pulled the trigger and heard the discharge of guns, followed by a piercing then burning pain that slammed into her body. The kick of the gun knocked her off balance. Elizabeth slammed down onto her hands, the pistol thudding against the floor of the boxcar as it was knocked from her grip and tossed in front of her.

Yuri wailed as the bullet ripped into his flesh. Elizabeth's ears rang from the sudden screams. Her eyes became cloudy. "Did I get him?" she asked Nikolai, struggling to push herself up from the hay-covered floor.

Nikolai scampered to his gun. Jerking up his Smith and Wesson, he yelled, "Go to hell!" Nikolai pulled the trigger.

The old pistol made its mark. Yuri stumble back feeling a bullet pierce his chest. His lung collapsed. His ghostly smile suddenly twisted and faded. His cold gray eyes fell on Nikolai in defeat. His gun in his hand, he fell next to Sergei's body. Yuri struggled to push himself back up.

Nikolai's breath became heavy as he watched Yuri fighting to rise. He looked toward the broken doorway to the flatbed as footsteps ran up the metal stairs.

Entering the boxcar, Ivan stared down menacingly at Yuri, his gun fallen from his grasp. Yuri glanced up as he gasped for air, his eyes swollen with pox. Ivan saw his razor drop in the palm of his hand. Ivan kicked both weapons away.

"Ivan, handcuff him. Arrest him for crimes against humanity!" Nikolai shouted his command.

With the last of his strength, Ivan pulled the government issued handcuffs form his belt loop. Yanking Yuri's arms behind his back, he snapped the plastic restraints tight on his wrists. Pushing his weight onto a still struggling Yuri, he repeated the action, snapping on the cuffs at his ankles. With a deep, primitive voice that came from within and the taste of victory in his eyes, Ivan spoke to Yuri. "I told you I'd get you. I can promise you a quick conviction that carries with it the death penalty. I'll be honored to be part of that firing squad." Ivan spit on the wooden floor near Yuri's face.

He brushed his pox-covered hands on his uniform. Ivan fell to his knees, sweat rolling down his face. The virus weakened him. He braced against the door frame for support. Ivan glanced at Nikolai and Elizabeth. "What now?" Ivan asked, wincing in pain.

Dmitry, pushing himself to anyone man's limit, rushed through the rear boxcar doorway, the back of his shirt soaked in blood, his gun pulled. His eyes fell on Yuri's restrained, blood covered body. His brow rose at the twisted arms and pox-covered wounds.

"He got what he deserved." Dmitry rested his gun at his side and sat down on the boxcar floor, rolling onto his back. "It's over," he sighed, closing his eyes. His breath was slow and heavy.

"Elizabeth," Nikolai called out to her, crawling to her side. He put his hand on her shoulders to pull her up and felt warm blood filtering between his fingers. He gently turned her over, pulling her up against his body, finding a wound on her arm. A flesh wound, where Yuri's bullet had skimmed her.

She groaned, sitting up. "My medical bag." Nikolai handed the black leather satchel to her. She opened it. "Thank God. It's here." She pulled out the brown bottle of prototype serum. "It didn't shatter."

"Is that it? The antidote?" Nikolai asked. "Hurry, give it to us."

Elizabeth winced, looking at the contents of the bottle. She said, "I can't. There is only enough serum for one injection."

Nikolai glanced at Ivan and Dmitry. "Give it to them. Make it enough for both. It's my fault for all of this. I should have known about Yuri. About Sergei. Damn! The virus has taken hold." Nikolai fell back, clutching his stomach in pain. He closed his eyes. "Do it, Elizabeth." He pressed her.

Her breathing strained, she took out her syringes. "Sorry, Mr. President." She sat next to Nikolai. He barely had the strength to move when he saw the needle coming toward him.

His eyes were fixed on her. Struggling, he raised his hand in protest. "Not me." Nikolai drew back.

Dmitry spoke, "Nikolai. She's right. Mr. President, you first." Summoning the last bit of his strength, Dmitry pulled his gun and aimed on his brother. "It's my sworn duty to protect you. Even from yourself. Give him the shot."

Nikolai held out his arm.

Elizabeth ripped the sleeve of his shirt down, exposing his arm. She was astonished at the number of lesions that covered it. "Why didn't you tell me you were so bad? Damn it, Nikolai. Nearly your entire arm is crimson with infection," she scolded.

"It wouldn't have helped," Nikolai replied.

"I could have treated the infection! Slowed it down at least. Made you comfortable." Wiping the skin with an antiseptic out of habit, she took Nikolai's arm and injected him with the last of the prototype serum. She sat back on her haunches. "Hold out your arm. I'll clean the sores." She rummaged through her medical bag. She stopped as a deep voice broke over them.

"I want that bottle of serum you have in your hand, Dr. Blake."

The voice startled her. She turned toward the doorway. Limping toward the open cargo door, Mus'ad pointed his gun at Nikolai. He glanced at Ivan and Dmitry, whose guns were both drawn on Mus'ad. He laughed. "This is a sight. Put your guns down. You think I am alone?" He nodded and several of his fully armed men showed themselves. Ivan and Dmitry lowered their guns. They knew they were outnumbered.

"It's empty," Elizabeth said.

"Give me the bottle." Mus'ad glanced at Yuri. "I see Yuri is of no use to me. I leave him to his fate. However, I will start to shoot the youngest Stepanov brother up to the oldest, which is you Nikolai, unless I get that bottle."

Elizabeth swallowed hard. "You'll go without any more bloodshed?" she said. Mus'ad nodded. "Here then. Take the bottle." She tossed the empty brown bottle to Mus'ad. He caught it and slipped it into his pocket.

"Thank you, Dr. Blake. It seems you are the smart one. I'll keep my word to you and leave you to your deaths in this wilderness." Mus'ad looked at Nikolai. "But, Mr. President, you will be coming with us. You will ensure our safe travel out of what is left of your country since Yuri is unavailable to help in the matter."

Nikolai shook his head. "I don't think so Mus'ad. Listen!" Nikolai pointed to the clearing sky. Mus'ad gave him a confused look. A moment later, gunfire rained down around the overturned box car. One of Mus'ad's men swore in Arabic from on top of the wrecked boxcar as footsteps sounded above them.

Mus'ad looked up. "This isn't over, Nikolai," he cried out. "Hurry!" He and his men fled from the box car as the roar of helicopters pierced the silent night air.

"Who are they?" Elizabeth called out, leaning out of the boxcar, struggling to see the choppers.

"Not Russian. I can't make out the markings," Dmitry replied.

"If Mus'ad escapes, we're in for more trouble later." Nikolai pulled himself up and motioned to his brothers to arm themselves. He handed Elizabeth his Smith and Wesson and picked up Yuri's gun from the floor. "If we have to, we'll make a last stand here. Then go after Mus'ad."

Elizabeth ducked back into the boxcar. The noise of the chopper blades whirling covered the roof of the car as they passed over. They heard several choppers land not far off. The Stepanov brothers waited as they heard men moving outside. Nikolai motioned for them to aim. Moving silently, they raised their guns toward the open door. A deep voice broke the silence.

"Dr. Blake! Dr. Blake, this is United States Special Ops Officer Harrison," he called into the boxcars.

Waves of relief crashed over Elizabeth. Scrambling to the cargo door, Elizabeth hung her head out and waved. "Here, here! Hurry! Harrison." She turned with a smile that outshined any pain she was feeling. "They are Americans!"

Her smile faded as she saw Nikolai double over, vomiting. "No! Damn. Harrison, did my uncle send any of my serum with you?"

Harrison hurried onto the boxcar with his team. "Yes. I have it here. That stuff works miracles, Dr. Blake."

"Let's hope so." Elizabeth took the medical supplies from Harrison. She filled fresh syringes and repeated the injections on Nikolai and his brothers.

"We were all infected, but that little liquid you whipped up took effect on the bacteria immediately. The symptoms disappeared within 24 hours. That little bug was not going to keep us from our duties," replied Harrison.

She knelt next to Nikolai, putting his Smith and Wesson back in his holster. "No blood is in the vomit. That means the virus hasn't progressed to the final stage. I think it's the serum that's making you sick. It's a side effect. Hold on. We'll get you to a hospital. American soldiers are here."

Nikolai nodded in a haze. "Yes," was all he could manage to say as he clenched his stomach.

"When did you get here, Harrison?" Elizabeth asked, checking on Ivan and Dmitry.

"President Blake set this up. We were holed up at the old western Siberian base. Arrangements were made when the evacuation of Moscow began. Our unit was waiting for the activation of our orders, orders to find you, Dr. Blake. They came sooner than expected when we lost total contact with the Eclipse. We've set up two chemical/biological protective shelters not too far from here. President's Stepanov's men can be treated there." Harrison tilted his head towards Ivan and Dmitry. "You and I have to leave immediately. I have to get you back to U.S. soil as ordered."

"I am not leaving until President Stepanov is stabilized," Elizabeth replied.

Harrison nodded. "I am leaving a team behind." He gave orders to the groups of American soldiers. "You have clean up duty. Your team: Capture Mus'ad and his men. Treat them like the Syrian terrorists they are." Harrison half-grinned. "The rest of you, get these men on board and get them back to the CBPS unit." Harrison turned to Nikolai. "Can you return with Dr. Blake, President Stepanov? President Blake would like you to join him at our Alaska base."

Nikolai was unable to answer.

Harrison realized the situation. "We'll take you with your FSB team as soon as you can travel." He turned to Elizabeth. "We will have transportation waiting to take him to Fairbanks when he can travel. You're not equipped here in the open fields of Siberia. They can stabilize him at the CBPS."

Elizabeth nodded that she understood. "And what about Mus'ad and his men?" she asked.

"Mus'ad had only a handful of men here with him, but there may be more nearby. We'll get them. We are in control," Harrison assured her.

"And Yuri?"

"President Blake wants them all tried on American soil for crimes against humanity. The Hague is under quarantine. It'll probably have to be burned and the International Criminal Court permanently shut down. You will have to ask President Blake yourself. I am not privy to his plans," Harrison replied. "My men will take care of Nevsky, transport him for trial. The whole world will want to see him pay."

Elizabeth moved to Nikolai's side as the soldiers pulled him off the wrecked boxcar. He reached for her, motioning for her to come closer. Elizabeth dropped her head and placed her ear near his mouth. She gave a slight smile at his words.

"I lied. Those eight months, fourteen years ago. They were something. If your uncle hadn't walked in on us that night, I was planning to go back to America with you," he whispered.

She gazed at him. She lifted one palm and gently stroked his face softly. Bending down, she placed a gentle kiss on the back of his hand. "I know," she whispered back.

"Dr. Blake." Harrison cleared his throat, uncomfortable with the scene. "May I remind you that you are an American and he is Russian?" His deep Montana brawl didn't hide the fact that he didn't like what he saw.

Elizabeth shot him a look. "Harrison, that is none of your business."

"Like hell it isn't!" he mumbled to himself. He called out the remaining orders to his teams. "Secure the injured and the prisoner. Let's move out!" Harrison looked at Elizabeth. "President Blake is waiting at the Fairbanks base and I have strict orders to get you there. How did he put it...To 'get your ass over there immediately'."

They boarded a fully-armed chopper. As Elizabeth secured her flight belt, a private administered first aid to her. Looking out the window, she saw that the storm had passed. The sky was clear. It was like a postcard to her, the Russian white night reflected on the flower filled-fields and the old castles of the Vladimir province. A peaceful smile rose to her face. Humans, for all the misguided superiority of their short history, had beaten out extinction once more.

EPILOGUE

Day Nine. 4:00 p.m. Alaska Standard Time (AKST). Fairbanks Military Base.

"We're spraying the fourth round of your antiviral serum from crop dusters and specially out-fitted helicopters today," Harrison explained as he escorted Elizabeth to her apartment at the base. "Your uncle called in the remainder of the National Guard. They are covering the cities' spray trucks. Most of the victims of the SV121R have been sent to designated cremation location C. Clean up is slow. The cities are quarantined until we are sure your viricide has done its job."

Elizabeth nodded as she unbuttoned her white medical coat. Her name was embroidered in blue script across the pocket. She opened the apartment door.

"President Blake has offered the formula to any country willing to accept help and work with our government on rebuilding. The new treaties are sound. Starting with utilities, and communication and transportation systems." Harrison continued, "Elizabeth you and your team of scientist did something no one could. The viricide formula is easy to use and mass produce." He took off his beret. The formality of his voice left. "Your uncle said you needed a break," Harrison folded his beret in half, "and I told him I'd take care of it." He smiled. "I was wondering if you'd like to have dinner with me tonight." He extended his hand to her.

"I believe she's busy tonight."

Elizabeth and Harrison glanced into the apartment. Nikolai was standing in the doorway in faded blue jeans and a simple cotton shirt.

"What are you doing here?" Elizabeth asked.

Harrison unfolded his beret and placed it back on his head. "That's what I'd like to know," he grumbled.

"William let me in," Nikolai replied. He saw envy appear in Harrison's eyes. He pressed. "Jealous, Officer Harrison?"

"Not on your life Mr. President." He nodded to Elizabeth. "I'll be going now, Dr. Blake. I'll see you tomorrow."

She watched Harrison in his buffed and polished uniform vanish around the corner. Elizabeth entered her apartment, shutting the door. Nikolai returned to looking out Elizabeth's apartment window at the barren Alaskan tundra. The apartment was crisp smelling. Inuit paintings hung on the walls behind simple wood furniture. A faux bear rug covered the wood floor.

Walking over to Nikolai, she stood next to him. "It won't be long now," Elizabeth said. "I see you are stabilized enough to fly. I can't believe you went from ICU to discharged from Fairbanks Memorial Hospital in 48 hours." She paused. "When do you think you'll go back to Russia?"

"Go back? Go back to what?" Nikolai said, frowning. "Ivan is not out of the woods yet. Anton is recovering from burns along with remnants of the virus. It is a miracle he survived. Dmitry lost a lot of blood. They are tough. I have to believe they'll make it." He sighed. "I lost all of my life as it was before. My wife, my son. If it wasn't for you, my brothers would have joined them in death." He shook his head. "And Sergei. It's unimaginable how he and my father betrayed the family all those years," he said in remorse.

Putting her hands on his shoulders, Elizabeth gave him a little squeeze. "I'm sorry. The amount of loss hasn't even begun to surface. The world has changed. It has a long, hard grieving period ahead of itself."

Nikolai turned to face her. She glanced up and saw a few remaining pox scars left on his handsome face. The laser resurfacing technology use to cauterized the open wounds and kill remaining bacteria was an added success.

"I have to tell you something," he said after a moment. "It's about your uncle and me. We've formed a temporary federation government under the United Nations flag. We wrote a new charter to help rebuild the world's cities. Most world leaders are behind it. With what little resources we have left, we all need to pull together until we can reclaim our old borders. Your uncle needs my voice to convince the remaining skeptics to join in the rebuilding of our world. If we don't form alliances, there will be a battle of political wills. The problem is that men like Yuri and Mus'ad have an unquenchable thirst for power. They will see this worldwide moment of weakness as the time to push a political agenda and be difficult to sway. I am afraid we haven't heard the last of Mus'ad's movement. I'm sure he's groomed a replacement. We have to regroup to defend our freedom. It will be a difficult undertaking. We already are re-charting a new International Criminal Court. The vote passed to reinstate the death penalty. William and I agree Yuri will be placed on trial under these new international laws."

"Why are you telling me all this?" Elizabeth asked with a puzzled look, twisting her necklace. She took a step back. "What about Russia? I thought it was agreed that you were to return as soon as you are fully recovered." She frowned.

"Change of plans," Nikolai responded with raised brows.

"What kind of change?" she pressed.

"I am staying in America," he stated. Her mouth parted. Mixed feelings ran over her. He took Elizabeth's hands in his and said, "I'm not going back to Russia."

"Who will rebuild Russia?" Elizabeth inquired.

"There is no place to go back to. There is nothing left after the bombings. St. Petersburg might be saved, but Moscow is gone along with all her history. Your capital, too. Gone. Your uncle and I will govern this new federation from what remains of the governing body of the United Nations. We moved the New York location to upper New York state until your city is rebuilt as well." He shoved his hands in his jean pockets. "We need your help."

"My help? So this is why my uncle let you in, to smooth talk me into what you two have planned."

"It's not like that, Elizabeth," he explained. "No one can do the work you can. Several from your international team who survived the virus are willing to work on programs on behalf of the World Health Organization, on one condition."

"And what is that one condition?"

"That you lead it."

Elizabeth crossed her arms. "You and my uncle aren't giving me a choice, are you?"

He raised his brows. "I'll understand if you say no. I lost everything. But William lost his son, too, your cousin, and the world lost half of your international team, half of the top medical researchers in the world. I'm not the only one who has to start over. We have a chance here to change the world, to recreate a vision for the future, to make sure this can never happen again. A peaceful world." He reached out to touch her face. "I want to do those things with you. You're the only one left who means that much to me."

"Stop." She turned away, looking out the window again. The harsh barren tundra matched her mood. "I agree to head the new World Health Organization." She looked back at him. "As for us... I make no promises. It's too soon, Nikolai."

He felt a sting at her rejection, a rejection he would not accept so easily. He turned the conversation back to what he really was there for. "I am pleased you're on board for the new U.N. leadership. The first meeting is set for tonight at seven p.m." He grabbed his jacket and put it on while walking to the door. He opened it and turned back to her. With a determination he said, "Elizabeth, it's never too soon. We have a second chance. Think about it. The virus has changed everyone's destiny, even yours." Nikolai quietly shut the door.

Elizabeth dropped onto the living room couch and sat alone in the room filled with his cologne. As the lingering spicy scent of her past wafted through the air, she thought about her future, his future. He was right. Destiny would call again.

THE END